THE BEST OF TEMPTATION COLLECTION

Too hot to handle? Maybe a little,
but this 2-in-1 collection of sassy, sexy romances
will have you captivated from page one.

Filled with steamy nights and sizzling days,
these classic stories explore what happens when
a fun, flirty woman meets an irresistible man.
The result of such chemistry is often explosive,
usually unexpected and always unforgettable!
We're sure you'll agree....

These tempting tales prove that sometimes reality
can be even better than your most private fantasies!

VICKI LEWIS THOMPSON

New York Times bestselling author Vicki Lewis Thompson's love affair with cowboys started with the Lone Ranger, continued through Maverick and took a turn south of the border with Zorro. Fortunately for her, she lives in the Arizona desert, where broad-shouldered, lean-hipped cowboys abound. Vicki has won numerous awards including the Nora Roberts Lifetime Achievement Award from Romance Writers of America. Visit her website at www.vickilewisthompson.com.

New York Times Bestselling Author

VICKI LEWIS THOMPSON

Pure Temptation

and

Old Enough to Know Better

HARLEQUIN®
THE BEST OF TEMPTATION COLLECTION

Recycling programs
for this product may
not exist in your area.

ISBN-13: 978-0-373-60627-6

PURE TEMPTATION AND OLD ENOUGH TO KNOW BETTER

Copyright © 2014 by Harlequin Books S.A.

The publisher acknowledges the copyright holder
of the individual works as follows:

PURE TEMPTATION
Copyright © 1999 by Vicki Lewis Thompson
OLD ENOUGH TO KNOW BETTER
Copyright © 2004 by Vicki Lewis Thompson

Printed in U.S.A.

CONTENTS

PURE TEMPTATION

To Alex Comfort, MB, DSc,
for celebrating the beauty of love and play.

CHAPTER ONE

Summer Project: Lose Virginity.

TESS BLAKELY ROCKED gently on her porch swing, a yellow legal pad balanced on her knee, a glass of iced tea on the wicker table beside her. She gazed at what she'd written and sighed. The beginning of a quest was the hardest part.

It was pitiful that a twenty-six-year-old, reasonably attractive woman found herself saddled with the handicap of virginity, but there it was, on paper. And her status had to change before she left for New York at the end of the summer, or she'd risk her credibility with the high school girls she'd been hired to counsel. Besides, she wanted to experience sex. She *longed* to experience sex.

She took a sip of iced tea and continued.

Goal One: Find knowledgeable candidate willing to deflower me.
Goal Two: Swear candidate to absolute secrecy.
Goal Three: Get it on.

Tess sighed again. Writing out her goals and objectives had been her cherished method for getting what she wanted, beginning at the age of eight when she'd yearned for her very own pony. But although she wanted to lose her innocence much more than she'd wanted that pony, her current project seemed about as likely of success as a personal rocket trip to the moon.

The little town of Copperville, Arizona, wasn't exactly crawling with "knowledgeable candidates," but even the few that she'd consider had been scared off long ago by her four very large, very overprotective older brothers. And not a one of those beefy brothers had moved away or relaxed his vigilance. They all expected their little sis to save herself for her wedding night. They were stuck in the Dark Ages, as far as she was concerned, but she loved them too much to openly defy them.

That was the reason for goal number two—for absolute secrecy. Now *there* was a definite sticking point. Even if she found a man her brothers hadn't intimidated, how could she ever expect him to keep a secret in Copperville? This was a town where you could wake up with a sore throat in the morning and have three kinds of chicken soup at your doorstep by noon.

Which meant she might never arrive at the third step— Getting It On. And she was ready for number three. Extremely ready. She'd driven all the way to Phoenix to buy research books, knowing that she couldn't be caught thumbing through *One Hundred Ways to Drive Him Wild* in the Copperville Book Barn, if the local bookstore even carried such a thing, which she sincerely doubted.

So much for her list. The goals were unreachable. She tossed the legal pad on top of the stack of books lying next to her on the swing. A list might have worked for the pony, but it was probably dumb to think it could cure a resistant case of chastity.

And to be honest, a list might have helped get her that pony all those years ago, but her best friend, Jeremiah "Mac" MacDougal, had been the real key. Her family lived in town and had no room for a horse, but Mac had talked his folks into keeping Chewbacca on their ranch. Tess's older brothers had always thought they had first claim to Mac, being boys, but Tess knew better. Ever since Mac, who'd been only five at the time, had saved her from a rattlesnake, she'd known he was the best friend she'd ever have.

Mac. Mac could help her find the right guy! She mentally slapped her forehead and wondered why she hadn't thought of him before. Unlike her brothers, Mac understood why she needed to take the job in New York and prove herself an independent, capable woman. Her brothers might have laughed at her when she asked for a light saber for Christmas, but Mac had saved his allowance and bought her one.

Surely Mac would also understand that she couldn't go to New York a virgin. Coming from a small town was enough of a handicap. If the girls she'd be counseling figured out that she was sexually inexperienced, she'd be a real joke. Mac would see that right away. And he'd help her find the right man to solve her problem.

THE SUN HAD barely crested the mountains as Mac saddled two horses. He'd left his bed this morning with a sense of anticipation. He hadn't had an early-morning ride with Tess in months. When she'd called to suggest it, he'd been happy at the prospect, although lately he'd been feeling a little jealous of her.

As kids they'd spent hours talking about the places they'd go when they were older. This September she was actually going to do it, while he was stuck on the ranch. His folks expected him to stay around and gradually take over what they'd worked so hard to build. As the only child, he couldn't foist off that obligation on anybody else.

Tess had it easier, although she was forever complaining about how hard it was for a woman to "go on a quest," as she put it. But she was doing it, and he wasn't. Her mom and dad hated having her leave town, especially for some faraway place like New York City, but they still had four sons, their wives and seven grandchildren. With such a slew of Blakelys around, Tess didn't have to feel guilty about grabbing her chance at independence. Mac envied her that freedom.

"Top 'o the mornin' to ye, MacDougal."

He buckled the cinch on Peppermint Patty and turned to smile at Tess. She used to greet him that way for months after she'd starred in Copperville High's version of *Brigadoon,* and hearing it again brought back memories.

They'd rehearsed her lines in the tree house in her folks' backyard. At one point he'd almost kissed her, but only because the script called for it, of course. Then they'd both decided the kiss wasn't necessary for her to learn the part. He'd been relieved, of course, because kissing Tess would seem weird. But at the time he'd kind of wanted to try it, anyway.

"Aye, and it's a fine mornin', lass," he said. She looked great, as always, but there was something different about her this morning. He studied her, trying to figure it out. "Did you cut your hair?"

"Not since the last time you saw me." She used her fingers to comb it away from her face. "Why, does it look bad?"

"No. It looks fine." In twenty-three years of watching Tess create new looks with her thick brown hair, he'd lived through braids, kinky perms, supershort cuts, even red streaks. Once he'd given her a haircut himself after she got bubble gum stuck in it. Neither set of parents had been impressed with his barbering skills. He liked the way she wore it now, chin-length and simple, allowing her natural wave to show.

"Is there a spot on my shirt or something?" She glanced down at the old Copperville Miners T-shirt she wore.

"Nope." He nudged his hat to the back of his head with his thumb. "But I swear something's different about you."

He stepped closer and took her chin in his hand. "Are you wearing some of that fancy department-store makeup?"

"To go riding? Now that would be stupid, wouldn't it?"

He gazed at her smooth skin and noticed that her freckles were in full view and her mouth was its normal pink color. Her eyelashes were soft and fluttery, not spiky the way they had been in high school when she'd caked on the mascara. Nope, no makeup.

But as he looked into her gray eyes, he figured out what was bothering him. They were best friends and didn't keep things from each other, or at least they hadn't until now. This morning, for whatever reason, Tess had a secret. It changed her whole expression, making her seem mysterious, almost sexy. Not that he ever thought of Tess as sexy. No way.

Despite himself, he was intrigued. Even a little excited. He didn't associate Tess with mystery, and it was a novel concept. He decided to wait and let the secret simmer in those big gray eyes of hers. It was fun to watch.

He tweaked her nose and stepped back. "I guess I'm seeing things. You're the same old Tess. Ready to mount up?" To his amazement, she blushed. Tess never blushed around him. They knew each other too well.

"Um, sure," she mumbled, heading straight for Peppermint Patty without looking at him, her cheeks still very pink. "We're burning daylight."

While he stood there trying to figure out what he'd said to make her blush, she climbed quickly into the saddle and started out. As he mounted he continued to watch her, and he could swear she shivered. With the temperature hovering around eighty-five on this June morning, he didn't think she was cold. This might be the most interesting morning ride he'd ever had with Tess.

MAYBE ASKING FOR Mac's help wouldn't be so simple, after all, Tess thought as she headed for the trail leading to the river. Here she was blushing over some offhand remark he'd made about mounting up. Or maybe she'd spent too much time reading those books, and every conversation had sexual overtones now. She certainly couldn't go to New York keyed up like this. It would be good to get this whole business over with.

Ducking an occasional overhanging mesquite branch, she rode at a trot ahead of him on the dusty trail. He knew something was up. She never could keep anything from him, so she might as well lay out her plan as soon as they got to their favorite spot by the river. As kids they'd used the sandy bank for fierce battles between their *Star Wars* action figures, and when they were older, they'd come out here to drink colas and talk about whatever was going on in their lives. Tess had never shared the hideaway with anyone else, and neither had Mac, as far as she knew.

The riverbank was where they'd gone after Chewbacca died. They'd talked about heaven, and had decided horses had to be there or they weren't interested in going. They'd headed out here after Mac broke his arm and couldn't try out for Little League, and the day Tess had won a teddy bear at the school carnival. Before either of them knew anything about sex, they'd spent time by the river talking about whether men and women made babies the same way horses and dogs and goats did.

Later on, Mac had put a stop to their discussions on that topic. Now Tess wanted to reopen the discussion, but she wasn't sure if she had the courage.

"So what's your summer project this year?" Mac called up to her. "I know you always have one."

A perfect opening, but she didn't want to blurt it out while they were riding. "I'm still thinking about it." She drew confidence from the familiar rhythm of the little mare, the friendly squeak of saddle leather and the comfort of breathing in the dry, sweet air of early morning.

"Really? Hell, you usually have something planned by April. I'll never forget that summer you got hooked on Australia—you playing that god-awful didgeridoo while you made me cook shrimp on the barbie."

"How did I know it would spook the horses?"

Mac laughed. "The sound of that thing would spook a corpse. Do you ever play it anymore, or are you taking pity on your neighbors?"

"Watch yourself, or I'll be forced to remind you of the time you mooned my brothers."

"That was totally not my fault. You could have told me the bridge club was coming out to admire your mom's roses."

Tess started to giggle. "So help me, I tried."

"Sure you did."

"The boys stopped me! I felt terrible that it happened."

"Uh-huh. That's why you busted a gut laughing and why you bring it up on a regular basis."

"Only in self-defense." She barely had to guide Peppermint Patty down the trail after all the times the horse had taken her to the river. The horses flushed a covey of quail as they trotted past.

She could smell the river ahead of them, and obviously so could Peppermint Patty. The mare picked up the pace. As always, Tess looked forward to her first glimpse of the miniature beach surrounded almost entirely by tall reeds. The perfect hideout.

As the mare reached the embankment and started down toward the sand, her hooves skidded a little on the loose dirt, but she maintained her balance, having years of experience on this particular slope. In front of them the river gurgled along, about fifty feet wide at this point. Other than a few ducks diving for breakfast and a mockingbird trilling away on a cottonwood branch across the river, the area was deserted.

There was no danger that anyone would overhear their discussion, and she trusted Mac to listen seriously without laughing as she laid out her problem and asked for his help. She couldn't have a better person in whom to place her confidence. Yet no matter how many times she told herself those things, her stomach clenched with nervousness.

MAC LET HIS gelding, Charlie Brown, pick his way down the embankment as Tess dismounted and led Peppermint Patty over to the river for a drink. This morning was exactly like so many other mornings he and Tess had ridden down here, and yet he couldn't shake off the feeling that this morning was like no other they'd ever spent together.

He watered his horse, then took him over to the sycamore growing beside the river. He looped the reins around the same branch Tess had used to tie Peppermint Patty and went to sit beside Tess on a shady part of the riverbank.

He picked up a pebble and chucked it into the water. "Did you hear from that teacher at your new school?"

"Yep." Tess plucked a stem of dry grass and began shredding it between her fingers. "I got an e-mail from her and she'll be glad to let me stay with her until I can find an apartment."

Mac glanced at Tess. He'd wondered when she'd suggested the ride if she had something specific on her mind. Maybe this move had her spooked. She'd been renting a little house ever since she got the counselor's job at Copperville High, but living on her own in a small Arizona mining town with her parents three miles away was a lot different than living alone in New York City, two thousand miles from everyone she knew.

"Would this teacher rent you a room in her apartment?" he asked.

Tess shook her head. "She doesn't have the space. I'll be on the couch until I can find an apartment of my own. Besides, I want my own place. After growing up in a house-ful of brothers, I've discovered I love the privacy of living alone."

"You just think you're living alone. Your family drops in on you all the time."

"I know." She sighed. "I love them, but I'm looking for-ward to being less convenient for a change."

Mac could understand that. It was one of the reasons he'd decided to get a private pilot's license. He looked for excuses to fly the Cessna because it was one of the few times he could be alone. "You might get lonesome," he said.

"I probably will." Tess began shredding another blade of wild grass. "But after living in a fishbowl for twenty-six years, lonesome doesn't sound so bad."

"Yeah." Mac tossed another pebble in the water. "I hear you." He breathed in the familiar mixture of scents—the dankness of the river, the sweetness of the grass, the light, flowery cologne Tess had worn for years, and the wash-line smell of sun on denim. Dammit all, he was going to miss her. He'd avoided facing that unpleasant fact ever since he found out that she'd gotten the job, but now it hit him all of a sudden, and he didn't like it.

Tess had been part of his world for as long as he could remember. So had the rest of her family, giving him the brothers and sister he'd always longed for. But Tess had always been the one he'd felt closest to. Maybe it was all those Halloweens together when she'd insisted he be Rag-gedy Andy to her Raggedy Ann, Han Solo to her Princess Leia, Superman to her Lois Lane. Or maybe it was the Easter-egg hunts, or the Monopoly games that lasted for days, or tag football—Tess had been there for everything. Every Christmas she dragged him out to go caroling even though he couldn't carry a tune in a bucket.

He'd die before admitting to her how much he'd miss

her. In the first place, they'd never been mushy and sentimental with each other, and in the second place, he didn't want to be a spoilsport right when she had this exciting chapter opening in her life. He was happy for her. He was jealous as hell and he'd have a hard time adjusting to her being gone, but that didn't mean he wasn't glad she had this chance.

"I'm glad you got the job," he said.

"Me, too. But I asked you to come here with me because I have this one problem, and I think you can help me."

"Sure. Anything."

"It's a different world there in New York, and I don't feel exactly...ready for it."

Her voice sounded funny as if she was having trouble getting the words out.

"You're ready." He broke off a blade of grass and chewed on the end of it. "You've been working up to this all your life. I've always known you'd go out there and do something special." He turned to her. "It's your ultimate quest, Tess. You might have butterflies, but you'll be great."

"Thanks." She smiled, but she looked preoccupied and very nervous.

He hoped she wasn't about to break their code and get sentimental. Sure, they wouldn't be able to see each other much, but they'd survive it.

She cleared her throat and turned to stare straight ahead at the river, concentrating on the water as if she'd never seen it flow before. God, he hoped she wouldn't start crying. She wasn't a crier, for which he'd always been grateful. He'd only see her cry a couple of times—when Chewbacca died and when that sleaze Bobby Hitchcock dumped her right before the senior prom. Good thing he hadn't had a date that night and had been able to fill in.

They'd had a terrific time, and he'd even considered

asking her out again, for real. She'd looked so beautiful in her daffodil-yellow dress that it had made his throat tight, and to his surprise he'd been a little turned on by her when they'd danced. He'd almost kissed her on the dance floor, until he'd come to his senses and realized how that would be received by the Blakely brothers. Then, too, he might gross himself out, kissing a girl who was practically his sister.

She continued to gaze at the river. "Mac, I—"

"Hey, me, too," he said, desperate to stave off whatever sappy thing she might be about to say. If she got started down that road, no telling what sort of blubbering he'd do himself. He chewed more vigorously on the blade of grass.

"Oh, I don't think so," she said in a strained voice. "The thing is, Mac...I'm still a virgin."

In his surprise he spit the blade of grass clear into the river. Then he was taken with a fit of coughing that brought tears to his eyes.

She pounded him on the back, but the feel of her hand on him only made him cough harder. Ever since he'd discovered the wonders of sex, he'd made sure that he and Tess didn't talk about the subject. Life was a lot safer that way, and he wished to hell she hadn't decided to confess her situation to him this morning.

As he sat there wondering if he'd choke to death, she stood up and walked toward the river. Taking off her hat, she scooped water into it and brought it back to him. She held it in front of his nose. "Drink this."

He drank and then he took off his hat and poured the rest of the cool water over his head. As he shook the moisture from his eyes and drew in a deep breath, he felt marginally better.

She remained crouched in front of him, and he finally found the courage to look at her. "So what?" he said hoarsely.

"I'm *twenty-six years old*."

"So?" His response lacked imagination, but she'd short-circuited his brain. If he'd ever thought about this, which he'd been careful not to, he'd have figured out that she was probably still a virgin. The Blakely boys had fenced her in from the day she'd entered puberty.

"I can't go to the big city like this. I can't counsel girls who've been sexually active since they were twelve if I've never, ever—"

"I get the picture." Much too graphically for his tastes. His mind had leaped ahead to a horrible possibility—that she would ask *him* to take care of her problem. And the horrible part was that he felt an urge stirring in him to grant her request. He pushed away the traitorous thought. "I think you could certainly go to New York without... experience. Chastity's catching on these days. You could be a role model."

"Oh, Mac! I don't want to be a role model for chastity! I didn't choose to be a virgin because of some deeply held belief. You know as well as I do that my brothers are the whole reason I'm in this fix."

Her brothers. God, they would skin him alive if he so much as laid a finger on her. "Well, your brothers aren't going to New York!" He knew the minute he said it that he'd stepped from the frying pan into the fire.

"No, they're not. And that's another point. I'll be clueless about sex and unchaperoned in a city full of sophisticated men. Is that what you want for me, to be swept off my feet by some fast-talking city slicker who'll play me for a fool because I don't know the score?"

This was a trap made in hell. And damned if he wasn't tempted. "Of course not, but—"

"I need a nice man, Mac. Somebody who can take care of this problem for me before I leave."

Oh, God. She was going to ask him. His heart hammered as he wondered if he'd have the strength to refuse her. "Listen, Tess. You don't know what you're saying."

"I know exactly what I'm saying. And you're the only person I trust to help me find that man."

CHAPTER TWO

"ARE YOU CRAZY?" Mac leaped to his feet so fast he knocked Tess over. The only thing worse than imagining him involved in this dirty deed was imagining some other guy involved. "Sorry." He reached down and gave her a hand up. Once she was steady on her feet, he released her hand quickly.

She dusted off the seat of her jeans. "Mac, please. I can't stay a virgin forever."

"Why not?" So he was being unreasonable. He couldn't help it. And dammit, now he'd caught himself watching her dust off her fanny and thinking that it was a very nice fanny. *Dammit.*

She sighed and lowered her head. "I was so counting on your help."

"Aw, jeez." Not only was he having inappropriate thoughts about her, he also felt as if he'd abandoned her. But he couldn't imagine how in hell he could diffuse either situation. "Tess, you know I'd do anything in the world for you, but I can't see how this would work."

Her head came up, and hope gleamed in her gray eyes.

He backed a step away from her. "Don't look at me like that."

"Here's how it will work. We'll brainstorm the possibilities and come up with a shortlist. Then you can find out if any of the guys are seeing anyone, because I don't want to break up any—"

"Whoa." Panic gripped him. "I never said I'd do this."

"You said you'd do anything for me."

"Anything but find you a lover!" Just saying it gave him the shivers. He'd worked so hard to keep from thinking of Tess in a sexual way, and now the barriers were coming down. For the first time he acknowledged the sweet stretch of her T-shirt across her breasts and the inviting curve of her hips. "I think that's a little more than a reasonable person should expect, don't you?"

"This is perfectly reasonable! Why should I search around on my own and end up with some clumsy nerdling who makes my first experience a nightmare, when I can rely on your advice and have a really nice time instead?"

There had to be a good answer to that one. He just needed a moment to think of it. And he couldn't think while he was picturing Tess having a "really nice time."

"See?" She gave him the superior little smile that she reserved for the times she'd won either an argument or a game of Monopoly. "You have to admit it makes sense."

"I don't have to admit anything. And why me? Why not one of your girlfriends? I thought women exchanged notes on guys all the time."

"They do, but you're a better source of info." She stuck her hands in her hip pockets. "You've dated more people around here than anyone I know. You'd know what women say about a guy, and you've had a chance to get to know the guys themselves and what they're really like. You'd know if they brag in the locker room, for example. Besides all that, there's not a single person, man or woman, I trust to keep my secret as much as I trust you."

He gulped. When she put it that way, he didn't know how he could refuse. And he wished she wouldn't stand like that, with her hands in her hip pockets and her chest thrust forward. He didn't like it. Okay, he liked it too much.

"Mac." She reached out and put her hand on his arm. He tried not to flinch. Tess had put her hand on his

arm a million times. She'd grabbed him for various reasons, usually to inflict injury, and he'd grabbed her back.
He'd held her hand when she was a little kid and they'd
gone trick-or-treating, and they'd clutched each other and
screamed when they rode the Twister at the state fair.
Touching had never been a big deal. Until now.

"Listen, Mac," she said. "You pulled out my first tooth,
remember?"

"Different case."

"And you taught me to drive." She grinned. "You also
gave me my first drink of whisky."

"You begged me for it, and then you threw up."

"And you held my head. You see, at all those important
moments in my life, you were there to guide me."

"This is *way* different."

"Not if you stop being a prude."

"I'm not a—"

"What about Donny?"

"Donny Beauford?" He snorted. "You can't be serious."

"Why? What's wrong with Donny?"

Mac couldn't say exactly, except that when he thought
of Donny in an intimate embrace with Tess, his skin began
to crawl. He passed a hand over his face and gazed up
through the leaves of the sycamore. Finally he glanced at
her. "He wouldn't…take care of you."

"Oh." Her cheeks grew pink, but she faced him bravely.
"You mean sexually?"

"In any way."

"Oh. Now, see, that's exactly what I need to know. How
about Stu?"

"Oh, God, he's worse."

"Buck?"

"Nope."

"I know who. Jerry."

"Definitely not! Jerry's a dweeb. He'd probably—" Mac

thought of some raunchy revelations he'd been privy to and decided to censor them. "Never mind. Not Jerry."

"Okay, then you make a suggestion."

He gazed at her as the silence filled with the sound of the river and the shuffling hooves of Peppermint Patty and Charlie Brown. The horses were becoming restless in the growing heat. Moisture trickled down his back, but he didn't think it was only the weather making him sweat. "I can't think of anybody." The truth was, he didn't want to think of anybody.

"Maybe you just need some time. I caught you by surprise."

"You certainly did that."

"Tell you what. Let's postpone the discussion. Maybe we could meet for dinner tonight."

"It's poker night."

"You're right. I can't, either. I'm playing pinochle at Joan's. Okay, then tomorrow night."

He decided a delay was the best he could hope for. He couldn't imagine what would occur to him to get him out of this mess in thirty-six hours, but maybe he'd stumble onto a miracle. "I'll meet you at the Nugget Café." He smiled. "It's meat-loaf night." Meat-loaf night at the Nugget was one of their shared treats.

"So it is. About six?"

"Yeah. Sounds good." He glanced up at the sun. "It's late. We'd better get back. I've got tons to do today."

"Yeah, me, too."

"Like what?"

"Research. I bought some books in Phoenix."

Mac had a feeling he shouldn't ask the question, but he did, anyway. "What sort of books?"

"On sexual techniques. When the time comes, I want to make sure I know as much as possible."

He felt as if somebody had kicked him in the stomach. "*This* is your summer project?"

"As a matter of fact, it is."

Mac groaned. It was even worse than he'd thought. When Tess settled on a summer project, a truckload of dynamite wouldn't dislodge her from her chosen path. If he knew Tess, and he thought he did, she would not be a virgin by the end of the summer. He could help her or not, but she would persevere until she'd checked off everything on her list.

TESS REALIZED HOW lucky she was that she liked each of the women her brothers had chosen to marry, and they liked her. When the guys got together for poker every Wednesday night, the wives hired babysitters and met at one of the other brothers' houses for pinochle. Tess was always invited. She'd miss the friendly, raucous evenings when she went to New York, but some sacrifices had to be made if she planned to live up to her own expectations.

Tonight the women were meeting at Rhino and Joan's. Rhino, originally named Ryan but indelibly stamped with a macho nickname in high school, was Tess's oldest brother and the acknowledged leader of the five siblings. He'd been the first to get married, buy a house and have kids.

From the moment Tess's niece Sarah had arrived in the world, Tess had decided being an aunt was the coolest thing in the world, although she was a little tired of being a maiden aunt. She arrived at Joan's early so she could see Sarah, who was now eight, and six-year-old Joe before Joan tucked them into bed.

After giving each of the kids the game she'd bought for them in Phoenix and joining in as Joan sang them silly good-night songs, she followed her dark-haired sister-in-law downstairs to the kitchen to help her get out chips and drinks for the party.

"Thanks for bringing them the game," Joan said as she took glasses out of the cupboard. "They're really going to miss you when you go to New York."

"I'm going to miss them." Tess emptied tortilla chips into a bowl and opened the refrigerator to search for the homemade salsa Joan always kept on hand.

"Oh, I don't know. You'll be living such an exciting life, I don't know if you'll miss anything from back here."

"Sure I will. I love this place, and my family and friends."

"Me, too." Joan turned to look at her. "But I'd give anything to be in your shoes."

"Really?" Tess gazed at her sister-in-law. With Joan's Hispanic, family-oriented background and her obvious dedication to her home and children, she seemed to have found her dream. "I thought you were the original Earth Mother."

"Don't get me wrong. I'm very happy. But the challenge has gone. When we first got married, everything was new. Sex was new, and then having kids was new, and then buying this house and fixing it up was new. But now it's all just a comfortable routine. And I want—" she paused to laugh "—more worlds to conquer, I guess."

"I so understand. That's the whole reason I'm going to New York. It's my Mount Everest." She hesitated, then decided to risk a suggestion. "Have you thought of going back to school?"

"I've already got the catalogs. I'm thinking—now don't laugh—of becoming a marriage counselor."

"No kidding! Joan, that would be wonderful. Obviously you know what goes into making a good marriage."

Joan gave her a rueful glance. "I wouldn't call me an expert. But I understand what happens when a couple gets to this point and sort of loses interest in each other."

Tess's jaw dropped. "You mean..."

"I mean things are getting really dull in the bedroom. I've been thinking of driving to Phoenix and getting some how-to books. I wouldn't dare buy anything like that in Copperville or the whole town would think I'd become a nymphomaniac."

"Amen to that. You know, I—" Tess stopped herself before she offered Joan a couple of her research books. She loved and trusted Joan, but she wasn't quite ready to tell her sister-in-law about her summer project. "I think that's a good idea," she said.

"I figured you would. Listen, I'm not saying anything against your brother. He's a great guy. It's just that we could probably both use some pointers."

"Sure. Most people can."

"I mean, you know how it is. You get used to a certain way of doing things, and then it all becomes mechanical."

"Absolutely." Tess felt like an impostor, having this discussion with Joan, who assumed Tess had some experience. If she needed any further proof she was doing the right thing, here it was.

Joan came over and gave her a hug. "Thanks for listening and encouraging me. Even though you're younger than I am, I always think of you as being more sophisticated, for some reason. Maybe it's your college degree."

Tess returned the hug. "Book learning isn't everything."

"No." Joan stepped back and smiled at her. "The ideal thing would be to have both."

"I couldn't agree more." And if Mac would help her, she would have both, at last.

THE POKER GAME was held at Tiny Tim's, the youngest and the largest of the Blakely clan. Tim was a newlywed, proud to show off the new digs he shared with Suzie in an apartment complex near the edge of town.

Mac had spent the entire day worrying the subject of

Tess's virginity, and the hell of it was, he could see her point. Her small-town background might make her seem unsophisticated to native New Yorkers. And if the kids she was counseling found out she had no sexual experience, either, that might become a credibility issue. Then there was the other problem—the very good possibility that some city dude, some fast-talking greenhorn, would take her virginity. Mac *really* didn't like thinking about that.

"Hey, Big Mac, are you in or not?" called Rhino from across the poker table.

Mac's head came up with a snap. Then he realized the question had to do with the cards in his hand, not whether he would help Tess find a lover for the summer. She'd sure ruined him for poker night. One of the things he loved about these weekly games was the simplicity of them. But nothing was simple tonight. No question was innocent. Even the name of the game, five card stud, had overtones he'd never noticed before.

He tossed his hand facedown on the table. "I'm out."

"Let's see what you got, Rhino," said Dozer, whose given name was Doug. Nobody called any of the brothers by their real names anymore. Doug and Hamilton, the two middle boys, had become Dozer and Hammer when they'd formed the heart of the offensive line for the Copperville High Miners.

The brothers were Mac's closest buddies, not counting Tess. Their mother and his were best friends, so the kids had naturally grown up spending a lot of time together. In high school the Blakely boys had literally covered his ass when he quarterbacked the Miners. But he saw them with new eyes tonight as he evaluated how each of them might react if they learned about the conversation he'd had with Tess this morning, and the fact that he hadn't turned her down flat.

"Read 'em and weep, Dozer," Rhino said, laying out

two queens and three sevens. At the tender age of thirty he was starting to lose his hair, and so he wore baseball caps a lot, even inside. Tonight's was a black one from the Nugget Café.

Rhino didn't miss much, which made him a damn good poker player. He'd likely be the first one to figure out if Mac had lined up some guy to initiate Tess, and he'd probably organize the retaliation against Mac and the poor unfortunate guy Mac had brought into the picture.

"Aw, hell," muttered Dozer, a redhead with a temper to match. He acted first, thought about it later. He'd been known to deck a guy who so much as looked at Tess wrong. "You must be living right."

"Nah," said Tiny Tim, pushing back his chair. "He's ornery as ever. Just lucky. Who needs a beer?" Tim didn't have a mean bone in his huge body, and couldn't even go hunting because of his tender heart. He'd do anything for anybody and never took offense—except when it came to somebody bothering his sister. Then all his tenderness evaporated. Mac had seen it happen.

"Hit me," said Rhino with a tug on his cap. "And don't be bringing out any of that light crap, either."

"Yeah, he wants something to put hair on his head," said Dozer.

"Funny," said Rhino. "Real funny."

"Don't blame me for the light beer," said Tim as he headed for the kitchen. "Suzie bought it. Said I needed to watch my waistline."

"Yeah, Deena's been giving me that old song and dance, too," said Hammer, the third and smallest of the brothers, although at six-three he was no midget. He was Mac's age and they'd been in many of the same classes in school. Logically he should have been Mac's best friend in the family, but Hammer wasn't a thinker, and Mac had always found more to talk about with Tess. Mac had often suspected Hammer was a little jealous of Mac's special relationship with his sister. This new development could really set him off.

Hammer glanced at Mac. "You don't know how good you've got it, with no woman to nag you to death about your diet."

"That's the truth," added Dozer. "It's getting so bad that if I haul out a bag of chips for *Monday Night Football,* Cindy tries to grab them away."

"And you let her?" Rhino asked. "You wouldn't catch that happening in my house. I lay down the law with Joan."

Mac led the chorus of hooting laughter. "Are you kidding?" he said. "Joan's got you wrapped around her little finger!"

Rhino grinned sheepishly.

"In fact," Mac continued, "I've never seen guys crazier about marriage than you four. You could hardly wait to march down that aisle. Don't give me this bull about nagging wives. You love every minute of it." And he envied them, he realized. They'd all found happiness.

Rhino took the beer Tim handed him and popped the tab. "So when are you gonna round out this ugly bunch and make it five for five?" He watched Mac over the rim of the can as he took a drink.

Mac gave his standard answer. "When I find the right woman."

"Hell, you've had a passel of right women." Dozer brushed back a lock of red hair from his forehead. "Jenny was great. I dated Jenny, and there was nothing wrong with her."

"So why did you end up with Cindy?" Mac asked.

"Cindy knows how to handle my temper. But you don't have much of a temper, Mac. Jenny would've been fine for you."

"Yeah, she would," said Hammer. "Cute figure."

"Obviously I should have taken a poll before I broke up with her." Mac picked up his beer.

"And Babs," Rhino said. "I liked Babs, too."

Mac swallowed his beer. "Me, too. Just not enough to last forever."

"Aw, you're too picky, Mac," said Tiny Tim. "That's your problem. Nobody's gonna be perfect." He grinned. "Although Suzie's close." He ducked a shower of peanut shells.

"The newlywed nerd might have a point, though," Rhino said. "Maybe you are too damn picky. What kind of standards are you using, if you eliminated two nice girls like Jenny and Babs?"

Mac shelled a peanut and tossed it in his mouth. Then he glanced around the table. "You know, I'm truly touched that you all are so worried about my marriage prospects. Maybe we should hold hands and pray about it. Maybe, if we concentrate real hard, I'll see the light, and grab the next available female I run across."

Rhino's bushy eyebrows lifted and he glanced at Tiny Tim. "Seems to me this apartment complex has a pool."

"Sure does." Tim pushed back his chair, as did the other Blakely brothers.

Mac saw the look in their eyes and pushed back his chair, too. "Now don't get hasty, guys. I was just making a joke."

"So are we," said Hammer. "Right, Dozer?"

"Yeah." Dozer grinned, revealing the tooth he'd chipped in the state championship football game eleven years earlier. "I *love* jokes."

As he was carried unceremoniously out to the pool and thrown in, Mac thought he probably deserved a dunking, but not for the reason the guys were doing it.

CHAPTER THREE

TESS HADN'T SPENT much of her life in dresses, but tonight's dinner with Mac seemed to require one. She didn't want to wear anything too fussy, not when the late-afternoon temperature had topped out at a hundred and five. She ended up choosing a sundress with daisies on it because she knew Mac liked daisies.

As she stood in front of the mirror wondering if she needed jewelry, she remembered the single teardrop pearl on a gold chain that Mac had given her as a high school graduation present. She'd been touched that he'd bought something so delicate and feminine, considering the rough-and-tumble nature of their friendship. Because she saved the necklace for special occasions, she seldom took it out of the black velvet box it had come in. Tonight seemed like the perfect time to wear it.

Once she was ready, apprehension hit her again. If Mac had willingly fallen in with her plan, she would have been calmer at this point. Her project was nerve-racking enough even if Mac agreed to help. If he continued to drag his heels, she'd need to gather her self-confidence to stay on track.

Her rented bungalow wasn't far from the center of town, so she decided to walk the two blocks to the Nugget and work off some of her anxiety. She slipped on her sunglasses, hooked the strap of her purse over her shoulder and started out. A block into the walk, she knew she'd made a mistake. She'd arrive at the restaurant more cooked than the meat loaf.

Mac pulled into a parking spot in front of the Nugget as she passed the drugstore two doors down from the café. As she walked, she watched him climb out of his white pickup. Although the truck was dusty from a day spent on ranch work, Mac wasn't. He'd obviously changed into a clean shirt and jeans, and he was wearing a dove-gray Stetson she'd never seen on him before.

He looked damn good, with his cowboy-slim legs encased in crisp denim and his broad shoulders emphasized by the cut of his gray plaid western shirt. Every so often in the years they'd known each other, she'd paused to notice that her best friend was a hunk, but she hadn't done that lately. She was noticing it now.

Maybe all her reading was affecting her. She suddenly wondered what sort of lover *Mac* would be. Then she quickly put the thought out of her mind. Mac was like a fifth brother to her. She shouldn't be having such thoughts about him. He'd be horrified if he knew.

As if sensing her eyes on him, he glanced in her direction before going into the Nugget. He paused. "Did your car break down?"

"I decided to walk."

He scratched the back of his head as he stared at her. "But it's June."

"So I discovered. I have to admit I'm a little warm." Up close she could smell his aftershave and noticed there was no stubble on his square jaw. For some reason the fact that he'd showered and shaved for this dinner made her stomach fluttery.

He looked her up and down from behind his sunglasses and then shook his head. "I thought I taught you better than this. Now after that hot walk you'll hit that cold air-conditioning. It's not good for your system."

"Oh, for heaven's sake. You sound like my mother. Could you at least mention that my dress looks nice? I wore it because you like daisies."

"Your dress looks nice. And you're going to catch your death of cold in that restaurant."

It wasn't the reaction she'd expected. As her irritation grew, she realized she'd secretly hoped he'd be dazed and delighted by her appearance, the way guys in movies reacted when a tomboy type like her showed up in a dress. "Let me worry about that."

"Fine. Just don't come crying to me when you catch a summer cold."

"I promise it won't be your responsibility."

"I'm glad to know at least something's not my responsibility." He held the door open for her and the brass bells hanging from the handle jangled.

She stayed where she was. "Look, if that's going to be your attitude, maybe we should just forget the whole thing."

"And then what?"

"In or out, you two!" called Janice, a waitress who'd been working at the Nugget ever since Tess could remember. "We don't aim to air-condition the entire town of Copperville!"

Mac let the door swoosh closed again and turned back to Tess, his expression impassive. "What'll it be?"

She didn't really want to call the whole thing off. She needed Mac to help her, and besides, he'd shown up for dinner all shaved and showered. It would be a shame to waste that effort. "Let's have some meat loaf," she said.

MAC HELD THE door for Tess a second time and tried not to drool as she walked past him trailing her cologne like a billowing scarf. When he'd seen her coming down the street in that flirty, daisy-covered dress he'd almost swallowed his tongue. Then she'd gotten close enough that he could see the moisture gathering in her cleavage, right where the pearl nestled.

He fought the crazy urge to lean down and lick the drop of moisture away before it disappeared into the valley between her breasts. He must be out of his mind. Fantasies like that didn't apply to Tess, the girl who could ride her bike no-hands down Suicide Hill, a girl who could throw a baseball so hard that it stung when it hit his glove. *But the girl is a woman now.* He couldn't ignore the truth any longer. He'd had glimpses of the fact over the years, like the first time he'd seen her in a bikini and she actually filled the thing out. And the prom had been another revelation, but he'd come to his senses before he'd done something stupid like kissing her. Sure they'd kissed when they were little kids, just to see what all the fuss was about, but it hadn't meant anything.

Funny, though, he still had a vivid memory of the spring day down by the river when they'd decided to try kissing. If he concentrated, he could still feel her soft little-girl's mouth that had tasted like pink bubble gum. When he'd pulled back to get her reaction, she'd looked sort of dreamy and sweet. Then she'd grinned at him and blown a big bubble that popped all over her face, destroying the moment.

He followed her through the restaurant to the back booth, the one they always took at the Nugget. Along the way he managed to return greetings from the others in the café, people he'd known all his life. But his attention was claimed by the sway of Tess's hips under the flared skirt covered with daisies. The dress zipped in the back, and he figured she had nothing but panties on under it. The combination added up to what he and his buddies used to call a good make-out dress.

Damn. He had to stop thinking like this. Late this afternoon he'd finally decided maybe he should try to fix her up with someone. He'd come up with a couple of possibilities and had told himself he'd rather have Mitch or Randy be the lucky guy than some sleaze in New York.

Now he didn't want Mitch or Randy anywhere near her.

But if he didn't help her, no telling what harebrained thing she'd do. He'd seen her get a bee in her bonnet enough times to know she wouldn't give up her summer project easily. The year she'd decided to learn how to use in-line skates, she'd sprained her ankle and bloodied both knees, but she hadn't given up. And she had learned.

He slid into the booth across from her and tried to pretend this was like all the other times they'd shared a meal or a milk shake at the Nugget.

"Hungry?" she asked.

"You bet," he lied. He wondered if he'd be able to force anything down. He'd never look at her the same way again, he realized in despair. No matter what happened, the friendship had been changed forever. He'd made the mental leap and begun to think of her as a desirable woman—more desirable than he ever would have imagined. He could hardly believe that all these years he'd managed to screen out her sexuality.

"Have you been thinking about...what we discussed?"

"Some." He blew out a breath. "A lot."

"Any ideas?"

Yeah, and all of them X-rated.

Janice sauntered over to their table, notepad in hand. "Hey, you two."

Tess smiled at her. "Hey, Janice. How's that grandkid?"

Janice reached in the pocket of her skirt. "Take a look." She tossed a snapshot of a baby down on the table.

"Oh, Janice, she's gorgeous."

"Isn't she?"

"Cute kid," Mac said, although he was more interested in the look on Tess's face than the picture of Janice's grandchild. As Tess gazed at the photo, her expression grew soft and yearning. Only a fool would misinterpret that expression, and Mac wondered if Tess knew how much she wanted a baby of her own. Hell, that was another thing he'd never connected with Tess, but she'd make a great mother. Which meant she had to find somebody who'd be a great father. The whole idea depressed him.

Janice scooped the picture up and slipped it back in her pocket. "So, are you guys having meat loaf or something else?"

"Meat loaf for me," Tess said.

"Same here." Mac hoped he'd feel more like eating when their order arrived.

"The usual on the salad dressing?"

"Yep," they both said at once.

"Iced tea?"

"Yep," they said again.

Mac thought about Tess going to New York, where the waiters wouldn't automatically know she liked honey-mustard salad dressing, coffee in the winter and iced tea in the summer. He thought about her eating alone at a restaurant, or worse, eating with some guy. Some guy who would be having the same thoughts Mac was having right now.

"I'll be back with your tea and salads in a jiff." Janice headed back toward the kitchen.

Mac stared at Tess, not sure what to say for the first time in all the years he'd known her. They'd always been able to talk to each other. They'd been able to hang out without talking, too. She was the sort of girl you could take fishing, because she'd sit, her line in the water, and let the peacefulness of the day wash over her. But there was nothing peaceful in the silence between them tonight.

"It was pretty hot today," he said. Then he rolled his eyes. They'd been reduced to talking about the weather. "Forget I said that."

She smiled. "Okay." She leaned forward, which made the pearl shift and dip beneath the neckline of her dress. "Remember the time we put pennies on the train tracks?"

He gazed at the spot where the pearl had disappeared. Then he glanced up again, aware that he shouldn't be looking there. They were in a public place. Anyone could walk in and catch him at it. One of the Blakely boys, for example. "Yeah, I remember."

"I never told anybody."

"Me, neither."

"That was twenty years ago, Mac. You and I have kept that silly secret for twenty years, because we both have the same sense of honor. That's why I'm asking you for help. I know you won't tell."

"I swear, you two look like you're hatching a plot," Janice said as she set down two iced teas, then plopped a salad plate in front of each of them and a basket of rolls in the center of the table. "Aren't you a little old to be painting water towers and such?"

"My folks' anniversary is coming up," Tess said. "Thirty-five years."

"Aha! And you're going to give them a surprise party." Tess looked secretive. "Could be."

"My lips are zipped," Janice said. "But be sure and invite me."

"I will."

After she left, Mac leaned closer to Tess. The scent of her cologne worked on him, giving him ideas he shouldn't be having, but he didn't want anyone to overhear him. "You see how complicated this can get? Now you're going to have to give your parents a party to cover your tracks!"

She shrugged, and the straps of her dress moved. "No problem. It's a good idea, anyway."

His fingers tingled as he imagined slipping those straps down. Slipping the sundress down. With a soft oath he leaned back against the booth. "I'll bet you're freezing in here, right?" He wasn't freezing, that was for sure.

"Not really." She reached up with both hands and combed her damp hair back from her face with her fingers. The motion lifted her breasts under the cotton of the dress, and there was no doubt that she was braless.

Mac told himself he wasn't getting turned on. Definitely not. "Let me get that old flannel shirt I keep in the truck."

"I don't need your old flannel shirt. I'm fine."

But he needed her to cover up. "I could get it anyway, just in case." He started to leave the booth.

"Mac, I don't want the blasted shirt, okay? I want to get this project going. So sit down and tell me what you've got."

He stared at her, his mind in turmoil. He should tell her about Mitch and Randy. He really should.

"Meat loaf's here!" Janice announced. "Goodness, you haven't touched your salads. Must be some party you two are cooking up."

"You don't know the half of it," Tess said. She moved her salad plate to one side. "Just set it down there, and I'll eat everything together."

"Me, too," Mac said, following suit.

"Better clean your plates," Janice said. "Or no dessert for you. And Sally made fresh peach pie today."

Mac patted his stomach, which was in no mood for a meal, let alone dessert. "Sounds great. You know I love peach."

Once Janice had disappeared, Tess leaned forward again. "That reminds me," she said in an undertone. "I've been learning the most amazing things from my reading. For example, the use of flavored oils. Did you know they make peach?"

"No." His jeans started growing tight. Mind over matter wasn't working.

"Have you read any books on the subject?"

"No." He stabbed his salad, determined to get through some of this food if it killed him.

"There are some wonderful ideas in there. You might want to take a look."

He lost control of his fork and it clattered to the plate. "I don't think so."

"Oh, for heaven's sake. Men and their egos. I'll bet even you could learn something."

He picked up his fork and returned to his meal with a vengeance. "Thanks, but I think I'll just blunder along on my own."

"Okay, but this is a perfect opportunity to check the books out without anybody knowing you're doing it. When I leave, I'll be taking those books with me and you'll be SOL."

"I won't be likely to forget you're leaving."

The light of amusement faded in her eyes. "Oh, Mac. I'm sorry. I didn't mean to say it like that. I know you'd love to do the same."

He clamped down on his emotions. There was no point in wanting what you couldn't have. "I wouldn't say that. And somebody has to take over the ranch. I noticed this past winter that my dad's already slowing down."

"Have you ever given them the slightest hint that you don't want to take over?"

"I do want to take over. They've struggled so hard to build that place and keep it going. It would kill them to have to sell it to strangers when they can't work it anymore." He looked into her eyes. "If you were an only child, would you be heading for New York?"

She seemed about to say yes, when she hesitated. Then she sighed. "Probably not. It really helps that my brothers look like they're going to stay in Copperville forever." She sent Mac a look of deep sympathy. "You can come and visit me anytime you want. I'll show you New York in style."

"Thanks. Maybe I'll take you up on that."

"We could have a great time. The top of the Empire State Building, the Statue of Liberty, Central Park, Times Square. Promise me that you'll come to visit me, Mac. It would be so wonderful to have that to look forward to."

"Okay, I promise." His heart wrenched at the thought of how much they probably would enjoy themselves. And then he'd have to come home again and leave her there. Well, he'd just have to get over it. His life was here, and hers would be there, and that's the way it was meant to be.

"I feel so much better, knowing that you'll come to visit me." Her eyes glowed. "I guess I always pictured seeing some of those things with you. Maybe I'll wait until you get there before I do some of that tourist stuff, so we can both experience it at the same time. I've heard Ellis Island is very moving. And the Metropolitan Museum of Art will be beautiful, and we could save our money and eat at one of those pricey restaurants, at least once, and—"

"I'm not taking you to a pricey restaurant unless you can do better on the food than you're doing here."

She glanced at her plate and picked up her fork. "I guess I'm distracted. I can't seem to think of anything except this move, and getting ready for it." She pushed her food around and glanced up at him. "Mac, I know you think I'm crazy for wanting this one thing before I go."

"Not crazy." He laid down his fork and gave up all pretense of eating. God, she was beautiful. Not cute, not attractive, not passable. Beautiful. He'd never admitted that to himself before, but he'd probably always known it on some unconscious level. He'd been entranced watching her talk about their future adventures in New York.

"Then you understand?"

"Yes."

She sagged against the table, and her sigh was heavy with relief. "Thank goodness. I wondered if I'd ever convince you."

"I'm convinced."

"Then you'll help me? You'll find someone and introduce us?"

Maybe he'd known all along what he had to do. Maybe he'd just needed time for the inescapable truth to settle upon him. But now he could see no other way. It was dangerous, extremely dangerous. A great deal was at stake. Still, it was the only answer, and he was man enough to accept that, along with the consequences.

He took a deep breath. "I don't have to look for someone. I already know who will do it."

"You do?" Her eyes grew bright, her cheeks pink. "Who?"

"Me."

CHAPTER FOUR

Tess gasped and put her hand over her mouth. She felt as if someone had dumped a bucket of warm water over her. Oh, God. Mac. Could she do it? Her imagination quivered and danced around the idea, unable to focus on the possibility. Her heart beat so loudly she thought he might be able to hear it. Mac. Oh, dear. How delicious. How impossible. How frightening. How lovely.

"Unless you don't want me to."

She was having trouble breathing, let alone talking. "I—I—"

"It's okay if you don't. I might not be...what you want."

"I...have to think."

"Sure."

Although she was caught up in her own turmoil, she sensed his vulnerability. "I'm honored," she choked out.

"Honored?"

"That you'd even consider...that you'd even be willing..."

"Better me than anybody else I can think of."

"Is it..." She paused and squeezed her eyes shut. "Such a sacrifice, then?" At his astonished laughter, she opened her eyes.

"Are you kidding?" He stared at her in wonder. "If word got out that you were in the market, the line outside your door would stretch all the way to the Nugget."

"You think?" He'd never, ever given her such an extravagant compliment about her sex appeal. His compliments on that score had been nonexistent, come to think of it.

"You could have your pick," he said. "You don't have to settle for me. I just thought—"

"That I'd feel more comfortable with you. Thank you, Mac. And I probably would. Once I get over the shock."

"Take your time."

"You won't change your mind?"

He shook his head.

"But what about my brothers?"

He let out his breath in a great gust. "I won't pretend that won't be tough. But I've kept our secrets from them before." He gazed at her. "I guess I can do it again."

She'd never been so impressed with another human being in her life. "I don't deserve such a good friend."

He gave her a crooked smile. "Don't go giving me too much credit. This wouldn't be the worst assignment I'd ever drawn in my life."

"So you think you could have...fun?"

"I think I could manage that."

Tess leaned back in the booth and fanned herself with her hand. "Wow. This blows me away." She glanced at him with his fresh shower, shave and clothes. "Did you decide this before you showed up tonight?"

"No. I honestly didn't know what I was going to say to you when I got here. Then, while we were talking, I finally decided this was the only solution I could live with."

She hesitated, feeling unbelievably shy. "The reason I asked is that I wondered, considering that you're all cleaned up, if you thought that we'd just...take care of it."

He coughed and cleared his throat. "Is that what you want?"

She couldn't seem to control her racing pulse, and every breath was a struggle. "I don't know. I realize this is my project, but I'm not feeling very much in charge right now."

He gazed at her. "I have a suggestion."

She swallowed. He was the sexiest man she'd ever seen in her life. How had she missed that in all these years? "Okay."

He leaned forward and beckoned her to do the same. He lowered his voice and his eyes grew smoky blue. "Maybe we need to work up to this. We could take a drive, park somewhere, do some old-fashioned making out and see how it goes. And to take the pressure off, we'd agree not to go all the way this first time."

He was so close that his breath caressed her face. His hands—hands that had positioned her grip on a baseball bat, picked her up when she fell off her bike and pinched her when she'd dropped the frog down his back—had taken on a whole new significance. And they lay less than an inch from hers on the Formica tabletop. As she looked into his eyes, her heart beat so fast she thought she might have a heart attack. This was a Mac she'd never met before. "I g-guess we could do that, but…"

"But? And how were you envisioning the process?"

Her cheeks grew hot. "Honestly?"

"Honestly."

She kept her voice to a low murmur, which increased the sense of intimacy in the booth. "If you'd set me up with someone, I envisioned a one-night stand, to get it over with."

He winced. "That's a terrible idea."

"It is?"

He held her gaze with those electric eyes. "I thought you wanted to have a nice time."

"I do." She drew a shaky breath. "But couldn't I have a nice one-night stand?"

"Not you. Some women, maybe. Not you. You need to ease into it."

"That's why I've been reading all those books. And I'm a quick study."

His eyes twinkled and his mouth twitched as if he wanted to smile, but he didn't.

"What?"

"It's just so you, to thoroughly study a subject before you get into it."

He had her totally off balance, and she wasn't used to feeling that way with Mac. She tried to equalize the situation. "I could probably teach you a few things, Mr. Know-It-All!" she whispered a little louder than she'd meant to. Then she glanced around quickly to see if anyone was listening. Nobody seemed to be paying them any attention, which wasn't surprising. Seeing the two of them huddled over the table in the back booth of the Nugget was commonplace.

Mac leaned back against the worn seat, amusement in his eyes. "No doubt you could." As they continued to gaze at each other in silence, his expression became more guarded. He picked up his spoon and balanced it on his forefinger. "The question is, do you want to? Last time I checked, the ball was still in your court."

"I don't know, Mac. This is very…personal."

"That's a fact." He concentrated on the perfectly balanced spoon.

"You know me so well."

"About as well as anybody."

"Things would never be the same between us."

He laid the spoon down. "They're already different." He glanced at her. "Am I right?"

Oh, yes. The blue eyes she'd always taken for granted now had hidden secrets, and she was already wondering how those eyes would look filled with passion. Passion for her. The thought made her body tighten and throb in ways that had nothing to do with friendship. "You're right," she said.

"Let's get out of here."

Anticipation leaped in her, making her shiver. "What about your dinner?"

"I wasn't hungry to begin with. But if you want, we could have Janice box it up."

"Let's not bother. It won't last in this heat."

"Probably not." Mac reached in his back pocket for his wallet. "We don't need a bill. As long as we've been eating this Thursday-night special, we should know what it costs."

"Right." Tess opened her purse.

"Put your money away, Tess."

She glanced at him. "But we always split the bill. I don't want you to think that just because—"

"New game, new rules. You're my date tonight, and dinner's on me."

The gesture thrilled her more than she was willing to admit. "Aren't you taking this a little too literally?"

"Nope." He slid out of the booth. "I would expect any man in my position to have the courtesy to buy you a meal."

Her feminist conscience pricked her. "What, as some sort of barter arrangement?"

He took his hat from the hook at the end of the booth and settled it on his head. "No, as an expression of gratitude."

Her breath caught in her throat at his gallantry. No wonder he'd had women falling at his feet. She'd never quite understood it, but then, he'd never turned the full force of his charm on her.

Janice ambled over toward them. "Leaving so soon?" She glanced at their plates in surprise. "Was something wrong with the meat loaf?"

"No," Tess said. "We—"

"Goodness, you're flushed." Janice put her hand against Tess's cheek. "You're feeling feverish, child. I'll bet you're coming down with the flu."

"I think she might be, too," Mac said. "That's why we decided to leave."

"My Steve came down with the flu last week. You wouldn't think a bug could survive in this heat, but it seems to be going around. Best thing to do is stay in bed."

Tess felt her face heat, and she didn't dare meet Mac's gaze. "Right."

"Look at you!" Janice exclaimed. "You're burning up! Better get on home."

"What's wrong with Tess?" called Sam Donovan from his stool at the counter.

"Flu!" Janice called back.

"Flu?" asked Mabel Bellweather, popping up from the booth where she'd been sitting with her sister Florence. She hurried to Tess's side. "Should I call your mother, honey? She'd want to know if you've come down with the flu."

"I'll call her, Mrs. Bellweather," Mac said.

Mabel patted his arm. "You're a good boy, Jeremiah MacDougal. Anybody'd think you were kin to Tess, the way you've watched out for her over the years. I know she'll be in good hands."

Tess looked at the floor, at the walls covered with Frederic Remington prints, at the golden light of sunset outside the café windows. Anywhere but at Mac.

"Just get along now," Janice said, guiding them toward the door.

Although she wanted to run out the door, Tess made herself walk like a sick person as she preceded Mac through the restaurant. They exited to a chorus of get-well wishes.

Mac helped her into the truck. "Well, at least we're being inconspicuous about this."

"We can't go through with it," Tess wailed. "Soon everybody in town will know that you took me home from the Nugget, and—"

"And what?" He started the truck and switched on the air-conditioning. "You're letting a guilty conscience run away with you. They aren't the least bit suspicious of us being together." He backed out of the parking space and headed down the street toward her house.

"You're sure?"

"I'm sure. You saw the way Mrs. Bellweather patted me and told me I was a good boy."

Tess glanced over at him. "And is that what you intend to be?"

He pulled up at the town's only stoplight and gave her a look that threatened to fry her circuits. "Depends on your definition."

STAY COOL, MAC told himself. He was supposed to be the experienced stud, the one who knew the score. If he gripped the wheel tightly enough, Tess wouldn't know that his hands were shaking. And if she noticed he was sweating, then he'd blame it on the hundred-degree temperature.

The reaction they'd gotten at the Nugget had convinced him of one thing—nobody would suspect that he and Tess had progressed to more than friends for the same reason he'd taken so long to come around to the idea. It was totally out of character for both of them. Even the Blakely brothers wouldn't guess, if he and Tess could keep from tipping them off.

But oh, God, what had he done? His whole world was turning upside down. If Tess agreed, then they would become lovers this summer, assuming he didn't turn out to be like his old dog George, who'd been taught to stay out of the living room when he was a puppy and now couldn't be dragged in there. Mac wasn't sure how deep his hands-off conditioning ran, but he might find out soon.

He'd already discovered he was more possessive about Tess than he'd ever dreamed. If he made love to her this summer, that possessiveness could get out of control. And he couldn't allow that, because she was going to New York, and she'd meet other guys there. And that would lead to… he didn't even want to think about where that would lead. He was setting himself up to go crazy, that's what he was doing.

But he couldn't see any other way around the problem.

"Are you really going to take me to my house?" she asked.

He glanced at her. She still hadn't committed to anything. "Do you want me to?"

"Not really." She was staring straight ahead, holding on to her little straw purse for dear life. Sunglasses hid her eyes, but her cheeks gave her away. They were the deep pink of the sunset lining the horizon. Her chest rose and fell quickly, making the pearl quiver in the valley where it lay against her golden skin.

The air in the cab grew sweet and thick with desire, until Mac felt as if he could lick it like a cone of soft-serve ice cream. "So you want to take that drive?" His voice was slightly hoarse.

"Yes, but I've figured out what we should do. Let's go to my house and sit in the driveway for a little while, in case anybody notices. Then I'll get down on the floor of the cab, and we can drive away to…wherever you had in mind."

Instantly he became aroused. Apparently the old dog would be able to learn new tricks. "All right."

She still didn't look at him. "You know, we might not be able to do anything. We might start laughing or something."

"Laughing's okay. Laughing usually means you're having a good time."

"I mean because we feel ridiculous."

That hadn't occurred to him. "Do you think you will? Feel ridiculous?"

"I don't know. Maybe I should pretend you're someone else."

"Don't do that." The idea incensed him more than it probably should have. "That would be insulting."

"Okay."

He pulled into her driveway and glanced at her. The pretending statement had him going. "Who would you pretend I was?"

"Nobody, because you don't want me to."

"Yeah, but if I didn't care, who would you superimpose over my face? Brad Pitt?"

She turned to him and took off her sunglasses. "I don't know. I hadn't really thought about it. Forget I said anything."

"Tom Cruise?"

"Mac, I won't be doing it, so let's drop the subject."

He couldn't drop it. He had to know who she thought was sexy. "Antonio Banderas? Mel Gibson?"

"All of them!" she said, clearly exasperated. "In a rotating sequence! With Leonardo DiCaprio thrown in for good measure! There, are you happy now?"

He stared at her. Good Lord, he was jealous that she'd imagine a movie star making love to her instead of him. He was in big trouble. "Sorry," he said. "Feel free to imagine anybody you want."

She looked at him as if he'd gone around the bend, which was pretty much true. "Okay."

"Just don't tell me about it."

"If you say so. But if you've never tried it, you might want to reconsider. Some men get very turned on by hearing their partner's fantasies about other men."

"Somehow I don't think I'd fall into that category."

"If you say so," she repeated. She seemed to be relaxing, if her superior little smile was any evidence. It was the kind of smile that told him she didn't think he had the foggiest notion what he was talking about.

Maybe he'd have to take a look at those books of hers, after all. She definitely had him at a disadvantage. Sure, he'd glanced through his share of sexy magazines when he was a teenager, but he'd been concentrating on the pictures, not the text. He'd thought he'd be the teacher and she, the student, the way it had been all their lives. The idea that she might know more about sex than he did wasn't entirely comfortable.

She unsnapped her seat belt. "I guess I'd better get down on the floor of the cab now," she said.

"Wait a minute. It's all dirty down there. You'll mess up your dress." He opened his door and reached around behind the seat where he always kept a soft blanket. He handed it to her. "Put that down first."

"I remember this! We used to make a tent with it in your backyard!"

"Yeah, that's the one."

She arranged it on the floor at her feet. "It's like meeting an old friend, seeing this blanket again, still so soft and blue. The binding's getting a little worn, though. What do you use it for, now?"

"Uh...different things." Suddenly he didn't want to tell her that he'd made love to several girls on that blanket. He kept it washed and tucked behind his seat to have handy if the weather was nice and the woman in his truck was willing. And now, dumb as it seemed, he felt as if he'd betrayed Tess by using the blanket that way.

She gazed at him. "It's all right, Mac. I know you've had a lot of women."

He shifted in his seat. "I wouldn't say I'd had a *lot*."

"Then my brothers must be lying. According to them, you've been to bed with more women than—"

"Does it matter?" He didn't like the direction the conversation was taking.

"I guess not. In a way it's a good thing. You've had lots of experience, so I assume you'll know what to do."

"And what I don't know, you'll be able to teach me."

She looked at him, eyes narrowed. "You don't like that idea much, do you, Mac?"

Damn, but she could read him like a book. She was the only woman who'd ever been able to do that. "Hey, I'm always open to new things."

"I know you. You like to be the one who has all the answers."

"That's not true. I can take suggestions as well as the next man."

"The experts all warn that sex is a sensitive topic, especially for guys. Maybe it would be best if I didn't mention any of the things I've learned. I wouldn't want to give you a complex."

That did it. "A complex! Hell, woman, make all the damn suggestions you want! My ego can take it!"

"See? You're already upset."

"I am not upset!"

She always seemed to know when to stop arguing and just gaze at him quietly, reflecting his behavior back to him.

Finally he gave her a sheepish smile. "Okay, so I'm a little intimidated."

"Wouldn't you like to learn more, if you could?"

"Sure. Only a fool wouldn't."

"Good." She looked extremely pleased with herself. "Then I can contribute something, after all."

That made him grin. "You think your biggest contribution will be from a book?"

That seemed to shake her poise and she blushed bright red. "Well, um, I guess not."

"I guess not, either."

She met his gaze for a fraction longer before she glanced away, obviously rattled. She took a deep breath. "I'm scared to death, Mac."

"Even with me?"

She nodded. "Especially with you. I know you have high standards. What if I disappoint you?"

He reached out and took her hand. It was different from any other time he'd held her hand, and they both knew it. He waited until she turned her head and looked into his eyes. "I wouldn't have offered to do this if I didn't want to, Tess. There's no chance that I'll be disappointed."

The uncertainty eased in her gray eyes. "Thank you."

He squeezed her hand and released it. "We're giving each other the jitters, sitting here thinking about it. We'll be better off once we get started."

"You're probably right. So here goes." She turned on the seat and started hunching down so she could fit on the floor. "Take a look and make sure nobody's around to see me doing this."

He scanned the tidy little neighborhood. "I don't see anybody. Most people are probably inside having dinner right now."

She tucked herself down onto the blue blanket. "Punch it, cowboy."

And so it began. He took a deep breath and put the truck in Reverse. He'd done some wild things in his life, but this had to be the granddaddy of all risks he'd ever taken. He hoped that this time he hadn't finally bitten off more than he could chew.

CHAPTER FIVE

KNEELING ON THE BLANKET on the floor of the truck, Tess felt more wild and crazy than she had in years. She had developed a taste for reckless adventure after tagging along after her brothers and Mac when she was a kid. Lately she'd been missing that adrenaline rush.

She rested her arms on the seat and pillowed her head on her arms. She had two choices—either she could look at the passenger-side door on her left or Mac's thigh on her right. With her feeling of adventure still running strong, she looked to her right.

His muscled thigh flexed as he stepped down on the gas, making the denim of his jeans move in subtle and tantalizing ways. Just beyond was the ridge of his fly. Her pulse quickened as she contemplated the ramifications of her decision. Of course, if they discovered they had no talent for making out with each other, they could call a halt to the whole program.

Mac clicked on the radio and a soft country tune filled the cab. She'd ridden in Mac's truck with the radio on hundreds of times. They'd sung along with the music, even rolled down the windows and turned up the volume when they were feeling really rowdy and wanted to stir up the neighborhood. She realized now that she'd always felt more alive when she was with Mac.

She certainly felt alive right now. Every nerve ending was checking in and registering the soft blanket under her knees, the tweed fabric of the seat beneath her arms, the waft of the air-conditioning over her bare back. The scent of Mac's aftershave used to be a comforting presence, letting her know her friend was nearby. Now it signaled something else entirely. The man who would soon take her in his arms was sitting very close to her.

"We're going to be on a dirt road in a minute," he said. "I'll try not to jolt you too much. Once we've gone a ways, you can probably sit up again."

"Where are we going?"

"A little road I found a couple of years ago. It goes out to the edge of a plateau where you have a nice view of Anvil Peak. Hold on. Here's comes the turnoff." He touched his booted foot to the brake, causing the denim to ripple again.

Watching Mac drive from this vantage point was quite an erotic experience, Tess decided.

He turned the wheel with one hand and reached over with the other to grip her shoulder as the truck bumped down off the pavement and onto the dirt. His hand was warm and sure as he held her steady. There was nothing seductive in his touch, and yet her heartbeat began to thunder in her ears and her whole body reacted to that point of contact. When he took his hand away, she wanted to have it back. Maybe his embrace wouldn't feel as awkward to her as she'd feared.

"Okay, I think you can sit up now. Nobody ever comes out here."

"Except you. You seem pretty familiar with the place." She crawled up to the seat and straightened her dress.

"I've been here a few times."

"Making out?"

"Now don't start asking me questions like that, Tess. You're going to spoil the mood for sure."

"Making out," she concluded.

He sighed and switched on the headlights.

"Well, I'm not dumb, you know. I understand the reason guys search for lonely roads." She looked around. Sure enough, there were no signs of civilization, just a road stretching to a point in the distance where the scrub-covered ground dropped away. Across the green swath of the river valley, Anvil Peak was silhouetted against a brick-red sky. To the right of that, the smokestack of the Arivaca Copper Mine sent a gentle plume into the air. "This is very pretty."

"I think so."

"So who did you bring out here?"

"Tess!"

"You pestered me about movie stars."

"And I shouldn't have. When two people are together, they should be concentrating on each other."

"Unless they want to explore the fantasy angle."

"Could we forget the fantasy angle? For all you know, being out here with you is my fantasy!"

She caught her breath and stared at him. "Is it?"

"No. Or at least I don't think so. I don't know what made me say that. Forget it."

But of course she couldn't forget it. And she remembered a dream she'd had about five years ago, one she'd put out of her mind as being silly. "Have you ever dreamed about me?"

"Of course I've dreamed about you. We see each other all the time. I dream about all the people in my life. Everybody does that."

"No, I mean, have you ever dreamed of me in a sexual way?"

He hesitated. "Yes. Once."

"So have I. About you."

He kept his attention on the dirt road. "That's probably normal."

"I didn't say it wasn't. What did you dream?"

"I...I can't remember."

"I don't believe you. Are you going to tell me what it was?"

"Nope."

"Do you want to know what I dreamed?" When he didn't answer, she smiled. "I'll take that as a yes. We'd gone out for ice cream at Creamy Cone one summer night, and mine was melting all over the place, and you'd forgotten to get napkins, like you always do."

"Not *always*."

"Most of the time. Anyway, I was a mess, and I didn't want to go home like that, so you decided the only solution was to lick the ice cream off me. We'd magically gotten down to the river by that time, and we were sitting on the sand in our special place. You started cleaning me up, like a cat would, and then…you started kissing me instead of licking, and…then you took my clothes off…" She wondered how much detail to include, but she felt dishonest leaving anything out.

"You kissed my breasts," she continued quickly, "and I said I was surprised you wanted to do that. You said you'd always wanted to, and you kissed them some more, and then you kissed me…all over." She decided to leave some details to his imagination. "Then right at the moment you were finally going to…well, you know…I woke up."

Her heart was pounding by the time she finished, and she had total recall of what she'd felt like in that dream, all warm and melting like the ice cream. She was definitely in the mood for a kiss. For more than a kiss.

Mac stopped the truck and switched off the lights and the engine. "That's…quite a dream." His voice sounded strained.

"Now you tell me yours."

"Maybe later."

"Was it anything like mine?"

"No."

She sat in the truck as the silence grew more and more intense between them. The air-conditioning was off, but the outside heat hadn't penetrated the cab yet. The warmth she felt was all coming from inside her, and she was ready to do something about it, but she didn't know whether she should make a move or let Mac be the first one. From the corner of her eye, she could see him sitting there, staring into space. He seemed hypnotized. At last she decided to say something. "What next?"

"Give me a minute. Then we'll take the blanket in the back."

She peered at him. "Are you feeling sick or something?"

"No, I'm feeling aroused."

"You *are?*" She glanced down at his jeans but it had become too dark to see much. "Cool. Was it my dream that turned you on?"

"Sure was. But then you probably knew that would happen, after all your reading about fantasies."

"No, I didn't." She felt thrilled with herself. "I wondered if you'd laugh."

He groaned. "I guess you don't know me as well as you think you do, then."

"Then you...really want me right now?"

He looked over at her. "Yeah. I really do. What a surprise, huh?"

"Oh, Mac." She put a hand against her racing heart. "That makes me feel so good."

He gave her a slow smile. "I guess this isn't going to be as difficult as we thought."

She smiled back. "I guess not. Want me to put the blanket in the back and wait for you?"

He took a deep breath. "I'm okay now."

"Are you ever going to tell me your dream?"

He took off his hat and laid it on the dash. "Not right now. It's a little more graphic than yours."

"And you said you didn't remember!"

"I've tried my damnedest to forget all about it. I thought I had, until you started talking about dreams." He opened his door. "Stay there. I'll come around and help you out. I don't want you stepping on a snake in those sandals."

"I've lived here all my life, Mac." She picked up the blanket from the floor. "I certainly know enough to check for snakes before I get out of a vehicle after dark in the middle of nowhere." She opened her door.

"Hey." He turned back to her. "Could you pretend that you're a timid female for a few minutes and give a guy a chance to be a big brave he-man? It's good for the ego."

"Oh." She grinned and pulled her door shut again. "All right, but I think it's stupid."

He shook his head. "Maybe this will be exactly as difficult as we thought."

Tess sat obediently while Mac rounded the truck and opened her door, although waiting for him to take care of things wasn't her style. But if that made him feel more romantic, then she was all for it.

He held out his hand. "I'll take the blanket first and then come back for you."

"I can take the blanket."

"Tess."

"Oh, okay, here's the blanket, Mr. He-man, but this is dumb. We could make it in one trip."

"Yeah, if we're going for efficiency. I was after a different effect." He walked around to the back of the truck, pulled down the tailgate and climbed in.

She listened to him arranging the blanket. A couple of years ago, he'd installed an all-weather cushioned pad in the bed of his truck. At the time she'd wondered if it had anything to do with his love life, but she'd decided not to ask. Now she was pretty sure she knew the answer.

He hopped down from the truck and came back to where she was waiting.

"Can I put my dainty foot on the ground yet?" she asked.

"Not yet." He gazed up at her. "Have you ever been lifted down from a pickup?"

"Not since I was six years old. Once I could manage by myself, it seemed silly when I was perfectly capable of—*whoa!*" She gasped as he took her by the waist and lifted her out of the truck. Instinctively she put her arms on his shoulders, which was a good move because her feet still dangled in midair.

Balancing her against his chest and looking into her eyes, he let her slide down in a slow, sensuous movement. Warmth rushed through her as the friction of his body against hers gave her a complete and thoroughly arousing caress. At last her feet rested on the ground, and she let out her breath.

He held her close and gazed down at her. "Did that seem silly?"

Completely absorbed in the experience of being tucked so intimately against him, she shook her head.

"Think you're ready for a kiss?"

Oh. She gulped. "I…don't know."

"Let's try it." Holding her close with one arm, he reached up with his free hand and gently combed her hair back from her face.

She'd seen this tender side of him, usually when he was working around animals, or the times when she'd hurt herself and he'd been the one to doctor her up. But now she wasn't hurt, and his sensitive touch was meant to excite, not soothe her. He was succeeding admirably. She was trembling so much she wondered if she'd be able to stay upright.

"You're nervous."

"Yes."

"Me, too." He continued to comb her hair back, lightly massaging her scalp with his fingers.

"I can't tell." His touch felt awesome.

"Macho guys learn to hide their nerves. I'm hoping you like this."

"So am I."

He chuckled. "Do you remember the bubble-gum kiss?"

"Yes," she murmured. The more he stroked her hair, the less capable she felt of standing on her own.

"Did you like it?"

She took a shaky breath. "So much it scared me. So I started goofing around."

He began tracing the contours of her face with the tip of his finger, ending with her mouth, which he outlined slowly and with great care. "I still remember how your mouth felt that day."

She held as still as she could, considering the fine quiver that seemed to have taken over her body. She focused on his touch, wanting to record every subtle variation in pressure.

He brushed her lower lip with his thumb. "Your mouth is still as soft as it was then."

She gazed up at him, trying to make out his expression in the shadowy twilight.

He cradled her cheek. "The last time I touched you like this, I was putting an ice pack over your eye, where you got hit by a baseball."

She could barely see his smile in the darkness. "You didn't touch me like this," she murmured.

"Sure I did." He slid his hand along her jaw and leaned closer.

"No. You were rougher." Her heart thudded with anticipation. "You were mad at me."

"I was mad at myself." He tilted her head back ever so slightly. "I was the one who hit that ball."

"And I'm the one who bobbled it."

"Mmm. Your mouth looks sexy when you say *bobbled*."

"You can't even see my mouth."

"Yes, I can. There's a little bit of light left over. That's why I tilted your head back, to catch that light. I wanted to see your mouth, to know I'm going to kiss it soon. Say the word again."

Desire curled and stretched within her. "You're crazy."

"Yeah." He drifted closer. "Say it for me, Tess."

"Bobbled."

"Again."

She felt his warm breath on her mouth. "Bobble—"

His lips touched hers, and in that instant, she knew that the world as she'd known it had ceased to exist. For she was really, truly kissing Mac, and now nothing would ever be the same.

TESS HAS BEEN forbidden fruit for so long that when Mac placed his mouth on hers, he half-expected a lightning bolt to strike him dead. Instead, her velvet lips welcomed him so completely that he drew back, his heart racing. Damn, this was going to be good. Too good. A man could lose himself to a kiss like that. If he'd ever secretly wondered if she was a virgin because she wasn't sensual, he'd been dead wrong. She was on fire.

"Mac?" she whispered. "Is something—"

With a groan he returned to her full mouth, committing himself to the kiss, to what would follow the kiss. To hell with what it might cost him. But he had a sinking feeling it would cost him more than he could ever guess.

For her mouth was a perfect fit for his. He didn't have to think about kissing Tess—it happened as effortlessly as breathing. She opened to him as if they'd been doing this for years, and although his body pounded with excitement, her invitation to pleasure seemed natural, almost expected. And he accepted without hesitation—tasting her richness, probing her heat, shifting the angle so he could deepen his quest.

Joy surged within him as she responded, pressing closer, moaning softly as he made love to her mouth. He thought of all the wasted years when she'd been there, only a touch away. But she was here now, so alive and warm in his arms, so ready.

Very ready. As she molded herself to him, he could feel her nipples, tight and aroused, pressing against his chest. His erection strained against his jeans. If he didn't slow down, he'd violate the terms of tonight's agreement and make love to her out here in the desert. That couldn't happen, first of all because he believed what he'd said about not rushing the process, and second because he had no birth control with him.

With great regret he drew back, breathing hard. The sun had gone down, and the stars didn't allow him to see her expression very well. He wished he could, but maybe it was for the best. Tonight promised to be intense enough without being able to see desire written all over her face.

"I...liked that," she said. Her breathing was about as ragged as his.

"Yeah." He rubbed her back and took a deep breath as a chorus of crickets started up in the nearby sagebrush. "Me, too."

She wound her arms around his neck and leaned back to look up at him, although she probably couldn't see his expression, either. "You're aroused again. I can tell by your voice."

"Any guy would be aroused if you kissed him like that."

"Was I too...uninhibited?" She sounded genuinely worried.

"God, no. You were great."

"I wondered, because I don't usually get so..." She paused. "Excited."

Man, he loved hearing that. "Really?"

"Especially the first time I kiss someone. You're, um, very good at this kissing business. I guess it's all your practice that gives you such good technique."

"That wasn't technique." He loved running his fingers through her hair. "That was...I don't know. You inspired me, I guess."

"Oh." There was a world of self-satisfaction in that tiny syllable.

He began itching to kiss her again. And he had all the rest of the territory labeled as "making out" to enjoy. Even knowing he wouldn't have the ultimate experience tonight didn't dampen his enthusiasm for the next step. "Ready to climb in the back of the truck?"

"I've been thinking. Are you sure you should?"

He laughed. "I think we dispensed with that a while back. No, I probably shouldn't, but I will anyway, because it's still the best solution."

"No, I mean, with the way you react when we kiss. I'll bet you're not used to just making out with a woman and not finishing the job. You're liable to get awfully frustrated."

He grinned down at her. "So are you. That's the idea— to build up to the main event, so we're really ready for it."

"I can understand that strategy for me, because of my lack of experience, but I'm afraid I'll be torturing you. I know from my reading that some men are able to draw out foreplay for a very long time, but I'm sure they extend that time gradually, so their bodies are used to delayed gratification. You wouldn't be in that category."

He sorted through that little speech until he thought he understood. "Are you saying you're willing to sacrifice yourself for my benefit?"

"I…yes, I am. We don't have to stop with just making out if you find that you're too…uncomfortable."

Oh, God. Heaven was within reach and he'd been caught unprepared. He took a deep breath. "Well, as willing as you are to make the supreme sacrifice for me tonight, it won't be possible. I don't have birth control with me."

She met his declaration with stunned silence. "You don't?"

"Of course not. What, you think I carry a supply around with me at all times, just in case I get lucky?"

"Not even in your wallet?"

"Not since high school. These days I have a much better idea of what will and won't happen with a woman, and I plan accordingly."

She seemed to be digesting that. "What about in the glove compartment of your truck?" she finally asked.

"Are you kidding? My mom's been known to borrow my truck, and she's also been known to get a speeding ticket now and then. I can imagine how much she'd love finding condoms in the glove compartment when she's digging for the registration papers."

She gazed up at him. "You know, I'm glad to find out you don't keep some around at all times."

"You had me pegged as some sort of sex machine, didn't you?"

"Not exactly a machine, but everybody thinks you installed that spongy mat in the back of your truck so you could have fun with your girlfriends."

He let out a sigh of exasperation. "I put that mat in the back of the truck when Mom started refinishing antiques, so she could haul them around without damaging the finish on the furniture."

"Not for making love?"

"No."

"And so you've never—"

"I didn't say that. And this discussion's over." He swung her up in his arms before she traveled down that road any further. Of course he'd made love in the back of the truck, but he didn't want to talk about it now.

"What are you doing?"

"I'm taking charge and carrying you to the back of the truck. It's the manly thing to do." She didn't resist, so he concluded she had faith in his self-control. He was putting a huge amount of faith in it, himself.

"Then I guess you don't want to talk about your love life anymore," she said.

"You've got that right." Specifically he didn't want to talk about or think about any other women he'd been involved with, in the back of his truck or anywhere else. They'd been wrong for him, but he hadn't realized how wrong until a few moments ago...when he'd kissed Tess.

CHAPTER SIX

TESS SAT CROSS-LEGGED on the blanket and waited for Mac to crawl into the bed of the truck and join her. The night was still very warm, but she felt shivery with delight. Maybe it was partly the blanket, reminding her of the tent she'd shared with Mac as kids. They'd hauled comic books and snacks into their hideaway, and there had been nothing sexual about the cozy intimacy of being stretched out beside him in that tent.

Or maybe there had been, and she had been too innocent to realize it. At any rate, she had a delicious sensation now that reminded her of that intimacy, only magnified a hundred times. They were alone, closed off from the world, and ready, in a sense, to play.

"The sky's so clear," Mac said as he crawled up beside her. "Let's lie on our backs and look at the stars, like we used to."

"And not do anything?" She was hungrier for him than she cared to admit.

He gave her a swift kiss on the mouth. "I'll tell you my dream."

"Oh, all *right*." She pulled the skirt of her dress down underneath her as she settled back on the blanket and looked upward. "Big Dipper, Little Dipper, North Star," she said automatically as she searched them out.

Mac lay down beside her, his arm touching hers, his thigh against hers. "Orion's Belt, and the Seven Sisters," he added.

"And?"

"And nothing. That's all I ever learned."

"Still? I thought you took an astronomy class."

"I learned things for the test and then forgot it. I only remember what we figured out from that kid's book you had on the constellations."

"Slacker."

"Yeah."

Tess felt as if they could still be seven and nine, lying on their backs in the cool grass of the park on a summer's night. Tess's brothers would be racing around playing tag, and the grown-ups would be sitting in lawn chairs complaining about being stuffed. Meanwhile, Mac and Tess would be off by themselves looking at the stars, probably because they'd been the ones most captivated by *Star Wars* and galaxies far, far away.

She could almost imagine they'd gone back in time... until Mac reached for her hand, lacing his fingers through hers. Memories of childhood faded. They definitely weren't kids anymore, and the emotions coursing through her at the barest touch of his hand weren't the least bit childish.

But the basis of those feelings had been there all along, she thought. What was happening between them now had been simmering within her for years, waiting for a touch, a word, a gesture, to make passion flare to life. He rubbed his thumb along hers, and although it might have been an unconscious movement, she didn't think so. He had to realize that what they'd taken for childhood play had been more sensual than they'd ever admitted to each other, or themselves.

"Tell me your dream," she said.

He was silent for a moment. Then, with a little sigh that sounded like surrender, he began. "You'd been invited to a Halloween party, and you asked to borrow Peppermint Patty because you wanted to go as Lady Godiva."

"*What?* I would never do such a thing." She thought of riding bareback with no clothes on. It didn't sound comfortable, but it was sort of erotic. "Did I have long hair?"

"Down to your hips. You wanted to practice riding with no clothes on to see how it felt before you tried it at the party, so you talked me into riding along the river trail with you. You rode bareback, and you had this loose dress on with nothing on underneath. Halfway along the trail you took off the dress and tossed it into the bushes."

Tess shivered. It *was* a sexy image. "But my hair covered me up, right?"

"Not that well. And you know how the trail winds, so even though I was behind you, I got some side views. You were..." He cleared his throat. "You were beautiful. And riding like that, rocking back and forth on the horse, was turning you on."

"How could you tell?"

"Your skin was flushed, and you were breathing faster, and...your nipples were hard." Mac clutched her hand a little more tightly and cleared his throat again.

"Oh." Which described exactly the way she was feeling right now. When Mac didn't continue with the dream, she prompted him. "Did you wake up then?"

"No."

"What happened?"

"You had an orgasm."

"Oh!"

"Which turned *me* on, and I pulled you off the horse and made love to you right on the ground."

Tess wasn't sure who was holding on tighter, her or Mac, but they had each other in a death grip. "Was it... nice?"

His voice was hoarse. "It was a dream. You can't put dreams up against the real thing."

Disappointment shot through her. "Then it wasn't nice."

"No, it wasn't nice. It was wild and primitive, no holds barred. I bit your neck and you dug your fingernails into my back. It was…fantastic."

"Wow." She wondered what he'd think if he knew how her body was throbbing this very minute. Being thrown to the ground and ravished sounded perfect. She loosened her grip when she realized she might already be digging her nails into his hand.

He released her hand and turned on his side to face her. "I don't want you to be scared by that description, Tess. I would never be that rough in real life."

She turned on her side, too, pillowing her head on her arm. But her casual posture belied her racing heart. "Too bad."

He sucked in his breath. "You'd *want* that?"

"Would I want you to be so overcome with desire that you'd pull me from my horse and make love to me on the ground? Of course I would. But as you said, it was a dream. In real life—"

"In real life I want you even more than that."

She gasped. "You *do?*"

He lifted a hand to her cheek, and as he caressed her, his hand trembled. "In real life, I want to rip that dress away and take you now, right now. But I won't. It wouldn't be fair to you."

"It would so be fair!"

His laugh sounded strained. "No, it wouldn't."

She'd never heard that edgy tone in his voice, and it was more exciting than the tenderest of murmurs. She almost wished he would be that reckless, but of course he wouldn't, which was why she was lying here with him now. She trusted him. "But taking it slow doesn't seem fair to *you,*" she said.

He slid his hand to the nape of her neck, massaging gently. "Fair doesn't even come into it. I never imagined

I'd be lying here with you like this. It's like getting a present I didn't have sense enough to know I wanted." He fingered the clasp of her necklace. "What made you decide to wear this tonight?"

"It seemed right."

"It was," he murmured. His lips found hers and his kiss soon brought her to a fever pitch.

She didn't realize he'd begun unzipping her dress until the material loosened over her breasts and he drew back slightly, gently ending the kiss. She opened her eyes. His face was in shadow, but she could see the rapid rise and fall of his chest as he eased the zipper the rest of the way down.

"Stop me whenever you want," he said in a husky voice.

"I don't want to stop you." Her heart pounded as the thin strap of her dress dropped from her shoulder.

"Just know that you can." He took the strap carefully between his fingers and pulled it down, bringing the bodice of the dress with it, gradually exposing her breast. His breath caught. "Oh, Tess." He eased her to her back and expertly drew the dress down to her waist. Then he groaned and shook his head.

"What are you thinking?"

"That you're even more beautiful than in my dream. And that you've been right there, all along...."

Her mouth moistened with desire. "All covered up."

"Yeah. Damn. All these years."

"Aren't you going to...touch me?"

"I'm still caught up in looking." But at last he traced the aureole of one nipple, causing it to tighten even more. Then he cupped her so tenderly, so carefully, that she felt like precious china. She loved being cherished, but she wanted more. Perhaps she needed to show him. Arching her back, she pressed forward, filling his cupped palm.

"Ah, Tess." Taking a shaky breath, he dipped his head and brought her tight, aching nipple into his mouth.

Yes. She cupped the back of his head and lifted into his caress. Oh, yes. His was the touch she'd been waiting for—the swirl of his tongue, the nip of his teeth, the sweet pressure as he sucked, nursing the flames that licked at the tender spot between her thighs. Shamelessly she offered her other breast, and he lavished the same loving attention there while continuing to give a sweet massage to the damp nipple he'd just left.

As she twisted on the soft blanket, her skirt rode up. Or maybe he pushed it up, in that subtle way he had of making her clothes disappear. He slipped his hand between her thighs, pressing against the damp silk of her panties. The heel of his hand found the spot that ached, and pushed down. She trembled.

He kissed his way back to her mouth, then lifted a fraction away from her lips. "Do you want me to stop?"

"No," she said, panting. "But I don't...I've never..."

He paused, breathing heavily, too. "No man has ever had his hand there?"

"They didn't dare."

He leaned his forehead against hers. "But you must have done this...yourself."

"No, I—read about it."

"Not the same."

"I know but—promise not to laugh—I didn't want to be alone when it happened."

"Oh, sweetheart." He didn't laugh. Instead, he tenderly kissed her forehead, her nose, her cheeks, and finally her lips. "You're not alone now," he whispered between kisses.

And sometime in the midst of those bewitching kisses, he eased his hand beneath the waistband of her panties. When she felt his fingers slip through her damp curls, she gasped.

His hand stilled and he lifted his mouth away from hers. "Is that a no?"

She began to quiver and fought the urge to press her thighs together. His hand resting there felt wonderful, but frightening, too. "Just a...reaction."

"Should I stop?"

"No. But Mac, this is so personal."

"Yes, ma'am." There was a definite smile in his voice. "About as personal as you can get." He eased his hand down and began a slow massage.

Breathing became more difficult as her body responded to that easy stroke. "At least...it's almost completely dark."

"That can help. The first time."

She felt as if he was transforming her into a liquid, flowing state. "What if I make a fool of myself?"

"I hope you do."

"I hope I don't. You'll never let me forget it." She gasped again as one of his very talented fingers sought out the sensitive nub that sent shivers zinging through her.

"No, I probably won't," he murmured as he kept up the maddening, electrifying rhythm.

She felt like a watch being wound too tight, but she wanted him to keep on winding. "Oh, Mac." She clutched his shoulder as the tension grew.

"Won't be long now." He leaned down and feathered a kiss against her lips. "Let go, Tess."

"I don't know how."

"Your body knows. Get out of your head and live right..." He pressed down a little harder. "Right *there*."

She moaned as the pressure became unbearable and her body arched and quivered beneath him.

He leaned over and whispered in her ear as he deepened the caress. "Remember my dream? You rode naked to the river, becoming so aroused that you climaxed, and then I pulled you down, spread your legs and—"

She cried out as the convulsions swept through her, wave upon wave of glorious release. And all through it, she held on to Mac, the man who had offered to lead her into this land of magic, and then had made a miracle happen. And he held on to her equally as tight, covering her face with kisses and laughing softly in triumph.

MAC HELD TESS and listened with pride to her sighs of satisfaction as she nestled in his arms. He was tense with unfulfilled need, but he could stand the pressure. "So you liked it."

"I adored it." Her voice was lazy and sweet, an after-the-loving voice that didn't sound like the Tess he knew, but like a Tess he'd like to know. "Mac, you used fantasy on me, after all."

"Had to get you past that wall."

"See?" Her voice was whisper-soft. "Fantasy can work."

"You made a believer of me."

She sighed again. "I'm so glad you were the one, Mac."

"Me, too." Even when Tess had announced she was still a virgin, Mac had never dreamed that she'd never experienced what he'd just given her. Knowing that he'd introduced her to her first orgasm made him feel like a king. Of all the accomplishments in his life, this might be the one he was the most proud of.

On the downside, he was in real agony. Tess had been right that he was used to finishing something that started this way, and his body was demanding that he take care of things. Even without birth control, there were ways to gain mutual satisfaction. But she couldn't be expected to do that for him, considering her lack of experience. He wouldn't even ask.

Then he felt her fingers working at his belt buckle.

"Tess? What are you doing?"

"If you'd move back a little I could do it better." She fumbled her way through the fastenings of his button-fly jeans. It was obvious she'd never undressed a man in her life.

Suddenly he felt protective of her innocence. "Look, you're new at this, so please don't think that I expect you to—"

"Want me to stop?" She paused. "It's just that, in the dark, I feel…braver. And I want to, Mac. I really want to."

She'd nearly released him from the confines of the denim, which left only the cotton of his boxers between him and paradise. Consideration warred with urgent need. "Uh…"

"I'll confess I'm a complete novice when it comes to giving a man pleasure, but I've read extensively." Her words might be scholarly, but her tone was sexy as hell.

The combination of sex and innocence was dynamite. His erection stiffened even more, thinking of her untutored hands on him, practicing.

She rubbed him through the cotton. "Well?"

With a sigh, he kissed her deeply. "Considering it's dark and all, I'd love it," he murmured against her lips.

"Then lift your hips so I can push your clothes away. I'm too much of a beginner to deal with impediments."

His skin flushed with anticipation. He'd never in his life been approached this way, and he found it damn exciting. "Okay." He lifted up and she shoved his boxers and jeans down in one efficient movement.

"Goodness gracious." She sounded intimidated.

Well, at least he wasn't a disappointment to her. He took some satisfaction in that. "Change your mind?"

"No. I'm just…impressed. Lie back and let me get used to the idea."

He did, and realized he was quivering—like a first-timer. When she finally circled his shaft with one warm hand, he squeezed his eyes shut and gritted his teeth. He would not explode this very minute. He would not. Talk about making a fool of yourself. But even the thought of Tess holding on to him like that was enough to make him climax. The reality was so stimulating that he wondered how long he'd survive her attentions.

"Your skin here is so soft."

"Mmm."

"Let me just moisten it."

Before he realized what she was up to, she'd leaned down and started using her tongue. "Tess!"

She lifted her head. "Am I shocking you?"

"Yes! You're not ready for that stage yet."

"I'm not?" She moved her hand up and down his shaft. "Or you're not? Are you okay? Your face is all scrunched up."

"I'm trying to control myself. And when you do unexpected…things, I find it difficult."

"Oh. So you don't want this to be over too quick?"

"Right." He groaned as she settled into a rhythm that was uncannily good for someone who had never engaged in this activity. She must have some good books.

"Do you suffer from premature—"

"No!"

"Because there are techniques for that."

"Tess, I'm fine…usually." He clenched his jaw and fought the urge to erupt as she explored the tip of his penis with fluttering fingers. And he knew in a flash of certainty he was reacting this way because these were Tess's fingers touching him so intimately. "Maybe it's because I've wanted you for so long, without knowing."

"That's a nice thought." She leaned down and flicked her tongue back and forth against the spot she'd been caressing with her fingers.

He worked so hard to hold back his climax that he thought he might pass out. "Where…did you learn that?"

"A book." She blew on the damp spot. "Do you like it?"

He gripped the blanket in both fists and stared blindly up at the night sky. He'd never had an experience to equal this one. "Yeah. I like it."

"Too bad we don't have some ice."

"Ice?" He definitely had to get a look at those books. "What—what for?"

"It's supposed to feel fantastic during an orgasm if you put some right here." She pressed against a spot below his family jewels.

He didn't know about ice, but the pressure she was exerting was having a fantastic effect. He moaned softly.

"Having trouble holding back?"

"Yeah, you could say that."

"Then let's try this." She held him snugly at the base of his shaft with one hand, pushing down slightly, and took the tip in her mouth.

The effect was unbelievable. Intense pleasure poured through him from the action of her mouth, but her firm grip on his shaft kept his climax at bay. He moaned. He groaned. He thrashed his head from side to side.

Then she released her grip, took him completely into her mouth, and his control shattered. He tried to pull away from her, sure this wasn't what she meant to do, but she wouldn't let him. His world came apart as he surrendered to the most cataclysmic orgasm of his life. As his spinning universe slowly came back into focus, he drew her up and gathered her close to kiss her passion-flavored lips.

He felt as if he'd been poleaxed. This evening had started out to be an educational session with him as teacher and her as pupil. Somehow, in the past few minutes, she'd completely reversed their roles. And in the process she'd made him her slave.

"We can try the ice another time," she whispered.

"Sure." He held her close, unable to find the energy to do more than breathe.

CHAPTER SEVEN

TESS HAD NEVER SEEN Mac so still, not even the time he rode all day without a hat and ended up with sunstroke. He was usually brimming with energy, yet he lay slumped against her like an unconscious person, his eyes closed. On the other hand, the experience of loving Mac had stirred her up again. She'd finally experienced activities she'd only read about, and she felt as if a whole new world had just opened up for her. She was ready for…more. She wasn't sure exactly what form that "more" would take, but she was ready for it.

She peered into his relaxed face. "Mac, I didn't hurt you, did I?"

His mouth curved in a faint smile. "Nope."

She stroked his hair back from his forehead. "You're awfully quiet."

His lips barely moved enough to form the words. "Your books should tell you why."

"It was that good?"

"Yeah, Tess, it was."

"Cool." She smiled to herself in the darkness. "I was wondering if I'd done everything right."

"Extremely right."

"Good." She adjusted her position. "Is it okay if I kiss you again?"

His eyes drifted open. "Where?"

"On your mouth. Where did you think?"

"I wasn't sure. For a virgin, you have some amazing ideas."

She brushed her lips against his. "I'll take that as a compliment."

"It was."

She settled her mouth over his, coaxing his tongue into slow love-play with hers. At first his response was lazy, almost nonchalant, but gradually the tempo of his breathing picked up. As the temperature of his kiss changed from warm to sizzling, he cupped her breast, kneading it with sure fingers. Her body throbbed with new knowledge, and she whimpered and moved closer to his heat.

He drew his mouth back a fraction. "Oh, Tess. I'm getting hard again."

She reached downward. "Let me—"

"No." He captured her hand. "We have to stop. I thought I was so drained that I could just play around for a while more without getting too worked up. I was wrong. I don't trust myself if we get started again."

Her body tightened in anticipation. "You'd ravish me?"

"There's a good chance." He reached for the strap of her dress. "Let's put this back on."

"Mac..." She could hardly believe that she was about to make such a bold suggestion, but she wanted this night to continue forever. "I'm sure you have birth control stashed somewhere at home. You could take me back to my house, go get it, and then come back to my place."

He paused in the act of pulling the bodice of her dress back up over her breasts.

"You see, I want you, too," she murmured.

He trembled and bunched the material in his fist.

"There's still a lot of time before the sun comes up."

He drew a long, shaky breath and continued his task, reaching for the zipper of her dress. "It's probably stupid, but I want to stick with what I promised you. You'll only have the experience of giving up your virginity once in your life. I think…we should make it special."

"We could make it special tonight."

"Not special enough. Give me a chance to woo you a little. Let me bring you flowers, maybe a bottle of good wine."

Despite her frustration, she liked the picture he was painting. "Should I buy lingerie or something?"

"Lingerie would be very nice." He arranged the pearl in the cleft between her breasts. "But wear this. I love watching the way it nestles right there."

"I'll bet when you gave it to me you never imagined a scene like this."

"Not consciously." He ran a finger over the gold chain. "But maybe subconsciously. When I saw the necklace in the jewelry store, I knew immediately I wanted to get it for you for graduation." He looked into her eyes. "Maybe I wanted something that would touch you where I wasn't allowed to."

She smiled. "We seem to have overcome those restrictions without too much trouble. I'd say our makeout session was a success."

"Yeah, but now we have to go back and face the real world with all its guilt trips. And we still have the big hurdle to jump." He gazed at her. "Maybe when it comes to that final moment, I won't be able to do it."

Her smile widened. "Oh, I think you will, judging from tonight."

He grinned back. "You could be right."

"So, when?"

"Tomorrow night? Oh, wait. Damn. I promised to fly my mom up to an antique show in Flagstaff tomorrow. Dad's going along, and he and I have appointments to look at some horses while we're up there."

She wrestled with her impatience. "How long will you be gone?"

"Three days. Until Sunday. Damn. I don't think there's any way I can get out of it, either. It's been set up for months."

"Three days sounds like an eternity."

"Tell me about it."

She traced the line of his jaw. "We could go back to my original plan and have you come back to my place tonight."

He gazed at her for a long moment and finally shook his head. "No. I really want this time to be one you'll remember."

"I don't think there's much doubt about that, no matter when it happens. And to tell the truth, I'm...afraid you'll change your mind in three days."

"After tonight? Are you kidding?"

"You had a good time tonight?"

He cupped her face in both hands. "I had the best time I've ever had in my life. And I promise you I won't change my mind."

Her heart swelled with an emotion she couldn't name, but it was strong, and it brought happy tears to her eyes. "Thank you, Mac. You're a true friend."

"I do my best."

"What time of day will you be home on Sunday?"

"Probably around noon."

"So you could come over that night."

"I could do that."

Her heart thudded in her chest. "Then I'll expect you about eight."

LEAVING TESS AT her door that night was the toughest thing Mac had done in a long time. He hadn't told her, but he wouldn't have had to drive clear back to the ranch for birth control. He'd made it a practice to know where he could buy condoms on short notice, and there was a convenience store still open only five minutes from her house.

He was probably a fool for not taking her up on her suggestion and making love to her all night long. The thought of doing that made him ache. Now he had to wait three days for the chance. No matter that he'd been waiting all his life.

Wait a minute. *Waiting all his life?* Where had that come from? It couldn't be true. Surely Tess didn't have anything to do with his fruitless search for a wife. He just hadn't found the right woman yet. Oh, God. Maybe he had.

On impulse he swung into the Ore Cart Bar's parking lot and climbed out of the truck.

Suddenly a cold beer and a game of darts sounded like an excellent idea. He was still a young carefree bachelor. Bachelors were free to stop in for a beer whenever they wanted to, and he cherished that freedom.

Maybe tonight he sort of wished he could go back over to Tess's house instead of stopping for a beer, but that was only natural, considering how new the situation was. But the novelty would wear off with Tess, the way it had with all the rest.

That's what you think, taunted a voice that sounded a lot like Tess when she was bound to prove herself right and him wrong. Over the years she'd infuriated him, made him laugh until he could barely stand, and worried him sick. But she'd never bored him. Mac walked into the bar, hoping a beer would silence that know-it-all voice that told him he'd started something that he had no idea how to finish.

The bar was fairly well deserted on this weeknight, but it had one patron that made Mac consider ducking back out the door. Unfortunately Dozer Blakely saw him before he got the chance.

"Hey, Big Mac!" he called from his bar stool. "Come on over and let me buy you a cold one."

Mac walked toward the row of stools and glanced around. "Where's Cindy?"

"At home." Dozer shoved a wayward lock of red hair off his forehead with a beefy hand. "Waitin' for me to cool off. Hey, Dutch, set the man up with his favorite brand, okay?"

"Will do," the bald bartender said. "How're you doing, Mac?"

"Can't complain." Mac sat down next to Dozer, but he would have liked to put more space between them. He could still smell Tess's perfume on his clothes, and he was afraid Dozer might recognize it. "Listen, should you be fighting with Cindy, her being P.G. and all?"

Dozer smiled. "When we fight, I'm the only one who gets upset. Cindy's cool as a cucumber." His blue eyes twinkled. "Hot date tonight?"

This would be tricky, Mac decided. "Why do you ask?"

"Oh, you look a little mussed up. I figured you might have been out parking."

"Could be."

Dozer smiled and took a sip of beer. "So, did you take that dunking last night to heart and decide to make up with Jenny?"

"Uh, no." Mac grabbed the beer Dutch scooted in front of him and took a big swallow.

"Babs?"

"Nope."

"Somebody new?"

"You could say that."

"But you're not talking, are you, Big Mac?"

Mac grabbed the opening. "No, Dozer, I'm not. I don't want you guys riding herd on me with this one, pestering me as to when we're going to tie the knot." He glanced at the hefty redhead and decided to go on the offensive. "And speaking of the knot, you're a sorry poster boy for the institution of marriage, sitting down here at the Ore Cart nursing a beer while your wife sits at home."

"I'm only doing what she told me." Dozer shook his head. "She's something else. I fly off the handle, just itching for a fight, and she won't fight. She tells me to go grab a beer and come back when I have something nice to say. In the meantime, she works on her cross-stitch, calm as you please."

"How do you know?"

"Because I usually sneak back and peek in the window to see if she's pacing the floor or banging things around, at least. You know, upset because I left the house. The hell of it is, she's not. So I come down here, drink my beer, and go home. She takes me back like nothing happened, and that's the end of that."

"What was the fight about? Or I should say, the fight she refused to have with you."

"Damned if I can remember." Dozer grinned sheepishly. "Knowing me, it was probably over something dumb. I tell you, I picked the right one when I hooked up with Cindy. Any other woman would have divorced me by now, with my short fuse. But Cindy knows it's just a passing thing, and she sends me off until I get over it. I love that woman something fierce."

"I'm glad for you." Mac picked up his glass again. "Here's to you and Cindy, and your diamond anniversary."

Dozer raised his glass in Mac's direction. "I'll drink to that." He took a long swallow, draining the glass before he set it down.

"Another beer, Dozer?" Dutch called.

"Nope. One's all I need, thanks." He turned to Mac. "Of course, if she ever threw me out for good, I'd drink the place dry."

"Sure."

"I've been meaning to tell you something, Mac."

"What's that?"

Dozer fished for his wallet and pulled out some money. "All kidding aside about Babs and Jenny, I can see why you didn't end up with them. They're both nice and all, and Jenny's built real sweet." He jiggled his cupped hands out in front of his chest. "Real sweet."

Mac didn't want to think about women's breasts, either. "And your point is?"

"You're a smart guy. You need somebody with brains. Babs and Jenny could never have kept up with you. You'd have been bored in a month or two."

"So I figured."

"Well, good. So, is this new girl smart?"

"Yeah, she's smart."

Dozer nodded. "Did you score yet?"

Mac winced. The type of evening he had planned for Tess didn't even begin to fit the definition of "scoring." He tried to imagine Dozer's response if he knew they were talking about his sister.

"Guess not," Dozer said, undisturbed by Mac's reaction. "Otherwise you would've grinned when I asked that." He laid his money on the counter and slapped Mac on the back. "Well, good luck with her, buddy. You deserve to find yourself a real nice lady. Maybe this is the one."

"Maybe." *Not.* As Dozer headed home to Cindy, Mac sipped his beer, determined to think of something else besides Tess lying alone in her bed. He even carried on a conversation with Dutch about the Arizona Cardinals' chances this year. When the beer glass was empty he added another bill to what Dozer had left and walked out into the warm night thinking how great it was to be a free man. He drove home with the windows down, a song on the radio… and Tess on his mind.

THE EVAPORATIVE COOLER had reduced the heat in Tess's little bungalow by the time she walked inside that night, but the place was still plenty warm. She closed the front door and with a sense of deep regret, listened to Mac's truck drive away. If only he still carried condoms in his wallet, then he could have stayed.

To make matters worse, he hadn't even kissed her goodbye. She understood why—nosy neighbors might have seen them and passed the word. She could spend all the time she wanted in Mac's company without arousing any suspicions, but one public minute in his arms would start every tongue in town wagging.

This particular business they had between them had to be kept private. She could still hardly believe he'd offered to take care of her problem himself. He was running a big risk that could potentially ruin his relationship with her brothers. And because she appreciated that so much, she intended to protect him as best she could. So she kept their goodbyes on the porch deliberately nonchalant.

But once she was inside the door and he was truly gone, she ran her hands over her breasts and closed her eyes, lost in remembering. Then she lifted her arms over her head and turned slowly in a circle, executing a subtle dance of celebration. By touching her and arousing her the way he had, Mac had given her a completely new sense of her body.

In the carefree days before puberty, she'd run and played with Mac and her brothers with no thought to the fact that she was a girl and they were boys. Then the changes had begun, and for the most part, she'd thought of them as a nuisance. As she developed, her body seemed to get in her way more than it helped her enjoy life. But now...now she understood what all those changes had been for. For *this*. Laughing in delight, she flung her arms out and whirled until she grew dizzy.

Feeling slightly drunk with the wonder of it all, she wandered into her bedroom, shedding her clothes as she went. She kicked off her sandals and padded barefoot into the bathroom, where she turned on the shower, adjusting the temperature until it mimicked the warmth of a lover's caress. She craved bodily sensation in a way she could never have admitted to anyone, least of all Mac.

She stepped under the spray, letting it beat down on her. Then she flung back her head and lifted her breasts to the coursing water. Her nipples tightened and she touched them gently, reawakening the memory of Mac's loving.

Then she slid both hands down her water-slicked body to the juncture of her thighs, where she throbbed for him still. Her erotic books had been very clear—she didn't need Mac or any man to give her the kind of release she'd found tonight. She could take charge of her own pleasure.

And maybe someday she'd follow that advice, she thought, skimming her hands back up over her rib cage to cup her breasts once again. But tonight she wanted to savor the remembered sensation of his hands caressing her, coaxing her to enjoy the wonders of her body. Perhaps she was being silly, but it seemed to her that to work the miracle herself at this moment would dilute that precious memory.

She turned off the shower and toweled dry, paying careful attention to the task. Her body was no longer exclusively her domain, and the thought made her shiver with delight. She smoothed lotion over every inch of skin she could reach, taking her time, anointing herself as if she expected Mac to return.

He probably would not. He was, as she knew from years of experience, a man of his word. Once he'd decided that her initiation should proceed a certain way, he would follow through on that decision, ignoring his own needs, and even her arguments to the contrary. She wouldn't see him again until three days from now, at eight o'clock on the dot.

And perhaps he was right about this, she thought as she rubbed the scented lotion over her body. Perhaps there should be some ceremony and ritual to what they were about to do. She had three days to prepare. Three days to find tempting lingerie and turn her room into a lover's bower. Setting down the lotion, she returned to her bedroom and surveyed the situation. Most of it would have to change.

Grabbing a yellow legal pad and a pen from her desk drawer, she sprawled naked on her bed and began making a list.

CHAPTER EIGHT

THE NEXT AFTERNOON as Tess pulled packages from the car after her shopping trip to Phoenix, her neighbor, Hazel Nedbetter, came hurrying over with a florist's vase full of daisies. Tess quickly shoved the Naughty But Nice lingerie box under the front seat.

"I took these into my house so they wouldn't wilt on your front porch," Hazel said.

"Why, thank you, Hazel." Tess took the vase and stared at the cheerful bouquet of white and gold daisies, exactly like the ones on her dress. They could only have come from one person.

"It isn't even from the Copperville Flower Shoppe. The van was from some big florist in Phoenix. Can you imagine? The delivery fee must have been huge!"

"Probably was." At least Mac had taken some precautions, Tess thought. If he'd ordered from the local flower shop, the news would have spread by now. She was thrilled that he'd sent a bouquet, but she didn't know how in hell she'd explain it to Hazel. And Hazel would need an explanation. The more mysterious Tess was, the more Hazel would speculate and the wilder the gossip would become.

The sun beat down on them, and Tess needed to buy some time to think of what she'd say. "It must be three hundred degrees out here. Let's go into the shade," she said, starting toward her front porch. Doggone Mac, anyway. He'd put her in a precarious spot, but his reckless gesture made her smile. She could just hear him—*I wanted to send you flowers. I figured you're a smart girl. You'll think of something to tell the neighbors.*

Setting the vase on the porch rail, she turned to Hazel and used the first explanation she could think of. "I'll bet they're from my new principal in New York."

"Really? How fancy! I don't think Mr. Grimes ever sends flowers to the people he hires at Copperville High. They must do things differently back East." Hazel eyed the small white envelope secured in the arrangement with a plastic holder. Clearly she wanted Tess to take the envelope out and open it to prove that the flowers were indeed from Tess's new principal, as she'd speculated.

The envelope wasn't sealed shut, so Hazel could have looked at the card, but Tess didn't think she had. Still, it was possible, so Tess decided to go for broke.

She could pull this off, although Mac had given her quite a challenge. He knew good and well that the neighbors would notice flowers arriving at her doorstep and he was probably sitting in Flagstaff chuckling as he imagined her predicament. Even if she'd been home, the delivery van would have attracted attention. Most of her neighbors in this older section of Copperville were retired and had plenty of time to observe the activities surrounding them.

Determined to convince Hazel, Tess boldly plucked the envelope from the plastic holder. "Let's just see if I'm right." She opened the envelope, figuring whatever Mac had said, she'd tell Hazel it was indeed from her principal.

As it turned out, Mac had come to her aid. The cryptic card read *Wishing you the best as you explore new worlds—M.* Tess knew exactly what new worlds he was talking about, and they all involved the bed she was about to redecorate. But Hazel wouldn't realize that.

"Yep, it's from my principal, all right," Tess said. She repeated the greeting for Hazel and on impulse decided she could even nail her story down a little tighter. "My principal's name is Emma Kirkwood, but most people call her Em, or they use the initial *M* for short. See?" She turned the card around for Hazel's inspection. Tess had no idea if anyone called Emma Kirkwood *Em,* let alone abbreviated the nickname to an initial, but the chances of Emma appearing in Copperville were remote.

Hazel adjusted her bifocals and peered at the card. "Sure enough." She glanced at Tess. "That's real nice, sending you a bouquet like that. Although I would have thought maybe roses or carnations would be more likely than daisies."

"M likes daisies."

Hazel nodded. "Been shopping?"

With the change of topic, Tess knew she was home free. The daisies were explained. "Yes. Picked up some things for the trip." And it would be some trip, considering the supplies she'd found today. She thought Mac would be pleased. Maybe more than pleased. She wanted him to salivate, actually.

"When does Lionel plan on putting up a For Rent sign in front of your house?" Hazel asked.

"Not until next month, I think. Don't worry, Hazel. Lionel is very particular who he rents this place to. You'll get good neighbors."

"I suppose, but I'll miss you, anyway."

"I'll miss you, too, Hazel." Tess lifted the hair off the back of her neck. Even the shade of her porch was darned warm, but if she invited Hazel in she might be there for another hour. She was a dear lady, and another time Tess might not have minded visiting with her, but at the moment she was eager to get her purchases inside before someone else showed up and noticed the lingerie box or the satin sheets.

"Your poor mother's going to cry her eyes out when you go."

"I know. I'll probably cry, too. But I have to spread my wings, Hazel. My brothers all got to be football heroes. This is a chance for me to shine."

"Oh, yes, your brothers. They might act like they don't care about such things, but they're going to hate having you so far away. And then there's Mac MacDougal. That boy's going to miss you something terrible. I noticed you two were out last night. I was surprised at that, because Mabel Bellweather told me you were feeling sick when you were at the Nugget for dinner."

Tess began to wonder if she and Mac had any chance of keeping their secret, after all. Copperville was a hotbed of gossip. "I was feeling sick, but after I left the restaurant I started feeling better, so we took a long drive. He, um, wanted to discuss the breeding program he and his father are starting. They're going to look at a few studs during that big horse show in Flagstaff this weekend. You did know they're in Flagstaff?"

Hazel nodded. "I heard. Nora's at one of her antique shows up there."

"Right." Tess decided she needed to prepare Hazel for Mac's next move. "I made Mac promise to come over when he gets home and tell me all about the trip," she said. "So you'll likely see his truck here after they get home."

"Now, see there?" Hazel wagged her finger at Tess. "You two have always been close like that, sharing your news. Who's he going to tell about his goings-on when you're in New York City?"

Tess hadn't wanted to face that, herself. "I guess we'll have to use the phone. Well, Hazel, I'd better let you get to your dinner preparations."

"Guess so." Hazel seemed reluctant to take the hint. "How was Phoenix?"

"Hot," Tess said.

"I'll bet. These nights have been so warm I can barely sleep."

Which means Mac and I had better close the blinds good and tight, Tess thought. "I know what you mean," she said. "Well, see you later, Hazel. And thanks again for preserving my bouquet."

"You're welcome. Enjoy it." Hazel headed back over the path worn in the grass between the two houses.

Tess picked up the flowers and went inside. The phone rang the minute she set the vase on her coffee table. She walked over to the little telephone table next to the sofa and picked up the cordless receiver. "Hello?"

"Where have you been?" Mac asked. "I tried about six times today and kept getting your machine."

The sound of his voice made her nipples tighten. He'd never had that effect on her before, but times had changed. "I was in Phoenix."

"Oh, really? Buying more books?"

"Not this time. This trip was for other things." Her first impulse, because it was the way they'd always interacted, was to tell him everything she'd bought. But the dynamics had changed and secrets were very appealing now.

"Anything to do with…Sunday night?"

"As a matter of fact."

"What did you buy?"

She smiled. "Oh, something very, very brief."

"Really." The timbre of his voice changed. "Care to describe it?"

"I'd rather surprise you. Use your imagination."

"That's been my problem today. I can't seem to use anything but my imagination. I've been so spaced out my dad keeps asking if I overdosed on allergy medicine, even though he knows I don't have allergies."

"So you've been thinking about me." Her body reacted,

moistening and throbbing as if he were right there beside her.

"That would be an understatement. I keep thinking about that daisy dress of yours, and...everything that happened last night."

"Me, too." She stroked the petals of her floral arrangement. "But the daisies were *very* hard to explain to Hazel Nedbetter, Mac."

His laugh was low and sexy. "I'll bet you came up with a story, though, didn't you?"

"I told her they were from my new principal, whose name is Emma, but she often goes by just the initial *M*."

He laughed again. "Damn, but you're clever. I wish I'd been there to hear you spin that yarn."

"Me, too."

His voice lowered, became soft and seductive. "I wish I could be there right now."

Tess sighed. "Me, too."

"What are you wearing?"

"A sleeveless blouse and shorts." Scenarios from her reading flashed through her mind, and she had the urge to experiment with her newfound power. "But it's very hot, Mac." She picked up the vase of flowers. "I think I'll just walk back into the bedroom and take my blouse off."

"Now?"

"Well, sure, unless you want me to hang up."

His tone was strained. "No, I don't want you to hang up. I might not get another chance to call you today. But Tess—"

"Just unfastening the buttons will help."

In her bedroom she set the vase down and started unbuttoning her blouse. "Ah. I can feel a little breeze from the air conditioner right here, blowing on my bare skin. By the way, did you find any good studs?"

"Uh, yes. No. Maybe. Have you got your blouse off yet?"

"I'm getting there. These buttons aren't the easiest in the world. I tell you, it's so warm here, Mac. This little trickle of sweat just rolled down between my breasts. I'll bet I'd taste really salty right now."

"You're..." He cleared his throat. "You're doing this on purpose."

"What? Taking off my blouse? You bet. Ah, there. That feels so much better." The joke might be on her. By teasing him, she was becoming incredibly aroused herself.

"What...color is your bra?"

"Ivory." Her breathing quickened. "Satin mostly, but the cups are a pretty lace. I like it because it hooks in the front, which makes it easier to take off."

His voice was low and dangerous. "Take it off now."

"You know, I think I will." She unfastened it with trembling fingers and released her aching breasts. "It's...off. Oh, Mac, I wish you were here."

"Believe me, so do I."

"The daisies are so beautiful." She snapped one from its stem. "So soft." Slowly she drew the petals over her rigid nipples. "I'm stroking my breasts with one of your daisies, Mac."

He groaned.

"Little bits of yellow pollen are scattered over my breasts and nipples."

"God, Tess. How am I supposed to stand this?"

"You'll be here soon."

"Not soon enough."

She continued to administer the sweet torture of touching her breasts with the daisy. She pretended it was Mac's gentle fingers stroking her. "And if it helps, I'm aching right now, too."

"I hope so." His breathing rasped in her ear. "You deserve to be absolutely miserable."

"Are you?"

"Denim doesn't give real well, if that's what you mean."

"Too bad I'm not there to help you."

"Yeah, isn't it."

"I'm going to hang up now, Mac."

"I guess you'd better." His voice was tight with strain. "I'm at a public phone at the fairgrounds, and I'll have to stand here with the receiver to my ear and my back to the folks for a long time."

"Goodbye, Mac. Think of me."

"As if I have a choice. Goodbye, you devil woman."

She broke the connection between them and pressed the daisy against her breast. Sunday night seemed an eternity away.

MAC LISTENED TO the soft click that ended the call, but he didn't put the receiver down. He hadn't been kidding about the bulge in his pants, and there was no way in hell he could turn around yet. He hadn't planned on the call turning into an erotic experience, not considering the thousands of times he'd talked to Tess on the phone. Mostly he'd been curious about how she'd handled the delivery of the daisies and if she was pleased with them.

I guess so, MacDougal, if she's rubbing them over that sweet body of hers. But he had to get that image out of his head or he'd never be able to leave this phone. Tess was amazing. When he'd suggested himself as her summer lover, he'd had no idea what a Pandora's box he was opening.

As he stood with the silent phone to his ear, he forced himself to think about something else. The exorbitant price that Stan Henderson wanted for his stallion, for example. And the fact that his father was seriously considering paying it. Finally he was able to hang up the receiver and turn around.

His father was standing not ten feet away, watching him.

"Hey, Dad." He walked over with what he hoped was a nonchalant smile. "I figured you'd be haggling with Henderson over that stud for the rest of the afternoon."

"I decided to take a break and let him think about my last offer." Andy MacDougal was a tall, lean cowboy who didn't look his age any more than Nora MacDougal looked hers. Most people assumed Mac's parents were younger, but they'd suffered through several miscarriages before he'd come along when Nora was almost past childbearing age.

"I'm guessing you've got girl trouble," Andy said. "Am I right?"

Mac grinned. A partial truth was probably his best approach. "You could say that."

"I also have a feeling she might be a serious girlfriend this time around."

Mac didn't like hearing that. "Nah. I'm not ready to settle down."

"Oh, I think you are. I've seen the way you look at the Blakely boys and their families. I also realize you're choosy, and that's fine. But I've never known you to be this distracted. So if the woman you've been trying to call all day long is ready for a home and family, then I suggest you go for it."

"She's not."

"Oh." Andy gazed at his son for a long moment. "Want to grab a hot dog and a beer and talk about it?"

"A hot dog and a beer sounds great, Dad, but there's really nothing to talk about."

Andy nodded. "If you say so. But the offer stands, anytime."

"I know that, Dad, and I appreciate it." Mac swung an arm over his father's shoulders. "Let's go eat. I'm starved."

THE OVERNIGHT MAIL TRUCK arrived in Tess's driveway the next morning. As she signed for the package, she noticed the Flagstaff postmark. Well, at least he hadn't sent another bouquet of flowers. She'd be hard-pressed to explain a second floral delivery from her new principal.

Once she'd bid the deliverywoman goodbye, she closed the front door and ripped open the package. Inside were a pair of unbelievably soft, furry gloves. She put them on and discovered they were too big for her, but inside one glove she encountered a folded slip of paper. She pulled it out.

Dear Tess,
I saw these in a clearance sale. I could have brought them with me Sunday night, but I decided I'd rather send them so you can spend the next thirty-six hours imagining how you will feel when I put them on and run my hands over every inch of your naked body. In the meantime, enjoy the daisies.
M.

With a cry of frustration she clutched the gloves to her chest. What an evil man. What a wonderful, delicious tease of a man. She smiled to herself. Just like when they were kids, they always had to get each other back. He'd sent the daisies and she'd tortured him over the phone. Now this. The score was definitely in his favor at this moment.

She put on one of the gloves and ran it experimentally over her bare arm. *Oh, Lord.*

"Knock, knock, can I come in?"

Tess leaped to her feet as her mother came through the unlocked front door, a habit she'd developed that Tess had seen no reason to change—until now. Heart pounding as if she'd been caught raiding the cookie jar when she was five, she shoved Mac's note in the pocket of her shorts and pasted on a welcoming smile. "Hey, Mom! How's it going?"

"I hadn't heard from you in a few days, so I thought I'd drop by and find out what you're up to. Darling, you look guilty as hell. What's going on?"

"Nothing, Mom."

Debbie Blakely raised her eyebrows, obviously not convinced. She was a small woman, and Tess had taken after her in height and hair color, although her mother's warm brown now came from a commercial product instead of nature. She was what Tess always thought people meant when they described someone as "pleasingly plump." Tess wouldn't have wanted her mother to lose an ounce, but she sure wished she'd be a little less perceptive.

Debbie glanced at the coffee table littered with the remnants of the overnight package and then at the gloves, one on Tess's hand and the other clutched against her chest. "What's that, a joke? Gloves in the middle of a heat wave?"

Tess thought fast. "That's what it is, all right. Mac sent them. It's his way of saying, 'Nanny, nanny, boo, boo, I'm in Flagstaff where it's cool and you're not.'"

Debbie Blakely laughed. "That would be Mac. And if I know you, you're planning your revenge even as we speak. Now I may have an idea what you're looking guilty about. Don't smuggle ants into his bed this time, Tess. It took Nora weeks to get them out of the ranch house."

"Right. No ants. Maybe I'll solder his boots to the horse trough, instead."

"Well, I promise not to tell. Want to do lunch?"

"Uh, sure." She'd planned to spend the day transforming her bedroom, but she could probably take time out for lunch.

"Good. I was thinking today that I won't be able to pop

over here and invite you to lunch much longer, so I'd better take advantage of your being here while I can."

Tess walked over and gave her mother a hug. "I'll come home whenever I can. And I want you and Dad to visit me in New York whenever you can get away."

"Oh, we will, but…it won't be the same. My, those gloves are soft."

Tess had forgotten she was still wearing one. "Um, yes. I might actually use them in New York."

Debbie examined the glove. "Kind of big, aren't they?"

"Well, yeah, but it's the thought that counts."

"And no doubt Mac's thought was to torture you while he's enjoying the cool mountain air. He probably didn't care if they fit or not. Men."

"Scoundrels, all of them," Tess agreed.

"But we couldn't live without them, could we?"

"Guess not." Or so Tess was discovering. This was turning into the longest three days of her life.

"If you'll excuse me, I'll freshen up in your bathroom before we go," her mother said.

"Sure. Help yourself." Tess sent thanks heavenward that she'd decided to watch a movie last night instead of starting her renovations then. Satin sheets would have been a little difficult to explain to her mother, not to mention the angled mirror she planned to install.

"Oh, so these are the flowers you got from your principal," Debbie called out as she passed through Tess's bedroom into the bathroom. "Why don't you have them out on the coffee table?"

"I was enjoying them before I went to bed last night," Tess called back. Oh, my. Word traveled as fast as always around this place. She and Mac would have to have their wits about them. But they'd had a lot of practice being co-conspirators. Maybe she could think of this secret project as an extension of the pranks they'd pulled together over the years.

She looked down at the gloves. Then again, maybe not.

CHAPTER NINE

WITH SOME EFFORT Mac managed to smuggle a small cooler
on board the Cessna Sunday morning without his parents
noticing. Inside rested the bouquet of daisies he'd bought
on the sly in Flagstaff and he'd used motel ice to keep them
fresh in the cooler. Ice had never been an erotic substance
to him until Tess had mentioned placing it against certain
parts of his anatomy. Now he couldn't even look at an ice
bucket without getting turned on.

And now, at long last, he was flying his parents back
to Copperville. His rendezvous with Tess was only a few
hours away, yet it was too many hours for his comfort. He
hadn't dared call her again, considering the condition she'd
put him in the one time he'd tried it. But she'd been on his
mind constantly. He wondered what she'd thought of the
gloves, and if she'd run them over her skin.

Picturing her doing that, his mouth went dry. Maybe
she'd always been a sensuous person, but her reading had
stoked up the fire in her. He wasn't going home to a timid
virgin, that was for sure. But she was still a virgin, and
no matter how she plotted to drive him insane, he had to
remember to go slow and be gentle. That might not be as
easy as he'd thought at first.

When he and his folks arrived home, Mac and his father unloaded the suitcases from the car while his mother
went inside to check for messages on the answering machine. Mac walked into the kitchen in time to hear Tess's
voice coming from the speaker.

This message is for Mac, she said, sounding like the Tess he'd known for twenty-three years, not the new Tess he'd just discovered. *Mac, don't bother to eat dinner before you come over tonight. I'll feed you. Something simple, finger food probably. Oh, and don't worry about ice. I have plenty. I might be out back or something when you get there, so just come look for me. See you tonight.*

Mac nearly dropped the suitcases he was carrying.

His mother turned to him with a smile. "You're seeing Tess tonight?"

"Yeah." Mac tried his best to look nonchalant, which wasn't easy while he was thinking about Tess feeding him some exotic food while dressed in whatever sexy outfit she'd bought. And then there was her subtle reference to ice, and the fact that she wanted him to walk in the unlocked door and come look for her. He'd bet a million dollars where he'd find her, and it wouldn't be "out back."

She'd cleverly created the whole message to sound normal, when it was filled with suggestive ideas that only he would understand. That was so like her. She'd done it to get him back for the gloves, no doubt. He cleared his throat. "I promised to drop by and let her know how the trip went," he added, realizing he was standing there staring into space. Not good.

Nora gazed at him, a speculative light in her blue eyes. "You're upset that she's leaving town, aren't you?"

"Not really. I'm happy for her. It's what she's always wanted."

"I know, and of course we're all happy for her, but you're agitated about it. I could tell by the expression on your face just now. Your color was high. I think you're upset because she's going off and leaving you."

"I absolutely am not." Mac set down the suitcases, walked over and took his mother by the shoulders. "That imagination of yours is working overtime." Then he gave her a quick kiss on the cheek and noticed the tiredness around her eyes. Three days of being constantly on the go had taken its toll on both her and his father. He couldn't ignore the fact that they were both nearly seventy. "I think I'll ride out and check the stock tank Dad's worried about," he said.

"Wasn't he going to do that after we got unpacked?"

"Yeah, but why don't you two take the afternoon off? You both got a lot accomplished on this trip. Relax for the rest of the day."

His mother nodded. "I'll see if I can get him to do that. I think he's more worn out than he admits." She glanced at Mac with gratitude. "Thanks. I don't know what we'd do without you."

"Hey, no problem." Mac smiled at her and headed out the door. On the way, he passed his father coming in. "Try and get Mom to take it easy for the rest of the afternoon, will you? She's bushed."

"I need to check the stock tank."

"I'll do it. No point in both of us heading out there in this heat."

His father laid a hand on his shoulder. "Thanks. If I don't watch your mother, she'll run until she's exhausted."

"My thoughts exactly." Mac crossed the back porch and started toward the corrals with a sense of relief. The solo activity was just what he needed to get him through the next few hours.

HE'D NEVER BEEN so nervous and excited in his life as he drove toward Tess's house a little before eight. The sun was down and the streetlights on, but heat from the day still rose up from the pavement and he had the truck's air conditioner going full blast. Considering his heated condition, he might have to run the air conditioner in the dead of winter if he had a negligee-clad Tess waiting at the end of the line. Which wouldn't happen, because she'd be gone by winter.

The cooler beside him with a bottle of wine inside had been easy to pass by his parents. He'd taken wine over to Tess's house before. But he'd sneaked the daisy chain he'd made into the cooler when no one was around. His mother did seem to be watching him a little more closely, so he'd have to be careful about similar preparations in the future.

The future. A terrible thought came to him. Maybe tonight was all there would be. After all, once he'd taken care of Tess's virginity problem, she wouldn't need to continue this risky business, even though she'd be in Copperville for the rest of the summer. For some reason, he hadn't figured that out. He'd been "hired" for a specific job, and after tonight the job would be over.

Hell, he couldn't think about that or he'd be too depressed to enjoy himself. And he definitely planned to enjoy himself. If her brothers ever found out about any of this, his goose was not only cooked, it was fried, so he might as well make the reward worth the risk. Tonight would be one for the record books.

He parked in her driveway and discovered he was shaking like a newborn colt. The lights in the living room were muted, but he doubted that's where she was. Heart pounding, he got out of the truck with the cooler and walked up the steps to her front porch.

Sure enough, the front door was unlocked. He walked in, his chest tight from the effort to breathe normally, and stepped on a daisy. A trail of them led from the front door down the hall. He turned and locked the door.

Quietly setting the cooler and his hat on the coffee table, he opened the cooler and took out the daisy chain and the wine. First he glanced at the unopened bottle and then at the trail of daisies leading, no doubt, to her bed. If he didn't open the bottle now, it might never be opened.

Sidestepping the daisies, he walked into the kitchen, found the corkscrew and opened the wine. His hands weren't completely steady, but he managed to take two goblets from the cupboard without dropping them. With the daisy chain looped around one arm, the wine in one hand and the glasses in the other, he took a deep breath and started down the hall, following the daisies.

He'd prepared himself for the tempting sight of Tess lounging on her bed with very little on. After all, they'd gone swimming together hundreds of times, so he knew what she looked like in a bathing suit. This wouldn't be all that different, probably.

Wrong.

The scene she'd created left him breathless. His blood hammered through his veins as he gazed at every man's fantasy—a virgin trapped in a bordello.

Red velvet swags and red bulbs in the lamps gave the room a glow of sinful pleasure. His furry gloves lay waiting on a bedside table. On the other, a tray of food that could have been plucked right out of an orgy offered plump red tomatoes, velvet-ripe peaches, chilled asparagus, and clusters of moist grapes.

Whether it was the fruit or some exotic fragrance Tess had added, the room already seemed to smell of sex, and a stereo played soft, yet subtly persuasive music with an underlying beat that mimicked the rhythm of lovemaking. Gilt-framed mirrors propped at various angles all reflected the centerpiece of the room, a bed covered in virginal white satin and mounded with satin pillows of all shapes and sizes.

Reclining on that nest of pillows was a woman Mac barely recognized. Although the scraps of white satin covering her breasts seemed inconsequential, they managed to emphasize her cleavage, where the pearl necklace lay cradled by her soft body. His gaze traveled to the white lace garter belt and panties, which defined her femaleness in ways he'd never imagined. The garters were fastened to white silk stockings with a sheen like pearls and lace tops circling her thighs. Last of all he absorbed the fact that Tess, the woman who believed in no-nonsense running shoes and well-worn boots, was wearing a pair of white sandals with four-inch heels.

Tess gave him a slow smile. "What do you think?"

"I don't—" He swallowed. "I don't believe this is about thinking."

"True." Her gaze traveled to his crotch. "I have the reaction I wanted. Would you like…to get out of those clothes? They seem a bit…tight."

"Um, yeah." He looked down and realized he was still holding the wine bottle, glasses and daisy chain, but his brain was so fuzzy he couldn't decide what to do with them. It was a wonder he hadn't poured the wine on the carpet.

She held out both hands. "I'll hold the bottle. And the daisies. I can pour us some wine if you want while you're taking off your clothes."

He gazed at her holding out her arms to him in that welcoming fashion and had the urge to toss the wine and glasses over his shoulder and join her immediately on that tempting bed. He groaned softly and shook his head to clear it. He'd need every ounce of control at his command in order to make this the slow seduction he'd planned.

"Is anything the matter?" she asked.

"Only that you've blown me away, and I'm struggling to get my bearings."

"I really did that?"

"Yeah, you really did that." He handed her the bottle and glasses. After she set them next to the tray of food, he gave her the daisy chain. "I'm usually a little more suave when I walk into a lady's bedroom with wine and flowers. I usually present them instead of waiting for her to ask."

"Oh." She grinned, and he caught a calming glimpse of the other Tess, the one who loved climbing trees and eating cotton candy. "Thank you for the wine and flowers," she said demurely. Then she put the daisies around her neck. They draped her breasts like a lei, drawing attention to the provocative swell above the tiny garment she wore. "How's that?"

"More exciting than I could have predicted."

She looked into his eyes, her own filled with an intensity to match his. "It is exciting, isn't it? Us, and...all of this. Who would have thought?"

"Not me."

She glanced at the wine. "The books say alcohol dulls sensual pleasure."

"I thought you'd need to relax." He chuckled. "Maybe I need it more than you do. You don't look nervous at all."

"I have a million butterflies inside."

"You do?"

"Of course. I've never acted this way with a man in my life."

He was humbled as he thought what a gift she was giving him. "That makes tonight very special. For me, too."

"I'm glad. You know, maybe a little wine wouldn't hurt."

"I'm so keyed up I can guarantee it won't affect me."

"And I don't want to be inhibited."

He laughed. "This is inhibited?"

"Sort of. The books say that a woman can drive a man crazy if he comes into the bedroom and finds her...touching herself."

He gulped. "Really." From the painful bulge in his jeans, the books must be right. "And some wine might encourage you along those lines?"

"Maybe."

"Then drink up."

Her cheeks grew pink. "Just a little, then." She reached over to the nightstand and poured them each half a glass. Then she picked hers up and leaned back against the pillows. "Now undress for me, Mac. And make it slow."

His jaw slackened. "What do you mean, *slow?*"

"Tease me a little. Build the suspense." She swirled her wine in her goblet and took a sip, watching him over the rim of her glass.

His body quivered in anticipation while his mind balked. "What suspense? You've seen every part of me. And I can say that with conviction after the other night. What difference does it make how I take off my clothes now?"

"Believe me, it makes a difference. And keep your eyes on me the whole time you're doing it."

Suspicion made him frown. "How do you know it makes a difference?"

"A friend of mine in college had a male stripper for her twenty-first birthday party. He was very good."

"I'm not a male stripper!"

"Your body is even nicer than his." She rubbed the wineglass slowly back and forth across her lower lip. Then she circled the rim with her tongue and licked an imaginary drop off the side of the glass. She turned to him with a smile. "I'll make it worth your while, cowboy."

He wanted to laugh and make light of her blatant attempt to remind him of what she'd accomplished the other night. But the laughter stuck in his throat as he gazed helplessly at her mouth and remembered. With that gesture of her pink tongue moving over the wineglass, she probably could have persuaded him to drink arsenic.

He settled for drinking the wine she'd poured. Walking over to the nightstand, he picked up his glass and drained it. He set down the empty glass, took off his watch and laid it next to the glass. Then he emptied the condoms out of his pocket and put those on the table, too.

She glanced at them and back at him. "I have some, you know."

"How did you know what size?"

"I had a good idea."

He remembered her hands on him, her mouth taking him in, and agreed silently that yes, she probably did know.

"So, will you strip for me, Mac?"

He gazed at her. "Swear to me you'll never tell anyone," he said as a last attempt at self-preservation.

"I swear on the tomb of old King Tut, take a willow switch to my butt."

That crazy rhyme they'd made up as kids took on erotic meaning when spoken by a sexy wench reclining in her red velvet and white satin room of seduction. "Is that a suggestion?"

"Not exactly. I haven't done much research into spanking fantasies." She picked up a remote control and pushed a button. The volume of the music increased a fraction, the beat becoming more insistent. "Now do it, MacDougal. Make me squirm."

TESS TRIED TO LOOK composed as she lay against the pillows and waited for Mac to undress, but inside she was churning with anticipation. He had no idea what a beautiful body he had, and in the past she hadn't allowed herself to admire it much, either. But that was then. This was now.

He'd worn a long-sleeved western shirt even though it was summer. Like most cowboys, he kept mostly long-sleeved shirts in his closet, because they'd protect his arms from whipping branches on a wild cross-country ride. If he got too hot, he'd roll the sleeves back, but Mac had come to her tonight in dress mode, the sleeves snapped at his wrists.

Slowly he unsnapped them, his habitual movements executed with tantalizing care. Her heartbeat quickened. He was really going to do this for her.

She sipped her wine as he started on the top fastener of his shirt. Keeping his gaze on her, he made his way gradually down the row. Each soft pop of a snap was like the flare of a match lighting a new fuse. She hungered for each snap to release, each section of newly exposed skin.

He languidly pulled the shirt from his jeans so it hung open. She waited for him to take it off. Memories flashed by, more potent than she'd realized, of Mac stripping off his T-shirt and using it to mop his face when he'd helped her parents paint their house one summer, of Mac lying bare-chested beside the river one hot afternoon, his fishing pole anchored in the sand, his hat over his eyes.

She'd enjoyed the view then—she wanted it now. Instead, as if to gently torture her, he walked over to a chair and sat down. He drew off one boot with great deliberation, and then the other, all the while keeping his attention on her. His socks followed.

He's undressing because he's going to make love to me. The thought washed over her like a caress, moistening her with need.

He stood and walked toward her. "I've decided two can play this game."

"You have?" Her voice was breathy, not at all the way she normally sounded.

"You did a good job on the phone. If you unhook your bra for me now, I can watch."

She trembled. Darkness had protected her during their first encounter, distance and a telephone line the second. She wanted to be bold and daring this time, to experience the wonders she'd only read about. Mac was asking her to do that.

Following his lead, she drank the rest of her wine and set the empty glass on the table next to his.

"And do it slow," he murmured.

Heart pounding, she leaned back against the pillows and eased her fingers over the clasp holding the silken cups. Then she waited as he took off his shirt and she could finally admire his sculpted torso. With her eyes she traced the scar on his shoulder from a scrape with barbed wire, another on his arm from a run-in with a bull. The scars only made him seem more masculine.

He was magnificent. No wonder she'd loved wrestling with him when they were teenagers. She wanted to do more than that now.

He stood, hands on hips, and lifted his eyebrows, clearly indicating it was her turn.

She applied pressure to the clasp and it gave way, but she held it closed as she reached up and slid one shoulder strap down. Then she slid the other strap down. Slowly, slowly she allowed the garment to part and fall away, leaving only the pearl necklace and his daisies. The chain of flowers caught on one nipple, causing it to pucker. Instinct prompted her to brush the daisy chain across her other nipple, arousing it, too.

His gaze darkened and he sucked in a breath.

She paused and flicked her glance toward his belt.

His attention never left her breasts as he eased the buckle open and pulled the belt slowly from the loops. "Now touch them," he whispered.

Her heartbeat ratcheted up another notch. Sliding both hands up her rib cage, she cradled the weight of her breasts, lifting them as if in offering. Then she drew her thumbs down over the nipples, caressing herself.

"Oh, Tess." His hands shook as he unfastened his jeans.

The effect of sliding her thumbs over her breasts while he watched was incredible. Sensation poured downward to the juncture of her thighs, pooling and throbbing there, demanding satisfaction. Now she knew what fulfillment felt like, and she wanted it again.

He shoved jeans and boxers away, no longer measuring his movements.

The sight of his aroused body brought a quiet moan from her lips. Her desire had a shape now, as instinct made her aware of a hollowness that ached for what he could provide. More than release, she wanted to be filled.

He came to the edge of the bed. "You said you'd feed me."

"Yes." Her breathing was quick and shallow. "Whatever you want."

"That's good to hear." His voice was husky as he put a knee on the satin sheets. "I see what I want." He gently moved her hand aside and replaced it with his own.

At the remembered touch, her heart thundered in her chest. "Is there…anything I can do?"

"Arch your back," he murmured.

She did, lifting her breasts.

He used his teeth to lift the daisies away. When he drew her nipple into his mouth, she gasped with the realization that she was nearly at the point of climax. He'd had to coax her before, but no longer. Apparently this time she'd need only the fantasy they created in this room to become a wild woman. She hoped Mac was ready for that.

CHAPTER TEN

FOR THREE DAYS Mac had been dreaming about Tess's body. To taste and caress her breasts, to kiss and nibble and suck to his heart's content, was heaven. As the tempo of her breathing quickened, he lightened his touch, not wanting to bring her to the brink too fast. They had hours to enjoy each other. And besides, he knew where he wanted to be when she climaxed this time.

"You're so beautiful," he murmured.

"You, too." She ran her hands over his chest, brushing his nipples until they became as taut as the rest of him. She reached lower.

"Not yet." He drew back, knowing he couldn't tolerate her hands on him there until he was more in control. He teased the daisy chain over her skin, tinged rose by the lamps, and caused her to flush even pinker. Pollen scattered over her breasts and he licked it off. Then he took the pearl in his teeth.

Still fondling her breasts, he eased up and transferred the pearl to her mouth. As it lay against her tongue, he toyed with it with his own tongue in a blatantly suggestive way. He wondered if she knew that he was telling her, if she understood what he had in mind. If not, she would find out very soon. He was hungry for her.

With one last flick of his tongue over the pearl, he lifted it from her mouth and eased downward, depositing it, moist and shining, in the valley between her breasts.

"Do you know what I want now?" he whispered against her skin.

"I...think I do."

"Are you ready for that?"

Her breathing grew ragged. "If you are."

"I crave you. All of you."

Her breath caught. "But I...might go crazy."

"That was my plan." Heart racing, he began his journey, kissing his way along her downy soft skin to her navel. The scent of her cologne mixed with the perfume of crushed flowers and the heady aroma of arousal as he dipped his tongue into the small depression. She moaned and twitched beneath him.

He moved lower. The silk of her stockings and the ridiculously high heels excited him more than he wanted to admit, and he decided not to disturb any of it yet. The damp scrap of lace covering the object of his quest was easily drawn aside. Ah, she was so pretty. So drenched with need.

He touched her gently with one finger and she gasped. He kept his caress subtle as he planted lingering kisses along her inner thigh and ran his tongue over the lacy top of her stocking. Desire surged through him as he lavished the same attention on her other thigh, moving ever higher, ever closer to his goal.

At last he kissed her dark curls, and she moaned. When he finally touched his tongue to the delicate pearl nestled there waiting for him, she writhed beneath him. Suddenly impatient with the thin strip of lace denying him total access, he held it between his fingers and tore it with his teeth. Now.

Easing his shoulders under her silk-clad thighs, he sought his reward. The taste of her made him groan with delight. As her cries of pleasure filled the room, he immersed himself in sensory overload, relishing the stockings, the shoes, the rosy light, the satin sheets, the erotic music, and most of all, the passionate woman coming apart in his arms.

Her climax came quickly, too quickly for him. She lifted her hips and he took all that she offered, but as she sank back, quivering and gasping, he settled in for a more leisurely exploration. She tried to wiggle from his grasp but she was weak in the aftermath of her release. He held her easily and continued along his chosen path. Before long her slight resistance faded and she opened to him in a wanton gesture that nearly brought him to the boiling point.

And he learned her—the touch that made her whimper, the stroke that pushed her closer, the teasing flick that drove her wild. As he coaxed her toward the precipice a second time, a fierce possessiveness took over. Rational thought played no part as he boldly claimed her, drawing from her the most intimate of sounds as she gave herself up to wave upon wave of shattering convulsions.

He brought her gently back to earth with feathery touches and light kisses over her thighs and dew-sprinkled curls. At last he drew slowly up beside her and brushed the hair back from her flushed face.

She gazed up at him, her gray eyes filled with dazed wonder. Her lips parted, but no sound came out.

He smiled. She looked the way he'd felt the other night. He was gratified that he'd created that sort of expression in her eyes. He trailed a finger down the curve of her throat and over her breastbone until he encountered the pearl on its golden chain. He brought it up slowly to his lips and kissed it before settling it back between her breasts.

Her gaze grew smoky and she ran her tongue over her lips.

He was glad to see a return of desire in those gray depths, for he was far from finished. And he loved knowing that the pearl necklace had become a symbol for the intimate activity they'd just shared. If he had it his way she'd wear it forever, and each time it moved against her skin she'd relive the sensations his tongue had given her.

"How do you feel?" he asked.

Her voice was low and throaty. "Like a concubine. How do you feel?"

"Like the luckiest man on earth."

She sighed. "That was way better than they described it in the books, and the books made it sound very nice."

He brushed his finger against her lower lip. "But you're still a virgin."

Her smile was pure seduction. "Feel free to take care of that anytime, cowboy. In case you can't tell, I'm putty in your hands."

His erection throbbed. She made the next step sound almost casual, and he tried to keep the same tone in his voice. "How about now?"

"Now's fine," she said lazily. She ran a fingertip down his shaft. "Unless you'd rather have me—"

"Not this time." He heard the edge in his voice. Damn, he was strung tight as a roped calf, and he figured there was only one way he'd be able to unwind. But in the process he didn't want her to absorb his agitation and tighten up herself. The whole point behind the way he'd just loved her was to ease her into this moment. Well, part of the point. In truth he hadn't been able to help himself. She was luscious.

"Do you want me to put the music on again?" she asked.

He became aware that the music had ended. He'd been so absorbed in her that he hadn't noticed. He thought about the music, considering. "Let's not," he said, combing his fingers through her hair. "I think this is a moment when we should listen only to each other, to anything we might say, to how we breathe…and the cries we make."

Her eyes darkened. "Okay."

He reached across her and took a packet from the bed-side table.

"I could put that on for you. I've practiced."

"Practiced?" Jealousy hit him, swift and unyielding. "On who?"

"Mr. Cucumber."

He started laughing. "Only you, Tess."

"You think it's funny?" She grabbed the packet from him.

"Yes, I think it's hilarious." He give her a swift kiss and made a grab for the packet, but she held it out of reach. "Give it here." He kissed her again. This was sort of fun. Then he started chuckling all over again as he thought about her sitting in her kitchen studiously rolling a con-dom down a cucumber, over and over, until she got it right.

"I want to show you how good I am!" she protested, ripping the packet open.

"No." He made another grab but she evaded him. "Come on, Tess. I'm too worked up. If you fumble around you could set me off."

"I won't fumble."

"You will." He tackled her in earnest, laughing and kissing her everywhere he could reach as he tried to get the condom away from her. In the process he pulled off both her shoes so she wouldn't injure anything important.

"I'm good at this. Let me do it, Mac." She used the satin sheets to her advantage, wiggling away from him.

The wrestling match was putting him in even greater danger of exploding, but between sliding around on the sheets and coming into constant contact with Tess's bare skin, he was having a great, if risky, time of it. He'd always loved wrestling with Tess. "If you don't hold still and give me that condom, I'm going to tie you to the bedposts," he warned with a grin as he paused to catch his breath.

"I don't care." She was breathing as hard as he was. "The books say that's fun. Ever done it?"

"No." He looked down at her, his pulse racing at the vivid picture of her lying spread-eagle on the white bed, silken ties holding her wrists and ankles. He could barely breathe. "I was kidding," he said hoarsely.

"I wasn't. That seems like the perfect time for you to use the furry gloves."

He gazed into her eyes and saw the fire there. "You'd let me do that?"

Her chest heaved with her rapid breathing, making her breasts quiver. "I would let you do that, Mac, because I trust you. And you would let me do the same with you. It would be exciting."

"Oh, Tess." He began to tremble as a new picture formed—Tess tying him down and then…trying out all that she'd learned in her books.

"Lie down. Let me put the condom on."

"All right." She was messing with his head, making him want to surrender his role of leader again and let her tempt him into all sorts of new and fascinating sensuality. He lay back against the pillows. "But don't…play around."

"Don't worry. I understand your problem."

"I don't have a problem! Any guy in this situation would be struggling to keep it together."

"So you've had a good time so far?"

"You don't even have to ask. I—" He nearly choked as she leaned over him and took his erection into her mouth. "Tess!"

She lifted her head and smiled at him. "Lubrication." Then she expertly rolled the condom on in less time than he'd ever managed it and lifted her hands like a cowboy in a calf-roping event. "Done."

Despite her speed, the contact made him gasp and grit his teeth.

"Wasn't that pretty good?" she asked.

"Sure was."

"Want me to be on top? I've seen pictures of how—"

"No." He grabbed her and rolled, pinning her to the mattress. Then he reached for the garters and unfastened them. "And it's time to get rid of these."

She gazed up at him, her breath shallow and her lips parted in anticipation. "If you say so, macho man."

"Sometimes a guy has to take charge." He rolled each stocking down and pulled it off. Then he worked her out of the garter belt and what was left of the panties.

Her cheeks flushed as she lay there under his gaze. "Now do you approve? Am I ready?"

He was so overcome by the picture she made wearing only the daisy chain and the pearl necklace that he could barely speak. He lifted his gaze to hers and swallowed. "You're perfect," he said in a tight voice. He swallowed again. "And I should probably let you be on top and in control, since you've never done this, but I…don't want to."

Her question was breathy, seductive. "Why not?"

"Because I think I'd feel…secondary."

"Sort of…used?"

"Exactly."

"I wouldn't want that."

"Thank you." He stroked her breast, loving the softness beneath his palm as he cradled the supple weight and brought the nipple to a firm peak. "I'll be careful."

"I know you will." She closed her eyes and arched into his caress. "Oh, Mac, I could get addicted to having you touch me like that."

He paused, unsure how to respond. "We have all summer," he said at last.

Her eyes opened slowly, and excitement glowed in their gray depths. "Do we dare risk it? Making love like this all summer?"

He would risk just about anything to spend the summer loving Tess, but he didn't want to pressure her into anything she might regret. "That's up to you. It's your project. You said all you needed was deflowering."

"That was when I thought…it would be someone else. Mmm. That's good, Mac."

He rolled her other nipple gently between his thumb and forefinger. "The more we make love, the greater the chance someone will find out."

"Mmm. Yeah." She closed her eyes again and ran her tongue over her lips. "We should think about that."

"So think about it." He leaned down and drew one pert nipple into his mouth.

She sighed and lifted upward, encouraging him to take more. "Oh, sure. While you're driving me insane."

He tried his best to do exactly that, hollowing his cheeks as he drew her more fully into his mouth, letting her experience his hunger for several long seconds before he kissed his way to her other breast. "You don't have to decide now," he murmured against her skin as he slid a hand down to the damp triangle between her legs.

"That's…good." She drew in a quick breath as he tunneled his fingers through her curls and reconnected with her flash point. "And so is that."

Caressing her now took on a different meaning, because now, at last, he would know the wonder of being inside her. His blood sang in his veins as he stroked her, preparing her for that sweet invasion. And he would be the first. God help him, he was filled with joy at that thought.

TESS SENSED THE change in Mac's touch, as if the promise of completion gave new urgency to every caress. And though she'd tried to seem casual about what was about to happen, in reality she felt like a canoe being carried down the rapids toward a thundering waterfall. If anyone but Mac had been touching her, arousing her, she would have leaped from the bed, unsure if she truly wanted this change in status, after all.

But Mac was there, making her ache, making her long for the firm thrust of him, deep inside her. Perhaps there would be pain. She no longer cared if only he'd finally claim her, complete her in ways she'd never dreamed of until this moment.

He lifted his head, a question in his eyes as he slipped his finger deep inside.

It was the penetration she longed for, but not nearly enough. A sudden shyness overtook her, causing her to close her eyes before she asked for what she wanted. "More," she whispered.

He eased two fingers in, placing soft kisses on her mouth. "Tell me how that feels."

"Different." Her breath caught as he moved his fingers gently back and forth. "Wonderful," she said, letting out a trembling sigh. "Mac, I'm going wild inside. Deflower me. Please."

His kiss was soft and lingering, but still she felt the barely leashed power of him as he moved between her thighs and propped his arms on either side of her head. Quivering with excitement, she wrapped both arms around his back and felt his muscles flex. She couldn't tell for sure because of her own trembling, but she thought he was shaking, too. His breathing was affected, at any rate, as he probed her gently with the blunt tip of his erection. She braced herself. No matter how much she might want him there, he would be substantial and might take some getting used to.

"Tess." There was a smile in his voice. "Open your eyes."

She gazed up at him, astonished by the tenderness in his

blue gaze. She'd thought a man in his position would be in the grip of passion and appear much more fierce. "What?"

"You look just the way you used to before the roller coaster started. I'm going to go easy. You don't have to clench your jaw like that. And keep your eyes open. If you're looking at me, I'll be able to tell how I'm doing."

"How can you be so…calm?"

"Believe me, I'm not calm," he said quietly. "But I am paying attention."

"Oh, Mac. Thank you for being here."

"I'm here." He eased slowly forward and his eyes darkened. "Right here."

She noticed the flicker of uncontrolled desire in his eyes before she became totally absorbed by the sensation when he entered her. She registered warmth and size. He withdrew and eased in again, and she moaned in pleasure at the friction that was unlike anything he'd provided before.

"Tess?"

"That was a happy moan," she murmured, looking into his eyes. There was that flicker of primitive need again. She found it thrilling.

His breathing was labored, but he kept his movements slow. "I'm going a little deeper."

"Yes." Everything else, she began to realize, no matter how delicious, was only a lead-in to this, the ultimate connection. Nothing in her world had ever felt so right as opening her body to this man and being filled by him.

He slid forward, and met resistance. He stopped immediately and looked into her eyes. "This is it."

Her heart thudded wildly. One movement and her life would be forever changed. She would be a virgin no longer. Ah, but then she could welcome the whole length of him and know the wonder of joining intimately with another person. And not just any person, either. Mac. One movement and she could be fully with him, in every sense.

She slipped her hands down to his buttocks and gripped firmly. "Let's go for it."

As he pushed gently forward, she rose to meet him, determined to share in the moment. The sharp pain brought a cry to her lips.

"Damn." He stopped, his gaze troubled.

"It's okay." She trembled against him. "It's going away. Don't hold back. It's over now. Love me. Love me the way a man loves a woman."

With a groan he pushed deep, locking their bodies together, his hips cradled between hers. And the fierceness she'd expected to see earlier flared in the depths of his eyes as he gazed down at her.

As she met that gaze, she felt an answering intensity rise within her. She'd expected them both to be naked tonight, but she hadn't guessed he'd also strip her to the essence of her soul, and she him. She looked into his eyes and realized they were both seeing depths they'd never imagined before. And her world shifted, for she knew the connection they were making would not end with this night, or even with this summer. It would last forever.

CHAPTER ELEVEN

PERFECT, MAC THOUGHT. He'd never been anywhere in the world that had felt so absolutely right as being here, as close as he'd ever been to Tess. It seemed as if their entire lives had been leading to this moment. Linked in spirit ever since they were children, they had finally created the ultimate link, and a sense of destiny washed over him.

Mindful of her tender condition, he moved carefully, but still he moved, needing to define and redefine that sword-to-sheath perfection they made together. "Okay?" he murmured.

"Very…okay." Her eyes shone.

He eased back and edged forward again. Yes. And again. *Oh, Tess.*

"Mac…Mac…"

The wonder in her eyes and the richness she poured into his name told him all he needed to know. She was with him. He cupped a hand beneath her bottom, steadying her as he transmitted a new, more urgent rhythm. She caught on quickly, rising to meet his thrusts. Her bottom was soft and yielding, sweet to hold, sweeter yet to knead gently with his fingers. Yet the flex of her muscles against his hand when she truly began to participate drove him wild.

Very wild. Soon. He changed the angle, brushing the tips of her breasts with his body, pressing against the sensitive nub between her thighs that would bring her with him.

Her breathing grew shallow and he knew he'd found the spot, if only he could last long enough. This first time, he wanted to give her the gift of knowing how good it could be, how much higher she could climb when he was deep within her, coaxing a response that would vibrate down to her toes.

Her eyes widened and her breathing quickened. He played to that response, urging her on. So good. He'd never dreamed making love could be like this. Her body rose to meet his thrusts, tightening around him. As the moment built in the depths of her eyes, exultant laughter bubbled from him.

"Yes," he cried.

"Oh, Mac!" She arched against him. "I'm—"

"Yes." His voice was hoarse with need. "You're a woman now." *My woman.* With one final thrust he brought heaven raining down upon them.

TESS SAT PROPPED up against the pillows next to Mac, the tray balanced on another pillow across their laps while they sampled the snacks she'd prepared for the evening. Mac was eating with gusto, but Tess felt too happy and pleased with herself to be interested in food.

She looked at Mac for about the hundredth time, a grin on her face. "We did pretty good, huh?"

He lowered the peach he'd about to bite into and gazed at her. A slow smile eased across his face, and he nodded. "Yep. You look damn pleased with yourself, too."

"I am." She picked up a cluster of red grapes and plucked one off its stem with her teeth. "I'm proud of us. I think we were awesome. Better than I ever expected."

After swallowing his bite of peach, he gestured around the room. "I don't know. Looking at all this, I'd say you expected a lot."

"The books say a man is a visual animal, so I was trying to make sure you'd be properly aroused."

He laughed so hard he almost choked on his peach. "Overkill," he gasped. "Major overkill."

She lifted her chin. "I don't know how you can say that, considering how well everything worked out. Maybe if I'd left the bedroom the way it was, and worn an old T-shirt and boxers, you wouldn't have been able to get an erection."

He stared at her. "Tess, I had an erection driving over here just knowing what we planned to do tonight."

"Yeah?" She smiled. "So the phone thing worked?"

"I *knew* you did that on purpose!"

"Of course. Just like you sent the gloves on purpose."

"And you put that double-meaning message on the answering machine. I stood there listening to it with my mom watching me the whole time, if you don't think that was tough!"

"Well, I didn't want you to lose interest!"

"Fat chance of that, twinkle toes."

"Seriously, Mac. According to what I've read, women are a lot better at sustaining lustful feelings in the absence of the lover than most guys. Guys are more the out-of-sight, out-of-mind type. I didn't want you to lose interest."

"For your information, there was no chance I'd lose interest. I didn't need that phone conversation or the message on the answering machine and your cute little reference to ice in order to get excited."

"Oh! I didn't remember the ice! I was planning to give you a special treat with that ice trick. But I was so carried away that I…forgot."

He gave her a long glance. "I'll take that as a compliment."

Her heart beat a little faster, remembering the glory of the moment when she'd felt completely united with him, as if their souls had fused. She'd lost all track of techniques and tricks in the wonder of loving Mac. "It is a compliment. I couldn't think of anything but what was happening between us." She held his gaze and heat invaded her secret places once again. "I guess we didn't need the ice."

"No. We didn't need anything but each other."

Even now, she could barely believe that he really and truly wanted her. "This is so new. Then you're really turned on by me, the girl you've known forever?"

"Uh-huh."

"Wow."

"In fact, I'm getting in the mood again."

And so was she, but she'd been hesitant to admit it. "I thought it took a while for men to recharge."

"It does. It's been a while."

"Not that long. From what the experts say, a man would probably need some stimulation before he could manage another episode."

Mac chuckled. "That reading may get you into trouble yet. Take my word for it, I could manage another episode. Maybe several. I wish I could stay here and make love to you all night, but I don't know how we'd ever explain my truck being parked outside your house all that time."

Tess glanced at the clock and sighed with regret. "You're right. The neighbors would wonder and the gossip mill would start running."

He nodded. "I could park outside somebody else's house all night with no problem, but not yours. And we sure don't want to awaken anybody's suspicions." He moved the pillow and the tray of food and swung his legs over the end of the bed.

Tess couldn't resist glancing at the part of his anatomy that had recently delivered her from her virgin status. "You *are* ready again!"

"Surprise, surprise." He reached for his clothes.

"Want a quickie?" Her blood raced at the thought.

He turned back to her, a smile on his face. "And what do you know about quickies?"

"Everything. You just forget about the foreplay and go for it." Her nipples tightened in reaction. "It makes for variety. What do you think?"

He paused, his boxers in one hand. "Sounds tempting. But I guess I need the answer to my question first."

"What question?"

He faced her. "Well, you're not a virgin anymore."

"No, I'm not."

"So your project's technically finished, right?"

Her stomach clenched with sudden anxiety. "You mean we could stop right here and never…make love again?"

"That's what I mean. I need to know if this is the end of the fun and games or not."

"What do you want to do?"

He gave her a wry grin and gestured toward his groin. "I think that's obvious."

"I'm talking about the long-term risk." But as she spoke, she wondered if she fully understood the long-term risk. She'd been concerned about their families and people in town finding out. Maybe that wasn't the biggest problem. After tonight she felt bonded to Mac in a way she'd never experienced before, and yet she'd have to break that bond at the end of the summer. The more they made love to each other, the stronger the bond would become.

"I'm willing to accept the long-term risk," Mac said quietly.

A world of meaning lived in that statement, she thought. "And we'll still be…friends?" She wondered if that was the most foolish risk of all. If they made love all summer, could they possibly continue to be just friends?

His reply was soft and deliberate. "We'll always be friends."

He looked magnificent standing there, she thought. No

woman in her right mind would turn down the chance to spend the summer loving Mac, no matter what the consequences. "I wouldn't want to lose your friendship," she said.

"You won't."

"Promise?"

He smiled. "I swear on the tomb of old King Tut, take a willow switch to my butt."

She took a deep breath. "Then I guess…" She paused and blushed. "I guess I'd like to expand my summer project and get more…experience."

His smile faded, and he gazed at her with that unfamiliar fire in his eyes. "Okay. Then that's what we'll do." He started to put on his clothes.

"Wait. I thought we were going to have—"

"A quickie?" He pulled on his jeans and winced as he started buttoning his fly.

"Well, yes."

He reached for his shirt. "If tonight had been the end of the road, we would have. In fact, I might have turned it into something a little longer than that." He gazed at her as he buttoned his shirt. "But if we have all summer, then I don't want to settle for a quickie."

She wanted him so much she trembled, but she swallowed the words that would have begged him to stay. Still, she couldn't let him go without knowing when they'd make love again. Her hunger for his touch both startled her and warned her of the dangers ahead. "When are you…free again?" she asked. No matter how hard she tried, the neediness in her voice seeped through.

He crossed to the bed and sat down. Leaning toward her, his shirt half fastened, he cupped her face in one hand. "Are you going to get all prissy and try to pretend you don't want me so much you can't see straight?"

Of course he could read her like a book. She should have realized that. "I—"

"Because that's how much I want you. I'm practically blinded by how much I need you, how much I want to be inside you again. I don't want to leave tonight, but we both know I have to, and the sooner I go, the easier it'll be for both of us." His thumb brushed her lower lip. "I want to see you again tomorrow night, and the night after that, and the night after that. Hell, I want to spend all summer here in your bedroom."

"You do?"

"I can't think of anything sweeter. But we have to watch it or we'll make people suspicious. We need to wait a while before we get together again."

She moaned in frustration.

"That's better. At least you're being honest about what you want."

She gazed into his eyes, helpless in the grip of passion. "I didn't realize making love would be so...so good."

"It isn't always."

"I figured that, from the cautionary tone of the books. The first time is supposed to be pretty awkward because the couple isn't used to each other."

He caressed her cheek. "That's where we have the advantage. We already know how the other one thinks."

"Maybe not completely. You see, I was afraid that familiarity would make me boring for you."

"Oh?" His eyebrows raised. "Why? Am I boring for you?"

"No, but I've never done this before. You have."

"But not with you."

"So having sex with me is not boring?"

He smiled. "Not by a long shot."

"Good." She smiled back. "Then how about we do it again Tuesday night?"

He shook his head. "Too soon. And Wednesday's poker night. That should be quite a test, come to think of it."

"Mac, you're torturing me."

"No more than I'm torturing myself. Listen, Thursday night's a full moon. Let's take a ride to the river."

Her pulse rate skyrocketed. "Am I supposed to wear a dress with nothing on underneath?"

He grinned. "Good memory."

"As if I could ever forget that dream of yours!"

"Well, I won't ask you to do that. You'd be uncomfortable, and your hair's too short for that particular fantasy, anyway."

"I could wear a wig."

His smile widened as he combed his fingers through her hair. "I like your hair the way it is. But you might wear as little as possible without making a big deal of it. And don't worry about being thrown to the ground. I'll bring a blanket. And a couple of towels."

"Towels?"

"Ever gone skinny-dipping?"

"Of course not. My brothers would have had a fit if they thought I was swimming nude in the river." She gazed at him. "Have you?"

"A time or two."

"With a girl?"

"Maybe."

She was insanely jealous, but she didn't want him to know. She glanced away. "It's naive of me to think you wouldn't have. Did you take them…down to our hideaway?"

He guided her chin around until she had to look at him again. "Do you honestly think I would take someone else to our spot? To go skinny-dipping and…other stuff?"

She hoped he wouldn't, but she'd never asked him not to. "It's a good spot."

"It's *our* spot. I wouldn't feel right taking someone else there. I'm insulted that you could even think such a thing."

"Oh, Mac." She couldn't help the happy smile she gave him. "I would have so hated you taking someone else there, even if you didn't go skinny-dipping or have sex with her."

"I know. That's why I'd never do that. But I want to make love to you there, on the sand. And maybe even in the water."

Her body moistened, imagining exactly that. "I don't know if I can wait until Thursday night."

"Me, neither. But we don't want to ruin everything. In the meantime…" He leaned closer and kissed her, his tongue taking firm possession of her mouth.

She grew hot and dizzy from the suggestive movement of his lips and tongue and the memory of all the pleasure he'd given her. By the time he drew back, she was struggling for breath.

"Come to the corral about seven-thirty Thursday night," he murmured.

"I will." She tried to pull him back for another kiss, but he left the bed.

His voice was hoarse. "I really have to go, or we'll be tumbling around on that bed all night and we'll both be in trouble." He finished dressing. "I'll see you Thursday night."

It seemed like an eternity, but she knew he was right. People were used to them doing things together, but not constantly. "Okay. Thursday night it is."

He started out of the room and turned back. "I suppose you'll have to change the room, in case anybody shows up."

"I probably should. But I could put it back again sometime if you'd like."

"Oh, I'd like. We have some unfinished business in this room—something to do with silk ties and furry gloves."

She was going wild inside. "Mac, if you drove your

truck down to the bar, and walked back, maybe we could—"

"No." He gripped the door frame as if to keep himself from walking back into the room. "Leaving is best. I don't want anybody reporting my truck was at the bar all night, either. And there's always the chance I'd be seen leaving your house in the early-morning hours." He glanced at her. "If we really want this secret to keep all summer, then we have to be careful not to blow our cover."

She sighed. "I guess you're right."

"Aren't I always?" He gave her a cocky grin.

"No, you are not, you arrogant man!" She laughed and threw a pillow at him.

He caught it in one hand. "Your aim's off, Blakely. You must be out of practice. When was the last time you threw a baseball?"

"I don't know. Want to practice Thursday night instead?"

"Not on your life."

"Then get out of here. I have more reading to do."

The comment had the desired effect, making the flame leap again in his eyes. "You really know how to get to a guy."

"I promise to tell you all about what I've read when we get together Thursday night."

"Want to bring a flashlight and a book along? We could glance over it together."

"Sure, why not? Sort of like reading comics together in the tent after dark."

He laughed. "Not even close. Oh, and by the way, congratulations on your new status."

"Thank you. I think I'm going to like it."

"I know I am. This is by far the best summer-project idea you've ever had." With a wink, he walked down the hall.

Tess listened until she heard the front door close. Then she got up and threw on a robe before walking down the hall. Maybe he'd change his mind and come back in, needing to hold her again as much as she needed to hold him.

Unfortunately he really seemed to be leaving. After he slammed the truck door shut, the engine roared to life and the headlights flicked on. She automatically walked over and flashed the front-porch light, their goodbye signal. He flashed the headlights of his truck in return. Then he backed the truck down the driveway.

She could hardly stand to have him go. He'd taken her from innocence to knowledge, and now she craved him with an intensity bordering on obsession. Maybe she would have felt this way about any man who had introduced her to the wonders of physical love, but she doubted it.

For one thing, not any man would have known her well enough to make this such a mind-bending experience for her. Not any man would have had the tenderness and caring Mac had demonstrated every step of the way. And she couldn't imagine any other man looking so beautiful in the act of love.

As she stood in the living room listening to the fading sound of his truck's engine, she discovered the fatal flaw of her great plan. If she couldn't bear to have him leave after one night of lovemaking, what condition would she be in when the summer came to an end?

CHAPTER TWELVE

TESS WAS LOOKING for any distraction to get her through until Thursday night. When Hammer's wife, Deena, called Tuesday morning to suggest a day at the community pool with whichever Blakely women and kids could make it, Tess jumped at the chance.

Deena, a freckle-faced brunette who had been one of Tess's best friends in high school, was a teacher's aide. She had summers off, which was a schedule she intended to keep until five-year-old Jason and four-year-old Kimberly were older. Joan brought Sarah and Joe, and Cindy found somebody to work her shift at the auto-parts store so she could ease her pregnant self into the cool water. Only the newlywed Suzie, a bank teller, couldn't get off.

"And wouldn't you know, she's the one who looks the best in a bathing suit," Deena said as the group of women staked out a corner of the fenced pool area with lawn chairs, beach towels and a cooler containing sandwiches and juice.

"Oh, I don't know that Suzie wins the bathing-suit competition," Joan said. Like everyone else, she'd worn her suit under her T-shirt and shorts and was now stripping off her outer layer. "Tess is looking pretty buff in that red tank suit."

Tess glanced down at herself, suddenly self-conscious. "Hey, it's the same old me."

"Maybe so," Deena said. She grabbed Jason and swiped

some sunscreen lotion on him. "But you're looking real good, chick. Been working out or something?"

"Nope." She hoped she wasn't blushing. Surely the fact that she was no longer a virgin didn't show somehow. Inside she felt like a changed woman, but outside she must look exactly the same. Mac wasn't that much of a miracle worker.

"They're right," Cindy chimed in. "There's a certain glow about you." She laughed. "People say pregnant women get that, and I'm still waiting. Mostly I just feel fat."

"I think you're all seeing things." Tess felt desperate to get out of the spotlight. "Come on, kids! Who's ready to go for a swim with Aunt Tess?"

A chorus of *me, me, me* followed immediately.

Tess had helped teach all of them to swim, and consequently they were all fish, even four-year-old Kimberly. Tess gazed down at their eager faces and felt a pang of regret. They would grow so fast while she was gone. She must remember to cherish days like today, and not count them as time-fillers until she could see Mac again. "Last one in's a rotten egg!" she called, and leaped into the pool.

Three hours later the women gathered their tired group together, put more sunscreen on pink noses and decided the perfect ending to the day would be treats all around at the Creamy Cone. Tess pulled on her shorts and sandals, ran her fingers through her hair and decided not to bother with the T-shirt. In the summertime, shorts worn over a bathing suit became almost a uniform for patrons at the Creamy Cone.

Everyone piled into Joan's minivan for the four-block trip, and on the way Tess sat in the back with the kids and led them through "The Itsy Bitsy Spider" and "I'm a Little Teapot."

"Carry me, Aunt Tess," Kimberly begged when they arrived at the bustling ice-cream shop.

"Too many cannonballs into the pool for you," Tess said, hoisting the little girl out of her seat and propping her on her hip.

"I *like* cannonballs," Kimberly said, snuggling against Tess.

"Yeah, you sprayed me all the time," added her brother, Jason.

Tess laughed. "Me, too. This girl's a regular spray machine."

"Hey, look!" shouted Joe, Joan's six-year-old. "Uncle Mac's here!"

Uncle Mac. Of course the kids had always called him that, considering that he was an honorary Blakely, but today, after she'd been hearing herself referred to as Aunt Tess for hours, the title struck her differently. Aunt Tess and Uncle Mac.

The idea hit her with more force than any cannonball jump of Kimberly's. Uh-oh. She hadn't subconsciously been having *that* little fantasy, had she? If so, she could forget it right now. Mac was only helping her out. Sure, he might be having a good time in the bargain, but if he'd ever considered having a relationship with her, he would have spoken up long before this.

And he certainly could have spoken up on Sunday night, she thought as she watched him get out of his truck. Instead, he'd been more intent than she was on keeping their secret. Nope, he definitely didn't have dreams of happily-ever-after with her.

"Hey, Uncle Mac!" Joan's daughter, Sarah, called. She started to run across the parking lot.

"Sarah!" Joan yelled a warning and bolted after her as a low-slung car pulled quickly into the lot, apparently oblivious to the running girl. Sarah had a good head start on her mother.

Still holding Kimberly, Tess ran forward, too, knowing neither she nor Joan would make it in time.

At the last minute, when Tess was too horrified even to scream, Mac hurtled into the path of the car, snatched Sarah out of the way and leaped to safety.

The driver, a teenage boy, slammed on the brakes and jumped out of the car. "Oh, God! I didn't see her!" he wailed. "Is she okay?"

Mac held a quaking Sarah tight in his arms. He was breathing hard. "I think so." He leaned away from the child. "You okay, sweetheart?"

Her voice was muffled against his shirt. "I...think so."

"Sarah!" Joan reached them and wrapped her arm around the girl's shoulders. "Did you get bumped? Does anything hurt?"

"N-no." Sarah sounded close to tears.

Joan sagged with relief as Cindy and Deena came up and put comforting arms around her. Everyone started talking at once, exclaiming over the close call, while Joan took several deep breaths and the color seeped back into her face.

Finally Joan held up her hand for silence. "Put her down, please, Mac. She and I are going over to that tree and having a little talk about running in parking lots."

"I don't run," Joe announced.

"Me, neither," said Jason.

"Me, neither," piped up Kimberly from her perch in Tess's arms.

"And we're going to hold you all to that," Mac said, glancing at each of them with a stern expression.

The teenager stepped toward Joan. "I'm sorry, Mrs. Blakely. I shouldn't have driven in so fast. I just got the car today, and I was all like, wow, I want to show my friends. But if anything bad had happened to her..."

Joan took Sarah's hand and gave the teenager a weary smile. "Fortunately it didn't. It's Eddie, isn't it?"

"Yes, ma'am. Eddie Dunnett."

"Well, we're lucky, Eddie. Hopefully we've learned something without suffering a tragedy in the process. Sarah shouldn't have been running without looking, and you should probably remember how dangerous parking lots can be around here, especially this one in the summer."

"Yes, ma'am." Eddie glanced at Mac. "Thanks, Mr. MacDougal. Thanks a lot."

"I'm glad I still have some reflexes left," Mac said.

"Yeah, no quarterback at CHS could run the option play like you. My dad still talks about it."

Mac looked uncomfortable. "That was a long time ago. So, is everybody ready for some ice cream? I'll treat."

"In that case, I'll have the jumbo banana split," Deena said with a grin. "I was going to settle for a small cone, but if the gentleman's buying—"

"Okay, but I'm gonna tell Hammer you took advantage of me," Mac retorted.

Deena laughed. "You're lucky he's not here. He'd order the Earthquake."

"If he was here, I wouldn't have offered to treat. Come on, everybody. Let's see what kind of bill you can run up."

"Sarah and I will be in shortly," Joan said. "Joe, you go with the rest of them so I can talk privately with Sarah."

"Come along, Joe," said Cindy, holding out her hand.

Tess had always liked the way members of the family accepted responsibility for all the children, not just their own. A Blakely grandchild had a host of adult role models, and from where Tess sat, they were all good ones. Then if you added Uncle Mac, a true hero, a kid would have no excuse for not turning out well.

As for Sarah, she looked completely miserable for ruining the mood of the day. For a sensitive little girl, that was punishment enough. "Come on, gang," Tess said, adjusting Kimberly on her hip. "I'm in the mood for vanilla dipped in butterscotch."

"That's my favorite," said Mac, falling in beside her. He reached over and tugged gently on Kimberly's blond curls. "How's Kimmy today?"

"Uncle Mac! You're messing up my hair!"

"It's already messed up! You've been doing cannonballs in the pool, haven't you?"

Kimberly laughed. "Yep."

Tess wondered if Mac realized that in reaching over to tease Kimberly his arm had brushed Tess's breast. But if Mac didn't realize it, Tess did. All at once she became aware of her own unkempt hair, her pink nose and her wrinkled shorts. Until a few days ago, she'd never thought about what she looked like when Mac was around. Now she wished she'd at least taken time to comb her hair.

"We all got a little messed up today," she said.

"That's okay." He reached over and tweaked Kimberly's nose, getting a squeal in response. "I like my girls messed up."

This time she was sure he was aware that he'd brushed against her. The movement might have seemed accidental to someone else, but Tess felt the deliberate nature of it. He held the door of the shop open for her, and as she walked by him, she registered the heady scent of a slightly sweaty, thoroughly masculine Mac. He wore a T-shirt and jeans today and looked sexier than any man had a right to. She fought her reaction to him, knowing that she couldn't let any of her feelings show in front of her sisters-in-law.

"So you can take a break any old time and sashay into town for ice cream?" she asked, glancing at him. Oh, but he looked good, with his hat tilted at a rakish angle and a gleam in his eye. "Must be a cushy job you have, MacDougal."

"Not as cushy as yours," he said. "Frolicking in the water with this bunch all day while I'm out there busting my butt repairing fence."

Kimberly leaned over Tess's shoulder to peer behind Mac. Then she giggled. "Your butt's not busted, Uncle Mac."

That's for sure, Tess thought, remembering the muscled firmness she'd gripped when they'd…whoops. Dangerous territory. Thoughts like that would make her blush, and blushing wasn't something she normally did when Mac showed up. She stepped into line at the counter behind Cindy and Joe. Mac stood behind her, and she could feel his presence as clearly as if he'd pressed his body up against hers.

Kimberly peered over Tess's shoulder at Mac. "When I grow up, I'm gonna marry you."

"That makes me one lucky guy," Mac said.

Tess shivered, remembering those words in a far different context than playful banter with a little girl.

"Unless I marry Buddy in my Sunday school instead," Kimberly added solemnly. "He's always trying to kiss me."

Tess jiggled her and spoke with mock sternness. "Hey, you little heartbreaker. You can't propose to one guy and then announce you're marrying somebody else the next minute. You have to make up your mind."

"Okay. Then I choose Uncle Mac."

"Thanks, Kimmy. Can *I* give you a kiss?"

"Oh, sure. Just don't slobber like Buddy."

"I'll try not to." Mac leaned forward and kissed her on the cheek. "There, it's official."

They were all just kidding around, Tess told herself. There was no reason for this tightness in her chest, no reason for her to feel suddenly grief-stricken at the thought that Mac would have a real engagement one of these days.

No doubt he'd even ask Tess to be in the wedding. After all, they were best friends.

Her turn came to order, and she got a butterscotch-dipped cone for herself and a chocolate-dipped one for Kimberly.

"That's all?" Mac said as she stepped aside so he could order. "No triple banana split or Earthquake for either of you?"

"I like chocolate-dipped the best. I always get that," Kimberly said with authority.

"Tess? You're going to let me get away with just a butterscotch cone?"

"Yep." She set Kimberly down and handed her the chocolate cone before taking the freshly dipped butterscotch one from the counter clerk, a young woman named Evie Jenkins. "Thanks, Evie."

As Kimberly walked over to the table where the rest of the group had gathered, Tess turned back to Mac, who looked more tempting than any ice-cream cone. She realized that her sisters-in-law were engrossed in eating their ice cream and keeping their children from becoming sticky disaster areas. They wouldn't pay any attention to her and Mac, especially considering they were used to seeing the two of them tease and joke with each other.

A devil took temporary possession of her, and she gave Mac a sultry glance. "As much as I'd like to take advantage of you, this is my all-time favorite." Then she swirled her tongue around the top of the cone.

Mac stared at her.

"Then if you nip off the top—" she bit through the butterscotch coating "—you can suck the ice cream right out." As she demonstrated her technique, she glanced up at Mac.

He continued to stare at her while gripping the counter so hard his knuckles showed white against his tan.

"Mr. MacDougal? Are you ready to order?" asked Evie.

Mac didn't take his gaze from Tess. "Uh, yeah." His voice was gravelly. "I'll have…what she's having."

"Coming up."

"I can't believe you're doing that," he murmured to Tess.

"Eating ice cream?" She smiled innocently. "That's what everyone does at the Creamy Cone."

"Not like that."

"Exactly like that. I've eaten one of these like this a million times."

"But not after we've just…"

She took a quick inventory of the area below his belt and was gratified with the slight bulge there. "I can't imagine what you're talking about."

"Oh yes you can," he said in a low voice. "Imagination is your long suit. You love to torture me, don't you?"

"What's good for the gander is good for the goose. You were playing games with me as we walked in here, while you were pretending to fool with Kimberly."

"That was only—"

"Mr. MacDougal? Here's your cone. Oh, and the other ladies said you were paying for everyone."

"That's right." It seemed to take great effort for him to turn away from Tess and focus on the task of paying the bill.

Tess moved a little closer. "I'll see you over at the table," she said softly. "And thanks for the dipped cone."

He slipped his wallet back in his pocket. "If I'd known what you were going to do with it, I never would have agreed to buy you one," he muttered without turning around.

"Fair is fair." Feeling much better than she had when she'd been mired in thoughts of his eventual marriage, Tess walked over to join the others.

MAC PLAYED ABYSMAL poker the following night, and the Blakely brothers finally figured out that a woman must be distracting him. Although they teased him about being lovesick and pestered him for the name of his latest conquest, he managed to outmaneuver their questions. By the end of the evening no one was the wiser.

His latest conquest. He chuckled at the irony of that as he stuffed a blanket and two beach towels in his saddlebags Thursday night in preparation for his ride with Tess. Tess had conquered *him,* more like it. He was afraid to put a name to what he was feeling in relationship to Tess, but he craved her nearly every waking minute, and that wasn't a good sign. He'd thought tonight would never get here.

No other woman had ever made him come unglued so fast. Maybe it was all the reading she'd done, or maybe she was a natural when it came to exciting a man. In any event, her instincts would do justice to some Hollywood sex kitten, and yet she had no real experience with men other than him. Oh, how he loved knowing that. He loved it way too much, considering that the status quo would change. More men lived in New York City than in all of Arizona. She had a damn good chance of finding at least one who was to her liking.

He pushed that notion out of his head, not wanting to ruin the night. And it was one hell of a beautiful night. The moon sat just below the mountains, creating a glow that threw the familiar ridge into stark silhouette. Any minute now the moon would poke its head over, looking huge and golden as it crested. Mac hoped Tess would get here before that happened, so she could see it with him.

He'd always liked sharing stuff like that with her because she was so passionate about the beauty around her. He should have known that she'd transfer that passion to anything she did, especially making love. Passion and curiosity—it was quite a combination. He wondered if she'd remember to bring any of her books.

The sound of her car pulling in beside the barn made his pulse rate go up. She rounded the barn just as a sliver of the moon eased up over the ridge.

"Come over here and see the moon," he said.

She quickened her steps. "I hoped I'd get here in time." She reached his side and leaned her forearms against the top rail of the corral as she watched the sky. "Oh, wow."

He leaned casually against the rail next to her, his arm barely brushing her arm, as if to prove to himself he could be alone with her and not grab her, as if he were in no hurry to leave and go down to the river. As if he didn't want her with every fiber of his being.

When she'd hurried toward him, he'd figured out from the lovely jiggle under her T-shirt that she wasn't wearing a bra. If he had to make a guess, he'd say she'd skipped the panties under her shorts, too. She held a book and a small flashlight in one hand. All of that made a potent combination, and he was more than ready to forget about the moon.

But he'd promised her they would always be friends, and Tess was the sort of person who remembered promises like that. She'd expect that someday they'd be able to stand here and watch the moon rise as friends, the way they'd done many times before. He might as well start practicing now.

But the air was filled with her scent, and his heart raced as he thought of holding her soft body again. He hungered for the taste of her lips, although he wouldn't dare kiss her here. Either one of his parents could come out and catch them.

"How was poker?" she asked.

"I lost every hand."

"Mac!" She turned toward him. "That's not like you. In fact, you usually come out ahead of everyone else."

"Your brothers were extremely happy about it. They

wanted the name of the girl I was seeing, so they could thank her. They figured that was the only thing that would make me completely hopeless at cards."

"But it wasn't really me that was the problem, right? It was having to face my brothers after having sex with me."

"I guess so." Although he wasn't quite sure about that. He'd suffered some guilt pangs for the first half hour or so of the poker game, but after that, the guilt had seemed to wear off. From then on he'd lost because he was day-dreaming about Tess, but revealing that might give away more than he wanted to right now.

"So what did you tell them?"

"Nothing. I just let them speculate."

"Do you think they'll try to find out who you're see-ing?"

"Oh, they'll ask around, but I don't think anyone will think of you. As I've said before, no one would ever sus-pect what's going on between the two of us. We could prob-ably kiss in the middle of the park in front of the whole town, and they'd think it was brotherly and sisterly affec-tion going on."

"Do you feel like kissing me now?"

He stared at the moon. "Yeah, I do."

"More than kissing?"

His groin tightened. "Yep."

"I just wondered. You seem so cool and collected. Weren't you the one who told me not to get all prissy and pretend I didn't want you so much I couldn't see straight?"

He looked at her and saw a beautiful face silvered by moonlight, sparkling eyes that drew him like a moth to flame, moist lips that made him crazy to taste her again. "I want you so much I can't see straight."

"Then what are we doing standing here gaping at the moon?"

"Beats the hell out of me." He pushed away from the fence. "Let's go."

CHAPTER THIRTEEN

BEING ON A horse in his current condition wasn't the smartest move he'd ever made, Mac realized as they went down the trail, but riding to the river was the only option. Walking would take too long, so he had to make a compromise between speed and comfort.

The moon lit their path and gave him an arousing view of Tess moving along ahead of him, her hips swaying gently in rhythm with Peppermint Patty's brisk little walk. When the trail curved so he caught her in profile, he became more convinced that she didn't have a bra on under her shirt.

And then she took off the shirt.

He could hardly believe she was doing it and wondered if he was having another potent dream, complete with crickets chirping and an owl hooting in the distance.

A few moments later the shirt came sailing back toward him, and he was so dumbfounded he was barely able to snag it before it dropped to the ground. "Hey!"

"What?" She turned in the saddle, giving him a breathtaking view of her breast bathed in moonlight.

"What are you doing?"

Even from this distance, the mischief was obvious in her smile. "Getting you hot."

"I'm already hot!" Squirming in the saddle, to be more accurate. Panting, lusting, longing for relief from this agonizing need to be deep inside her.

"Then hotter."

"Damn, Tess." Her shirt was scented with her cologne, and something even more erotic, the fragrance of Tess, aroused and ready for love. He bunched it in one fist and held it to his nose. Oh, Lord. That scent...memories of lying between her thighs, of tasting her, whirled through his fevered brain. "Why does your shirt smell so...good?"

"A little trick I read in the book I brought along tonight."

"What trick?"

"Oh, you just find a way to convey your own...special perfume to your lover. They say it works better than any manufactured perfume from the store."

He watched her through a haze of desire. "They would be right. You're not wearing panties under your shorts, are you?"

"No."

"So you took this shirt and put it—"

"In a very special place. Then I sent it back to you. You know, the motion of this horse is...*very* nice."

Mac groaned. "Ease up on me, Tess. I'm a desperate man."

"The book says anticipation is everything."

"Bull. Anticipation is excruciating." He heard the gurgle of the river ahead. Almost there. Smelling the water, the horses picked up the pace, and he tortured himself with imagining the sweet jiggle of Tess's breasts in the moonlight. He reached down and pulled the blanket out of his saddlebag and tucked her shirt in its place. He had no intention of wasting time once they got to the river.

Tess headed Peppermint Patty down the embankment and was off her horse in no time. She left the mare groundtied, as she and Mac always did when they came down here at night. The horses weren't going far in the dark, and they provided a good warning system for snakes.

Mac's view of Tess was blocked by her horse as he dismounted holding the blanket. But when she stepped out from behind Peppermint Patty into a pool of moonlight, Mac lost his grip on the blanket. She was naked.

"Does this come close enough to your fantasy?" she murmured.

As he gazed at her standing in the silvery light like some nymph from a fairy tale, the water rippling and flashing behind her, his throat tightened with desire. "It goes beyond it," he said huskily. "I don't think I could dream something this beautiful, so I sure hope you're real."

"I'm real." She walked toward him across the sand and he noticed the small book in her hand. "And I want to make love with you, Mac."

Make love. His throat ached with emotion as he faced the truth—making love was exactly what he'd be doing, perhaps for the first time in his life. But for Tess, this might only be a stepping stone, an initiation into pleasures she would one day enjoy with another man. He had to protect his heart. "I see you have your reference book, there," he said, trying to keep his tone light.

"You said you wanted to see it."

"Oh, I do." But technique didn't seem to matter so much now. Still, she wanted an education, and he'd been chosen to help her learn. That in itself was an amazing gift he'd been given, and to expect more would be greedy. He leaned down, picked up the blanket and shook it out, settling it on the sand. She stretched out on it while he started taking off his clothes with shaking hands.

The process took longer than he wanted because he couldn't stop looking at her lying there like some sort of nature goddess. He never would have guessed that their old meeting spot by the river could turn into such a seductive place. More than seductive. Tess made his heart ache with her beauty.

Sunday night she'd totally captivated him with her white satin and rose-colored bedroom, but there was something even wilder about this scene. Not far away a pack of coyotes howled and yipped, hunting, perhaps even mating by the light of the full moon. The sound stirred basic instincts deep within him. He'd do well to ignore them. They could only get him into more trouble.

"Coyotes," Tess said.

"Yeah." He took off the last of his clothes and reached in the pocket of his jeans.

"They sound so…primitive."

He caught the note of urgency in her voice, as if her reaction was the same as his. Heart pounding, he knelt beside her on the blanket. They were only playing at this, he told himself. He would be crazy to get serious. "So, professor, what do you want to try?"

She opened the book and leaned away so that moonlight fell across the page. "This."

The coyotes howled again as he gazed down at a black-and-white artist's drawing of a couple mating in the way that wild creatures mated. He sucked in a breath, knowing that was what had filled his mind as he'd listened to the coyotes' song, yet never imagining she would want such a thing, too. But oh, to love her like that, with the night sounds around them and the river rushing by…he ached with the wanting of it.

He glanced at her and a tremor passed through him. This primitive mating would have great significance for him, which made it dangerous, but for her it might simply be a unique experience. "You're…sure?"

Slowly she closed the book. Then she sensuously rolled to her stomach. Before he realized it, she'd risen to her hands and knees, offering her round bottom in the age-old invitation of a female to her chosen male.

His body could not refuse. Hot blood thrummed through his veins as uncivilized needs took hold of him. Grasping her hips, he moved into position behind her. A guttural, untamed sound rose from his throat and he fought the urge to drive deep and claim her in the way of the wilderness. Instead, he probed gently, not wanting to frighten her.

Desire surged in him when he found her moist and ready. Still he held back, slipping his hand around her waist and down, massaging the tight nub that heightened her response. With a little cry that was almost a plea, she tilted her hips, and he could restrain himself no more. He slid smoothly into her waiting channel.

And for the second time in his life he felt an incredible sense of connection, even stronger than the first time. And with that arose an urge he'd never known—the compulsion to pour himself into this woman and watch her grow round with child, his child. His body chafed against the barrier he'd placed between seed and womb and called for him to complete the connection and fill her with his essence.

And he could not. With a groan of pleasure mixed with deep frustration, he drew back and pushed forward with more force, lightly slapping her with his thighs. She murmured encouragement, and he increased the pace, pummeling her gently yet firmly as the sandy clearing filled with the sounds and scents of mating. They became slick with sweat in the heat of the night air as the slap of flesh against flesh grew faster and more defined. Their gasps and soft cries melded with the call of night creatures, the wind in the trees and the ripple of water over stones.

She tightened around him a moment before she was rocked with convulsions. Her undulations drew him into more frenzied movements as instinct told him now was the time, the time to plant his seed. He erupted in a forceful climax, crying out her name and holding her close to receive him. And the mating dance that had shaken him to his soul came to a powerful…and fruitless…end.

TESS LAY ON the blanket, curled with her back nestled against the protective curve of Mac's body, and wondered how she'd created such a terrible problem. She'd fallen madly, passionately, desperately in love with her best friend. What had started out as fun and games, a fine adventure together before she headed off to her new life, had become more important than anything else in her world.

She didn't believe a woman should sacrifice a bright future in order to be with a man. Yet that's exactly what she wanted to do. She knew that Mac wouldn't leave Copperville as long as his parents needed him on the ranch, so any woman who wanted to be with Mac would have to stay in Copperville, too. And she wanted to be with Mac, to make love with him, to laugh and play with him and make babies with him.

Especially make babies. She wanted to be his mate, to make love again the way they had a little while ago, only without protection. She'd leaped from being a virgin only days ago to wanting it all—marriage, motherhood, years of lovemaking with this man.

It wasn't the way she'd pictured herself. From as long as she could remember, she'd been determined to escape the confines of this small town, to be sophisticated and worldly. She'd vowed to live in a big city, travel to exotic places, have many lovers.

Then, when she'd tired of all that, she'd settle down, probably right here in Copperville, and raise a family.

Now all her worldly plans seemed hollow and lonely. What good was any of it, if she couldn't have Mac there to share it with her? She'd rather stay here and be a ranch wife than lose Mac.

Not that Mac was asking. He'd never given any indication that he thought of her in those terms. He didn't act as if he wanted to settle down and marry anyone, as a matter of fact, let alone her. He'd never even been engaged.

He stroked her hip. "Whatcha thinking about, twinkle toes?"

She decided on a partial answer. "Oh, just that it's too bad I'll be heading for New York the end of August."

He kneaded her thigh. "Because this is so much fun, you mean?"

"Yes." More than fun. She'd become involved, heart and soul, but she dared not tell him.

"It's fun, but in a way it's a good thing we have a limit on the time we can be together. We'd never be able to keep it a secret if it went beyond August."

"True." Perhaps he was happy with the secret arrangement, considering that he wanted to keep his status with her brothers intact. The only way her brothers would tolerate a sexual relationship between Mac and Tess was if they were getting married. Immediately. Mac didn't want marriage at the moment, apparently, so the secret had to be kept.

"Ready for a little skinny-dipping?"

She turned toward him. "We're really going to?"

He gave her a quick kiss. "Sure. We're all hot and sticky. It'll feel good. And besides, it's part of your education."

"Mac, I don't think we can have sex in the middle of that river."

"Why not?" His grin flashed in the moonlight. "Because it isn't in your book?"

"Because you won't have a pocket to stash your condom in."

"Tsk, tsk. You take away a girl's virginity, and suddenly she thinks sex is only about intercourse." He got to his feet and pulled her up with him. "Come on. Let's see what happens when you stand thigh-deep in rushing water without a bathing suit on." He took her hand and led her toward the riverbank.

Excitement swelled within her. That was another thing

she loved about Mac. He had a heck of an imagination. Still, she wondered if he'd thought of that sort of stimulation on his own. "Have you been reading my books?"

"Nah. But I went down to the drugstore and bought one of those magazines they keep behind the counter. The article was about hot-tub jets, which we don't have, so we'll have to improvise."

And improvise he did, although there was much laughing and splashing and playful groping before he finally had her positioned the way he wanted her. He'd so awakened her sensuality that he easily convinced her to accept the river as a teasing lover. Holding her steady, adding his own caress to that of the water, he coaxed her to let the current stroke her intimately, bringing her to a crescendo of feeling. At the moment of release she couldn't tell whether the bubbling water or Mac's caress had sent her over the edge.

While she was still gasping in reaction, he swept her into his arms and carried her back to the blanket. He made love to her while they were both still wet and slick as otters, so their bodies slid together as if they were oiled. She'd never known such triumphant freedom. She felt lithe and supple, capable of anything. They twisted and turned on the blanket, exploring different positions, alternate ways their bodies could move and shift yet still give unbelievable pleasure.

She was sure Mac was enjoying himself. His murmured words told her so, and when his tone roughened, she knew he was in the grip of fierce passion. When at last he surrendered to that passion, she held him tight and absorbed the strong tremors that shook him. She couldn't imagine living without this, without him. Perhaps, if she loved him well enough and thoroughly enough this summer, he'd realize he couldn't live without her, either.

THE SUMMER PASSED far too quickly for Tess. For every creative lovemaking scheme she dreamed up, Mac came up with one to match it. She suggested a day trip to Phoenix. They checked into the honeymoon suite of a hotel where no one would know them and spent the day in bed. He flew them up to Flagstaff where they hiked to a mountain meadow and made love in a field of daisies under a bright summer sky.

They experimented with velvet ropes, furry mittens and feather dusters. While they were in Phoenix they stopped into an X-rated boutique and dared each other to buy something. They came out of the shop with body paint and flavored massage oils.

The charged hours Tess spent with Mac seemed painted in brilliant color, while the rest of her life seemed to be cast in shades of gray. She went through the motions of a normal summer, playing cards with her sisters-in-law every Wednesday night, babysitting for her nieces and nephews, having lunch with her mother, planning the surprise anniversary party for her parents. But none of it seemed quite real, because she couldn't tell those she cared about that a most significant and wonderful thing had happened to her—she was completely in love with Mac MacDougal.

And she wanted to tell the world. She especially longed to confide in her mother, who would be a great source of advice. When her sisters-in-law discussed their husbands, whether in frustration or delight, Tess wanted to be a part of that conversation, to join the ranks of women openly, proudly in love.

Mac seemed just as involved with her as she was with him, although not a word of commitment ever came from his mouth. During the hot weeks of summer, they shared everything, it seemed, except a future. It was as if she were about to be shipped off to war and might never come back, so the subject of a happy ever after could never be broached.

Aside from that, she thought they were no different from any other couple just discovering passion and love, except that their relationship was known only to themselves. At first she'd thought secrecy was essential to her summer project. Sharing the secret with Mac had felt delicious and naughty. Now she was sick of it. But she couldn't tell. Not ever, unless Mac agreed, and she couldn't imagine him agreeing. And that made her soul ache.

By THE FIRST WEEK in August, Mac had come to the painful conclusion that he should break up with Tess. He should have ended their affair long before this, in fact. He was obviously good enough for her in bed, but not good enough to consider altering her career plans for, not good enough to let the world know about their love affair. He'd watched for any wavering on her decision to move to New York, and there was none.

As he headed to her house for another night of lovemaking, the truck splashing through puddles left by a heavy afternoon rain, he cursed himself for being weak. If he couldn't treat sex with her as a casual roll in the hay, fun while it lasted but forgotten when it was over, then he should get out now and start putting himself back together.

In fact, that's what he'd do, by God. Tonight. He wouldn't make love to her. He ignored the sick feeling of disappointment in his gut at that thought and vowed to carry through with what was right, what would ultimately save his sanity.

He'd walk into her house and tell her this activity was eating into his time, causing him to get behind on some paperwork for the ranch. That much was true. He'd taken over the books for his parents a couple of years ago, and at the moment he was making a sorry job of it.

He arrived at the town's traffic light as it turned red, and although his was the only vehicle at the intersection, he stopped anyway. As he sat waiting for the green, a horn beeped behind him.

Glancing in the rearview mirror, he spotted Rhino Blakely's truck with Rhino driving and Hammer in the passenger seat. Mac raised a hand in greeting and fought down the guilt that swept over him every time he unexpectedly met members of Tess's family. Tonight he didn't have to feel guilty, though. He was going over to Tess's house, but he wouldn't be there long. It was over.

Rhino hopped out of the truck and ran forward to knock on Mac's window.

Mac rolled it down. "What's up?"

"Joan and Deena went to a movie, and me and Hammer feel like a darts tournament at the Ore Cart tonight. What do you say?"

Mac hesitated only a split second. If he had somewhere to go, that would force him to make the break with Tess. "Sure. I have to swing by Tess's house for a few minutes, but I can be there in a half hour or so."

"Great. Light's green." Rhino ran back to his truck.

Mac rolled up the window and crossed the intersection. Fate must have stepped in to make him take this necessary step, he thought. Here he'd been thinking of what he needed to do, and along came some help in the form of Rhino and Hammer. If he ended it with Tess tonight, the brothers would never find out about the wild activities going on under their noses.

Even Tess probably needed some time to regroup before she went to New York. She might not realize it, but she'd probably have a tough time giving up what they'd shared this summer.

The rest of the way to Tess's house, Mac ran through all the reasons to end the affair. They were all good reasons, yet he felt as if someone had dropped a load of copper ore on his chest as he walked up the steps to her porch and opened the door. Walking away from another night of wonderful lovemaking and knowing he wouldn't make love to Tess ever again might be the hardest job he'd ever given himself. He'd have to be strong.

CHAPTER FOURTEEN

EXOTIC MUSIC WITH a pulsing beat drifted from Tess's bedroom, and automatically Mac became aroused just wondering what she had in store for him. Whatever it was, he'd resist.

Not that resisting would be easy. With each rendezvous they planned, he always wondered what she'd come up with that would surprise the hell out of him. And totally turn him on. He and Tess had tried stunts that had never crossed his mind with any other woman.

Yet now that he thought about it, sexual adventure suited Tess perfectly. She'd tempted him with bold ideas when they were kids, too. The raft they'd built and almost drowned trying to ride, the wild-horse roundup, the cave-exploration trip—Tess had thought of every one of those.

God, it wouldn't be easy walking back out of here tonight and giving up the excitement of loving Tess, the pure fun of just being with her. But that was short-term thinking. For the long term he needed to start learning to do without Tess's soft mouth, her warm, moist body, her... He stood in the doorway and felt his resolve slip away.

Tess was dancing. And not just ordinary dancing, either. She wore filmy pants that hugged her hips, a jeweled bra dripping with gold coins, a gold armband and a veil across her nose and mouth. She was a vision straight out of a sheik's harem, complete with tiny cymbals attached to her fingers. She kept time with them as she rotated her hips in the most mesmerizing rhythm he'd ever seen.

"Surprise." Her grin was faintly visible behind the veil. "I've been practicing for weeks." She continued to dance as she motioned him to a straight-backed chair in the corner of the room. She'd obviously placed it there for her audience of one. "And now I'm going to dance for you and drive you insane. Enjoy."

The light veil had the most incredible effect, emphasizing the sultry look in her eyes and making him hungry for her mouth simply because he couldn't see it very well. By covering her lips, she made them seem more exciting and forbidden, more of a prize when they were finally claimed.

Not that he would be claiming them. He had something to say, and that would eliminate the chance of kissing those temptingly disguised lips of hers.

But he couldn't make his announcement immediately. After all, she'd been practicing this dance for weeks to surprise him. He ought to at least let her show him what she could do. Courtesy demanded it.

Besides, he couldn't seem to take his eyes off the circular motion of her hips. He wondered what that would feel like if…no. He wasn't going to make love to her tonight, so it didn't matter what that would feel like. Fantastic, probably. But he was ending it. Definitely. Once she'd finished her dance.

He slouched in the chair and tried to look slightly bored as she danced slowly around him. When the beat became faster, so did the motion of her hips. He swallowed. Then she began adding a new dimension, a gentle shimmy of her breasts that made the dangling coins dance. He licked his dry lips.

She drew closer, brushing his arm with her hip as she danced. Her shimmy increased in speed, and she leaned forward, shaking her breasts so close to his face he could see the tiny drops of perspiration in her cleavage. The pearl necklace rested there, as it had all summer. And looking at it never failed to get a response from him.

"Unfasten your jeans," she whispered.

He glanced quickly into her eyes. This wasn't going at all the way he'd thought it out. "No, Tess, I—"

"Do it," she whispered more urgently, dancing around him, her hips keeping that maddening, erotic rhythm. "I want you now, Mac. And I can tell you want me."

"But—"

"Now." Still dancing, she took off the finger cymbals and reached beneath the snug band around her hips for a small package she'd obviously hidden there earlier. She swayed closer, her arms undulating with the music, and tucked a condom in his shirt pocket.

He was lost. If he didn't go along with her plan, she would be very disappointed. She had this scene all worked out and had gone to a lot of trouble to make it happen. Besides, he was so aroused he was in pain. He couldn't walk out of this room now if his life depended on it. He worked clumsily at the buttons of his fly, his heart pounding as he focused on the fascinating shimmy of her breasts and the amazing rotation of her hips.

He took the condom out of his shirt pocket. Then he nearly dropped it when she reached between her legs and somehow made the crotch of the filmy harem pants come undone without missing a beat.

"Are you impressed?" she asked softly.

"Oooh, yeah." And shaking with need. He managed to get the condom on as she danced closer, the coins jingling from the quivering rhythm of her breasts.

"Hold perfectly still," she whispered. "I'm going to do it all."

Incredible as her body looked as it moved, he was completely captured by her eyes. Emphasized by the veil, her eyes seemed to smolder with more fire than ever before. He couldn't look away.

Still keeping time to the music with her hips, she braced both hands on his shoulders and straddled the chair. Then she slowly lowered herself in a sensuous, rotating movement that made him gasp with pleasure. Yet he wouldn't, couldn't close his eyes. As she used all the sensuous dance movements to make unbelievable love to him, he focused on the blazing heat in her eyes, searching for the depth of emotion that rocked him whenever they came together like this.

And he found it. As her rhythm increased, her eyes told him that yes, she felt what he felt, that her heart had been branded as surely as his.

"I love you," he said. For the first time in his life the words meant something special, something so real he could almost touch it.

Her eyes were pure flame. "I love you," she murmured.

Joy surged so intensely through him that at last he closed his eyes, afraid she'd see his tears of relief. She loved him. Everything would be okay. As her movements grew more uninhibited and her cry of release filled the room, he held her tight and abandoned himself to a soul-satisfying climax.

They stayed locked together for many long minutes, Tess's veiled cheek resting on Mac's shoulder. He gently stroked her back, unsure what to say next. He really wanted the first words to come from her—something along the lines of *I've decided not to go to New York. I love you and I want to stay here with you.*

They'd honeymoon in New York, he decided. They'd take lots of trips, in fact, to make up for the loss of her big adventure. They'd—"Yo, Big Mac! Where are you, buddy?" The unmistakable sound of Rhino's voice came from the direction of the living room.

Tess scrambled from Mac's lap and ran to the bedroom door. She slammed it and plastered herself across the door frame, her eyes wide.

"Oh, God." Mac stared at her. He'd completely forgotten he'd promised to meet Rhino and Hammer at the Ore Cart, and that he'd told them where he was headed in the meantime.

"Hey, Mac!" Rhino called again, this time obviously from the hallway. "What's going on?"

Mac swung into action, jumping from the chair. "We'll... I'll be out in a minute!" he called. "Lock that," he muttered to Tess.

"Why can't you come out now?" Rhino sounded suspicious.

"Just give me a minute, okay?" When he heard the lock click Mac headed for Tess's bathroom.

"What's going on in there, Mac?" Rhino's tone had changed from suspicious to angry. "Is Tess with you?"

"Yes, I'm with him, Rhino. Go on out to the living room. We'll be there soon."

Mac finished quickly in the bathroom. "God, I'm sorry, Tess," he said as he returned, buttoning his fly on the way.

"It's not your fault." She'd taken off her jeweled bra. Topless, she pulled a plain one out of a drawer.

"Yes, it is my fault. I met them when I was driving over here. I told them I was on my way to your house but I'd meet them in a half hour for darts."

She turned in the act of fastening the front clasp of her bra. "Why would you—" She paused. "You weren't planning to stay, were you?"

"No."

Her face grew pale. "You were going to end it, weren't you?"

"Well, yes, I was, but I—"

"Never mind the long explanation." Her voice quivered

and she turned away from him. "Just get out there and talk to them while I get dressed."

"Tess, dammit, I—"

"Go! I mean it, Mac!"

A knot formed in the pit of his stomach. "What do you want me to tell them?"

"You might want to start with the truth." She cleared her throat. "There's no way we can make up a story they'll buy at this stage. We got caught, Mac. There isn't any way we can pretty it up so they'll like it."

"The hell there isn't. We could tell them we're in love with each other."

She pulled a T-shirt over her head. "Thanks for the thought, but I'd rather you didn't."

Raw as he felt right now, he didn't have the courage to question her. Maybe she didn't want anyone to know she'd fallen in love with the guy who was merely doing her a service before she left for New York. And the way she was acting right now, he was pretty sure she would go. Maybe she loved him, as she'd said. But she'd leave him anyway.

Without another word, he unlocked the bedroom door and walked down the hall to face his inquisitors.

HE'D BEEN ABOUT to break up with her. Tess fought tears and struggled to get dressed. Oh, he might love her, as he'd said in the heat of passion. He'd probably told several women he loved them over the years, especially when they pleased him sexually. He still hadn't felt the urge to marry one of them. She was just another of his conquests, fun for the summer but not the one he wanted to spend a lifetime with.

There was only one thing Mac could say that would placate her brothers, and that would be to announce their engagement. And he wasn't going to do that.

Angry voices from the direction of the living room told

her things weren't going well. Stuffing the harem outfit in a drawer, she ran a brush through her hair and padded barefoot down the hall.

Rhino sounded furious. "So you stand there and admit that you took advantage of our sister's innocent nature?"

Hardly, Tess thought, wondering what sort of story Mac was spinning out there.

"That's exactly what I'm saying." Mac's tone was lower and more controlled. "And if I hadn't, some city slicker in New York would have. She couldn't stay innocent forever, dammit. I convinced her she needed to be prepared before she went off to the big city."

"You *convinced* her?" Hammer bellowed. "You *seduced* her, you mean! That poor girl didn't have a chance!"

Tess hurried into the room. "I did so have a chance. I—"

"Tess." Mac turned to her. "You can't assume the responsibility for this. I took advantage of your lack of experience. Simple as that."

"You most certainly did *not*." She realized he was trying to protect her, but she couldn't let him do that. If he had any chance of saving the relationship with her brothers, the truth had to come out. She glanced at her brothers. "I don't know what he told you, but this whole summer project was my idea. I decided back in June that I wanted to lose my virginity before I left for New York."

Rhino and Hammer stared at her, their jaws slack. Rhino was the first to speak. "Summer p-project?"

Mac snorted. "Don't listen to her. You know Tess. She could always make up wild stories on the spur of the moment, and most of the time it was to save my sorry ass. She's doing it again."

"I am not! I came up with my plan and asked Mac if he could fix me up with someone. He offered to take care of it himself."

"Oh, I'll just bet he did!" Rhino advanced on Mac. "And

how did she get this idea in the first place, huh? She's never been worried about stuff like that before, so who was putting ideas in her head, buddy-boy?"

Tess stepped between them. "I've been thinking about stuff like that since I was fourteen years old, Rhino! It wasn't Mac's idea, it was mine."

"He probably made you think it was your idea," Hammer said, joining his brother as they faced Mac, fists clenched. "We've always known this is one slick character when it comes to women. We just never thought he'd go behind our backs and prey on our little sister, right, Rhino?"

"That's right. Guess we have to take you outside and work you over, Mac."

"You will not!" Tess pushed a hand into each one of her brothers' substantial chests.

"I can take care of myself, Tess." Mac rolled his shoulders. "You don't have to protect me from your brothers."

"She can't stop us, anyway," Rhino said. He gently nudged Tess aside.

"Yes, I can!" Tess pushed her way between the men again. "If you touch one hair on his head, I'll tell Mom and Dad about the time you guys drove over the border, got drunk on tequila and spent the night in a Nogales jail."

"I don't care," Hammer said. "No biggie."

"And what about the time I found the marijuana in your bedroom, Hammer?" she added sweetly.

"You had pot in your room?" Mac asked. "You never told me that. God, your dad would have had a fit."

A flush spread over Hammer's face. "I only smoked a little of the damn stuff, and it made me puke!"

"So that's what I'll tell the folks," Tess said. "I'm sure they'll understand. Although they might wonder what happened to the rest of the joints, since I found about six."

Hammer's flush deepened. "I sold them at school."

Rhino turned to him, his eyes wide. "You *peddled* those things? You told me you flushed them!"

"Who flushed what?" called out Tim as he came through the front door. "And what's up with the darts tournament? Suzie said you called, so I went and picked up Dozer, but when we got to the Ore Cart they said you'd come down here."

"Yeah," Dozer said, walking in behind Tim. "Are we gonna play or not?"

Rhino crossed his arms over his chest. "It seems somebody's already been playing." He glared at Mac. "Our friend here, the one we all thought we could trust, has been playing house with our sister all summer."

"What?" Dozer looked from Tess to Mac. "Tess, is this true? Did this guy…?"

"It was a mutual decision," Tess said, "so don't go—"

"That's it." Dozer started across the room. "He's toast."

"Hold it, Dozer." Rhino grabbed his brother by the arm. "It's not that simple."

"It *is* simple," Tess said. "I'm the one to blame here, not Mac. I asked him to do this!"

"And he couldn't pronounce the word *no?*" Hammer said.

"I didn't want him to say no! I wanted to finally experience sex!"

Tim's face grew red. "Aw, Tess! What did you have to go and do that for? There's plenty of time for that after you're married!"

"Oh, really?" Tess lifted her chin and surveyed her four brothers. "And I suppose all you guys waited until after you were married?"

There was a general clearing of throats and glancing everywhere but at Tess.

"That's different," Rhino said. "We're guys."

Tess stared at them. "Hello? Can any of you say *wom-*

en's rights?" She threw up both arms and paced across the room. "I can't believe we're almost to the millennium and you're still making such outdated statements. In case you hadn't noticed, women aren't considered helpless little flowers anymore."

"Hey, we know all about that stuff," Hammer said. "We got women in the mines now. Women driving the big ore trucks. Women everywhere. But, dammit, Tess, you're our *sister*."

"Yeah, and guys can be real sleazy!" Tim added. "We didn't want you getting hurt or anything! A lot of guys only want to fool around. They're not into the marriage thing."

"Which reminds me of a very critical point." Rhino narrowed his eyes at Mac. "Just what are your plans, now that you've had a real fun summer fooling around with a sweet and innocent young girl?"

"I'm twenty-six, Rhino!"

"That's very young!" Rhino shouted back.

"Not *that* young," Tim said. "I'm twenty-seven."

"We're off the subject," Rhino said. He fixed Mac with an intimidating look. "What are your intentions, Mac?"

Tess panicked. She didn't want to listen to Mac fumble around and try to dodge the question. Suspecting he had no interest in her as a wife was not as bad as hearing him say it. "No plans, folks! *Nada.* Have you forgotten that I'm going to New York in a couple of weeks to start a new job? I'm in no position to make a commitment at this point. In fact, Mac and I had that understanding from the beginning, didn't we, Mac?" If she expected him to look at her with relief and gratitude, she was disappointed.

The blue eyes that had been filled with such passion not so long ago gazed at her without any expression at all. "Yes, we did."

"That probably suited lover-boy right down to the ground," Hammer muttered. He glanced at Tess. "And I still say you're covering for him and he came up with the idea first. He probably figured this deal was too sweet to pass up—a girl who was leaving town at the end of the summer. Perfect, right, Big Mac?"

Mac's nonchalant shrug broke Tess's heart. That's probably how Mac had thought of their lovemaking. A summer romance. Fun while it lasted. "Well, that was the beauty of it for me, too," she said, forcing the words past a tight throat. "I couldn't afford messy entanglements when I was about to leave."

Rhino looked at her, his gaze far too perceptive. "I don't buy it, Tess."

She squared her shoulders. "Well, I don't give a damn whether you buy it or not. It's the truth."

"Let me get this straight," Dozer said. "On the one hand we have a guy who's been romeoing his way around the county ever since he was fifteen, and on the other we have a girl who's lived like a nun until the age of twenty-six. What—"

"I didn't live like a nun by choice! You guys scared off all my prospects!"

"They were all terrible prospects!" Rhino said.

"And I'm trying to make a point, here," Dozer continued. "Tess says this is all her fault, but I wonder how that could be, considering she had zero experience and the stud-man over here has more experience than anybody in this room. I mean, who do you suppose was in control of that situation?"

"I was!" Tess said.

"Not likely." Dozer started toward Mac again. "And I'm itching to land a few punches."

"Sounds like a plan," Hammer said.

"Might as well get it over with," Rhino added.

Tess grew desperate. She couldn't have her brothers beat up the man she loved. She lowered her voice to deliver her ultimatum. It had always worked for her mother, so maybe it would work for her. "If you do this, I'm through with all of you," she said.

They turned to her with expressions of disbelief.

"I mean it. No brother of mine would gang up on an innocent man. And Mac is innocent."

"Hah!" Dozer said.

Rhino stroked his chin and gazed at her. "Does he mean that much to you, Tess?"

Trapped. There was no answer except the truth. Tears of frustration pushed at the back of her eyes. "Yes, dammit, he does."

Rhino nodded. "Then maybe you ought to stay home and marry him instead of traipsing off to New York."

But he doesn't want that, she longed to say. Instead, she swallowed the lump of emotion in her throat and lied. "Just because you care about someone and don't want them hurt doesn't mean you're ready to give up your dream for them. My dream is to experience some other place besides Copperville, and I finally have the chance to do that." She blinked to hold back the tears.

Rhino studied her for a while longer. "Well, I guess that settles it. We can't very well beat up on Mac and make our sister cry, now, can we?"

"I wouldn't cry." She sniffed. "I just would never speak to you again."

Tim frowned and came over to put a hand on her shoulder. "You look like you might cry."

She sniffed again and glared up at him through swimming eyes. "Well, I won't."

"We've got another thing to think about," Hammer said. "Is this information going to leave this room?"

"No." Rhino fixed each of his brothers with a stern look. "Nobody tells. Not even your wives. Got that?"

Everyone nodded.

Tess gazed at them all with a heavy heart. She wanted this little scene over with. "Don't you all have a darts tournament to play?"

There was a moment of silence. Finally Rhino broke it. "Guess we do. Come on, Mac."

"Thanks," Mac said, "but I think I'll take a pass."

"Like hell you will." Hammer grabbed one of Mac's arms.

"Yeah." Dozer grabbed the other one. "You don't think we'd leave you here, do you?"

"I'll make it even plainer," Rhino said. "Unless Tess changes her mind and decides to marry you, I don't want you around this house again. You may have gotten away with it all summer, but the party's over, buddy. The Blakely brothers are back on duty. Now let's go play some darts."

Tess watched with great misgiving as they escorted Mac out of the house. "You do understand I meant what I said," she called after them as Dozer demanded Mac's keys so he could drive Mac's truck. "If you hurt him, I'll find out, and there will be hell to pay."

"We won't hurt him, Tess," Rhino promised as he climbed into his truck. "We just won't let him within ten feet of you ever again."

CHAPTER FIFTEEN

MAC WISHED THE Blakely brothers *had* started swinging at him once they were out of Tess's sight. A nice little brawl would have been an improvement over what was happening at the Ore Cart. As he sat at the bar and nursed a beer, he wondered if they were trying to get him to throw the first punch. He wasn't about to do it.

He felt numb, which was another reason he'd love to get in a fight just so he could at least feel something and know he was still alive. But he wouldn't be the one to start it. Like someone in shock staring down at a gaping wound, he should be feeling tremendous pain knowing that he'd never hold Tess in his arms again. He had no doubt he would feel that pain eventually. But the reality of losing his best friend and the love of his life hadn't hit him yet.

"Hey, Benedict Arnold, you're up." Hammer pulled the darts he'd just thrown from the board and handed them to Mac, points out.

Mac took them, gazing stoically at Hammer as one of the points seemed to accidentally dig into his palm. "Thanks."

"Whoops, did I stick you with that dart? Jeez, I'm sorry, man. Oversight on my part."

"No problem."

"Check where he's putting his feet," Dozer said. "A guy like him could edge over the line to get an advantage."

"I'm watching him," Rhino said. "All the time."

Mac clenched his jaw and threw the darts. He sensed

that the brothers were testing him, trying to get him to crack. If he challenged them, either by starting a fight or leaving the bar, that would be the end of the relationship. If he stayed and took everything they had to dish out, the day of forgiveness might eventually come.

Unfortunately he was starting to win the damn darts tournament. Throwing darts felt exceedingly good right now. He'd give anything to be out on the field throwing a football right now. He could probably heave it seventy yards with no problem. He deliberately made a bad toss of the dart.

"Hey, lover-boy!" Dozer called out. "Having a little trouble with your concentration?"

"No doubt," Rhino said. "The boy has a lot of things on his mind. No wonder he hasn't been winning at poker this summer."

"I still can't believe it," Tim said. He of all the brothers seemed more hurt than angry. "I can't believe you'd sit there every Wednesday night like always."

"Sort of makes you lose your faith in your fellow man, doesn't it, Tim?" Hammer said.

Mac threw his last dart dead in the middle of the bull's-eye and turned to face the brothers. He gazed at them and pain started sneaking into his heart, like the pinpricks after an arm or leg has fallen asleep. Nothing would ever be the same. Nothing. "I'm sorry," he said softly.

They returned his gaze silently.

Finally Tim spoke. "Would you marry her if she wasn't going to New York, Mac?"

He saw nothing wrong with telling them the truth. "Yes."

Rhino made an impatient noise deep in his throat. "Then why the hell don't you get her to stay?"

"I don't think I could," Mac said.

"You could," Rhino said. "She might pretend she's one

of those women who takes her fun where she finds it, but she's not. We always figured she'd fall hard for the first guy she got involved with because she's not the type to take sex lightly, no matter what she says. That's the main reason we've been protecting her all along. She could have wrecked her life with the wrong guy."

"Maybe I'm the wrong guy."

Hammer drained his glass of beer and set it down on the bar with a loud click. "Maybe. I can't say I'd relish having a lying son of a bitch for a brother-in-law."

"He didn't exactly lie," Tim said.

"No, it's more like he betrayed our trust," Rhino said. "Now, that's not good, but I'm telling you, Tess has probably lost her heart, just like we thought she would when she became involved with someone. I think you need to convince her to stay here and marry you, Mac. It's the only answer."

Mac considered the idea, and for a brief moment hope gleamed in his heart. He knew Tess loved him. If only she'd given him some indication that she didn't really want to go to New York…but she hadn't.

He took a deep breath. "You're right, I might be able to convince her to stay. But I can't do it. All her life she's talked about leaving small-town life behind and experiencing the excitement of a big city. She could easily start blaming me for taking that away from her." He should know. Despite how much he loved his parents, he couldn't completely eliminate the resentment that cropped up whenever he thought of how they'd tied him to the ranch.

"Hell. You have a point." Rhino gazed at the floor. "I hate this. I purely hate it. If you were some other guy, we could all have a great time taking you apart."

Mac laid the darts on the bar. "Have at it."

"We can't beat you up, Mac," Tim said. "Not after the

way you said you were sorry, and that you'd marry Tess if you thought it would work out."

"Maybe it would work out," Dozer said. "Maybe she'd forget about this big-city thing after a while. Like the sofa Cindy wanted. She thought she'd die if she didn't get it, but we couldn't afford the darn thing. Then after she got pregnant she forgot about the sofa."

Mac's smile was sad. "I wish you were right, Dozer. But I've listened to Tess go on about this for years. You guys got so much recognition with your football that she felt overshadowed most of the time."

"Yeah, but she was in those plays," Tim said.

"I know, but Copperville folks don't get as excited about plays as they do about football games. You know she once considered trying to make it on Broadway."

Rhino groaned. "We were all having a heart attack over that plan, too."

"That Broadway idea was because of us?" Dozer asked.

"In a way. It would have made a splash. At any rate, thinking about a career on Broadway got her hooked on the idea of New York, but she finally realized she didn't want to act for a living, so she decided to get a job in New York as the next best thing. Because no one else in the family has done anything remotely like that, it'll be her badge of honor. I think she needs to go."

"I can't believe she's been jealous of us, when she was so smart, pulling down A's all the time," Hammer said.

"Pulling down A's doesn't rate a picture in the paper. Don't get me wrong. She's proud as heck of all of you, but she wants her own claim to fame. This is it."

Rhino stroked his chin. "You seem to know her pretty well."

Hammer coughed. "A little too damn well, if you want my opinion. Why didn't you just tell her you wouldn't do it, Mac?"

"I should have. God, I know I should have. But she seemed so determined to make this happen. She was considering Donny Beauford."

A strangled noise came from Rhino, and Dozer choked on his beer.

"God bless America," Hammer said. "Beauford?"

"I'd ten times rather have Mac than Beauford," Tim said. "Make that a hundred times."

A silence fell over the brothers as each of them seemed to be contemplating the horrors of Donny Beauford with their sister.

"I guess it had to be somebody, sooner or later," Tim said at last.

"We knew that," Rhino said. "But we wanted to make sure it was the right guy."

"I've been wondering about something," Mac said. "How were you planning to supervise Tess's dating life once she moved to New York?"

Rhino grinned. "We had a special picture made of all four of us and we planned to give it to her as a going-away present."

"And we had the photographer squat and point the camera up, so we all look *huge*," Tim added.

"We're going to tell her to keep it right by her bedside to remind her of her family," Dozer said. "Any guy who sees that might think twice, especially if we pay a few surprise visits to New York now and then."

Mac shook his head. "Amazing."

"We might not have to worry so much now," Rhino said. "If we want to look on the bright side of this disaster, Mac might have done us a favor."

Hammer glared at Mac. "I can't buy that."

"Think about it," Rhino said. "You know how she is once she settles on someone or something. Like a little bulldog. If she's carrying a torch for Mac, she won't be interested in any of those city slickers."

Mac thought that was one of the best things he'd heard all night. Unfortunately it didn't change the fact that Tess would be leaving and he would be staying. His life was about to become very empty, more empty than he could imagine. So if he wanted to keep his sanity, he wouldn't even try to imagine life without Tess.

TESS KNEW THAT her last two weeks in Copperville would be rough, but she hadn't understood the half of it. She ached from wanting Mac, but she'd expected that. The need for him was always there, a subterranean current that sometimes bubbled to the surface and threatened to drown her. But the moments she hadn't expected were worse—moments when her first impulse was to share some little detail of her life with Mac, until she realized she could no longer do that.

There was the time she rescued Sarah's kitten from a tree, and the hysterical sight of Mrs. Nedbetter riding around on her new mower, even though she had a postage-stamp lawn. Tess would hear a good joke or read an article about a new technique for breeding horses, and pick up the phone. And then the truth would hit her. No matter what he'd promised about always being friends, their friendship was dead.

The most exquisite torture of all lay ahead of her. Her parents' anniversary party was no longer a surprise—surprises seldom worked out in Copperville. Once the secret was out, her family had decided to combine an anniversary barbecue in the park with a going-away party for Tess. Most of the population of Copperville would be there... including Mac.

By the day of the party, Tess had packed most of her belongings, including many of her clothes. Too late she realized that the only thing she hadn't packed that was festive enough for the event was her daisy-patterned dress. Mac would probably think she'd worn it on purpose. The only reason it still hung in her closet was that she hadn't gotten around to stuffing it in the bag of discards she'd collected to give to charity.

As she zipped the dress, she realized that the pearl necklace she'd continued to wear probably would be another red flag for Mac. For the past two weeks she kept meaning to take it off for good, although she couldn't make herself give it away. But each time she'd reached for the clasp so she could put the necklace back into her jewelry box, she'd decided to leave it on a little longer.

Putting the necklace away seemed so final, as if that would sever the last tie with Mac. Besides, her mother had mentioned how nice she thought it was that Tess was finally wearing the lovely gift Mac had given her. Her mother might notice the necklace was gone and comment, Tess decided. Better to leave it on. Mac would just have to deal with it.

She arrived at the park early to help her brothers and sisters-in-law with the preparations. They worked steadily for two hours in the heat, tying balloons to lampposts, firing up the barbecue grills and chasing rambunctious children. Tess welcomed the sweaty, frantic activity and pushed thoughts of Mac to the back of her mind.

But her pulse started to race right on schedule when he backed his truck up to a ramada and started unloading the kegs of beer that had been ordered for the party.

"Guess I'll go help him," Rhino said.

"Don't sample the wares until we're finished here," Joan called after her husband.

Tess kept sneaking glances at the two men as they laughed and joked with each other while unloading the kegs. Pretty soon Hammer, Dozer and Tim wandered over and joined them. Everyone acted like the best of buddies, and she began to hope that her brothers had made a temporary peace with Mac. Once she wasn't around, they might be able to put the whole incident aside.

"Hey, Dozer," Cindy called over to the group. "Time for you and Tim to start cooking. People are beginning to arrive and the anniversary couple will be here any minute."

"Coming," Dozer said.

Deena continued tying the last of the balloons on an adjacent ramada. "Hammer," she called. "I need you to check on Jason and Kimberly at the swings. Suzie's been playing with them over there, but I'll bet she could use a breather."

Hammer headed toward the swings. "Jason, let Kimberly have a turn, son!"

Tess pretended not to notice that Mac had tagged along as Tim, Dozer and Rhino approached the table. Instead, she concentrated on filling a large wading pool with ice to hold the salad bowls. She'd never followed through on her plan to use ice during lovemaking with Mac, but ice never failed to remind her of the passionate adventures they'd shared this summer.

"Cindy, which cooler did you put the hamburgers and hot dogs in?" Dozer asked.

"The red one," Cindy said.

"*Which* red one?"

"Oh, for heaven's sake." Cindy got Dozer by one arm and Tim by the other and propelled them over to a nearby ramada. "Come on. I'll show you."

Tess dumped the last bag of ice in the wading pool. "This is ready, Joan."

"For what?" Mac asked.

Tess glanced at him and could tell by the challenging look in his eyes that he'd meant for the question to rattle her. It did. Her cheeks warmed. "We, uh—"

"It's for the salads, so you don't get poisoned by the mayonnaise," Joan said briskly.

"That's not all it's for." Rhino grabbed a piece of ice and slipped it down the back of Joan's dress.

She shrieked and scooped up a handful of ice, pelting him with it as she chased him across the park.

And just like that, Mac and Tess were alone.

He picked up an ice cube and tossed it up and down in his hand. "We never did get around to this, did we?"

Her throat felt so tight that she couldn't speak. She shook her head.

"Guess we never will." He tossed the ice on the ground and moved closer. "How are you doing?"

"Okay." She risked one look into his eyes and glanced away again. Too potent. She cleared the huskiness from her throat. "How about you?"

"Okay. I thought about calling you to see how you were holding up, but I thought that might make things worse."

"Yeah. It probably would have." She watched the ice cube melt in the grass at their feet. "Mac, did my brothers—"

"Beat me up? No. In a way I wish they had. It might have made me feel better."

Tess glanced across the park. Joan and Rhino were walking back toward them. They didn't have much time. She lowered her voice. "Dammit, I will not have you taking the blame for this. It was my idea and I should be the one feeling guilty, not you."

"Like they said, I could have turned you down."

"You knew I was going to nab somebody for the job, and you were afraid I'd end up with a dweeb."

"Yeah. And then there was that dress."

She glanced at him.

"Why did you wear it today, Tess?"

Because I was selfish enough to want you to look at me like that one more time. "I'd packed everything else."

"And what about the necklace?" he asked softly. "Didn't get around to packing that, either, did you?"

Her heart ached so fiercely she could barely breathe. "Mac, I—"

"Promise me something."

"What?"

"That you'll wear that necklace in New York."

"Loafing, are we?" Joan said with a grin as they walked up. "Boy, I can't leave my staff for a minute without discipline going to hell."

Rhino's glance shifted from Mac to Tess and he frowned. "I'll put Big Mac to work for you, sweetheart. He's probably distracting Tess so she can't get anything done."

"Oh, I don't really care," Joan said. "After all, we won't have Tess around here much longer, so I'm sure everybody wants a chance to spend a little time with her today. Technically, I shouldn't be making her work at all, since this is also supposed to be her party."

"I wouldn't feel right sitting around," Tess said. She'd caught the brief look of disapproval on her brother's face. He might have shelved his anger for the time being, but he wasn't about to let Mac spend any more time alone with her.

"None of us are going to sit around," Rhino said. "Come on, Mac. I have a bunch of lawn chairs in the van. Let's go take them out and set them up."

"Sure thing." Mac glanced at Tess.

She realized she was clutching the pearl in one hand. She released it and turned away. His request completely confused her. He knew that wearing the necklace would be a constant reminder of him, preventing her from moving on to someone else. That sort of dog-in-the-manger attitude wasn't worthy of him, and she couldn't quite believe that was his motivation. Yet she could think of no other reason he'd want her to continue wearing the necklace.

The more she thought about it, the angrier she became. Who did he think he was, branding her like that when he didn't have the slightest intention of making a commitment himself?

Her parents arrived soon afterward. Once the party was in full swing, Tess focused on making this a special day for her parents. More than once she felt the tug of tears as she realized that by next week she wouldn't be able to see them and talk to them every day as she could now. She wondered if she'd made a terrible mistake taking the job in New York, but she couldn't change her course now, and besides, she needed to get away from Mac. If she stayed around much longer, he would surely break her heart for good.

Although the festivities took most of her attention, she couldn't forget that Mac was there, although she really tried. Despite her efforts, she always seemed to know where he was, whether he'd stripped off his shirt for the volleyball game, or had taken yet another kid for a ride on his shoulders, or was challenging one of her brothers to a game of horseshoes. His voice, his smile, his laughter drew her as if they were connected with an invisible string.

Finally she decided the pearl necklace was part of the problem. She couldn't take it to New York, let alone wear it while she was there. And Mac needed to know that.

She excused herself on the pretext that she needed to head for one of the park restrooms. When she was away from the crowd, she took off the necklace. Unclasping it wasn't easy because her hands were shaking. Once she'd done it, she felt as if someone had wrapped her heart in barbed wire.

But this was what she had to do. She found Mac eating some of her parents' anniversary cake while he talked with a couple of ranchers who lived on the outskirts of Copperville.

"Excuse me, Mac," she said.

"Sure." He glanced at her bare neck and his gaze grew wary. "What is it?"

She reached over and dropped the necklace in his shirt pocket. "I need you to keep this for me." Choking back a sob, she turned and hurried away.

CHAPTER SIXTEEN

MAC WANTED TO throw the necklace away. In the tortured days that followed, right up to the morning Tess was scheduled to leave, he tried to make himself pitch it in the garbage, in the river, over a cliff. He couldn't do it.

The day she left, he drove to a bluff overlooking the highway winding out of town and waited there until he saw her car go by. He thought he'd fling the necklace over the bluff once he knew she was really and truly gone. But long after her car and trailer had disappeared from sight, he still clutched the necklace tight in his fist.

In the weeks that followed he kept the necklace in a drawer and fell into the habit of tucking it into his jeans' pocket before starting the day. He'd meant for her to keep it on as a reminder of him and what they'd meant to each other. He'd held on to the slim hope that after some time of living in the big city she'd grow tired of it and come home. If she wore the necklace until then, he might have a chance. But she'd turned the tables on him...again.

He handled his ranch duties like a robot. The work had always seemed confining to him, but he'd been able to bear it while Tess remained in Copperville. Now the daily routine was intolerable without her. She'd been the one who had kept his life interesting, and the fact that she shared his desire to go out into the world had kept that fantasy alive for him. Now she was out there and he was left behind.

As the heat lifted in late September, he was rounding up strays down by the river one afternoon when he came to a life-changing realization. Once his parents were gone, he'd sell the ranch and travel the world. That wouldn't take the place of losing Tess, but it would have to do. And if he was planning to sell the ranch eventually anyway, his parents' dream of keeping it in the family and passing it down through the generations was doomed from the beginning.

Suddenly the whole charade seemed stupid. To pretend he wanted a ranch that he wouldn't keep after his parents died was unfair to all of them. Telling his mom and dad the truth after all these years wouldn't be easy, though. Still, he was determined to do it and end the hypocrisy.

He waited until dinner was nearly over. He'd barely been able to taste his mother's prized beef stew, but he'd forced himself to eat every bite and carry on a conversation about the antics of the stud they'd bought from Stan Henderson in Flagstaff.

From the moment he'd come into the ranch house that night he'd seen the place with new eyes. Now that he'd decided the ranch would not be his ball and chain, he could appreciate the beamed ceilings and rock fireplace, the heavy leather furniture grouped around the hearth and the carved oak table and chairs in the dining room.

It wouldn't be such a bad place to live…someday, and with the right person. But he couldn't expect his parents to keep it going without him, holding on to it for when he was ready to settle down. And before that day came, he had many things to do.

Finally he pushed his plate aside and gazed at them. "I need to talk to both of you. It's…pretty serious."

"At last," his mother said with a sigh.

Mac stared at her. "What do you mean, *at last?*"

"Your mother's been worried sick about you ever since Tess left," his father said. "I've been a mite concerned, myself. You've been moping around like you've lost your best friend, and I guess you have."

Mac felt his neck grow warm. It showed how self-absorbed he'd been lately, that he hadn't even realized how his mood had been affecting his parents. "I'm sorry if I've been a pain in the butt."

"You have," his father said.

"No, he hasn't, Andy." Nora sent her husband a reproving glance. "He's been sort of glum, that's all."

"Which translates to being a pain in the butt, in my opinion," Andy said.

"I agree," Mac said. "But I'm about to be even more of one." He took a deep breath. "I know you've both worked hard all these years to build up this ranch."

"It's been a labor of love," his mother said.

She wasn't making it any easier for him. Mac cleared his throat. "I appreciate all that you've done, and I realize the goal was to pass the ranch on to me someday, but—"

"You don't want it," his father finished, his voice husky.

Mac met his father's gaze and his resolve nearly crumbled at the deep disappointment he saw there. "I might," he said gently. "Eventually, when I get some of the wanderlust out of my system. It's a beautiful place, and tonight I really began to realize just how beautiful it is. But right now the ranch feels like an elephant sitting on my chest, choking the life out of me."

"You want to go to New York, don't you?" his mother asked quietly.

"Maybe." *Yes.* He hadn't allowed himself to get that far in his thinking, but now that his mother had put the idea into words, he knew immediately that he wanted to start with New York. He wasn't sure how Tess figured into any of this, or if she even wanted to figure in, but he would never know if he didn't go there and find out.

"What in hell would you do in New York?" his father asked. His tone of voice betrayed the depth of his hurt.

"I'm not sure." The ideas started coming to him, and

he realized they'd been simmering in his subconscious for years. "I'd probably try to get on with one of the small commuter airlines there. If that didn't pan out I'd find some job at one of the major airports and work my way up until I could fly. I love airplanes, Dad. I always have."

"You have a damn airplane! You can fly it around all you want!"

"Andy." Nora laid a hand on her husband's arm. "That's not the point. He wants to go out on his own, the way Tess has. Plus, he misses her like crazy. I don't know if something more than friendship is involved, but I'm beginning to think there is." She glanced at Mac. "I didn't want to interfere, but I had a strong feeling that you and Tess went beyond the boundaries of friendship this summer. Debbie thought so, too."

"You and Tess's mom talked about it?" Mac felt the heat climb from his neck to his face.

"To be honest, a lot of people in town had their suspicions," his mother said. "We wondered if Tess might decide to stay home, after all. When she left, I felt so bad for you."

"I knew it." Andy threw his napkin on the table and pushed back his chair. "This is all about chasing after a woman. If Tess had had the good sense to stay in Copperville, then you two could get married and you wouldn't be comparing the ranch to some damn elephant."

"Don't blame it on Tess!" In his agitation, Mac rose to his feet. "I've always felt this way. Both of us have, Tess and I. We spent hours as kids talking about the places we'd see, the exciting things we'd do once we left Copperville."

"Lots of kids talk that way," his father said. "Then they grow up and realize that what they have is better than anything they could find out there!"

Mac gazed at his father and tried to put himself in Andy MacDougal's shoes. After nearly thirty years of breaking his back to create a legacy for his son, his son was rejecting that legacy. Mac hated hurting his father. "It probably is better, Dad," he said gently. "But I'll never appreciate that if I don't see something of the rest of the world."

"Of course you must," his mother said.

"Maybe we should just sell the ranch right now," Andy said. "No point in killing ourselves if it's not going to be passed on."

"Oh, Andy, for heaven's sake!" Nora looked disgusted. "Forget your hurt pride for five seconds and listen to what your son is saying. He needs time to explore. And he needs to be with the woman he loves."

Mac's heart clutched. "Now, Mom. Don't jump to—"

"I'll jump to any conclusion I want, thank you very much." She glanced at him. "And Tess feels the same about you, unless I miss my guess. I also fully believe that both of you will eventually get homesick for Copperville and come back here to raise your children."

"Children?" Mac almost choked. "Last I heard, Tess had no intention of getting married, let alone having kids. I think you're getting ahead of yourself."

His mother smiled. "No, I think you're behind. Time to catch up. Go to New York and ask those questions. See what kind of response you get." She looked over at her husband. "All we need to do is hire someone to help out for a while, until these two come back home."

Andy scowled. "And what if they don't? Then it'll all be for nothing."

"Now that's the dumbest thing I've ever heard you say, Andy. Nothing? This ranch was your dream all along. You hoped it would be passed down, as a lot of parents do who work to build something, but you wanted it for yourself, too. You've had a wonderful time living this life, and don't you dare pretend it was nothing but selfless sacrifice for your son!"

Gradually Andy's expression changed from belligerent

to sheepish. "Guess you're right, Nora. I can't imagine any other place to be. That's why I can't figure why anybody in their right mind would want to live in that rat's nest they call New York City."

"We're all different," Nora said. "As for these two, they were both born and raised here, and I say they'll be back."

"I can't make any promises," Mac said. But he couldn't help weaving a few fantasies, either. Maybe he could have it all, a few years of adventures with Tess and then a family and security right here in Copperville with the only woman he'd ever wanted. But Tess might not be interested in such a plan. After all, she had given back the necklace.

"You don't have to make any promises to us," his mother said. "But I think you need to make a few to Tess."

NEW YORK WAS everything Tess had imagined and more. She'd used her weekends to walk Manhattan from end to end, and each excursion brought new delights. She'd become addicted to pretzels sold by sidewalk vendors, and corner deli markets, and the ride up to the top of the Empire State Building.

But she'd never expected to be so completely, utterly lonely. She'd made friends with people on the staff of her school, but *friend* didn't seem like the right word to describe someone she'd only known a couple of months. Friends were people you'd known for years, people who knew your family and all your other friends. Friends were people like…Mac.

She'd thought the ache for him would have begun to wear away by now, but if anything, it grew stronger. Today was worse than most days, because it was both Sunday, a time for families, and Halloween, a holiday she and Mac had shared for twenty-three years. They'd never considered themselves too old to dress up. A year ago they'd gone to a party together as a couple of Beanie Babies.

Tess had been invited to a party given by one of the teachers at school, and she'd accepted, but as she sat in her tiny apartment trying to come up with a costume, she couldn't get excited about it. Her simplest option was to wear the harem outfit she'd bought for the belly-dancing demonstration she'd given Mac. She thought she'd thrown it away, but she must have been in a real fog when she'd packed, because it was in the bottom of a box. Once she discovered it, she'd been so desperate for any reminders of Mac that she'd kept it.

Wearing it, however, might present a few emotional problems. Yet she didn't have any other great ideas for a costume, and this one was complete. With a sigh she started putting it on for a test run to see whether it made her cry, or worse yet made her hot and bothered. Sexual frustration had been a constant companion along with loneliness, but of the two, loneliness was the worst. She missed having Mac to talk to even more than she missed his lovemaking.

Still, she'd give anything to be held and caressed by him again, and it was definitely *his* lovemaking that she wanted. She'd turned down several dates already. The thought of even kissing someone besides Mac made her shudder.

If that attitude persisted, she might have to resign herself to staying single all her life. Damned if she wasn't beginning to believe she was a one-man woman. She'd never have believed it before the scorching events of this summer, but it seemed that Mac had taken not only her virginity, but her heart. And she wasn't getting it back.

After putting on the filmy harem pants and the jeweled bra, she stood in front of the mirror in her small bedroom and fastened the veil in place. Heat washed over her as she remembered the look in Mac's eyes as she'd danced for him. She'd never felt so sensuous as when she'd leaned over him and shimmied her breasts practically in his face.

He'd meant to end their affair that night without making love to her, but she'd tempted him beyond endurance and even made him forget he'd agreed to meet her brothers for a darts tournament. In all the turmoil that had followed, she'd forgotten that her seductive dance had succeeded beyond her wildest dreams. She had made him lose his mind. Maybe he didn't want to marry her, but for that moment, he had been completely, utterly hers.

And he'd said that he loved her. It had turned out to be an empty pledge, and now she wondered if he'd only meant that he loved the fantastic sex they'd made together. But when he'd said it that night, he'd filled her heart to overflowing.

She couldn't wear the harem outfit to the Halloween party. It made her long for Mac in every conceivable way—physically, mentally and emotionally. Maybe she'd skip the party altogether and rent a video. She reached for the hook on the jeweled bra just as the doorbell rang.

Probably her next-door neighbor, she thought. She'd moved clear across the country, yet some things stayed the same. The woman in the next apartment reminded her so much of her neighbor, Mrs. Nedbetter, back in Copperville, that several times she'd called her by the wrong name.

She glanced at herself in the mirror. Oh, well, it was Halloween. She'd explain that she was trying on costumes in preparation for a party. She really should make herself go, she thought as she walked toward the front door. A simple costume like a gypsy or a pirate wouldn't be that hard to create.

The doorbell chimed again. Then a voice that made her breath catch called out "Trick or treat."

"Mac!" She raced to the door and unlocked it, fumbling in her eagerness. So what if he'd only come for a visit and would leave her worse off than she was now? She didn't care. She flung open the door and gasped.

He was dressed as a sheik, complete with rich-looking robes and a gold piece of braid holding a white flowing turban on his head. When he saw her, his jaw dropped. "Wow. This is just plain scary."

"Yeah." She held his gaze, her heart pounding. "Scary as hell."

"Are you going to a Halloween party?"

"No. Well, maybe. I was invited and I was trying to decide if I wanted to go or not, so I put this on in case I could wear it." She gulped for air. "But I can't."

"Funny, but you seem to be wearing it. Or is that an optical illusion?"

"I—listen, come in." She stepped back from the door. "Do you have bags? How long can you stay? When did you—"

"No bags. I left them at the hotel."

Her hopes died. "H-hotel? You're not…planning to stay…with me?"

He walked through the doorway, his sheik's robes swaying, and closed the door behind him. Then he turned to her. "I didn't want to impose on you. I'm sure you have all sorts of things going on."

So he had come for a visit, with a capital *V*. He probably wanted someone to show him the sights, and she was handy, but he'd distanced himself from her by checking into a hotel. His sheik's outfit was a little joke, not a significant statement of his intentions.

"Well, of course I have things going on." She was determined to hide her pain. "But I'd be glad to adjust my schedule. If you'd told me you were coming, I might have been able to arrange a couple of days off, but on short notice, I'm not sure."

He waved a hand as if that didn't matter to him. "I don't

want you to interrupt your work for me." He hesitated. "You said you were invited to a party." His voice became husky. "Do you have a date?"

For a split second she considered lying, but she'd never been good at that, especially with Mac. "No. It's just some people from work. Not a couples sort of thing."

"And you're thinking of going in *that?*"

She bristled. Deciding not to wear it because of the memories it evoked was one thing. Having him question her choice in that tone of voice was quite another. He didn't have that right. "Why not?"

"Because it's indecent!"

"You didn't think so that night I danced for you!" She blew the veil impatiently away from her face. "You enjoyed this outfit so much your tongue was hanging out, mister!"

"And it still is! And so will every other guy's at that party!"

Her chin lifted. "What's it to you?"

He stepped forward and grabbed her. "Everything."

Her breath caught as the space surrounding them seemed to glow and pulse. She became lost in his gaze.

He squeezed his eyes shut. "Damn. I didn't mean it to come out like that."

"You didn't?" Some of the luster faded.

"No." He looked into her eyes. "I meant to go slow, find out if you had a boyfriend."

The luster returned.

"Well?" he prompted.

Wherever this conversation was leading she wanted to go along, but he'd taken his time about having this talk with her. She decided not to make it too easy and ruin the challenge for him. "Well, what?"

"Do you have a boyfriend?"

What a beautiful day. What an absolutely gorgeous day. "I think so."

"You *think* so?" He scowled down at her. "What kind of an answer is that?"

She was glad she still wore the veil. It hid her smile. "He's not being real clear about his intentions, so it's hard for me to know whether he's my boyfriend or not. But I'm pretty sure he is."

Mac's scowl darkened. "So he's one of those wishy-washy types?"

"Let's just say he's a little confused."

"And how do you feel about him?"

"I'm crazy about him."

His eyes blazed and his grip tightened on her arms. "You can't be."

"Why not? He's terrific."

"Terrific? What do you mean by that?" His eyes narrowed. "Tess, have you and this guy…made love?"

"Not recently."

"I don't give a damn if it's recent or not! Tess, how could you make love to another man? How could you—"

"In fact, I haven't made love to this guy since August," she added gently. "I was wearing this outfit at the time."

Understanding slowly softened the fierce line of his eyebrows and the glitter in his blue eyes. "Oh." He swallowed. "Did I hear you say you're crazy about this guy?"

She nodded.

"I can't imagine why." His voice was hoarse. "He's an idiot."

"No." She reached up and touched his cheek. "Just confused." She stroked the curve of his jaw with a trembling hand. She wanted him, no matter how long he could stay or what his terms might be. "Would you like to cancel that hotel reservation? No one in Copperville has to know that you stayed here during your visit, if that's what you're worried about."

"I'm not visiting."

"What?"

"I'm job hunting, looking into a couple of commuter airlines. I've come here to live."

She reeled from the news. "Mac! What about the ranch? What about your parents?"

"They've hired someone to take over my part of the work. Telling them that I needed to go out on my own wasn't easy, but it was the right thing to do. I should have told them sooner, but I guess I needed you to blaze a trail for me."

"I'm stunned."

His eyes grew shadowed. "Look, this puts you under no obligation. I'm not asking you to change your life just because I decided to come here. I mean, sure, I'd like to see you, and everything, but—"

"And what do you mean exactly by *and everything?*" She moved her hips boldly against his and felt his instantaneous response. "This?"

He groaned softly. "Tess, I—"

"And this?" She pushed the material of his sheik's robe aside and brushed her jeweled bra against his bare chest.

His gaze smoldered. "You drive me insane, Tess. I've missed you so much I can barely think straight."

She pressed her body against his. "If you can't think straight, then maybe you don't remember what you told me when we made love that last time."

"Oh, I remember that, all right."

She gathered her courage and continued. "I need to know if it was just something you said in the heat of passion, or if it meant more than that."

He held her tighter. "You want all my cards on the table, don't you?"

"Yes."

"Then take off that damn veil."

She reached up and unfastened it immediately, tossing it to a nearby chair.

He gazed down at her, his glance warm as it roved over her face. Then he reached beneath his robe and pulled out the pearl necklace. "I think it's time you put this back on."

Her heart thudded wildly at the implication. She trembled as he fastened the clasp around her neck and nestled the pearl between her breasts.

"Okay," he said softly. "I was going to lead up to this, but if you want everything all at once, that's what you'll get. I love you. Maybe on some level I've always known you were my mate, but so many things got in the way. I'm going to marry you someday, Tess, when you're ready. I realize that might not be for a while, but—"

"I'm ready."

"I'm willing to wait until you've experienced all…" He paused, as if finally registering what she'd said. He looked into her eyes.

She nodded.

"Oh, God." His mouth came down on hers, and he kissed her until they were both breathless. "You're sure?" He held her face in both hands, his gaze probing. "I mean, you just started this new life, and maybe you need to stay single for a couple of years, to—"

"To what? Nothing could be as exciting as living with you as your wife. I think I've known that since I was three years old. I love you, Mac, desperately, completely and forever."

His smile was tender. "Yeah, but do you swear on the tomb of old King Tut?"

"You bet. And now let me give you some vital information. The bedroom is through that door on your right. Do you think we could go in there and make mad, passionate love for about ten hours? I'm feeling very neglected."

He grinned and lifted her up in his arms. "Only ten hours?"

"For starters."

He feathered his lips over hers. "Got ice?" he murmured.

EPILOGUE

PLEASANTLY FULL AFTER a meal of fried chicken and potato salad, Mac lay back on the picnic blanket, closed his eyes and sighed with contentment. No New York traffic, no jackhammers, no jet engines. Only the gurgle of the river, the call of a quail, the rustle of the breeze through the reeds.

He'd visited beaches and riverbanks in many parts of the world this past year, but he'd recognize the baked-sand and wet-moss scent of this one blindfolded. The breeze moved over him like a caress. How he loved summer nights in Arizona.

Something tickled his nose, and he swatted it away. The tickling resumed, and he opened one eye.

Leaning over him, Tess brushed a feathery tip of a wildgrass stalk over his mouth.

He gazed up and noticed that when she leaned over, her blouse gaped open quite nicely. Taking the stalk from her fingers, he slipped it down the front of her blouse and stroked it over the swell of her breasts. "They already seem fuller."

"It's probably your imagination. I'm barely three months along."

"I'll never forget the look on our folks' faces when we told them." He could see desire stirring in her eyes as he continued to tickle her breasts with the grass.

She smiled. "I think they were even happier about the baby than when we told them we were home to stay."

"I'm pretty happy about that baby, myself." He brushed the grass up the curve of her throat and tickled under her chin. "Any regrets about leaving the big city?"

"Only that we never did it on top of the Empire State Building."

"We'll visit someday and do it then."

She shook her head. "Nah. We don't have to. Making love to you for the rest of my life is all the adventure I need."

"You mean that?"

"Absolutely."

"Then take off your blouse," he murmured. The sight of Tess unfastening buttons was one of the joys of his life.

She obliged him and tossed the garment aside before gazing down at him, a question in her gray eyes.

"Keep going." His erection strained his jeans as she flipped open the front catch of her bra. In another moment her breasts spilled into view, her nipples already taut. He stroked the grass across them anyway, loving the ripple of desire that went through her, the surrender in her sigh.

His voice grew husky. "Lean down."

She moved over him and he filled both hands with the weight of her breasts, kneading gently as he began to taste her.

While he feasted, she managed to wiggle out of her shorts, open his jeans and free his erection. He groaned with pleasure as she slid down over his rigid shaft. How miraculous to make love this way, without barriers. Releasing her breasts, he guided her down for a long, satisfying kiss.

She drew back and gazed into his eyes as she initiated a slow, sensuous rhythm. "I love you, Mac."

"And I love you," he said. Above her the cottonwood leaves dappled the twilight sky. Heaven couldn't be any better than this. "I love you more than life." His climax was building quickly, and from the way Tess was breathing, she wasn't far behind him.

"Stop," she said, panting. "I just remembered."

His fevered brain wasn't working. "Remembered what?"

"Hold on a sec." She reached toward the small picnic cooler near the edge of the blanket.

He squeezed his eyes shut, teetering on the edge. "I don't know if I can." He felt the pulsing begin. "Tess, I can't—" Something cold pressed against a critical part of his anatomy and he erupted, sensations crashing over him in waves, ripping moans of ecstasy from deep in his chest.

Finally he lay still, spent and quivering, while she sprinkled kisses over his face.

"What…was that?" he asked.

She sounded very smug. "Ice."

* * * * *

OLD ENOUGH TO KNOW BETTER

The book is dedicated with gratitude to all the
Temptation editors who for years have helped
make my books the best they can be,
with special affection and thanks to Claire Gerus,
Margaret Carney, Lisa Boyes, Susan Till,
Birgit Davis-Todd and, of course, Brenda Chin.

CHAPTER ONE

"HOTTIE ALERT!"

Kasey Braddock glanced up. While the two guys in the office made remarks about female chauvinists, all the women hurried to where Gretchen Davies, a gutsy woman with a great laugh, had her nose pressed to the glass of the second-floor window. Moans of appreciation sounded in chorus.

Deciding from everyone's reaction that the view was worth checking out, Kasey punched the save button on her computer and walked toward the window. She'd been working on a PR campaign for a lingerie shop that wanted to shift its image—more Victoria's Secret, less Frederick's of Hollywood.

Hours of careful research on the subject of lace teddies and thong underwear had reminded her that she'd been seriously neglecting the goal she'd set for herself: to become the woman she'd always wanted to be. Sure, she'd worked on her appearance but she had yet to launch her personal campaign to act as sexy as she now looked. The nerd that still lurked inside seemed to be giving orders to the babe she'd become on the outside. Maybe ogling a fine example of Phoenix manhood would jump-start the new Kasey.

"Okay, my turn." She approached the cluster of five women blocking her view. "Two of you aren't eligible, anyway, so give a single girl a break."

"I was only saving you a good spot." Brandy Larson's

fiancé, Eric Lassiter, was out of the office on an appointment, and she looked suitably guilty as she moved aside to make room for Kasey. "Try not to drool on the window," she murmured.

"Hey, Brandy, I'm telling Eric." Ed Finley leaned on the watercooler and observed the commotion.

"Don't go being a tattletale, Ed." Kasey gave him a warning glance, hoping he wasn't serious.

"Aw, I'm just kidding, Kase." Ed flashed her a peace sign.

"Glad to hear it." Kasey held her own in this boisterous office, but she wondered if that would still be the case if everyone knew she was only twenty. She'd finished college at eighteen. After thoroughly evaluating all the PR firms in the Valley, she'd targeted Beckworth, landing the job before her nineteenth birthday. Only the big boss, Mr. Arnold Beckworth himself, knew her age. She wanted to keep it that way, so she'd continue to be treated as an equal.

"Ten bucks says he takes his shirt off in the next five minutes." Gretchen clutched a file folder to her ample chest as she stared outside.

Kasey finally took a look. "My God, it's Tarzan with a chain saw." Right at eye level, a really cute dark-haired guy stood balanced in a large mesquite tree. As the pruned branches toppled to the ground fifteen feet below, a couple of other workers cut them into smaller sections and loaded them into the back of a trailer.

His square jaw clenched, safety goggles making him look seriously macho, Trimmer Guy gripped his chain saw and made precision cuts. His muscles bunched under a sweat-stained T-shirt.

"I'll take that bet," said Amy Whittenburg, a fortysomething divorcee with very red hair. "That's a company logo on the back of his shirt. Ashton Landscaping probably requires their employees to keep the shirts on to promote the company."

"I have to say he's promoting that company in a mighty fine manner," said Myra Detmar, the receptionist. "Mighty fine. Look at those shoulders. Too bad he's wearing gloves. We can't check out his ring finger."

"There you go again, making a sex object out of some poor slob," called Jerry Peters from his desk across the room. "If a bunch of guys acted the way you women act, we'd be crucified." Balding and on the pudgy side, Jerry always chimed in with a dose of indignation during a Hottie Alert.

"Oh, bite me," Gretchen shot back. "Between the insulation and the noise of his saw, he can't hear a word we say, and with the reflective coating on this window he can't even see us. It's like watching a movie."

"More like *Candid Camera*," Jerry said. "I think I'll wander out there and ask him if he knows there's a huddle of rabid females on the other side of the glass pretending he's the star attraction at Chippendale's."

Gretchen turned to glare at Jerry. "You do and you'll never get another double chocolate espresso on my coffee run, bub."

"Well, Tarzan's adorable," said Robbi Harrison, who'd returned from her honeymoon a week ago, "but I'm so spoken for. I'll have to leave him for the rest of you." She walked back to her desk. "I just had to take a peek for old time's sake."

"I tell you, that Ashton Landscaping shirt is comin' off," Gretchen said. "It's gotta be at least ninety out there, and handling that chain saw can't be easy. Look, he's turned it off and propped it in the crotch of the tree."

"I love it when you talk dirty." Kasey winked at her.

Gretchen laughed. "Mark my words, he's thinking about losing the shirt."

"I'm betting another ten that he does," Kasey said, joining in the ever-popular game. She studied the shirt in question. Ashton Landscaping was stenciled on the back in green script. She tried to think why the name Ashton sounded familiar. Even the guy looked like someone she should know. Information was working its way in from the far reaches of her memory, but it wasn't quite there yet.

"As long as we're throwing down bets," said Amy, "we might as well draw straws for him, too, in case he turns out to be available."

"Un-freaking-believable," Jerry muttered. "It's the straws again."

"It's the only fair way to handle a Hottie Alert," Gretchen said. "Robbi, we need you back over here. You can be the designated straw holder."

Kasey's heart began to pound. She'd have to take part in the straw thing or lose face. So far, she'd never ended up with the long straw, so she hadn't been required to go out and ask whatever hottie they were ogling for a date. Mostly she'd been relieved not to be forced into doing it. Then again, maybe peer pressure was the best way to launch her new persona.

"Here you go." Robbi came up beside them. She held out her hand, and four stubs of paper sprouted from her closed fist. "May the best woman win."

Kasey gazed at the stubs of paper. It was like a game of chicken. The idea was for the lucky gal to go out with the guy and make him drool without her handing over the goods. But twice since Kasey had started working at Beckworth, a woman had taken the dare and ended up engaged. Kasey wasn't about to let that happen to her.

Yet she was at a distinct disadvantage considering her

age and the fact that until she'd graduated from college she'd been nerd girl. She wasn't a virgin, but she'd never been assertive with guys and never been in demand. Her first job had seemed like the perfect time to start over and create a whole new Kasey Braddock, though, so far, she'd really done nothing more than change her look.

A long straw would put her goal to change her image to the ultimate test, and maybe it was time. Taking a deep breath, she reached for a stub of paper and hoped for the long straw.

SAM ASHTON LOVED taking a mangy-looking mesquite with good bones and transforming it into a sculptural work of art. He'd turn over other pruning jobs to his workers, but he didn't trust anyone else to make the right cuts on a beauty like this one. Besides, he'd never outgrown the joy of climbing trees.

While he worked, he thought about the woman he'd noticed this morning parking her little red Miata in the lot next to the building. He'd been lounging in his truck drinking coffee while he waited for his employees to arrive at the job site. During down times, he usually thought about ways to boost business.

More business would be good for him, but even better for his little brother's band, which desperately needed a backer. Although Colin and the other band members operated on a shoestring, the Tin Tarantulas had created a Gen-Y fan base in the Phoenix area, and Sam would love to help them buy better equipment and record a demo. They had the potential to make it.

He'd been daydreaming about that when here came trouble, pulling into a space in the next row, lining up exactly in front of him. The red convertible said *look at me,* but as if that weren't enough, the vanity plate announced that the blond woman driving it was SO REDY.

Sam's pulse rate had picked up. He'd always been a sucker for a woman in a red ragtop, and one who announced she was "so ready" had real promise. He'd sipped his coffee as she'd flipped down her visor, pulled off her shades and run a comb through sleek hair that hung straight to the shoulders of her white suit jacket. When she'd dabbed on some lip gloss from an applicator wand, he'd figured it was likely as red as the car, even though he couldn't see for sure.

He hadn't dated much in the past few months, mostly because he was getting picky. These days if a relationship had no potential, he backed away much faster than he used to. At thirty, he didn't care to waste time on dead ends anymore. His last girlfriend hadn't been ready to settle down, partly because of her age. He had to admit there was a big gap between twenty-three and thirty.

But even though he'd started thinking in terms of the *M* word, he was still a typical guy, and visuals snagged him first. Yeah, he should be willing to ignore the figure and see into a woman's soul. He wasn't quite that evolved yet.

Therefore he'd waited to see what kind of body went with the red car, the shiny hair and the saucy license plate before he committed himself to being interested. At last she'd opened her door. With his first glimpse of leg, his interest had shot up exponentially.

He'd returned his travel mug to its holder in the console and wrapped both arms around the steering wheel as he'd leaned forward. What followed was an outstanding view of the cutest ass ever to grace a bucket seat, wrapped in a short white skirt that was barely legal. Thank God, the mini was still in fashion.

After closing her door, she'd reached over to grab her

shoulder bag from the passenger seat. Excellent. Sam watched with relish as the white material stretched across her bottom. Yowza. He'd gazed, enjoyed…and leaned on the horn. Immediately he'd backed off the wheel and the damned horn. He'd driven through a rural area yesterday and a bunch of bugs had done a kamikaze number on his windshield. He'd hoped that would keep her from seeing him clearly.

She'd turned and glanced over at his truck. Fortunately, because of the angle, she wouldn't have been able to see the Ashton Landscaping lettered on the cab doors. He'd picked up the contract for today's job and pretended to study it while he'd kept track of her from the corner of his eye. God, how uncool was that, to accidentally honk the horn. She'd shrugged and started toward the building, her hips swaying, her high-heeled sandals tapping on the asphalt.

Sam let out a breath. Before he finished today, he needed to find out who she was. If nothing else, he could leave a note taped to her steering wheel, but he'd rather talk to her face-to-face. As he pruned the mesquite tree, he wondered where her office might be, which one of the building's tenants she worked for. Too bad the windows all had reflective glass, because from his perch he would be able to see into several of the building's offices.

Then again, maybe the reflective glass was a good thing. If he got another eyeful of her, especially if she happened to be bending over a file drawer, he might tumble right out of the tree. She was one hot babe.

And speaking of hot, thinking about her while working like a farm animal had spiked his internal temperature. Sweat stung his eyes and rolled down his spine. Life would be a hell of a lot more pleasant without his shirt.

After turning off the saw, he propped it carefully in the crotch of the tree. Then he took off his work gloves and goggles and tucked them in beside the saw. Finally he braced his knees against the trunk for balance and reached for the hem of his shirt.

KASEY TUGGED ON a stub of paper. And tugged, and tugged some more, until she stood holding the eight-inch strip that was clearly the long straw. The other three women groaned with disappointment.

Before Kasey could get her mind around the fact that she'd won, Gretchen gasped. "The shirt!"

All attention focused on the window once again as Tarzan of the Chain Saw took off his goggles, peeled his shirt from his back and draped it over a tree limb. A collective sigh went up from the group of women.

"I can see his ring finger," said Myra in hushed tones. "No ring."

Amy cleared her throat. "Didn't notice. Too busy looking at his body to notice his fingers. Girls, behold a work of art."

"Wouldn't you know." Gretchen gestured toward the window. "There's the answer to my prayers, and here I stand with a freaking short straw."

Kasey's first impulse was to trade straws with Gretchen. This guy was way out of her league. Her dates had been few and far between, but they'd all been with braniacs, not jocks. And not a one of them had possessed a build to equal this. But trading straws was not an option, not if she wanted to polish her so-far-undeserved rep as a happening chick whose license plate announced she was SO REDY. A happening chick would use that long straw to claim her prize.

"He's beyond gorgeous," said Amy. "Look at that. Even a tattoo."

Kasey screwed up her courage to take another look at

her challenge du jour, who was currently mopping his face with his shirt. Sure enough, he had a tattoo on his upper arm that looked like a ring of barbed wire.

As she stared at that tattoo, her memory delivered the information she'd been trying to retrieve ever since her first glimpse out the window. She'd seen that tattoo twelve years ago, wrapped around the arm of her stepbrother Jim's high school buddy, a dreamy guy by the name of Sam Ashton.

She could still picture the two teenagers out by the family's budget-sized swimming pool, radio blaring as they worked on their tans before prom. She'd been the eight-year-old brat who'd spent the afternoon splashing them from her vantage point in the pool. Finally Sam had responded, diving in and giving her a thorough dunking.

The cut at the corner of her mouth had been totally her fault. If she hadn't flailed around so much, she wouldn't have whacked herself in the mouth with her secret decoder ring. The minute Sam had noticed she was bleeding, he'd rushed her into the house, both of them dripping all over her mother's clean floor. Then he'd insisted on going with her to the emergency room, where the doctor had given her two small stitches.

Sam had sat right there, even though he'd looked decidedly green during the stitching process. He'd apologized about a hundred times. The next day he'd sent her a bouquet of flowers. That was when she'd fallen hopelessly in love as only an eight-year-old can fall for a sophisticated older man of eighteen.

After that she'd asked Jim endlessly when Sam was coming over again, but apparently finals and graduation had kept him too busy and he hadn't made it back to their house that spring. Then Jim told her Sam's family had moved to Oregon, and that's where Sam would be going to college in the fall. Jim had left to join the Marines and the two friends had lost touch. Kasey hadn't seen Sam again…until now.

"So, Kasey, what's your game plan?" Gretchen asked.

Kasey blinked, pulling herself from the past, when she'd had a mad crush on Sam, to the present, when she was the designated Bad Girl from Beckworth out to put some serious moves on the guy. Aside from fighting her internal panic, she had to decide if there was the remotest chance he'd recognize her.

Probably not. Jim was her stepbrother, so they had different last names, and what were the chances Sam would remember a little pain in the ass named Kasey? Besides, she didn't look anything like that eight-year-old. The scar was barely visible. Braces for her teeth, straightener for her frizzy blond hair and tinted contacts for her nearsightedness had all made a difference. Hormones and the good advice of Jim's girlfriend Alicia, now his ex-girlfriend, had taken care of the rest.

Kasey had worked hard to look older and more experienced than she was. From her little red car to her sassy clothes, she'd created an image that required her to take charge of this assignment to snare Sam's interest, and take charge fast.

"I think he looks hot, don't you?" she asked Gretchen.

"Oh, honey, don't you know it. And I need to hear what you intend to do about it. We have to live vicariously through you, so tell us your plan."

"No, I mean he looks *really* hot."

"That's what I'm saying! So how are you—"

"I'm going to take him a nice cold bottle of water straight from the machine in the break room. I'll get his attention first and then toss it up to him."

Gretchen smiled. "Brilliant."

"But then won't he know we've been watching him?" Myra asked.

"He'll know Kasey's been watching him," said Amy, "and I think that's part of her strategy, right, Kase?"

It hadn't been, but caught off guard, Kasey was happy to gather any words of wisdom on the art of seduction. "Of course." She walked to her desk, grabbed some change from her wallet and headed for the break room, trailed by Gretchen, Myra and Amy.

"How's your throwing arm?" Amy asked. "You don't want to heave it up there like a weakling."

"My arm's good." Kasey put the money in the machine and punched the button for bottled water. "My brother taught me to throw when I was a kid."

"That's lucky." Gretchen nodded as the bottle thumped down the chute. "A wimpy throw wouldn't help your cause."

"You'd better get out there quick," Myra said. "He's starting up the saw again. He might not notice you down there if he's cutting tree limbs."

Sure enough, the whine of the chain saw drifted into the break room. Kasey thought fast. "Okay, I can deal with that." She handed her bottle to Gretchen. "Hold on to this for a sec, okay?"

"Anything for you, toots."

Kasey slipped out of her white suit jacket. Underneath she wore a stretch-lace shell that made the most of her breasts.

"That oughta do it," Amy said. "Let him have it with both barrels, kid."

Kasey had never been fond of the word *kid* as a nickname, maybe because it had been applied to her so often in the past. But she knew Amy didn't mean it literally. Amy thought Kasey was in her mid-twenties, because that's what Kasey had led everyone to believe.

"Thanks," she said. "I will." She took the bottle from Gretchen, then walked back into the office and tossed her jacket over her chair.

She didn't even glance toward the window as she left the office, afraid seeing Sam there looking so yummy would weaken her nerve. The women in the office called after her with words of encouragement, while Jerry and Ed carried on some more about female chauvinists. Those taunts didn't bother Kasey. She'd spent enough time observing her big brother to know that women had a long way to go before they caught up with the guys in that department.

What bothered her was fear, plain and simple. In theory, she was perfectly willing to do her share of ogling and assertive date-making. But to begin with Sam…that was more of a challenge than she could have envisioned in her wildest dreams.

If she could carry this off, though, without his ever knowing that she was the scrawny little pest he'd dunked in the pool all those years ago, that would be amazing. Making Sam drool would be more than a feather in her Bad Girl's cap. Snagging the attention of a guy like Sam would be on the order of a damned plume.

CHAPTER TWO

ALTHOUGH SAM REQUIRED his workers to wear earplugs when they used the saw, he hated the damn things, so he fudged and left them out whenever he could get away with it. Fifteen feet in the air he could get away with it. That was probably the only reason he heard Carlos yelling at him over the loud buzz.

Turning off the switch with his thumb, he glanced down at his assistant. "What?"

"The lady wants to know if you'd like a bottle of water." Carlos gestured to his left.

Sam pulled off his safety goggles and let them dangle around his neck as he peered through the branches. He almost dropped his saw. It was her, the woman with the red Miata.

Her blond hair gleamed in the morning sun. Not only that, she'd ditched the white jacket. That move was understandable in the heat, but the resulting view of twin beauties outlined by stretch lace had Sam grabbing for a tree limb to steady himself.

She lifted her beautiful face toward him, squinting in the sunlight. "Nice job!"

"Thanks!" Talk about *nice*. He was staring down at the most wonderful view of nice he'd seen in a long time.

"I thought you could use some water!" She held up a plastic bottle.

He could use a whole lot more than water. A cold shower

would be good, and not because he was sweating, either. His strong attraction to her was a little embarrassing, to be honest. By his age he was supposed to be over this sort of reaction to a pretty girl. He'd seen plenty of pretty girls, even plenty of naked pretty girls. Yet he was mesmerized by this particular woman.

Maybe he'd developed heat stroke. He forced himself to engage in normal conversation instead of the caveman-speak that occurred to him. "Sure," he said. "I'd love some water." Now wasn't the time to let her know he had several bottles of the stuff in a large cooler in his truck.

"I'll toss it up," she said.

"No, I'll come down." The way she'd messed with his concentration, he didn't trust his hand-eye coordination right now. Nothing would be worse than missing the bottle she threw up to him.

Correction. Worse would be missing the bottle and falling out of the tree at the same time. Besides risking serious injury to his body, he could destroy his pride forever, not to mention his chances of dating this woman.

He left the saw propped in the tree. Then he took off the goggles and hung them on a branch before grabbing his shirt and pulling it on over his head. At last he started the climb down.

He'd never descended from a tree in front of an audience before, and self-consciousness made him clumsy. His foot slipped and he nearly fell. Grabbing a limb with both hands, he dangled for a humiliating second or two before finally relocating a supporting branch with one foot.

He could imagine Carlos and Murphy snickering behind their hands during this stellar performance. They both knew he had plenty of water in the truck. They knew because he always brought enough for all of them. Dehydration was a real danger working outside in Arizona.

But he was willing to look foolish in front of the guys and accept the bottled water from a woman he desperately wanted to meet. He would have liked to meet her when he was a little less fragrant, but he'd stand downwind of her and hope for the best.

No sense missing a golden opportunity because he was sweaty. If all went as he hoped with this woman, they might end up sweaty together, eventually. Yes, he was getting ahead of himself, but this connection had fate written all over it.

He dropped to the ground and headed toward her, ignoring his two employees. If either of them took this moment to go to his truck and pull a bottle of water out of the ice chest, they'd be on fertilizer duty for the rest of the summer.

"I didn't mean to interrupt your work." Her voice had a silky quality to it.

He liked silky. Silky usually meant a woman had a sensuous nature. "That's okay. I needed to take a break, anyway."

"I'll bet. You look hot."

So do you, sweet thing. Her eyes were a startling shade of blue, possibly helped along by tinted contacts. He liked the blue, although he wondered what color her eyes were, really. "But it's a dry heat."

"Yeah, right." She laughed and held out the dripping bottle. "Here. This should help."

"You're a lifesaver." He took the bottle, his hand brushing hers. He figured that was the idea. She'd obviously brought the water so they could have an interchange. As a way to meet a guy, it was clever.

"That's me," she said. "Kasey Lifesaver."

"Kasey?" He unscrewed the top of the bottle. "Is that all one word or initials?"

"One word. *K-a-s-e-y*. Kasey."

"Nice to meet you Ms. Kasey Lifesaver. I'm Sam Grateful." He took a long drink of the water, gulping down half the bottle. Although he really was thirsty, the drinking moment gave him time to think. He'd ask her to dinner. Yeah, that was a good idea. Dinner. What about tonight? Did he have anything going?

Damn it, he did. The Tin Tarantulas had a gig in a little club downtown, and he'd promised to be there. He didn't think taking a woman to hear his brother's very loud rock band was right for a first date. So he'd ask for tomorrow night, although he hated to wait that long.

He took one last swallow, lowered the bottle and smiled at her. "Thanks. That was great."

"You're welcome."

"Listen, in exchange for the water, how about if I—"

"So how come you climb around in the tree? Wouldn't it be safer to use one of those cherry-picker things?"

Obviously he hadn't impressed her with his coordination. "You mean because I almost took a header a minute ago? Usually I'm smoother than that."

"You did give me a scare, but that isn't what I meant. It seems dangerous to me, being up in the tree with a chain saw."

"Well, I'm a professional." That sounded stuffy, so he grinned and added, "Don't try this at home."

"Don't worry about that! Just watching you makes me nervous."

"Don't be. I've logged a lot of hours in plenty of trees." But her comment made him realize she probably worked in the office next to this tree and had been observing him from her window. That was gratifying. "I do use a cherry picker for some jobs, like palms and eucalyptus, but for big mesquites like this with an elaborate canopy, I'd rather get right into the tree so I can see how it needs to be shaped."

"Oh." She glanced over at the mesquite. "I guess there's more to it than I thought."

"Believe me, there's more to it than I thought when I first started out." He didn't want to talk about his work, though. He wanted to ease back around to the subject of having dinner tomorrow night. "Listen, would you—"

"Are you by any chance free for dinner tonight?"

Oh, hell. Now she'd beaten him to it. "Not tonight, but tomorrow night, I'd love to."

She hesitated. "Well, tomorrow night I have this…thing. Maybe the next night…no, wait a minute, there's—"

"Hold on." He could see they were losing steam, and he didn't want that. "Let me tell you what I have to do tonight. You might be willing to go with me."

"Okay." She looked wary. "What is it?"

"My little brother has this rock band, and they're playing tonight at the Cactus Club. It's not exactly my kind of music—they appeal to a younger crowd, but this is an important gig, and I want to show my support, so I promised I'd be there."

Instead of making a face, she actually looked interested. "What's the name of the band?"

"The Tin Tarantulas. I'm sure you've never heard of them."

"But I have! I heard them play when I was…um, when I just happened to be down at ASU last year. It was an open-air kind of performance. I…the college kids really seemed to love their music." She combed her hair back with both hands, a gesture that jiggled her breasts under the lacy top. "I wouldn't mind going, if that's your question."

"It's my question." He was careful not to let his gaze rest where it wanted to and looked into her eyes, instead. "So that wouldn't be too painful? We can have dinner first, of course, but I need to be at the Cactus Club by nine. Colin expects me to show up."

"That'll work." She smiled. "And don't forget I asked you to dinner, so that part's on me."

"Okay." He was so wrapped up in her smile that he didn't care to debate who would pick up the check. Her lips, decorated in the same shade of red as her car, made him think of hot kisses. But what made her mouth even more fascinating to him, a man who loved details, was the tiny scar in one corner.

It was so faint that someone would have to look close to notice, but that little scar made her unique, and he liked that. Maybe tonight he'd ask her how she got it. He loved hearing those kinds of stories about people. It gave him a handle on who they were.

"How about if I pick you up around seven?" she asked.

He thought about that and laughed. "That's okay. I'll drive. I'd probably need a shoehorn to get myself into your car."

She gazed at him. "How do you know that?"

Uh-oh. Oh, well. Confession was good for the soul. "I saw you get out of your car this morning."

"Really?" The light dawned. "Were you the person who honked?"

"I accidentally hit the horn." *Leaning forward to get a better view of your tush.* "Sorry if I startled you."

"I just thought somebody was trying to get my attention. But when no one called out my name, I figured it wasn't for me."

It was all for her, but he'd eat grubs before admitting that. "I didn't know your name then." He laughed. "I still only know half of it, Ms. Lifesaver."

She held out her hand. "Kasey Braddock."

He wiped his on his jeans. "Sam Ashton." He noted that her handshake was firm and her skin felt cool and incredibly soft. She met his gaze during the brief moment of touching, and he enjoyed the warmth of their eye contact.

What a great custom, the handshake. Sam thought of it as a sample of who the person was, like a taste of an ice-cream flavor served on a tiny pink spoon. In this instance, the sample made him want to take home a gallon's worth of Kasey Braddock.

KASEY WAS CONVINCED that Sam had no clue they'd ever met. After she gave him her full name and he didn't react, she knew she was home free. Of course, she hadn't expected him to react. He'd remember a buddy named Jim Winston, but the last name of Braddock shouldn't ring any bells for him.

"So I'll pick you up, then," he said.

Kasey hesitated, wondering if an assertive woman would insist on doing the driving, even if her car was a tight fit for her date. No, she'd let him drive. She knew the Miata was small, and Sam wasn't.

"Or maybe you'd rather meet at the restaurant," he said, obviously misinterpreting her reluctance. "After all, you don't really know me, so maybe you'd rather not give out your address to a perfect stranger."

But she did know him. Still, she couldn't say that. "You're Sam Ashton, so either this is your business or you're working for a relative."

"It's my business."

She'd thought as much from the way he'd talked about his work with the tree. "Then I can't believe you'd jeopardize your professional reputation by turning into some kind of stalker. I'd be glad to have you pick me up."

He smiled. "I promise I won't bring a truck."

"I'm not a car snob. You could bring a truck."

"Glad to hear it, but I'll bring my car, anyway. So let's head over to the truck and I'll locate a pen and paper."

"Okay." She walked beside him to the truck and trailer parked in the street next to the building, with orange cones set around it to divert traffic. Now she could see it was the same truck that had been parked behind her this morning. She liked knowing that he'd watched her get out of her car.

He opened the passenger door, grabbed a clipboard and closed the door again, but not before she noticed a cooler on the floor of the cab.

"Um, what's in the cooler?" she asked, thinking she already knew the answer.

He grinned sheepishly. "Bottles of water."

"I see."

"I couldn't very well tell you I didn't need that water after you'd gone to so much trouble, could I?"

"You could have." But knowing that he'd wanted to take the excuse to talk to her did a lot to calm her nerves. Maybe she was better at snagging a guy's attention than she'd thought. "But I'm glad you didn't."

"Me, too."

After giving him her phone number and address, she decided to get the heck out of there before she screwed something up. So far, so good, but her luck might not hold much longer. "See you at seven, then," she said.

"Absolutely."

She turned and walked toward the building, wondering if he was watching her. She did her damned best to walk like an experienced temptress. And she was well on her way to becoming one after successfully completing Phase One of the operation. Maybe her little red car had something to do with it, if he'd taken the time to notice her in the parking lot this morning. She thought of her license plate and wondered if he'd seen that, too.

The members of her family, especially her brother Jim, were not fans of that license plate. They'd predicted it would get her into trouble. No doubt they also wondered if that was exactly what she'd intended.

Her sexual experience so far couldn't be classified as getting into trouble. Losing her virginity in college—to another nerd—had been more of a social experiment than a night of grand passion. About a year and a half ago, she'd decided she needed a makeover to attract sexier dates, and Alicia had been there to help.

Coincidentally, her parents had sold the house she'd grown up in and moved to a condo in Gilbert, a good hour away. That small degree of separation had given her a surprising sense of freedom and had made changing her image even easier. By the time she'd started work at Beckworth Public Relations, she'd been transformed into glam girl.

To give her confidence a boost, she'd ordered the vanity plate. She'd told herself that any day now she'd start getting into that trouble her family was so worried about. Well, apparently she was going to start with Sam.

SEVERAL HOURS LATER, while dressing for her date, Kasey mulled over her game plan. After reading a ton of restaurant reviews online and interviewing her coworkers, she'd made reservations at a trendy Italian restaurant within walking distance of the Cactus Club. That way, Sam wouldn't have to worry about finding a downtown parking place twice.

Thank God she had fake ID. She'd felt like a criminal getting one in college, but it had come in handy. It would come in handy again tonight, because she wouldn't be allowed into the Cactus Club without it.

The trick to this evening, Kasey decided, was coaxing Sam to talk about himself. The less he knew about her, the less likely he'd figure out who she was, which could cause complications. Blowing her cover at work was only part of the problem. She didn't relish having Sam contact her brother, who would then fill him in on what his baby sister had been up to or, rather, *hadn't* been up to.

Therefore she wouldn't take this charade too far, only far enough to convince herself that Sam wanted her. This was simply a test of her abilities, one that would erase any lingering feelings of nerdiness she carried around and establish her new babe status for good.

At that point, she'd be ready to enjoy what the world of dating had to offer, maybe even juggling more than one guy at a time. Chances were that Sam, at age thirty, had moved beyond that exploratory stage. She'd seen the change in her brother, who'd been really serious about Alicia and hadn't dated anyone else since the breakup.

As for her, she had no illusions about holding on to Sam and zero interest in lasting relationships. She was only twenty, for crying out loud. No way would she tie herself down until she was really old, as old as her brother. As old as Sam. With tons of sexual experience.

Wiggling into the red slip dress she'd chosen for the evening, she thought about how much experience Sam must have had. A guy who looked like him must have gone horizontal with a bunch of women. She wondered what kind of lover he was.

A picture flashed through her mind—Sam sitting in the emergency room with her, Jim and her mom. Sam, looking remorseful every time he glanced her way. She'd tried to tell him it wasn't his fault, but talking made her mouth bleed, so she'd had to sit there silently and let him suffer. He'd bought her a can of root beer from the pop machine and rounded up a straw so she could drink it without moving her lips.

And then he'd sent the flowers the next day, pink, red and white carnations mixed in with baby's breath and lacy ferns. She knew now that it hadn't been an expensive bouquet, but because it was her first ever, she'd never forgotten how it had looked or how amazed she'd been when her mother had called her to the door to sign for the delivery. Come to think of it, the vase, her only one, was tucked into a cupboard in her apartment kitchen. She'd taken it when she'd moved away from home.

If he'd been that sweet at eighteen, he could be a wonderful lover with all the experience he'd surely collected since then. But she wouldn't be finding out. Way too risky. Once she'd made him drool, she was outta there and on to her regularly scheduled dating program.

She thought her outfit would be a good start. Alicia would approve of the slip dress, the high-heeled slides, the braided leather jewelry and the upswept hairdo. Sam would never connect her with the kid he'd wrestled with in the pool all those years ago.

Pacing her apartment, she reminded herself that she couldn't be too enthusiastic about the Tin Tarantulas, either. Even though she'd loved their music the one time she'd heard them play, they definitely appealed to the college crowd more than young professionals. And she was a young professional now. She should act slightly bored.

Maybe she needed to practice her slightly bored expression. After returning to her bathroom, she stood in front of the mirror and tried out a sigh and an upward roll of her eyes. Yeah, that was good. A world-weary, tolerant smile, perhaps. Excellent.

Her doorbell rang, and she yelped softly. World-weary disappeared as her heart pumped faster and her palms grew sweaty. Sam Ashton had arrived to take her out for the evening. How amazing was that?

She dried her shaking hands on a towel, took one last glance at her flushed cheeks, and decided she'd have to work on her bored expression later. Right now she looked and felt exactly like that little kid who'd received her first bouquet of flowers twelve years ago.

CHAPTER THREE

SAM STOOD AT Kasey's door holding a dozen first-cut red roses in a cone of green tissue paper. In his early and poor-guy dating years he'd gone for the bargain roses, not understanding that those had been trimmed at least three times and wouldn't last more than a few days. First-cut lasted much longer, long enough to make a real impression.

That's what Sam intended to do. He had a gut feeling about this woman. Although he'd be hard-pressed to explain why she seemed so right for him, he was letting his instincts dictate his actions. Thus the pricey roses on the first date. He wanted to let her know he wasn't kidding around.

When she opened the door and he got a look at her red slip dress and take-me-now shoes, he was doubly glad he'd brought the first-class roses. A woman who looked like Kasey Braddock had seen her share of bouquets, and he wanted his to stand out from the crowd.

"Hi," she said. "Wow, roses."

"And I'm sure glad I picked red." He handed her the bouquet. If she was used to getting flowers, she didn't let on. "I'm guessing it's your favorite color."

"It's my new favorite color. Come in and I'll find a vase for these."

"It should be your favorite color." He stepped inside the door. "You look terrific in it."

"Thanks." She gave him a quick smile. "Have a seat. I'll be back in a sec."

He nodded, although he had no intention of sitting down. He'd be able to get a better view of her apartment if he stood right where he was.

What he saw surprised him a little. It looked like a college pad instead of a career girl's place. Makeshift bookcases of bricks and boards overflowed with paperbacks, hardbacks and what looked like textbooks. A futon took the place of a regular couch, and over it hung posters from various art galleries. The women he'd dated recently had graduated to real furniture and professionally framed prints.

The place was neat enough, but it didn't look as if she'd spent lots of time thinking about decorating. One scraggly pothos in dire need of repotting hung from a hook in the ceiling, and the coffee table looked like a hand-me-down from her parents.

Okay, so she wasn't domestic, wasn't into nest-building. Was that such a problem? Reluctantly he admitted it might be. Nest-building instincts ranked pretty high on his list these days.

Then she walked back into the room holding the flowers, her cheeks flushed and the rosebuds a perfect match for her lipstick, and he forgot about his nest-building requirements. Hell, if this turned into something wonderful, he could build the damned nest. Roles were changing more every day. So what if she didn't own a decent crystal vase and had plunked his roses in a cheap glass one that looked like it had been stashed in a cupboard for years.

"Thank you for the flowers. They're gorgeous." From her expression, anyone would think he'd given her diamonds.

He found her enthusiasm sexy. Maybe she didn't bother

decorating her apartment or buying crystal because she had too many other exciting things in her life, like asking a complete stranger to have dinner with her.

"Okay." She set the vase of flowers on the coffee table and scooped up a small purse from the futon. "I'm ready."

He thought of her license plate. Yep, her vibrant approach to life really turned him on. "Then let's go."

HALFWAY THROUGH THE MEAL, Kasey congratulated herself on how well she was doing. Probably because the restaurant was upscale, the waiter hadn't carded her when Sam had ordered a bottle of red to go with the pasta. She was relieved about that. Although she had the fake ID, she didn't want to use it more than necessary, in case somebody spotted it as bogus.

As per her plan, she'd steered the conversation so they talked about Sam. During the antipasto, she'd confirmed what she already knew, that his family had moved to Oregon right after his senior year in high school. He'd gone to college up there but never could get used to the weather, so he'd decided to come back to Phoenix to build his landscaping business.

With a little prompting, she got him to talk about his business during the main course. She didn't blame him for being proud of what he'd accomplished, creating a thriving enterprise during tough economic times. Besides, she liked listening to him. There was a sexy, husky sound to his voice that hadn't been there when he was eighteen.

"The tree you worked on today looks amazing," she said. "Like a sculpture. How did you learn to do that?"

He put down his wineglass and gazed across the table at her, a little smile on his face. "Oh, I've had a lot of practice. Besides, it's fun. I like climbing trees. It's probably not much different from you designing a PR campaign. How do you go about that, by the way?"

Although it was an innocent enough question, she pegged it as an attempt to switch the topic to her. "Trust me, it's not half as interesting as what you do. So, what's the biggest landscaping challenge you've ever had?"

He grinned at her. "I'm beginning to think you've dated a bunch of egomaniacs."

"Why?"

"Oh, just the way you've made sure we talked about me all the time. Maybe the other guys wanted to bask in that constant limelight, but I'd love to hear something about you."

"I'm… I'm not all that fascinating." It was a truthful statement. She was hoping to *become* fascinating, but that would require more seasoning. He was to be part of the process, although he didn't know that.

"Come on. A woman who drives a red convertible with such an interesting license plate?"

So here was the fatal flaw in her plan. With the car, the dress, even the shoes, she'd presented herself as a daring *Sex and the City* kind of girl. She'd hoped that concentrating on him would prevent the spotlight from being turned on her. Spotlights picked up discrepancies. She wondered what she could offer up that would fit the image she'd projected without telling him too much.

Then she remembered her current project at work. "Well, right now I'm designing an image makeover for Slightly Scandalous."

His eyebrows rose. *"Really."*

"So you know the place?"

"Um, yeah, I've heard of it."

From his initial reaction she thought he'd had more intimate contact than that. At any rate, sexy underwear seemed to be a savvy topic that went with the red car and the license plate. She'd get some mileage out of it.

"They've seen how well Victoria's Secret is doing," she said, "and they want some of that market. They've rented mall space and they want a classier image when they move."

"So how do you do that? I mean, when I think of Slightly Scandalous, I think of G-strings and those bras with the cutouts…everywhere."

Having him mention such things changed the atmosphere of the table, and maybe that's what she needed. She wouldn't get him to drool over a discussion about trimming trees. "Exactly. It's all about branding. If I do my job right, when you think of Slightly Scandalous, you'll picture a runway model in silk underwear that's decent enough to be shown on national TV and yet still very sexy."

"So they're giving up on the other stuff?" He sounded disappointed.

"Pretty much. There's a niche market for the over-the-top lingerie, but apparently they were struggling to capture that." She decided a happening chick would be bold. "Face it, did you ever go in there?"

A flush stole up from the open collar of his silk shirt. "Maybe I should plead the Fifth on that one."

Which meant he had bought naughty lingerie at some time, for some woman in his life. Kasey wondered what that would be like, having a man like Sam bring her a present of underwear that he expected her to model for him. The idea gave her goose bumps.

"I have the feeling I've just incriminated myself," he said.

"Not at all." But he'd made himself seem even sexier, if that was possible. She reminded herself to keep playing the role of sophisticated city girl. "I know men have fantasies."

His gaze intensified. "I've been told women have them, too."

"Well, of course." She sounded nervous, damn it. She decided to retreat a little. "That's what my project's about, tapping into women's fantasies instead of catering to a man's. Women usually want their fantasies packaged more subtly."

"How about you? How do you like your fantasies packaged?"

I'm looking at it. "Oh, I'm probably like most women."

"I seriously doubt that. Play fair, now. I've pretty much admitted to buying something at Slightly Scandalous. The least you can do is confess that you've worn something from there."

As if. "Uh, well, I—"

"Your pink cheeks are giving you away, Kasey." He smiled. "I know a bad girl when I see one. But for the record, wearing an outfit from Slightly Scandalous is okay with me."

She knew she was in over her head. But the thing was, she'd nearly accomplished her mission. Sam looked like a man who could hardly wait to get her alone.

Picking up her goblet, she borrowed his line. "I'll have to take the Fifth on that." Then she drained the glass before setting it back on the table.

He let out a breath. "You know how to turn a man inside out, don't you?" He picked up the wine bottle and refilled her glass.

She made a command decision not to drink another drop. Finishing off her glass had seemed like a big-girl sort of gesture, but now she was feeling light-headed and giggly. Any more of that delicious red stuff and she was liable to tell Sam her entire life story. Nope, she'd stick with water from here on out.

In fact, a drink of water might settle her jumpy nerves. The way Sam was looking at her, she had the feeling she'd started something she might not be ready to finish. She picked up her water glass and took a cooling swallow.

"I've been dying to ask you—how did you get that little scar on your lip?"

She choked on the water. As an unplanned distraction, it worked well. Sam was out of his seat in no time, patting her back and murmuring words of concern.

Gradually she could breathe again, and she begged him to go back to his seat. Other diners had begun to stare and even the waiter had come by to make sure she was all right.

Sam eased back into his chair. "Sure you're okay?"

"Fine. Just embarrassed. You'd think by now I'd have learned how to swallow water."

"I hope it wasn't something I said."

"No, no, nothing like that."

"If mentioning that little scar upset you, I'm really sorry."

"Goodness, no. It's an old childhood injury. Most of the time I forget it's even there." She'd always cherished that scar, though, because it reminded her of Sam. He really had been her fantasy guy for years. That was one negative thing about running into him again. Chances were he wouldn't be able to live up to the image she'd created for him.

"I'll bet you were goofing around on the playground equipment," he said.

"Something like that." And they needed to get off this subject before she let some detail slip.

"I remember wrestling with my buddy's kid sister years ago in their swimming pool. I got too rough and she ended up needing stitches. I felt like a jerk."

She had to work very hard not to react. "You shouldn't have. I'm sure it wasn't intentional."

"Yeah, but I should have been more careful. She was just a kid—only about seven or eight. I can't even remember her name, but I can still see that little face, with an ice pack crammed against her mouth."

"I'm sure she recovered." *Although she missed you dreadfully and carried you in her heart for years.*

"Oh, I'm sure she did, too. I checked with my buddy after a couple of months, to make sure. But then he went into the service and we lost track of each other. I haven't tried to find him since I got back. I should. Maybe that's why we're having this conversation, to remind me to look up my old buddy Jim and see if he's back in town."

And Kasey couldn't stop him from doing that, either. One evening with Jim could be enough to blow her cover. She might as well enjoy this date with Sam, because there was a good chance she'd never have another one.

BY THE END OF THE MEAL, Sam hadn't made much progress in getting to know Kasey. And he wanted to get to know her, because physically she was driving him crazy. In the old days he would have given in to that physical urge and figured that he'd get around to the friendship part later. Now that seemed backward to him. He wanted to establish a relationship first.

Kasey wasn't helping. Being a mystery woman seemed to appeal to her, and that attitude had one-night stand written all over it. Maybe that's what she had in mind. After all, she'd made the first move and she'd insisted on paying for dinner. He'd tried to get the check, but she'd outmaneuvered him.

So maybe he was designated as her boy-toy for the night. He wasn't about to fall in with that plan. Of course he wasn't. Not even if he did find himself staring at her mouth and longing to stare at her cleavage.

He wanted to touch her…all over. As they left the restaurant, he settled for holding her hand. Even that simple contact aroused him. He should be offended at the idea that she might want him just for sex and nothing more. Instead he was challenged by it.

Unfortunately, the next part of the evening wouldn't allow much conversation between them. He had about three blocks before they'd be drawn into the noisy world of the Cactus Club. After that, they'd have to read lips.

"Do your folks live in Phoenix?" he asked, trying yet again.

"Uh, no. Gilbert."

"That area sure is growing. Is that where you went to school?"

"Not exactly. Whoops, the light's about to change. We'll have to hurry to make it." She tugged at his hand.

He resisted. "Maybe I don't care."

"Oh." She gave him a wary glance. "All right. We can wait until the light changes."

He decided the time had come for some gentle persuasion. Taking her other hand, he pulled her closer. "Kasey, why are you hiding from me?"

She laughed. "Hiding? Why would you say that?"

"Because every time I try to learn something about you, you find a way to avoid answering." He released his grip on her hands and cupped her shoulders. What silky skin she had. "I want to get to know you." He wondered if he was imagining the quick look of panic in her eyes.

Then it was gone, and she smiled. "In what way?"

In every way. "You know—the kinds of things you liked to do as a kid, the type of music you like, whether you have a favorite team or hate sports altogether."

"I like baseball, and my favorite team is the Diamondbacks."

"Me, too." But out of all the things he'd asked, she'd picked the least personal one to answer. Most everyone in Phoenix liked the home team. Nevertheless, although he really knew nothing more than he had before, he found himself caressing her shoulders and wanting to kiss her. Theoretically, he shouldn't get involved in a kiss with a woman who held her cards so close to her chest.

But what a chest it was, and he longed to know how it felt locked against his. "Okay, that's a start." He drew her closer. "How about music?"

"I like everything."

"Everything?" He couldn't take his gaze from her mouth. So tempting. "Even rap?"

"Some rap is okay."

He loved the way her lips rounded as she said the *o* in *okay.* "Can you sing?" It was a goofy question, but he was so focused on her mouth it seemed semilogical.

"Not very well." She looked up at him. "Can you?"

"Not very well." Then temptation overtook him. Forgetting why he didn't want to do this yet, he leaned down and kissed her.

And what a mistake that was, because she kissed him back. She might not want to tell him anything about herself, but she was perfectly willing to kiss him as if the end of the world had arrived. Her lips parted, her tongue became involved, and when he wrapped his arms around her and pulled her close, she settled against him with a soft moan of delight.

As kisses went, this one topped the charts. He tasted hunger as strong as his own, which filled his mind with all sorts of ideas he wasn't supposed to be having. In fact, much more of this kiss and they were liable to get themselves arrested. He pulled back with difficulty and looked into her eyes to double-check that he hadn't misread her level of involvement. Yep—eyes glazed, chest heaving, body quivering. Just like his.

"I...had a feeling about this," he said.

"N-not me."

"Boy, I did. Sometimes there's just...something between two people." Now there was a profound statement. Sheesh. He rubbed his hands up and down her arms, as if trying to restore the circulation, which was ridiculous. Judging from her reaction, her circulation was currently excellent. Speaking for himself, he could feel the blood whipping through his veins and arteries at warp speed.

"Something explosive." She still sounded out of breath.

"Right. But I believe in getting to know each other first."

She cleared her throat. "Okay."

"Unfortunately, going to my little brother's event won't give us much chance for that. The noise level will be horrific. And I can't leave too early or he'll think I didn't like it."

"Then we need to go and stay as long as necessary."

"I'm afraid so. But after that..." He didn't dare put what he was thinking into words. He hoped she was thinking exactly the same thing.

"After that, we'll...we'll see what happens."

So she wanted to hedge a little. He didn't buy her act. He'd been there during the fireworks and he knew she was flammable. "I think we both can guess what will happen, given half a chance."

"I thought you wanted to get to know me first."

"I do." He gave her a quick, hard kiss. "And I will."

CHAPTER FOUR

SOMEHOW KASEY CROSSED the street without getting run over. That probably had something to do with Sam's tight grip on her hand and his take-charge attitude. Thank goodness he was watching out for them, because she was too dazed by that kiss to notice traffic signals.

So when had kissing become such a big deal? She'd kissed guys before and been able to analyze the process in clinical detail, even during the act itself. She'd evaluated kissing techniques and rated them for firmness, taste and the all-important slipperiness factor. Then she'd taken into account the groping, or lack of groping, and whether that added to the experience or detracted.

Then along came Sam with a kiss that destroyed every analytical brain cell she possessed. Instead of being a mildly amusing mouth exercise, this kiss had thrown her into the center of a tornado where she'd clung helplessly to Sam as winds of lust tugged at her from every angle. Whatever he was offering, she wanted to be first in line.

All her sexual experiences so far had been motivated by curiosity. This driving urge was nothing like that. There was desperation mixed in with carnal desire, as if she might go crazy if she couldn't satisfy the need he'd created with one simple kiss. No, not *simple*. That had been a very complicated kiss. Because of it, she had to reevaluate her entire campaign.

Her original plan had included more control. She'd

judged her ability to stay in control based on her experiences with men so far. She hadn't factored in a kiss that would turn her knees to jelly. She'd always thought that was a silly expression, someone's wild exaggeration of normal sexual impulses.

Apparently not. Apparently there were men like Sam who could accomplish the knees-to-jelly thing. Who knew? In any case, she had a combustible situation on her hands. He wanted to sleep with her. That was the good part, because she really had made him drool. The bad part was that she wanted to sleep with him, too.

So now what? A big juicy flirtation was what she'd intended. A full-blown affair hadn't been part of the equation. Obviously that's what he wanted, though.

And so did she, but it wouldn't be a wise move. In fact, it would be an extremely foolish move. The deeper her involvement, the more likely he'd find out who she was. She didn't want that to happen.

Instead, she wanted to be the sexy mystery woman who got away. She might still be able to pull that off, but she'd have to keep her wits about her. No more of those high-octane kisses. And this would be their one and only date.

By the time she'd reached that conclusion, Sam had opened the door to the Cactus Club. A warm-up band had already taken the stage and the air vibrated with the sound of drums and acoustic guitars.

Kasey dug into her small purse and pulled out her fake ID. Showing it always made her nervous, but tonight provided a double dose of angst. Nothing could be more embarrassing than getting busted in front of Sam. Fortunately the interior was dim, the guy checking ID knew Sam, and there was no special scrutiny of her card.

"Colin's saved you a table up front," the guy said, leaning close to be heard above the music. "He also said the first round's on him."

"We'll see about that," Sam said with a smile. Then he guided Kasey to an empty table right next to the crowded dance floor.

Once there, he held her chair and leaned down to speak directly into her ear. "What do you want to drink?"

She turned to answer him and her mouth nearly collided with his. When she pulled back, he caught her chin with his hand.

"Hey, there." He stayed in close, a gentle smile on his face. "You're not having a shyness attack, are you?"

Shy was the last word she wanted him to associate with her. "Not in the least." She smiled back. "But I didn't want to be the cause of you getting teased, in case your brother's around."

"Let me worry about that." His expression grew warmer and he stroked her chin with his thumb. "I sure wish we didn't have to be here."

"But we do."

"Yeah. So what do you want?"

She'd watched enough movies and read enough books to know that a happening chick would pick up on that opening. "Whatever you're offering, Sam."

He groaned. "Later. Later you can have whatever you want. Right now all I can give you is a drink."

"Mineral water, then."

His smile widened. "I like that. A woman who wants to stay alert. I think I'll have the same."

"Don't abstain on my account."

"Oh, it's completely on your account. Normally I enjoy the band much more when I'm a little sloshed. But for tonight, I'll forgo that crutch."

"For heaven's sake, at least have a beer."

"Nope." He shook his head. "Considering what's at stake later on, this will be no sacrifice."

Her heart beat like crazy as she absorbed his meaning. If only she could go with the flow, but she didn't dare, not with this man. "You seem to have forgotten about getting acquainted first."

"No, I haven't." He dropped a slow, lingering kiss on her lips.

She couldn't stop him without making a scene. And from that first magic taste, she didn't want to stop him. Once again, she was lost to the world. The music faded and the crowd noise disappeared. There was only the sweet pressure of his mouth on hers, and she wanted more, so much more....

He ended the kiss and took a shaky breath. "There."

She opened her eyes, feeling like Sleeping Beauty. But this was no fairy tale and she was not going to be swept away by the handsome prince. Not if she could help it.

"I know you better already," he murmured.

"You can't find out anything from a kiss."

"Sure I can. For example—"

"Can I take your order, sir?" called out a waiter who'd appeared behind Sam.

Kasey glanced over Sam's shoulder and caught the waiter's eye. He winked at her. Being with Sam had already elevated her status. No waiter had ever winked at her before.

Sam straightened and turned around. As he gave the guy their order, Kasey took a moment to dredge up some of her famous self-discipline. She hadn't graduated from college at eighteen by allowing distractions to ruin her game plan. This was no different. Well, it was a little bit different. Okay, it was a *lot* different.

But if she'd been disciplined in her studies, she could be disciplined in limiting the amount of kisses that went on. No, not limiting—eliminating. She couldn't afford any more moments of oblivion. She quickly reviewed her list of reasons and vowed to keep them firmly in mind.

Sam took his seat across from her and plopped the waiter's ordering pad on the small table.

She raised her voice to make herself heard. "What are you doing with that?"

"Borrowed it for a while!" He scribbled something on the pad, tore off the top sheet and handed it across the table, along with the pen he'd apparently scrounged from the waiter.

She glanced at the paper, where he'd written, "Are you a morning person or a night person?" She started to laugh. No wonder he'd built a successful business. He was an extremely resourceful guy. She admired that in people, and she was gradually coming to admire Sam, not to mention wanting to jump his bones.

After writing "night person" on the paper, she handed it back. That kind of information shouldn't get her in trouble. Mainly she had to avoid biographical information like where she went to high school, which was also his high school.

Sam wrote "me, too" under her answer and held it up so she could see it. He seemed pleased to have that in common, but then he probably expected this was the start of something spectacular. She was starting to feel guilty, because it wouldn't be the start of anything. Unfortunately, she thought of him as sexual training wheels, and that wasn't fair to him or any guy. Maybe she should give some excuse about hating the music and make her exit.

She didn't need to hang around any more to see she had temptress potential or even to have stories for the women at the office. Her goal of making him want her had been accomplished and then some. She'd earned her first stripe as a Bad Girl, so she could stop the charade now.

He would be hurt and confused, would probably try to contact her again, but she could handle that. What she couldn't handle was getting in deeper with him and then forcing herself to back away. Right now she'd inflict only superficial wounds on his ego, but the longer she played this game, the worse it would be on him.

Meanwhile Sam was busy writing another question. He pushed the paper across the table and tossed her the pen.

This was her chance to leave. All she had to do was flip the page over and write "Have to go—music's giving me a headache." He wouldn't be able to leave with her, not when his brother's band was about to take the stage. He'd probably call her a cab, and that would be that.

If she meant to leave, she shouldn't read whatever question he'd come up with, because the question wouldn't matter. But she'd been born with an extremely inquisitive mind. The trait had been a blessing for the most part, but was a curse, now.

Chastising herself for doing it, she read his question. "What was your favorite book when you were seven years old?" Damn it, she knew she shouldn't have read his question. He wasn't just playing at this get-acquainted business. He really wanted to know who she was. Okay, she'd answer his question, and maybe that would send him running for the hills.

She picked up the pen and wrote "*Megatrends for Women*. Yours?" Then she scooted the paper across the table and waited for his reaction, the reaction she usually got from all except the genius-level guys.

Sure enough, his eyes widened and he glanced up. She could almost read his thoughts—*system alert: braniac in the house*. Then he smiled and picked up the pen. He continued to smile as he wrote down his favorite book and added another line, maybe another question.

When he pushed the paper over to her, she hesitated before picking it up. She was supposed to be out of here by now. Instead she was still trading notes with Sam. But she had to find out what he'd written, and what his next question would be. Without realizing it, he'd chosen a method of communication that tapped right into her curious nature. She found the suspense contained in each note irresistible.

Glancing down, she read "*Goodnight, Moon* was my favorite book. I think you're probably a lot smarter than I am. Is that a problem for you?" She looked up and saw the uncertainty in his expression. He wasn't rejecting her because of her brains—he was afraid she'd reject him.

Her heart turned over. She couldn't leave now. Instead she wrote "No way" across the bottom of the page and gave it back to him.

His face relaxed into another broad smile and he flipped the paper over to write something across the back. This time he didn't give her the pen, only the small sheet of paper.

When she read what he'd written, her pulse rate jumped. "I promise to compensate in other areas." Sweet heaven, the man was ready to guarantee that he'd love her so well she wouldn't care about his IQ.

THE TIN TARANTULAS' opening number put an end to the note writing for a while, but that was okay with Sam. Thanks to that maneuver, he was getting a handle on Kasey Braddock. What he'd taken as a standoffish attitude might be related to her heavy-duty smarts.

She hadn't wanted him to know she was a brain. Understandable. He wasn't oblivious to the problems that could have caused with the opposite sex once she started dating.

Some guys reacted poorly if they found out a woman was more intelligent than they were.

Sam happened to think it was cool. He liked hanging out with smart people. He'd discovered that early in his life during interactions with Colin, who had inherited more brains than he had. When discussing things with Colin, he sometimes lost his way in the conversation, but he was never bored. So if Kasey didn't mind the gap in mental abilities, he sure as hell didn't.

Good thing he'd thought up the note idea, or he might never have found out her secret. She must have decided to test him when he asked about her favorite book as a kid. Maybe she'd thought that would be the end of the attraction for him.

It was far from the end. This woman had beauty *and* brains. What a combo. He'd also decided something else about Kasey. She wasn't nearly as sophisticated as she wanted everyone to believe.

He wondered if she'd gone through school as a nerd, then transformed herself when she got into the working world. Tinted contacts, a different hairstyle, a new wardrobe, a sexy little car—they could be the props of her new image.

In the PR business, her brains wouldn't get her shunned, they'd get her promoted. In the dating game, unfortunately, there were still a lot of men who had to feel superior to woman in all ways. Kasey might have bumped up against a few of those, so she was careful how much she revealed about herself. And she might not have had the busy social life he'd imagined.

All that was good news as far as he was concerned. If she was searching for a guy who appreciated everything about her, including all that mental firepower, Sam was her man. This was turning into a very exciting evening, and it wasn't even half-over.

At one point Kasey leaned across the table to ask which member of the band was his brother, and Sam pointed him out. That reminded him that watching Colin was the reason he was here, and he needed to pay better attention. Colin played lead guitar. The band included a bass guitarist, drummer and a keyboard player who was also the vocalist.

The dress code for the Tin Tarantulas was black. Anything was acceptable if it was the color of soot. T-shirts, silk shirts, cargo pants and bell-bottoms appeared in various combinations.

Colin wore low-slung jeans and a plain black T-shirt. His long black hair flew in all directions and his gold earrings caught the light as he went wild on his electric guitar. The in-your-face musical style obviously satisfied the customers filling the tiny dance floor and crowding around the tables.

Sam hoped Kasey was tolerating it okay. At the end of the first number she applauded with such enthusiasm that he couldn't believe she was faking it. Much to his amazement, she actually seemed to like the music. That was a bonus—a surprising bonus, but a bonus nevertheless. He'd been afraid she'd be suffering through this club scene.

Instead, she tapped her feet and moved in time with the music. He was so fascinated watching her that it took a few minutes before he figured out she might want to dance. Standing, he held out his hand.

She seemed startled, and then quickly shook her head. "That's okay," she murmured. Immediately she stopped tapping her feet and twitching in response to the beat.

He leaned closer so he wouldn't have to shout. Man, did she smell good. "Oh, come on," he coaxed. "I'm no twinkle toes, myself."

"I'm definitely not a twinkle toes." She folded her hands on the table, as if that would keep her from moving with the music.

"Look, the floor's so small, all we have room to do is stand there and wiggle."

Apparently that got to her. She glanced up at him and grinned. "I'm going to risk embarrassing myself just so I can watch you do that."

"Good deal." He pulled her to her feet and they edged onto the crowded floor.

He hadn't done this kind of bump and grind in a while, so he felt a little self-conscious, but he wanted to give her every reason to let loose. That meant forgetting that his little brother was up on the stage and would no doubt comment on his dance moves at great length. Sam surrendered to that inevitability and began to shake his booty.

And praise the Lord, so did Kasey. She started out with small, tight movements, but when Sam challenged her by exaggerating his own moves, she laughed and threw herself into it. Before long she was making those gorgeous breasts of hers shimmy.

Sam wanted to stop dancing and simply watch, but then she might stop, too, and he couldn't have that. So he kept dancing and encouraging her with laughter and smiles. She was amazing. If he'd ever thought the bass was too loud, he didn't think so now. That rhythm echoed through his body and hers, linking them together in a way that was almost like sex.

He'd never danced like this in his life, not even when he was drunk. Tonight he was dancing under the influence, though—the influence of Kasey, a woman who knew how to shake his world.

CHAPTER FIVE

Kasey abandoned her slightly bored routine. She'd loved the bold music played by the Tin Tarantulas when she'd heard them at ASU. Sitting right up front at the Cactus Club, where the beat felt like tennis balls bouncing in her veins, made her long to move with it. But she hadn't meant to dance.

Then Sam had proposed that they could stand there and wiggle, as he'd put it, and she'd been unable to resist seeing how he'd look on the dance floor. Passing up that chance might lose her the Bad Girl's stripe she'd already earned. As it turned out, Sam knew how to wiggle.

Watching him lose himself to the music tripped a switch in her, and she abandoned herself to the heavy beat. Back in school she'd danced away her stress alone in the privacy of her dorm room where no one could comment on what she looked like doing it. Tonight the combination of the dress, the shoes and Sam gave her the confidence to shake it up in public.

When no one seemed to be pointing and laughing, she let herself go a little more with each number. What fun. What a huge relief to know she could play with the big boys and girls at the nightclub.

Sam looked at her as if he'd like to find a more secluded playground for just the two of them. She didn't know how she'd deal with that hunger in his eyes, especially because dancing to the wild beat was turning her on, too. But for now she wanted to revel in the feeling that she owned this dance floor. She'd never felt that way, and it was a big step in her evolution from nerd girl to hot babe.

They danced until the band took a break, then collapsed into their seats, panting. Taped music took over, but it wasn't nearly as loud or boisterous, so the dance floor emptied. She gave up on keeping her hair tidy and took the pins out so it fell to her shoulders.

Sam wiped his forehead with a napkin. "I'm getting too old for this."

That brought her up short. He thought he was getting too old for dancing at the Cactus Club, and she'd just found her dancing feet. She had to be realistic. No matter how wonderfully he kissed, he was too old for her, or she was too young for him, whichever way she looked at it.

But she wanted him to believe she was a contemporary, so she nodded. "I know what you mean."

He smiled at her. "I doubt it. You look fresh as a daisy. Like you can hardly wait for the band to start up again."

"I like how they play." She might as well admit that. After the way she'd reacted to their tunes, she couldn't pretend indifference now.

"And I'm glad you do!" Hair flying around his shoulders, Colin arrived. He grabbed a vacant chair, turned it backward and sat down between them. Then he stuck out his hand. "Hi, I'm Colin, the wayward little brother."

Kasey shook his hand. "Kasey Braddock. Your music's great." She figured he was in his early twenties, much closer to her age than Sam was. In theory, he'd make a more compatible date for her. When he wasn't onstage he'd be happy to dance the night away in a place like this. So why did she look at Colin and think he was way too young for her?

"Nice job, bro," Sam said. "Everyone seems to be eating this up with a spoon."

Colin beamed. "Yeah, I think they like us. Of course, all the guys made their friends come, but we counted familiar faces and only about half are people we know. The word must be getting out."

"It should," Kasey said. "I saw you when I happened to be down at ASU last year, and you gathered quite a crowd then."

"Yeah." Colin frowned. "I wish we coulda built on that, but we had some equipment problems."

Sam's jaw tightened. "Somebody swiped their amplifiers."

"And no insurance, 'cause we couldn't afford it." Colin clapped his hand on his brother's shoulder. "The big guy here saved the day and bought us new speakers, even though..." Colin paused and leaned closer to Kasey. "Don't tell anybody, but he really doesn't like our music."

"I do so like your music!" Sam looked offended. "When did I ever say I didn't?"

Colin grinned. "You don't have to say anything. It's the three beers you usually drink while we're playing that tipped me off. You aren't that much of a drinker." He picked up the glass of mineral water in front of Sam. "What's this, straight vodka?"

Sam folded his arms over his chest. "Water. So there. I don't need three beers when I'm listening to you, obviously."

Colin took a drink. "I'll be damned. It *is* water. Maybe you need either beer or a good-looking woman to dance with." He winked at Kasey.

"Quit flirting with my date, squirt." Sam sounded like he was kidding, but his eyes said he wasn't.

"Have I ever done that?"

"Yes, you have."

"Yeah, but not seriously." He turned to Kasey. "Still, I realize it must be embarrassing to hit the dance floor with an old guy like my brother. So if you ever—"

"Hey!" Sam grabbed Colin's shoulder. He was smiling, but his grip was firm and his gaze steady. "Cut it out."

Colin laughed. "Aw, I wouldn't really try to steal her, bro. Just fooling around, teasing the big guy. Listen, I really appreciate you coming out tonight, man. And I want you to order something besides water. Seriously."

"The water was my idea," Kasey said. "Don't blame Sam. We had wine earlier, and I'm not a big drinker, either. But thanks for treating us."

"You're welcome." Colin pushed himself upright. "Wish I could do more." He glanced at Sam, his cockiness replaced by vulnerability. "So how do we sound when you're sober?"

"Amazing." Sam looked into his brother's eyes. "I'll make another contribution to the cause real soon. I have an idea for attracting more landscaping clients, and I'm considering hiring Kasey to help me grab a different part of the market. Kasey's in PR."

"Hiring me?" Kasey panicked. That wouldn't work out at all. "I'm not sure that—"

"Hey, great!" Colin returned the chair to its rightful place and leveled his gaze on his brother. "But don't go thinking you have to do this so you can give the band more money. We're okay."

"Don't worry. I'll figure out a way to make it tax deductible. You'll be doing me a favor."

Kasey scrambled for a reasonable explanation as to why she shouldn't be part of Sam's publicity scheme. "You know, I'm not very informed about landscaping."

"I could bring you up to speed," Sam said.

"Just don't do anything radical, man," Colin said. "I'm the radical one, not you. Well, I gotta head back. Nice meeting you, Kasey."

"Same here." Still trying to gather her thoughts, Kasey watched him walk away in his low-slung pants and black T-shirt. No wonder Sam wanted to help him. He was a nice kid. Then she laughed at herself for thinking that. The nice kid was probably older than she was. And Sam wanted to hire her? She had to talk him out of that.

"Just so you know, he still chews bubble gum."

She swivelled back to discover Sam looking slightly worried, as if he thought there was a chance she'd be more interested in his little brother than in him. Hardly. She'd choose Sam any day ahead of a young guy like Colin, even factoring in Sam's reluctance to spend hours on the dance floor.

But talking about Colin could buy her some time to figure out a detour around this PR idea of his. "Don't tell me you're jealous."

"Jealous? Nah. I just don't want you to act on incomplete information. He's charming and I love him, but he's a flake."

"It's obvious that you love him. He's lucky to have you." She could recommend someone else in the firm for Sam's PR needs, but then she'd still have to see him. She'd have to suggest a totally different firm.

"I can't help worrying about Colin, though." Sam took a drink of his water. "I hope to hell he makes it as a musician, because he's hopeless at a regular day job. I tried to work him into my business, but I had to let him go before he maimed himself. He was using a chain saw to play air guitar and accidentally turned the damn thing on."

"Yikes. Surely the band doesn't bring in enough to support him?"

"No. He's had a bunch of different minimum-wage jobs. He's such a fun guy that he manages to get hired, but then he starts daydreaming and screws up something or other, so he gets fired. He moved down here because he needs family around, and he couldn't stay in Oregon because Mom and Dad were always on him about the job situation. I'm kind of a nag, but not as bad as the 'rents."

"He lives with you, then?"

"Nope. He lives with a couple of band members, who don't mind if he's something of a slob." He smiled at her. "So how'm I doing? Have I managed to discourage you from going out with him?"

"I never intended to go out with him."

"The thought didn't cross your mind at all?"

She shook her head.

"He's smarter than I am."

"So what?"

"And he's absolutely right that you'd have more fun dancing with him."

"I have fun dancing with you." She gazed across the table and forgot all about the PR deal, forgot everything but Sam, the guy she'd dreamed about for twelve years. And now he wanted her enough to fight for her.

The heat generated between them was enough to melt the ice in their glasses. Kasey wondered how on earth she would get out of this evening without kissing him again. And if she gave herself that pleasure, how would she be able to deny herself the pleasures that he'd offer after that?

SAM WAS ASHAMED of himself for making Colin look bad. Although everything he'd said was true, the only reason he'd told Kasey all that was to keep her from getting interested in his little brother. And that was extremely petty.

If Kasey was attracted to Colin, then that should be the end of that.

But she'd said she wasn't attracted, and from the way she was looking at him right now, he believed her. So now his conscience bothered him for saying all those things about Colin, who couldn't help being artistic and a dreamer unfit for regular work.

Sam cleared his throat. "Actually, Colin's a great person to have around," he said. "He's funny and a lot more optimistic than I am. People really enjoy being with Colin."

"That's probably a good thing if he's going to be an entertainer. You need charisma."

"Colin has that in spades."

"You're not so bad in the charisma department, either."

"Me?" Admittedly, he felt more studly when she looked at him like that.

"Uh-huh. I—"

The band chose that moment to start up again, blasting its way into their cozy conversation, so she shrugged and smiled, obviously giving up on trying to be heard. Instead she stood and angled her head toward the dance floor, her eyebrows raised questioningly at him.

"Why not?" He pushed back his chair. A guy with charisma should be able to dance another set. He'd show Colin he wasn't over the hill, not by a long shot.

One loud, fast tune followed another, and the only thing keeping Sam upright and in motion was the sight of Kasey, who seemed perpetually ready to boogie. She had the energy of a teenager. With her skin flushed and her lipstick gone, she even looked like a teenager. She might not appreciate looking young for her age now, but someday she'd be grateful.

Sam, however, was getting tired. Just when he wondered if he would collapse in disgrace, leaving Kasey to dance without him, Colin took the microphone to announce the last number of the night. Even more surprising, he said it would be a slow tune. As Sam sighed with relief, Colin added, "So my big brother can rest up."

If Sam had the energy, he'd climb up onstage and throttle the kid. Instead he turned to Kasey and drew her into his arms. Immediately he felt his vitality returning.

Ah, she was so warm and alive, still breathing fast from all the frenzied dancing. He nestled her head against his shoulder and it fit there perfectly. Then he laid his cheek against her silky hair and breathed in her scent—shampoo and perfume blended into a sweet mixture that made him forget how tired his legs were.

The song lyrics didn't make any sense to him, but then none of the lyrics written by the Tin Tarantulas did. He didn't care, as long as he could sway on the dance floor while holding Kasey tight. He savored the pillowy softness of her breasts pressed against him and the rapid beat of her heart.

She sighed and shifted her position slightly, so that she was even more securely tucked against him. That shift was all it took to put him in arousal mode. He worked to control an impending erection and succeeded…sort of. But if she should move again…

She moved again. Her pelvis rubbed across the fly of his pants. He groaned and fought for control, wondering if she was sending him a signal or if her movements were accidental.

Might as well know. The dance floor was wall-to-wall people, with other couples locked in similar embraces, oblivious to the world. Many of the guys had already taken the kind of liberties Sam was contemplating.

Deciding to go for the gusto, he slipped both hands down Kasey's back and cupped her bottom. And did she ever have a nice one, too. She felt even better than she looked, and that was saying something.

She reacted by snuggling closer. He reacted by getting hard. She couldn't help knowing, either, so the turn of events must be A-OK with her.

The thought came to him that making love to a high-IQ woman probably wasn't much different from making love to a woman with a normal IQ. Hormones made everyone semistupid, anyway. Still, he liked the idea that she was super smart and wanted him anyway. He liked that a lot.

He thought about his house and whether he'd cleaned it up enough before he left. He thought about whether or not he'd made his bed. Then he remembered that she hadn't come across as Ms. Domesticity and that helped him relax a little.

The main thing was whether or not he'd restocked the condoms in the bedside table drawer. He probably had. Although he hadn't had sex in several months, he always lived in hope and always kept a supply of raincoats just in case.

From the feel of things, his hopes were about to be realized.

KASEY HAD NEVER DANCED this way with a man, never pressed herself against him to make absolutely certain that he was rock hard and desperate for her. But she wanted to know that about Sam, because she was quickly reaching a decision that required his complete surrender.

Maybe she wasn't thinking clearly right now. Chances were she wasn't thinking at all. How could a woman think when she was getting hot and ready for the man who currently had his hands splayed over a very tender and erotic part of her anatomy? She could feel the imprint of every finger, and whenever he gave her a squeeze, she nearly climaxed on the spot.

Yet somehow, aroused though she might be, she had to make sure her next move was the right one. Sam had thrown a monkey wrench into her plans when he'd suggested he might hire her. Yes, she could direct him to another firm... *Oh, baby, was he ever firm....*

No, she had to concentrate on this problem, on the erection...er, the direction they should take now. She sensed he might be pigheaded. And hot-blooded. *Oh, yes.* Concentrate, Kasey! He might not take direction, might not go to another company, might insist on hiring her.

But he'd take direction in bed. Mm-hmm, would he ever take direction. And she would be so glad to provide that direction. She had never in her life been so drenched in lust, and if she didn't do something about that, she might end up in the loony bin.

She could see only one way out, both to save her sanity and take care of Sam's misguided plan to hire her as a PR consultant. That way out was through Sam's bedroom. They would have sex tonight—wild, wonderful, satisfying sex. A red haze settled over her brain as she contemplated Sam, naked and willing.

She hadn't meant for tonight to end this way, but he'd given her no choice. The way she saw it—when she could think at all—having sex with him was the only answer. Once they'd spent the night writhing on his sheets, he couldn't possibly consider hiring her for PR work. And once she'd satisfied this burning desire for him tonight, she'd thank him and move on.

Technically she was turning Sam into a one-night stand. She hadn't meant to do that, but, as she'd reasoned out, it was totally his fault.

CHAPTER SIX

ONCE SHE'D REACHED her decision, Kasey focused on making sure Sam was on board. Lifting her head from his shoulder, she wound both arms around his neck and gazed up at him, her eyes half-closed. Leaning back a little allowed her hips to move forward, accentuating the link between them. With the added height of her heels she was positioned exactly right. They could have sex against the nearest wall if everyone else would only disappear.

With his eyes glazed and his jaw rigid, he looked like a man ready to throw everyone else out, but she had to be sure. Earlier he'd spent time talking about how he needed to get to know her before sex could happen between them. She didn't want any last-minute hurdles ruining her plan.

She moistened her lips the way she'd seen models do on television. "Do you think you know me well enough?"

He blinked, as if he hadn't understood the question. "What?" His voice sounded gravelly.

"You said you wanted to get acquainted before we…" She caressed the nape of his neck. "You know."

"Oh. Yeah. I do."

"You mean you remember you said that? Or you think you know me well enough by now?"

"Both." He groaned softly. "You need to quit moving your hips like that."

"I'm just dancing." Yes, he was definitely on board.

"Then please stop dancing. I can't…I don't know how I'll make it back to the table."

"Or down the block to where you parked the car?" She took pity on him and just stood there.

"That, too." He sighed. "Thanks. That's a little better. Oh, hell, the music's ended, and I'm…don't go anywhere, okay?"

"I won't."

"The problem is, feeling you right there keeps me hard, but I can't let you go or everyone on the dance floor will know I'm in this condition. And my little brother's up on that stage."

"You might want to move your hands to a different location. That might help."

"Oh. Good point." He slid both hands up to rest at the small of her back. "But I'm still like a rock."

"Give yourself a minute."

"We don't have a whole lot of time before it seems kind of strange that we're still standing here."

"How have you handled this before?"

His smile was tight. "By sheer force of will. So far with you, I have zero willpower."

She realized that he was right about the time situation. They couldn't stay on the dance floor much longer. The cheers and clapping had subsided and people were returning to their tables. Soon she and Sam would look very weird standing there alone like a sculpture in the park. "Think of something else besides sex."

"I've tried. Doesn't work."

"Then I'll help. What was your worst subject in school?"

"Biology. I got sick to my stomach when we were supposed to dissect those frogs sophomore year."

"Me, too." She'd walked into the lab and walked right out again. "So how did you do in biology?"

"Almost failed the course."

She'd been able to get out of the lab work because she'd been only twelve, and the teacher had accepted a detailed report on the life of a frog instead. "So think about being in that lab, smelling the formaldehyde, picking up the scalpel, starting—"

"Yuck! Okay, you've grossed me out, and I'm much improved." Circling her waist with one arm, he turned and led her off the floor. He paused next to their table. "Hang on a minute while I leave a tip."

"I'm not going anywhere."

"Man, I hope not." He reached for his wallet, took out some bills and laid them next to his water glass. "I hope you weren't teasing me on the dance floor about wanting to continue this elsewhere."

"Nope. Not teasing."

He tucked her in next to him. "Then let's get out of here."

"You don't need to say goodbye to Colin?"

"If I know Colin, he's surrounded by admiring women and he wouldn't appreciate being interrupted while he plays rock star." Sam guided her through the tables toward the front door. "We always connect between sets. After that, we leave each other alone to do our thing."

"I see."

"And as it happens, I have something important to do."

Warmth coursed through her. "As it happens, so do I."

"That's good to hear." He gave her a squeeze. "Because your frog story is already wearing off."

THE NIGHT AIR FELT COOL against Sam's heated skin. That helped a little, but he still set a brisk pace as they covered the distance back to the car. "Am I going too fast?" he asked at one point as the staccato beat of her heels on the sidewalk made him realize she might be struggling to keep up.

"No, you're not going too fast."

Yet maybe he was, in the larger sense. This relationship had progressed to its sexual launching pad much quicker than he would have expected, but he wasn't a strong enough man to call off the countdown now. Besides, a woman as ready as Kasey seemed to be might not appreciate being left to her own devices.

He'd seen the look in her eyes out there on the dance floor. The woman needed to have someone ring her chimes, and she needed it very soon. These days ladies didn't take kindly to having a guy slow down right when they'd planned a race to the finish line.

A breeze picked up. The desert cooled off quickly after the sun went down, and the temperature could go from ninety-plus at noon to sixty at midnight. He was wearing a long-sleeved shirt, but she had no sleeves at all. "Are you warm enough?"

"Believe me, I'm plenty warm."

He chuckled and drew her tighter against his side. "I vouch for that. I'd go as far as to say you're plenty hot."

"I'd say you are, too. So don't slow down on my account, and don't worry about the temperature, either."

"Gotcha. We're making tracks." God, how he loved an eager woman. The way he was starting to see it, he and Kasey needed to get horizontal before they could make any more progress on the friendship front. Sex was getting in the way of having a decent conversation. So they'd take the edge off with a session between the sheets, and then they'd be able to talk, at long last.

He had lots he wanted to talk about, when the time came. Now that he knew she was a brain, he wanted to find out more about her childhood, which might have been way different from his. He wanted to learn about her friends, her family, her hobbies.

Besides that, he'd been serious about hiring her to do some PR. When she'd told him about changing the Slightly Scandalous store's image, it had dawned on him that he had a business that could use an image makeover. That would give him a great excuse to see her, besides potentially setting up more earning capability.

But before they could take care of business or friendship, they had to take care of pleasure. He knew sex would be fantastic with Kasey, especially if she plunged in with the same enthusiasm she'd given to dancing. Within the next hour, they would make each other very happy.

Once in his Mustang, they rode the distance to his university-area bungalow in cozy silence, holding hands across the console except when he had to shift gears. Words didn't seem necessary when they both knew exactly where they were headed and were equally interested in getting there. He didn't even bother with the radio, because the wrong song might come on and change the mood, which at the moment was perfect for what he had in mind.

The weeknight traffic was sparse, but he was careful not to speed even though he might have gotten away with it. He was taking no chances on messing this up. It could turn out to be the best sex of his entire life.

Even without speeding, he made good time to his house, an older home near ASU. "We're here," he said as he pulled into his driveway. He decided not to bother putting the car in the garage. He'd rather take her in the front door, anyway.

"You have a house?"

"The bank and I have a house. Mostly it still belongs to the bank." He'd bought the place so he could try out some landscaping ideas in the backyard, but once he'd moved in, the concept of having a serious relationship had moved right in with him.

He wondered if he'd look back on this night as the beginning of that relationship. So far, he had every reason to believe that one day he would do exactly that.

She opened her door and stepped out before he made it around to her side of the car. "A house seems so grown-up," she said.

"It has its advantages." He took her hand as they headed up a curving walkway to the door. A lamp he'd left on glowed from the living-room window. He thought it gave a welcoming look to the house, and he wanted her to feel very welcome. Extremely welcome.

"Like what advantages?"

"For one thing, no neighbors with common walls, so I can make all the noise I want." Right now he could hardly wait to get naked and vocal.

"Are you noisy?"

Heart hammering, he fit the key in the lock and turned to her. The light through the window illuminated her face. "Depends on what's happening," he said. "Are you?"

She gave him a look of pure seduction. "Depends on what's happening."

He trembled with the need to have her. "Come on." He twisted the key and shoved open the door. "Let's go in and make some noise."

KASEY HAD BEEN STARTLED to find out Sam lived in a house, much less a house he actually owned. Just when she'd decided there wasn't much of a gap between them, after all, here was more evidence that they were miles apart. She couldn't imagine renting a whole house, let alone buying one. She was years away from a step like that.

But it didn't matter, she told herself as she stepped into

Sam's living room. She was here to satisfy her craving and make sure that he changed his mind about hiring her for PR work. One would take care of the other, and whether his bed was located in a rented apartment or a cute little house near the campus made no difference.

Her sexual engines had been revving ever since this date began, and she'd worked herself into a lather on the dance floor. She was completely focused on climbing into Sam's bed. Once that happened, everything else would sort itself out.

Sam seemed to be of the same mind. She had a quick glimpse of large green plants, polished wood floors and furniture slip-covered in beige. Then the front door lock clicked into place, Sam pocketed his keys and took her hand.

"This way." His tone was urgent as he led her down a darkened hallway. Then he paused and sighed. "You know, I'm acting like a sex-crazed idiot. Maybe first you'd like something to drink, a chance to tour the—"

"Later." She didn't want to give herself any more time to think about this. Right now her mind and body agreed on a course of action, and she wanted to keep it that way.

"Great." He squeezed her hand and continued down the hall to a door at the far end of the hall. Inside the room he flipped a switch and two bedside lamps came on.

He had a grown-up bed, too—king-size mattress, solid wood headboard, plaid comforter. He threw back the comforter to lay bare the creamy sheets upon which she planned to get lots of satisfaction.

Then he drew her into his arms. "We didn't have the health talk." He slipped the straps of her dress over her shoulders as he looked into her eyes. "We should probably have the health talk."

She wrapped her arms around his waist and rubbed her

body against his, loving the way his eyes darkened. "Your equipment is safe with me," she murmured.

"As yours is with me." His voice was husky. "And right now, I'm really glad that I've been so damned careful all these years, because I'm free to love the living daylights out of you."

Her heart pumped wildly as she looked into his eyes. She had no doubt he was capable of doing that. "That's why I'm here."

"I know." He cupped one breast through the material of her dress. Slowly he brushed her nipple with his thumb.

She began to quiver, anticipating what lay ahead for them.

"I wanted to touch you like this on the dance floor, but I didn't dare. Dancing fast, in a dress like this, wearing no bra—you were tying me up in knots."

"Was that mean of me?" Desire thickened her tongue.

"Only if you'd told me no at the end of the night." He continued to caress her. "But you said yes. So you weren't being mean, just provocative."

She had trouble catching her breath. "I...liked the music."

"And I liked watching you like the music. To think I almost didn't take you to hear my little brother's band."

"But you did."

"And now here we are." His smile was slow and easy. "Tell me the best way to get this off. I'm feeling impatient, and I don't want to rip it."

She'd always dreamed of having a forthright lover instead of the tentative boys she'd stumbled into bed with in the past. In truth, she'd given that imaginary lover Sam's face. Now fantasy and reality had combined. And she already knew her lines.

"Better yet, let me show you the best way to get it off."

270 OLD ENOUGH TO KNOW BETTER

Moving a step back, she leaned down, clutched the hem in both hands and lifted the dress over her head. "How's that?"

Sam's quick intake of breath told her that she'd made the right impression standing there in only her black panties and her red shoes. She'd seen centerfolds in outfits like this, and she'd posed in front of a mirror to gauge the effect, but this was the first time she'd tried out the ensemble on a real live man.

As her dress slipped from her fingers to the floor, his gaze roamed her bare breasts and her erect nipples. She let him look. Putting herself on display excited her as much as it obviously excited him. She'd never exploited the power of her naked body before. It was more fun than she'd imagined it would be.

He gulped. "Kasey, you're...so gorgeous. I can't even find the words. You're—"

"Still not naked." She was ready for the next level of thrill seeking. She kicked off her shoes with a flourish and shimmied out of her panties.

He groaned and started ripping off his own clothes. A button popped, but he paid no attention. His focus remained fixed on Kasey as he tossed his shirt on the floor.

And there was that sexy tattoo, rippling as he hurriedly shucked his pants. At the age of eight she'd been mesmerized by that tattoo, the first one she'd ever seen up close and personal. Now the man with the tattoo was going to get very up close and personal with *her*.

She could hardly wait to get her hands on his beautiful body, but she didn't want to appear too eager. He didn't have to know that he was the best specimen she'd ever seen naked, not counting the guys in *Playgirl*. She hoped he wasn't quite as hugely endowed as some of the men in that magazine. A few of the centerfolds had dimensions that were scary for the average girl.

Anticipation had her gulping for air, so she covered that by walking to the bed and stretching out on the cool sheets. That put her at eye level with his package, which was currently straining to escape from its cotton prison. Judging from the bulge, Sam was plenty big, but any minute she'd know whether he carried around a large or a supersize model.

Then he peeled off his bikini briefs, and she was thrilled to discover he possessed wonderful proportions, proportions that could certainly satisfy but not intimidate. From this vantage point, Sam's manly attributes were truly inspiring, and her complementary parts had indeed become very inspired, responding with a rush of moisture.

Sam pulled out the bedside-table drawer, took out a box and set it down next to the lamp. "Now." He crawled in beside her. "Come here."

CHAPTER SEVEN

THE MOMENT WHEN Sam gathered Kasey's warm, supple body close and kissed her smiling mouth felt so incredibly right it made his head spin. He'd never believed in love at first sight, but this woman had slipped into his life, into his bed, like the missing piece of a puzzle. She had the perfect touch, the perfect scent, the perfect voice.

She belonged in this house, in this bed, in his arms. And he would show her exactly how much. Kissing her with all the certainty he felt, he rolled her to her back. She spread her thighs, and he could have taken advantage, burying himself inside her without stopping to put on a condom. He wondered if one day he'd be able to do that because caution wouldn't be important.

Maybe. But first many things had to happen. And at the head of the line was a night of pure pleasure. Although he wanted nothing more than to enter her and make that ultimate connection, he knew that most women expected to be led gradually to that point. And he was only too happy to guide her.

Sam intended to leave no sensual stone unturned tonight. Whatever she needed to make this an unforgettable experience, he'd provide. He lifted his lips from hers. "Tell me what you like. Tell me how I can make you happy."

Her breath came in quick little puffs, breaking up her words. "I'll bet...you already...know."

He nibbled her earlobe. "Generally, I might. I want specifics."

She moaned softly and wiggled beneath him. "And I want...something very specific."

"Then tell me."

Panting, she reached between their hot bodies and curled her fingers around his penis. "This."

His heart thundered in his ears. The pressure of her fingers was nearly enough to set him off. "Now?"

"Right now, Sam." She fondled him, creating havoc with his control.

He drew away, afraid he'd lose it. "But I was going to... What about foreplay?"

"We've had...hours of...foreplay. Do me."

He believed her. Only a fool would keep questioning when a woman spoke that plainly. "You've got it." He rolled to his side and made rapid work of opening a condom packet. By the time he returned to her, she was looking at him with undisguised longing.

Blood pounded through his veins as he moved between her thighs and braced himself on his knees and hands. "I thought it was only guys who liked to go straight to the main event."

She grasped his hips. "Wrong."

"I'm glad to be wrong." Watching her eyes, he probed gently, found that sweet door to nirvana and shoved home. There, that was what he wanted to see in her expression, the same sense of wonder he was feeling. He'd had plenty of sex in his life, but this was different, more significant somehow.

She felt wonderfully snug, as if the two of them had been created to make this connection with no room to spare. Somehow he'd known they'd fit like this. Maybe she had, too, and that's why she'd insisted they forget the preliminaries.

"Better, now?" he asked softly.

Her rapid breathing made her breasts quiver. "Much better."

"I still want to kiss you all over. You have such kissable breasts. I want to run my tongue over each nipple, and then—why are you smiling?"

"Thinking how nice that will be…later. But I can't wait for you to do all that."

He drew back and pushed in again. "Even if I kissed you until I made you come?"

That idea registered in her eyes. "I would like that."

"I think you would."

"But right now, I need you here inside me."

"Then I can guess what else you need." He began a slow rhythm. With the perfect fit they had, he suspected she'd feel every thrust in all the right places.

She moaned softly. "Good guess."

"Remember, no common walls." He picked up the pace. "You can be as loud as you want." He'd never tested that. This would be the first time in his house. He was glad she was here to test it with him.

"Mmm." She closed her eyes and lifted her hips slightly. "Ooh. Mmm, yeah. Right there."

He took his cue and snagged a pillow. "Lift up a little more."

She opened her eyes. "But it's…it's good like this."

"I know. But you'll get tired holding yourself up. Lift." When she did, he tucked the pillow under her. "Tell me how that feels." He slid slowly in and out, stroking steadily.

Her eyes became unfocused and her lips parted. "Like… heaven. Like we're doing it on a cloud. Oh, that's very *good*."

He felt ridiculously happy that he'd found a way to share some of his expertise with her and increase her pleasure. The angle did a few special things for him, too, so he'd have to exercise some control. Gliding back and forth like this was building the tension to a dangerous level.

When he felt her start to tighten around him, alerting him that she was on the brink, he bit down on his bottom lip to stop the surge of his own climax. She affected him so strongly that he'd have to work on his stamina when having sex with her. But what fun work it would be.

She began to whimper.

"That's it." He increased the tempo, but that made his own climax edge closer. He thought about frogs and kept going. "Come on, yell for me, Kasey. Show me what you're made of."

Her whimpers became cries, and she dug her fingers into his back.

He rode her harder, coaxing her into ever louder moans. "Let me hear you come!" he yelled, pumping faster. "Come for me!" And as if obeying his command, she came, shouting and laughing as her body bucked against his.

Only the image of frogs kept him from following right after. As she quivered beneath him, he thrust gently, absorbing the aftershocks, hoping to keep her on the edge.

She opened her eyes, a question there.

"Again," he murmured. "Show me that move again."

"I…I can't…"

"Sure you can." Easing slowly in and out, he reached down and rubbed his thumb over her happy spot.

She gasped.

"See?" He continued a circular motion with his thumb and watched her expression change from doubt to excitement.

This time she was loud from the get-go, groaning and

urging him on, wrapping her legs around him, abandoning herself to the possibility of another climax. Already the dynamic had changed between them. He could feel her trusting him now to take her where she wanted to go. And he would do that.

But as he pushed her closer, he knew that he couldn't hold back this time. The erotic sensation of touching her there, right where he could feel the pressure of each thrust of his penis, was too much stimulation. When she went off like a rocket, so did he, bellowing out his sexual satisfaction, loving the sense of privacy that allowed him to do it.

Sex in a house was good. Sex in a house with Kasey was *very* good.

NOT LONG AFTER THAT, Kasey took a tour of the house while wearing Sam's shirt and nothing else. She wasn't sure that a tour of the house was a wise idea, considering that she would end all contact with Sam after tonight, but he'd been like a little kid with a new toy. He'd admitted that he'd only had the house six months and she was his first female guest.

That had worried her, too. Sam might be putting too much importance on what was happening between them, even though she'd given him no reason to do that. She knew from talking with her friends that lots of couples enjoyed a night of sex with no strings attached. Sam was thirty, for heaven's sake. He had to know that was a possibility.

But you haven't said that, whispered a little voice in her head. She should have. She should have said it on the dance floor, or in the car, or before they walked into his house, or before he took off his clothes. But she'd never tried out that particular line, and it didn't come trippingly off the tongue, as Shakespeare would say.

She would tell him though, and soon, because this affair couldn't go anywhere. He was a thirty-year-old guy with a *house,* for heaven's sake. She was a twenty-year-old with no desire to settle down. They were very different.

She had to keep that thought front and center in her mind, especially considering how good the sex had been. She'd never had a multi before. Add that to the privacy of being alone in a house, another luxury she'd never experienced, and the comfy bed, and his trick with the pillow—way too much fun.

Then there was the other problem, the sense of belonging. She'd started this date already slightly in love with Sam, and he'd more than lived up to her expectations. They got along very well, considering how old he was. More than once she'd caught herself wondering if she could stretch this episode beyond one night. But she knew that would be a mistake that could get her in serious trouble.

Putting her thoughts temporarily on hold, she went for a tour of the house, because he seemed to need her to see it. Maybe that's the way new home owners were about their houses—they felt the need to show them off to anyone who would look around. She wouldn't know about that, but she had to admit it was a very nice house.

"I still have plenty I want to do to the place." Dressed in a pair of shorts he'd grabbed from a drawer, Sam held her hand as he took her back through the living room. "But at least the previous owners had already pulled up all the carpet and refinished the wood floors."

"They feel nice." She'd never walked on real wooden floors in her bare feet, and she liked the sensation.

He glanced down at her feet. "I know what you mean. I hardly ever wear shoes in here." His eyes traveled upward, to where the shirt skimmed her thighs. "Too bad I took down the drapes, or we wouldn't have to wear clothes, either." His eyes grew hot and his fingers tightened.

The thought of walking around Sam's house naked spiked her arouse-o-meter. "I'd probably feel weird doing that," she said. But she didn't really think so. She suspected she'd feel sexy.

"You'd get used to it. I never realized I was so sick of roommates and apartment living until I moved here. Come on, let me show you the best part."

She'd seen the best part, and it was his king-size bed, but she chose not to say so. The more she praised his love-making techniques, the less he'd understand when she told him goodbye.

He drew her through the dining room, which currently had only his computer desk in it, and into the kitchen, where he flipped on another light. "This is not the best part. Eventually the kitchen will have to be completely renovated, but I'm waiting. Kitchens aren't my specialty."

She could guess what he was waiting for—a woman who wanted to share this house with him, a woman who would have definite ideas about how she liked her kitchen arranged. "It looks okay to me," she said, so that he'd understand she wasn't mentally redesigning the space to suit her. She didn't even like to cook.

He shrugged. "It works for now. Which reminds me, would you like something? I have some wine and beer, plus I think there's cheese and crackers, if you're hungry."

"No, no, I'm fine." She turned down the goodies quickly, alarmed by her urge to accept them and watch him putter around this ancient kitchen. She was becoming entirely too involved with him. Time to get back to the sex.

"Okay, then let me show you the back." He unlocked the kitchen door and opened it. "Someday I'll have this widened and put in French doors, probably during the kitchen renovation. I'll also have somebody replace the bedroom window with French doors so it opens out here, too." Still holding her hand, he started through the door.

"Wait, are we going out there?"

He paused. "Why not?"

"I'm wearing nothing but your shirt, and there's a button missing."

"Doesn't matter. There's a flagstone patio and the yard is surrounded by a seven-foot solid wall. It's like a secret garden. No one can see in. This backyard was the main reason I bought the house."

"So you could have parties?" Somehow she didn't think so.

"I suppose, but more for myself. A hideaway." He gave her hand a tug. "It's okay. Trust me, nothing will get you."

She'd been an Arizona girl too long to walk casually outside barefoot. "What about scorpions? What about snakes?"

"No snakes in this garden. The wall's too high. And I patrol all the time with a black light and I've never seen a single scorpion. I think we're too far away from the actual desert here in the middle of town." He smiled at her. "But if it would make you feel better, I'll find you something to wear on your feet."

"No, I'll take your word for it." She almost wished he'd made fun of her fears instead of being so understanding. It was going to make dumping him extremely difficult. Of course, once she dumped him, he wouldn't be understanding. He'd pretty much hate her. What a depressing thought.

The cool night air tickled her bare legs as she stepped outside onto the flagstone. Low pagoda lights ringed the patio, which was furnished with a glass table and chairs on one side and a rope hammock hanging from a metal frame on the other. She smelled flowers and heard water splashing softly. Despite the seven-foot wall, which she could see dimly in the glow from the half moon, she felt daring being out here wearing only Sam's shirt.

"Isn't this fantastic?" Sam swung his arm to encompass the area. "Those two mesquite trees shade the patio during the day, and once I gave them a good trim they look really good."

Kasey glanced up through the delicate herringbone pattern of the mesquite leaves to the night sky, where the moon was the main attraction. City lights blocked out most of the stars. Although she could hear the muted drone of traffic, the trickling water and chirping crickets turned the yard into an oasis of calm in the middle of the city.

She could picture herself in the hammock reading a good book. She could also picture herself in the hammock with Sam, but she blocked that image. A hammock was for spending a lazy Sunday afternoon together, but impractical for sex. All she wanted from Sam was satisfaction, not long-term friendship.

"I can see why you like it," she said.

"I put in the pond and waterfall myself." He sounded very proud of that.

"I can hear it. Where is it?"

"Over here." He led her to the side of the yard, near the hammock. "I nestled it in between the lantana and the hibiscus, and tried to make it look as natural as possible."

Leaning closer, Kasey could see little silver flashes as moonlight reflected off water tumbling down levels of smooth rock into a small pool. "What a great idea. Do you have fish?"

"Not yet, but I've been thinking about it." He rubbed her palm with his thumb as he stood beside her, staring at the waterfall.

"Fish would be cool." In spite of her vow not to get

drawn into his life, she'd been captured by his excitement when he talked of this backyard.

"See, this is how I want to expand Ashton Landscaping. I'm known for creating and maintaining commercial installations, but I want to reach the individual home owner who would like something like this, a retreat. I think we're moving away from flashy showplace yards and toward increased privacy. I want that kind of business."

Now was the time to squash his next move. Then she could give her speech about spur-of-the-moment sex that meant nothing and went nowhere. "Sam, about hiring me, I don't think—"

"But I do think." He pulled her gently into his arms. "I never trusted the idea of bringing in a PR expert until I met you, but I know you'd do a great job. This new direction would take more than buying some ads. I need a new image." He slipped his hands under the hem of her shirt and cupped her bottom.

"That could be, but I can't be the one to give it to you." She wanted to give him something else, though. The moment he'd started caressing her, she'd remembered his promise to kiss her until she climaxed. From the way she felt right now, that wouldn't take very many kisses.

"Why not?" He started unfastening the buttons of her shirt.

"Because of this…what we're doing…" She closed her eyes and sighed as he pushed aside the shirt and stroked her breast.

"That's silly." He leaned down and nuzzled the side of her neck. "What happens here is a private thing," he murmured. "It doesn't have to affect our business relationship, except to make it better."

She felt confused, not to mention aroused. She'd thought there was some sort of rule about not sleeping with your clients. If there wasn't, there should be. Shouldn't there? "I don't think it's right. I don't—" She paused, unable to remember what she'd meant to say because he'd leaned down to flick his tongue over her nipple.

"Mmm." He licked her other breast. "You taste delicious."

A cool breeze made her damp nipples tingle. Vaguely she realized the shirt now hung open all the way to her thighs. "Maybe…maybe we should go in."

"Are you cold?"

Not even remotely. Now he'd started to suck on her nipples, and she was getting hotter by the minute. "I just thought, that if we're going to…get down to it…then we should go back to your bedroom." He was turning her knees to jelly again, and before much longer she wouldn't be able to walk.

He kissed his way back to her mouth. "Or we could stay here," he murmured.

"But—"

"Let's try this. Sit down here." He guided her to the edge of the hammock.

She was so wobbly that she sat down immediately. "Oh!"

"What?" He knelt in front of her.

"That feels very funky on my tush." Weird and on the kinky side, too, she thought.

He steadied her by bracketing her hips. "Bad funky or interesting funky?"

"Interesting." She was curious as to what he had in mind. She couldn't imagine having sex with him on this thing.

"Then let's go with it." He cupped her face and feathered kisses over her mouth. "I want you to lie straight back."

"And what will you do?"

"Stay right here."

She was beginning to get the picture, and it was quite a picture. He wanted her crossways on the hammock, her legs dangling over the edge, while he moved in. Her pulse rate accelerated. "You're sure no one can see us?"

"Positive." His voice trembled with obvious excitement.

"Not even the eye-in-the-sky police helicopter?"

"If I hear it coming, I'll throw myself across your writhing body."

She started to quiver. "And will I be writhing?"

"That's my goal." He nibbled on her bottom lip. "Only thing is, you can't yell out here."

She really needed to tell him that tonight was all they'd enjoy together, and she would, but not now, not before the hammock experiment. "Okay. I'll be quiet."

"Good. Now lie back." He leaned over her as he guided her down. As he did, he moved his mouth to her breasts, then on to her tummy. When her head rested on the far side of the hammock, he kissed the moist curls between her legs. "Perfect."

She couldn't believe she was doing this, lying in a rope hammock looking up at the moon, her shirt open, her heart racing because any moment Sam would…and then he did, using his warm tongue in a way that made her gasp. She pushed her fingers through the gaps in the hammock's weave and hung on for dear life. Oh, he was good. He was *very* good.

Then, when she thought the sensations rolling over her couldn't get any better, he thrust two fingers up through the open weave and buried them deep inside her. Incredible. As he used his tongue to swirl and lap, he stroked rapidly with his fingers until she was on complete overload. Her orgasm roared in with such force that she had to clench her jaw to muffle her groans of completion.

"Sweet," he murmured, trailing kisses along her thighs.

She lay panting, boneless and unable to move. Slowly her fingers uncurled from their death grip on the hammock. He'd have to carry her inside. No way could she walk there. Maybe he really did plan to carry her, because he lifted her hips to scoot her a little closer to the edge.

She took a shaky breath. "I can try to walk," she said.

"Not yet. Stay right there."

No problem. She would stay right there and look up at that beautiful, beautiful moon. Sex was the best thing ever, especially delivered by Sam.

"I'm going to hook your ankles over my shoulders."

"You're going to do what?" She raised her head as best she could and discovered that he was kneeling across from her, her ankles propped on his shoulders. He'd moved very close to the hammock. Then, she felt the smooth glide of his penis entering her. "Sam?"

"Hold still." His voice was husky.

"Did you put on a—"

"Yes. Put one in my pocket before we came out here."

"You had this in mind all along!"

"Not exactly this." His chuckle was low and sexy. "This was a recent inspiration. Now, I'm going to gently swing the hammock. It might not work, but if it does..."

"You're insane."

"Want to go insane with me?"

She should have picked someone else for her first one-night stand. Sam was more than she could handle. She felt his charisma wrap around her like the ropes of the hammock. With a guy like Sam, you always wanted to find out what would happen next.

"Sure," she said.

CHAPTER EIGHT

SAM WONDERED IF knowing about Kasey's super brain had spurred him to become more creative. Or maybe it was the house and this special garden he loved so much. They'd already done the wild thing on an ordinary bed. He thought they should try other options now.

And the hammock was some option. He didn't have to swing it very fast to get excellent friction. He'd read about something similar to this, some Asian rope trick, but the hammock worked just fine. More than fine.

Kasey was making soft little moaning sounds that he thought meant she was having a good time, too. But maybe he'd better check.

"You okay?" he murmured as he eased the hammock back and forth.

"Oh, yeah." She gulped for air. "This is…amazing. I don't have to…do anything and still I'm getting…my jollies."

"Then it's working for you?" It was working so well for him that he calculated about thirty seconds to blastoff.

"It's working. It's really, really working."

"Good." He tightened his grip on the edge of the hammock. The creaking of the metal support rings merged with the chirp of crickets. The flagstone was tough on his knees, but the rest of him was so happy he didn't care about his knees. "I'm…I'm close."

She groaned. "Me, too."

"Really close."

"Yeah. Like…right…*now*. Oh. Oh, oh, *oh*."

As her spasms rippled over his rigid penis, he steadied the hammock and let his own orgasm take over, clenching his jaw against the cries that rose from his throat. He'd meant to be quieter, but the pleasure was too intense to take it in silence. He hoped the neighbors were in bed asleep, because if they happened to be outside, they'd know exactly what was going on.

And maybe that didn't matter. At the moment, he really didn't care what the neighbors thought. He didn't care about a damned thing, actually, except enjoying this wonderful night with Kasey.

KASEY ALLOWED SAM to untangle them from their complicated position so she could stretch out lengthwise on the hammock. She murmured her thanks, feeling sexy and very sophisticated. Not every woman could say she'd had this experience. Kasey didn't intend to tell anyone about it, though, not even if it would give her hoochie mama status in the office.

Next to her, the waterfall babbled away, letting her imagine they were out in the woods next to a mountain stream. She didn't feel like moving, or thinking. "Let's stay here a little while," she said. Then she shivered as a breeze cooled her skin.

"We'll stay, but we need a blanket." Sam dropped a kiss on her mouth and headed into the house.

A blanket would be cozy, Kasey realized. Maybe too cozy. As the glow from her recent orgasm faded, she began to wonder when she should ask Sam to take her home. She really didn't want to do that, but she'd have to force herself at some point.

When he dropped her off at her apartment would be

the time to tell him she wouldn't be seeing him anymore. Bringing up the subject in advance wasn't smart. She might not have the willpower to make it stick. But at her front door, she could say what had to be said and then go inside, which would be easier on both of them.

She should probably think about leaving soon. The longer she stayed, the worse the parting would be. But now she'd agreed to this snuggle-under-a-blanket routine, and he'd gone to the trouble of finding a blanket.

It must be some trouble, because he wasn't coming right back. Finally he showed up, a plastic water bottle in one hand, a box of crackers in the other and a blanket under his arm.

"I thought we needed eats," he said.

"Nice idea." So he'd been getting refreshments. He was too sweet for his own good, plus she thought it was cute that he'd brought a bottle of water when that had been what she'd offered him earlier in the day. She really hated to think of dumping him when the night was over. She wondered if there was any way to avoid doing that. She quickly analyzed the situation. No, she had to dump him.

He set the water bottle and the crackers on the flagstone. "A man—not to mention a woman—does not live by sex alone." He grinned at her as he unfolded the blanket and draped it over the hammock. "But it sure would be fun trying."

"Uh-huh." Other than movie-star crushes, there'd never been a guy she'd choose over a plate of excellent pasta. Sam had demonstrated that sex with him was better than anything else on the menu.

Once the blanket was arranged, he attempted to crawl into the hammock beside Kasey and nearly toppled her onto the ground.

"Hey!" She started laughing as she hung on to the

wildly swinging hammock. "I thought you knew your way around these things!"

"Are you kidding?" He climbed out again and grabbed the edge to slow it down. "I just bought it last week. This is its maiden voyage."

"Really?" She wished he hadn't told her that. When she cut him loose, the hammock might be ruined for him, and here it was, brand-new.

"I bought it with the idea that I'd lie out here and read, but so far I haven't taken the time." He started to get in again. "This can't be that tough."

"Hold on. I have a suggestion." Kasey didn't know much about hammocks, either, but she was good at problem-solving. "I'll put one foot on the ground. When you climb in, leave one foot on the ground. Then we'll keep it balanced and lift both feet off at the same time."

"Makes sense." He waited for her to position her foot on the flagstone. Then he carefully eased in beside her, leaving one of his feet planted firmly on the other side.

"That's it. Now, on three—one, two, *three*." The hammock swayed slightly, but they were both in, snug as two bugs under the blanket.

"That's what I love about smart women," he said. "They're full of good ideas."

"Thanks." Not every guy thought she was full of good ideas. She'd met a few who insisted on doing things their way, even if their way wasn't working. Sam didn't seem to let his ego run the show. He'd make a good catch for some lucky woman.

"Now for the goodies." He reached down and picked up the water bottle. "Have a swig."

"Don't mind if I do." She popped the nozzle and took a drink. It wasn't water. "Wine?"

"Yeah. The connoisseurs would have a fit if they caught

me serving Chardonnay in a water bottle, but it's easier to drink this way here, and besides, the bottle's sort of symbolic of how we met."

Don't do that. She didn't want him getting sentimental. That would make the inevitable that much tougher. "It sure is a great delivery system if you're lying in a hammock."

"That's what I thought." He opened the cracker box and held it toward her. "I hope you like wheat crackers."

"Love 'em." She took one and popped it into her mouth. "Have some wine." She passed the bottle over.

"We could pretend this is one of those goatskin flasks they used to have in the olden days." He poured a stream of wine into his open mouth.

She watched him and smiled. "This is fun."

He swallowed the wine and turned to look into her eyes. "It is fun. Thanks for christening the hammock with me. That was incredible."

"Sure was." She still got quivers of sensation thinking about it. "Do you think anybody heard us?"

"If they did, at least they didn't call the police. But it's late. I'm sure everyone else is asleep."

"You should probably be asleep, too. Tomorrow's a workday."

He chewed and swallowed a cracker. "Ask me if I care."

"Do you care?" she asked, laughing.

"No. Do you?"

"No."

"Good. Have some more wine."

She drank it the way he had, directing a stream from the pop-up top into her open mouth.

"I'm getting the urge to kiss you again."

Swallowing the wine, she glanced over at him. He'd turned on his side and was looking at her the way she imagined a fox surveyed the henhouse. But if he acted on the impulse she saw lurking in his eyes, he'd send them both sprawling to the flagstone. "There is no way in hell we can get wild when we're both on this hammock," she said.

"I know. I've already tried to imagine whether it would be possible, and I think one of us would wreck something valuable in the process." He reached behind him to deposit the box of crackers on the patio. Then he slipped his hand under the blanket and explored until he found her breast. "I just want to make out a little," he said, caressing her gently. "Nothing heavy."

She loved being petted like that, and now that he'd planted the idea, she found herself wanting to feel his lips on hers again, too. "Okay." She set the water bottle on the other side of the hammock and turned to him.

"Okay." He cupped her cheek and edged closer. The hammock swayed but didn't threaten to dump them. "Hold still, now."

"I've heard that line before."

"You were wonderful to humor me about that." He touched his mouth to hers, then ran his tongue along her lower lip.

"I was curious to see if you could manage it."

"*We* managed it." Then he settled in and started seriously kissing her.

Nice, she thought as he applied exactly the right amount of pressure, all the while massaging her breasts and teasing her nipples. After that, she forgot to evaluate. Sam's brand of kissing bypassed her brain and headed straight for her nerve endings, making them sizzle and pop, creating aches and needs and urges that prompted her to caress him in return.

She knew full well where his central operation was located. When she rubbed her hand over the fly of his shorts, she discovered his claim that he only wanted to make out a little had not been truth-in-advertising. He was ready to rumble.

He lifted his mouth a fraction away from hers. "What are you doing?"

"Testing. I thought this was going to be low-pressure sex."

"I admit I can't kiss you without getting hard. So sue me."

She smiled. "Want to go inside?"

"Nope. I really like it out here. We'll take a break and drink wine. We'll have a conversation."

Conversations made her nervous. She unfastened his shorts. "I have a better idea."

"Kasey, we'll dump."

"If you lie still, we won't." Unzipping his fly, she gradually scooted toward the foot of the hammock. It trembled but didn't tip.

"Something tells me I'd be a wise man to follow orders."

"I think you would." She was no expert at this, but from her brief experience, she didn't think men required perfection. Hampered by the unsteady nature of the hammock, she couldn't move much, either. But she could take his penis into her mouth.

Apparently that pleased him, because he groaned in ecstasy.

Being careful not to rock the hammock, she did the best she could with her tongue. From the way he was breathing like a freight train, she must be accomplishing something worthwhile. Using gentle suction and a swirling motion with her tongue, she soon had him trembling so violently she decided to finish him off before they ended up in a heap on the flagstone, after all.

Applying greater suction, she moved her head up and

down just enough to provide some friction. That was all it took. His breath hissed out between his clenched teeth as he erupted.

He was still gasping for air when she inched her way back up and nestled in beside him. A man became so vulnerable at a time like this, she thought. She'd intended the move to delay conversation between them. Conversation could only lead to trouble, but as it turned out, she was in trouble, anyway. She was becoming very softhearted about Sam Ashton.

THEY WEREN'T GETTING much talking done, Sam had to admit. But he didn't know a guy in the world who would complain about that considering the way they'd occupied their time. He couldn't have guessed that Kasey would be willing to do what she'd just done so that he wouldn't be in sexual distress. What a woman.

"Wine?" she asked once his breathing had returned to normal.

"You're fantastic." He slipped his arm around her and kissed her talented mouth. "Thank you."

"I was a little hampered by conditions."

"I couldn't tell." He took the water bottle and drank a couple of swallows of wine, congratulating himself for thinking of a way they could have it out here without spilling it all over themselves. Maybe Kasey's intelligence was rubbing off.

As she settled into the crook of his arm, he passed the wine back to her. "Crackers?"

"Sure."

Wedging the box between them, he waited for her to take some before getting a handful for himself. "I think what I like about this garden is how simple everything seems when I'm out here."

"That's an illusion, you know." She munched on some crackers.

"Maybe, maybe not. Take the way we met. We saw each other today, made a date, and here we are. Everything just worked out."

"I guess that's true." She handed him the wine.

He took another drink, savoring the smooth taste that was only slightly tainted with plastic. All the exercise, good sex and now the wine was taking its toll. He was getting sleepy. He blinked to stay awake. Sooner or later he'd have to take Kasey home. They both had to work in the morning, and she didn't have a change of clothes here.

Someday that situation could be different. Ordinarily he wouldn't be planning a long-term relationship after one night, but this date had been far from ordinary. Certainly Kasey would agree with him on that.

"Would you rather sleep a little here?" he murmured, hoping she'd say yes. "I'm sure the birds will wake us up in plenty of time."

No answer.

"Kasey?" He turned his head to check on her.

She lay with her cheek pillowed against his outstretched arm, fast asleep.

Carefully he closed the cracker box and set it on the flagstone along with the water bottle. Then he settled back with a sigh and gazed up at the half moon. In a few days the moon would be full. He'd like to be right here on that night, snuggling with Kasey. With the way things had gone so far, he saw no reason that wouldn't happen.

A GARBAGE TRUCK in the alley behind the wall woke Sam from a most excellent dream in which he seemed to be getting married. In the dream, he'd been very excited about the idea. Then his night with Kasey came flooding back, and he knew how his mind had made that leap to a wedding.

But he had more immediate concerns, like getting her back home so she wouldn't be late for work. The garbage truck came about seven-thirty, so they had no time to waste. Still, he didn't want to startle her. They could both end up sprawled on the cold hard patio if she moved too abruptly.

He'd lost all feeling in the arm she'd used to support her head, so he reached over with his other arm and held her steady while he murmured her name.

"What?" She came instantly awake and tried to struggle upright.

"Easy, babe. Easy." Fortunately he had the presence of mind to slam one foot on the ground to anchor them, or they would have tipped. Her trick. He really did like knowing she was so smart.

She groaned and flopped back onto his numb arm. "What time is it?"

"About seven-thirty."

"Yikes! We have to get going! Omigosh. Help me out of here, Sam!"

He smiled to himself. "One foot out, just like we got in." Obviously he'd have to be the calm one in a crisis. That was okay. He liked that role.

"Oh. Right. Okay, I have one foot out. Do you have one foot out?"

"I do. Good morning, by the way."

"We don't have time for good mornings. Ready? On three. One, two, *three*."

He scrambled out of the hammock and stood shaking his tingling arm. "All right. Now we'll—"

"I'll be dressed in two minutes." She ran across the patio barefoot and threw open his kitchen door.

He shook his head. She was more panicked than he'd expected. Sure, being late for work wasn't a great idea, but it wasn't a total disaster. Ten years ago he might have thought that, but he'd learned that the world didn't revolve around him. Maybe she'd made a habit of being late in the past and had no leeway with her boss.

In that case, he'd do all he could to get her home in time. After picking up the water bottle and crackers, he walked into the house in search of his wallet and keys.

He didn't have to search far. She was already headed down the hall holding his shoes in one hand and his wallet and keys in the other. His dad had a saying for this— being given the bum's rush.

"I guess being late for work is a really bad thing," he said.

"I don't want my boss to think I'm irresponsible." She handed him his shoes.

Fortunately they were loafers, and he could slip right into them. He took the wallet and keys and decided he'd drive her there without worrying about a shirt. "Being late once would brand you as irresponsible?"

"Maybe not." She looked harried and young, especially now that most of her makeup was gone. "But I don't want to take that chance."

"I'm sorry I put you in this position, then." He unlocked the front door and ushered her out. "I'll get you home as fast as possible."

"Thank you."

He decided against conversation on the way to her place. Then she'd know he was putting all his concentration on his driving. He got her there in record time and was proud of himself. If she took a short shower and skipped breakfast, she'd make it to work on time.

She hopped out the minute he stopped the car. "Thanks, Sam."

"Can I see you tonight?"

She hesitated, uneasiness in her expression. "Well, the thing is, I—"

"Oh, yeah. You had something going on tonight. I remember now. So I'll call you later today. We'll work it out."

"Okay. See you." She hurried up the walkway to her apartment complex.

He watched her go and cursed himself for not waking up earlier. This wasn't how their fantastic night was supposed to end, with her feeling so rushed that they couldn't even say a proper goodbye or make another date. He wished she'd at least smiled and said she'd had a great time. Apparently her worry about being late wasn't allowing her to do that.

With a sigh, he put his car in Reverse and then drove home.

CHAPTER NINE

"DAMN, DAMN, DAMN," Kasey muttered as she whipped through her shower and threw on clean clothes. She hadn't been able to deliver the final blow, after all. How could she, when there was no time to spare, no time to break it to him gently?

Only a mean person would have been able to chop Sam off at the knees when there was zero time to give a compassionate goodbye speech. She hadn't planned on a long one, but at least long enough to explain that it wasn't his fault. So she'd reluctantly postponed saying what needed to be said.

Maybe she shouldn't be so paranoid about being late, but Mr. Beckworth had voiced reservations about hiring someone so young, claiming that a woman her age might not take the job seriously enough. It was a dumb prejudice on his part, but she'd proceeded to bend over backward to prove how responsible she was. Besides, there was a staff meeting this morning, and her lateness would be noticed for sure.

Because she couldn't explain all that to Sam without revealing her age, she'd had to let him think she was a nut case about punctuality. She did like to be on time, and at Beckworth, she'd made certain she was *always* on time. Mr. Beckworth had commented favorably on that more than once.

But what bothered her more than anything at the moment was that in the cold light of day, she realized she'd completely messed up her Bad Girl routine. All she'd meant to do was make Sam drool a little and then walk away. Instead she'd slept with him after convincing herself that having sex would ruin his idea of hiring her for PR work.

In fact, she'd been looking for an excuse, any excuse, to satisfy her lust. Her reasoning had been faulty, because Sam couldn't understand why having sex meant they couldn't work together. And he was right—if she didn't tell anyone what she'd done, which of course she wouldn't. Had she only flirted and walked away, she could have bragged about that to her cohorts. But she'd turned over the goods. No glory in that.

When she pulled into the parking lot next to the office building that housed Beckworth, it seemed impossible that only one day had passed. Just yesterday morning she'd parked her car here, vaguely aware of a man in a truck behind her, a man who might have accidentally leaned on the horn. Just yesterday she'd seen Sam Ashton, the object of her childhood crush, manicuring a tree in front of the Beckworth windows. And she'd drawn the long straw.

She was glad for the meeting this morning, which would give her an hour or so to rehearse her story. And she would be on time, just barely. Sam had navigated the streets with the intensity of a NASCAR driver so that she'd make it to work okay.

The tree he'd trimmed actually did look like a piece of sculpture now, with bare lower limbs undulating upward to a canopy of feathered branches. She remembered how hard he'd worked all day before spending a long, physically demanding night with her. He must be in pretty good shape for thirty, because he'd never complained about being tired.

She'd had a much easier day, and yet she'd been the

first one to fall asleep. His gentle voice and the music of the waterfall had lulled her into dreamland. What a night it had been. And what a mess she'd created.

She rode the elevator alone and slipped into the office conference room just as Arnold Beckworth opened the meeting. While Beckworth talked about aggressively pursuing new accounts, Kasey's buddies kept glancing at her, either smirking or waggling their eyebrows questioningly. They were obviously dying to pump her about her date with Tarzan of the Chain Saw.

How ironic that Beckworth would be on a tear about pursuing new business and she was trying to get rid of a potential client as quickly as possible. She'd have to wait for Sam to call her, though. Because he'd picked her up, she hadn't needed his home phone number, and during their exciting date she hadn't thought to ask for it. She hesitated to call him at work because he might be climbing trees again and answering a phone call would be difficult. Besides, she didn't want him to think she was eager to be in touch with him.

But when he called, and she knew he would, she planned to suggest another meeting tonight, but this time for something simple like coffee. If they met early, around seven, she might still be able to drop in on her mom's basket party later. She wasn't into collecting baskets or any of that domestic stuff, but her mother was, and Kasey had decided to order something for her mom's birthday. It wouldn't be a surprise, but it would help her mother's sales count and give her a gift she really wanted, all at the same time.

Sam needed a more domestic woman who cared about baskets and kitchen appliances and gardening. All Kasey cared about was sex. That might intrigue him for the time being, but eventually he'd expect her to develop more mature interests. After all, he owned a *house*. She kept coming back to that, hoping the thought of Sam Ashton, home owner, would blot out the thought of Sam Ashton, fabulous lover.

Of course the great sex wasn't all of it, either. He was just plain adorable, with his water bottle full of wine and his box of crackers. He'd been so proud of his little house, and the yard where he'd created an oasis of calm. They hadn't been particularly calm last night. They'd made that hammock creak pretty loud.

"Kasey? Kasey, are you still with us?"

Startled, she glanced up and realized Beckworth had addressed her directly. And she'd been dreaming about Sam. She cleared her throat and hoped her cheeks weren't as rosy as they felt. "Sure am, Mr. Beckworth. Just now I was brainstorming how I might pull in some additional business."

"And that was my question, Kasey." He peered at her over his reading glasses as light glanced off his polished head. His response to growing bald had been to shave the hair that was left. "All of us have contacts who could become clients—people in our congregation at church, friends we meet at our country club, even family members. So who have you come up with?"

She should have known he'd pin her to the wall. He was convinced the younger generation had no attention span, and he'd just caught her staring off into space when she was supposed to be hanging on his every word. "I'm already talking to a potential client, and he may lead me to other accounts in that field," she said.

"Excellent. Who would that be?"

Of course he'd ask. She whipped out another line of BS. "I hesitate to announce who it is until I've worked out a few more details." She had no intention of following through with Sam, but maybe she could buy some time.

Beckworth frowned. "Surely you could give us the name of the business, Kasey. We all understand that prospects can change their minds."

"Well, he asked me to keep our negotiations quiet until he'd decided for sure. It's a delicate situation." Was it ever.

"Very well." Beckworth obviously didn't like it, and he'd probably question her privately later, but he dropped the subject for now. "That means we've heard from everyone, then. I'll expect reports from each of you on your progress by the end of next week."

Sure enough, he spoke up before she could leave the conference room. "May I see you a moment, Kasey?" He stood and began gathering his papers into a leather briefcase.

"Of course." She straightened her shoulders and tried to look older.

Beckworth waited until the others had left the conference room. "In general, I've been very happy with your performance," he said. "You show remarkable ability in one so young."

"Thank you, Mr. Beckworth." She accepted his patronizing attitude because she owed him a lot. Beckworth was known throughout the Valley, and her work here would look great on her résumé if she decided to take a job outside Arizona. Her folks had begged her not to move for another couple of years, but someday she might try L.A. on for size.

Beckworth cleared his throat. "In fact, this morning is the first time I've seen you distracted. I'm not sure I buy your explanation. Is anything wrong?"

Omigod. He was showing his grandfatherly side, and she so didn't deserve it. She'd stayed out all night with a man and consequently wasn't at her best this morning. She didn't want him to be solicitous and kind.

She took the coward's way out. "I think I might be coming down with something." Like terminal stupidity.

"Then you should go home and rest." He looked as if he might even pat her shoulder, but seemed to change his mind at the last minute. "We're not running a slave galley, you know. And you do look a little flushed."

No kidding. Anyone would look flushed when faced by a disaster that was getting worse by the minute. She couldn't go home because then she might miss Sam's call, or worse, the receptionist would say where she was and he might come over.

When she had her talk with him they needed to be on neutral territory, someplace where he wouldn't be able to work his wiles on her. That expression had never made sense to her before, but it did now. Sam was loaded with wiles, and she was way too susceptible to them.

"I'll take it easy today," she promised Beckworth. "Thank you for being concerned."

"Of course I'm concerned. I'll admit I hired you against my better judgment, but you've proven yourself in the time you've been here. That's why I was so disconcerted by your behavior in the meeting today. It's not like you."

"It won't happen again." Kasey realized he'd spoken abruptly during the meeting because he'd been worried about her. "And thank you for keeping the secret about my age. I think it helps with office dynamics."

"I absolutely agree." He gave her a rare smile. "You have excellent potential in this field. Keep up the good work."

"Thank you." He'd never praised her like this. How ironic that he'd choose the moment when she felt like a complete dunce. "And speaking of work, I'd better get back to it." She smiled as brightly as possible and hurried out of the conference room.

Back in the main office she ignored the significant

glances from Gretchen and Amy as she headed for her desk and switched on her computer.

Within two minutes Gretchen approached, a file folder in her hand. Kasey knew it was a prop. Gretchen couldn't stand the suspense another minute.

Tapping the file folder against the desk, she spoke in a low voice, no doubt worried about whether Beckworth might stroll through. "Please don't tell me that you spent your entire date with that hunk selling him on the idea of a PR campaign."

Kasey bit the inside of her lip to keep from laughing. "Uh, no."

"Oh, goodie. That means you had a hot time on the old town and you were thinking about that very thing when Beckworth nailed you for spacing out."

"Something like that." No sense trying to fool Gretchen.

"Oh, God. Listen, Myra says that Beckworth's taking off for a round of golf soon, which means that you can fill us in once he leaves. Deal?"

Kasey coughed. "Well, there's really not a lot to tell." And most of it she'd take to her grave.

"Not a lot to tell, my ass. I've never seen you as dreamy eyed as you were during the meeting. I'm guessing that—" Gretchen's eyes grew round at something on the other side of the room. "Hel-*lo*. If I'm not mistaken, Tarzan of the Chain Saw just walked in the office. And he's heading this way."

Heart thumping, Kasey swiveled her chair around and stared straight into Sam's eyes.

She watched as he headed over, looking fresh as a daisy in beige slacks and a white knit shirt with Ashton Landscaping embroidered on the pocket. A person would never believe that he'd been up most of the night, in more ways than one. Once again, she felt her cheeks grow hot as she remembered precisely what activities she'd enjoyed with him in his cozy backyard.

"Hi," he said, giving her a warm smile. "I decided to come by this morning so we could discuss that PR campaign. The receptionist said it would be fine if I just came over here to talk to you, but if you're too busy right now, we can set up another time."

"Hi, Sam." Kasey recognized Myra's handiwork. The receptionist had no doubt taken great pleasure in sending Sam right over without buzzing her desk first. Myra loved surprises.

"Sam, I'm Gretchen Davies." Gretchen stuck out her hand. "All of us here really admire your work."

"Thanks." Sam shook her hand. "I guess you had a bird's-eye view of the process yesterday."

"That we did. Very inspiring."

Kasey watched Gretchen bat her eyes at Sam and had an inspiration of her own. "About that project, Sam, I think Gretchen's the person to deal with you instead of me. She's had much more experience than I have, and I'm sure she'd have some great ideas for your new direction."

"But you already have a grasp of my concept," Sam said. "No reflection on Ms. Davies, but you're the one I want to handle everything."

"And you should handle everything, Kasey." Gretchen, the rat, actually winked at her. "I wouldn't dream of taking your hard-earned business, not when Mr. Beckworth asked us just this morning to bring in new clients. Obviously this is the lead you mentioned during the meeting, and he's all yours."

"You mentioned me during the meeting?" Sam looked pleased.

"I didn't mention you by name." Kasey hoped this was a nightmare and she'd wake up very soon.

"You could have," he said. "I was absolutely serious about hiring you. I want to do that, and if you're being asked to bring in new clients, so much the better. Here I am."

"I'll leave you two to discuss the next step," Gretchen said. "Nice meeting you, Sam."

"Same here, Gretchen." Then he turned back to Kasey. "I really can come back later if now isn't a good time. You look a little harried."

A *little* harried? She felt as if someone had tossed her insides into a blender. "Uh, no, this is fine. Please sit down."

"Okay." Sam settled into the upholstered armchair next to her desk. Then he lowered his voice. "I really do plan to hire you, but mostly I wanted to see you again. Turns out the job we had scheduled for today canceled this morning, so I had some time on my hands. I wanted to apologize for making you rush out of my house this morning. We had no chance to talk."

She didn't want to discuss that now. "It wasn't your fault."

"It was my fault. I was the host, which meant I should have made sure we woke up in plenty of time."

In spite of his low tone, Kasey worried that Sam's voice might carry to the neighboring desks. If any of her coworkers caught the phrase *made sure we woke up,* she'd never hear the end of it. She needed to put an end to speculation. "I understand that you want to *wake up* your company image," she said very clearly. "What sort of a budget are you looking at for your campaign?"

He gave her a slow smile. "Whatever it takes."

Her heart, not exactly steady in the first place, skipped a few more beats. She had to face the fact she was being wooed. She'd have to put a stop to it, of course, but it might not be easy. She eyed him nervously. In fact, the determination in his expression made it clear it would be damned tough.

As if to drive the final nail in her coffin, Beckworth approached her desk. "Kasey, if I may interrupt for a moment?"

"Certainly, Mr. Beckworth." She could guess what this was about. He wanted to be introduced to the man at her desk because he'd guessed this might be the mystery client she'd referred to, and he didn't like being kept in the dark.

Beckworth confirmed that by pausing to glance pointedly at Sam.

She had no choice but to make the introduction. "Uh, Sam Ashton, I'd like you to meet Arnold Beckworth, the head of our firm."

Sam stood and shook the older man's hand. "Glad to meet you."

Beckworth glanced at Sam's shirt pocket. "Pleased to meet you, as well. Ashton Landscaping, eh? Interested in having some PR work done, by any chance?"

"Actually, yes. Ms. Braddock and I were just discussing some of the details. She's extremely creative. I probably don't have to tell you that."

Beckworth smiled, obviously happy to have his curiosity satisfied and a new client on board so quickly. "Extremely creative," he said. "You couldn't be in more capable hands."

"I couldn't have said it better."

Kasey wanted to crawl under the desk. If Sam hadn't been thinking about sex before, he definitely was now after Beckworth's remark about capable hands. "I appreciate the confidence you both have in me," she said. Man, did that sound stuffy. Then she remembered that Beckworth still hadn't stated his alleged reason for coming over to her desk. She looked at him. "Was there something you needed to talk to me about?"

"You know, it can wait. Sorry to have interrupted you. I have a ten-thirty tee time. I'll catch you tomorrow." He held out his hand to Sam. "I'm happy you've chosen Beckworth. I know you'll be pleased with our service."

Sam returned his handshake. "Thanks. I already am. Very pleased."

Kasey gulped. That's what she got for thinking she could play with the big boys. She was in so much trouble, it wasn't even funny.

CHAPTER TEN

"WERE YOU ON time this morning?" Sam asked. Kasey sure was acting strange, considering how sexy and open she'd been on their date.

"I was, just barely." She turned away from him and typed in something on her computer. Then she swiveled back to face him and tucked her hair behind her ears. "Would you prefer to pay by the hour or put me on a retainer?"

"What's the difference?" He tried to keep his mind on the business at hand, instead of the way her blue silk blouse clung to her breasts and how her blond hair rippled when she moved her head.

"If we go hourly, I'll bill you every time we talk about the project. If you put me on a monthly retainer, you'll have unlimited consultation time. If you think we can wrap this up in five to ten hours, then hourly would be the way to go. If you expect it to take more than, say, fifteen hours, then you'd be money ahead to pay the retainer."

"Then I want the retainer." Unlimited time with Kasey sounded perfect to him. Then he wouldn't feel guilty if the topic of business came up on a date. It wouldn't seem like he was trying to get free advice in a social situation.

That was why he'd come into her office ASAP, so she wouldn't ever think he was trying to take advantage of their relationship to get PR help for nothing. He was confused about her attitude, though. Apparently she'd been interested enough in the project to mention it to her boss this morning, and yet a few minutes ago she'd tried to turn his account over to her friend Gretchen.

"Retainer, then." She typed that into her computer. "I'll need your numbers—work, home, fax, cell."

"I can't believe I didn't give you all that yesterday." He took a business card out of his wallet and slid it across the desk. "That's another reason I came in. I realized you couldn't call me because you didn't have any of this information."

She scooted the card closer and filled in the little boxes on her screen. "Okay, then." Swinging back around, she faced him with all the eagerness of a mourner at a wake. "We need to do some preliminary work before I can outline a potential campaign for your approval. I can either ask you the questions now, or give you a questionnaire to fill out."

He leaned in a little closer. "Kasey, why don't you want to do this?"

"Of course I want to do this." Her jaw was rigid.

"No, you don't. And I need to understand why. Can we go get some coffee and talk about it?"

She looked wary. "Where?"

"I was thinking Coco's down the street." He'd love to take her home with him, but that might get her into trouble.

"Um, maybe that's a good idea."

"Then let's go." He waited for her to grab her briefcase, although she left her suit jacket hanging on the back of her chair as if to signal that she was coming back shortly.

Obviously she was a very conscientious worker, and he'd respect that. He paused by the front door while she spoke to the receptionist, a woman named Myra. Myra had been very nice to him when he'd arrived, much more welcoming than Kasey, come to think of it. Myra smiled at Kasey as if they shared some sort of secret. Maybe they did, because as Kasey turned and walked toward him, she was blushing.

"All I have is my truck," he said as they left the office and headed for the elevator.

"That's fine."

He thought of her climbing into his truck in that short skirt and hoped he'd be able to control himself. A gentleman would help a lady up in a situation like that, but hoisting Kasey onto the seat could create a host of problems for him. He'd have to think about dissecting frogs again.

Although they passed a couple of people in the hall, they had the elevator to themselves. Sam kept his distance, not wanting to start something he couldn't finish, but at least he could speak freely now. "I really am sorry that we were rushed this morning," he said. "When two people have shared as much as we did, they should have a chance to talk to each other before they go on about their day."

Her expression had closed down again. "Maybe that was for the best."

"Why would that be for the best?"

"Because now you're a client."

He didn't like the way she said that, as if he'd contracted a contagious disease. The elevator opened and he ushered her into the lobby. "And your point is?"

"I'll explain over coffee." Then she turned a smile on two businessmen coming through the front door of the building. "Good morning!"

They both greeted her in return, and Sam felt like a little boy who'd been chastised for talking during class. Once they were outside the building, he told her that.

"I just don't want my colleagues to get the idea that I have a personal relationship with a client." She put on her sunglasses.

"Why not?" Sliding on his own shades, he led the way to the parking lot, reaching for his keys as he walked.

"It's unprofessional."

"Oh, come on. Are you saying that if your dear uncle Morty wanted to hire you to do PR work, you'd refuse because you already know him?"

"That's not the same thing."

"Sure, it is." As they approached the passenger side of his truck, he clicked the button on his key chain and unlocked the door. "And I'm paying the retainer, so that simplifies our interaction, don't you think?"

"No."

He sighed. This was getting very complicated, but she was worth it. He opened the door. "I'll need to help you in."

"I can do it." She stepped up on the running board. Then she turned to him. "Go ahead and get in. I can make it."

They gazed at each other in silence. Finally he shrugged and walked around the truck. No doubt she could climb in just fine without him. He supposed he'd secretly wanted to help her because he would get to touch her, but he was out of luck.

She'd certainly turned into a prim and proper businesswoman today. He had a tough time believing she was the same person who had boogied on the dance floor and rubbed her body against his, the same person who had agreed to lie nearly naked in a hammock while he…

He groaned and shook his head. Thinking about that wasn't such a good idea. He could feel the repercussions of such thoughts as he stepped up into the truck cab. By the time he got behind the wheel she was already in with her door closed and her seat belt fastened.

"I'll put the air on. It's warm in here." He started the engine and punched a button to turn the air conditioner on high. If only he had a similar switch so he could turn himself off. Sitting with Kasey in the close confines of this truck reminded him of how much fun they'd had the night before. And he wanted to continue along those lines.

"Is Coco's all right with you?" he asked. *How about the nearest hotel room?*

"Coco's is fine."

"Then Coco's it is." He put the truck in gear and drove out of the parking lot, all the while trying to ignore the sexy woman in the passenger seat. He failed. Her perfume filled the cab of his truck and he was so sensitized to her that he could hear every breath, every rustle of clothing.

"You know, if my being a client makes you that uptight, we can forget that part," he said. "It's just that I think you could help me, and I don't trust anyone else to do the job. But I also don't want to ruin what we have going."

"You should probably—" She coughed and cleared her throat. "You should probably let me do your PR work for you. If your business grows, that will be good for you and good for your brother."

"I think that's all true, but something's happened to the connection we made last night. If the PR work is interfering, then I want to—"

"You passed Coco's."

"Whoops." He hung a U and drove back to the restaurant. "Anyway, as I was saying, our relationship is important to me." He turned into the parking lot and found a space near the door. "I don't want this idea I had for my business to cause problems between us."

"Sam, we would have had problems, regardless."

"We would?" An icy finger tickled his spine. Instead of turning off the engine, he put the gearshift in neutral and pulled on the emergency brake so he could leave the motor running and the air on. Then he unfastened his seat belt and turned to her. Whatever she had to say, he didn't want a restaurant table between them when she said it. "How come?"

She took off her sunglasses and looked at him, her expression sad. "We're at different places in our lives. You just bought a house, while I still live in an apartment, an apartment I haven't even bothered to decorate."

"Does that matter?" So maybe he shouldn't have given her a tour. "I don't care whether your apartment is decorated or not, Kasey. Maybe I gave you the wrong idea about me. I'm not obsessed about the whole house thing." *But I am becoming obsessed about you, wondering when I'll be able to kiss you again, and do other things.*

"Maybe we should consider last night a fun experiment, something we'll both remember fondly."

"Remember fondly?" He started to panic. "Look, I shouldn't have allowed us to oversleep. That wasn't smooth, and I apologize, but—"

"This has nothing to do with the oversleeping."

"Then what's the problem?" He took off his shades so he could see her expression better and she could see his. "You had a good time last night. I know you did. Or were you faking those orgasms?"

Her voice trembled slightly. "No, I wasn't."

"So you liked what I was doing."

"Yes."

"Then what happened? What did I do to turn you off? Am I some snore machine? Did I—"

"No, no, no! It's not you! It's me! I'm not ready for this kind of intensity, that's all."

He stared at her. So that was it. She was simply a good-time girl who'd enjoyed their sexual adventures and wanted a no-strings situation. On the other hand, he was coming on as a guy interested in a commitment of some kind. He'd taken her through his house, and she'd assumed he was casting her in some permanent role in his life. He wasn't…yet.

Apparently he had a skittish woman on his hands. He'd been in this situation before with Veronica, who had been too young to make a commitment. After handling that poorly, he didn't want to repeat the mistake and push Kasey into leaving.

He'd assumed she was close to his age, but maybe not. He could ask her, but that could backfire by emphasizing their differences. Maybe he should just let her go, but after what they'd shared the night before, he couldn't bring himself to walk away.

"All right." He took a deep breath. "All things considered, I can see why you'd think I want to tie you down. The truth is, I took you back to my house because I knew we'd have privacy there and that would make the sex better. But we could have gone to your place."

She swallowed. "I, um, got the impression this was about more than sex."

"Sorry if I implied that. This is very much about sex." He reached over and slipped his hand beneath her hair to cup the nape of her neck. "I want you, Kasey. I'm intense about that—I'll admit it. If I thought we could get away with having sex right here in the parking lot, I'd suggest it. From the way you acted last night, I thought you felt the same."

"I did, but—"

"But if I'm looking for a steady roommate, you're not that girl. Am I right?"

"Yes, you're right."

"Then let me put your mind at ease." He proceeded to lie through his teeth. "I'm not looking for a steady roommate." He massaged the back of her neck and felt her quiver. He was probably a sucker for trying to nurture something that had all the signs of being a repeat of his relationship with Veronica, but Veronica hadn't turned him inside out in the space of twenty-four hours. Kasey had. "I am looking for more amazing nights like we had last night," he said, and that much was true.

Heat flashed in her eyes. "But you're…you're a client."

"Want me to cancel that arrangement?"

"No. That makes no sense. I can't have you scuttling your whole plan because you want to have sex with me. There's also the little problem of Beckworth. I'd have to explain why I lost you as a client. I can certainly figure out some way to do that, but—"

"But why do it at all? Think win-win, Kasey. How about this? I'll stay completely out of your office. No one has to see us together. We'll work in private and play in private. You'll take care of the account and no one has to know that we're having mind-blowing sex at the same time. That will be our little secret."

Her breathing quickened. "I don't know…."

"I promise you, we'll be very careful."

"So you really won't tell anyone? Not even your friends?"

"No one. I won't drag you into my life and you won't make me part of yours. We'll just be getting together to discuss the PR campaign and have great sex." Although that wasn't the way he would have preferred it, he could tell the concept excited her. Now if only his suggestion was convincing enough to get her back into his bed. "What do you think?"

"I think you'd better take me back to the office."

His heart sank. "That's a no?"

She smiled. "It's a yes. And if you don't take me back to work immediately, I might jump you right here, which would blow our cover."

KASEY KNEW SHE was taking a huge risk, but if Sam kept his word, she might get away with having more sex with him and still not reveal her age or her identity. And she wanted to have more sex with him. Just sitting in this truck while he caressed the back of her neck was driving her crazy.

"All right, I'll take you back to the office." His smile was slow and sensual. "And somehow I'll control myself and not kiss you right now, which I really, really want to do."

"That would be a bad idea. We have to act as if we have no sexual interest in each other at all."

"That will be a trick, considering how much I want to strip you naked and lick your—"

"Sam, take me back to the office. Now." Heat flowed through her, dampening her panties and making her tremble.

He sighed and stopped stroking her neck. Then he turned and buckled his seat belt. "I'm not a patient man. How soon can I see you again?"

She loved his sense of urgency, especially now that he'd promised her it would lead to nothing permanent. Thinking about having sex with him again made her weak with lust. "I have this…thing to go to tonight."

"When can you get away?" He left the parking lot and drove down the street toward her office building.

She quickly calculated time and distance. If she left work soon after five, she could be at her mother's—even factoring in rush hour—by six-thirty, when the basket party was due to start. She'd put in her order and leave. The return should be much quicker. "I'll be free by eight-thirty," she said.

"Your place or mine?"

"Mine. An apartment complex is more anonymous. I'm afraid your neighbors might start to recognize me. My neighbors don't pay that much attention to the comings and goings of the tenants."

"We could find a way around my neighbors, but I'd be glad to come to your place. I would come to a tent in the middle of the desert if you'd let me use my tongue to—"

"How do you expect me to get any work done today if you leave me with that kind of image?"

He laughed. "I *want* to leave you with that kind of image. You're so damned dedicated to your job that I need to make sure you'll still want me when I show up at your apartment tonight."

There was no danger that she wouldn't want him. He had no idea how potent he was, and how tempted she'd been to throw all caution to the wind so that she could be with him. Fortunately he'd taken her protests seriously and created a situation where she felt relatively safe.

Now, even if he followed through on his idea of contacting her brother, he wouldn't mention the woman he was having hot sex with. He wouldn't discuss it with his own brother or with anyone. Neither would she. The girls in the office might guess, but they wouldn't know anything for sure. Maybe being mysterious was the best Bad Girl tactic of all.

In any case, she'd have a chance to find out if last night with Sam had been a fluke, or if she really was capable of being multiorgasmic. She'd find out if Sam could be as imaginative in her apartment setting as he'd been on his back patio, and if she had any creative ideas of her own on the subject of sex. Yes, continuing this fling with Sam could be dangerous, but the potential rewards were so exciting she couldn't resist.

CHAPTER ELEVEN

KASEY HAS A HARD TIME getting away from the basket party. Most of her mother's friends hadn't seen her since her makeover, and they kept her locked in conversation as they commented on how different she looked. At least she was no longer treated like little Kasey Braddock, girl genius. The image had weighed her down all her life and she was glad to be rid of it.

Except now, instead of fawning over her brains, the women zeroed in on her social life. So this was how it had been for the popular girls, she thought. Not so much better than being a brain, really. Having her mom's friends ask about her dates felt very strange, especially considering what her activities had been the night before and what they promised to be again tonight. On her way home from her mother's house she planned to buy condoms.

And she couldn't very well say she'd won an office lottery for the privilege of hitting on Sam. The idea would scandalize her mother, and besides, Sam was her secret, and she was his—at least she hoped to hell he would keep quiet about their liaison. So she smiled at the ladies buying baskets and deflected the questions about boyfriends. Then she ordered her mother's birthday present, gave everyone a hug and finally escaped.

By driving like a maniac on the way home and buying condoms in record time, she arrived at her apartment with twenty minutes to spare. She changed clothes quickly and

tidied the bedroom, remembering to stash all family pictures in a dresser drawer. Then she walked into her living
room and was hit by an attack of nerves.

Compared to Sam's house, her place wasn't much. She'd
put all her spare cash into her top priorities—a salon visit
once every two weeks, a new wardrobe and a zippy little
convertible. Her apartment hadn't seemed important, because she didn't invite men over to visit.

Until now. Glancing around, she groaned in despair.
Tacky furniture, half-dead plant, zero ambience except
for the vase of roses, courtesy of Sam. She should have
thought of chilling some wine and lighting some candles.
Wait—she had candles! All she had to do was find them.

Five minutes later, she'd torn through every kitchen
drawer and located two boxes of candles, one red and
one green. Someone had given them to her for Christmas
two years ago and she'd never used them. After suffering
through a summer in her apartment, they weren't exactly
ruler straight, but they were all she had.

Then she remembered why she'd never used the candles—no candleholders. Whoever had given them to her
must have assumed that everyone owned candleholders.
Kasey didn't. But she'd started on this candlelight kick
and she'd figure it out.

By the time Sam rang her doorbell, she had eight tapers burning in her apartment—two in the kitchen, two
in the living room, three in the bedroom and one in the
bathroom. She'd turned off all the lights, and what everyone said about candlelight was true. The apartment looked
tons better. Even her ratty furniture had taken on a romantic glow. Drawing in a deep breath, she opened her door.

Sam stood there holding another dozen roses, white
this time, and a long-necked bottle in a paper bag. "Hey,
Kasey." He swept her with a glance, his eyes hungry.

"More roses!" The heat in his eyes made her heart race. As she accepted the tissue-wrapped bouquet, she looked down at her khaki shorts and white tank top. "Now I feel underdressed for the occasion."

"Or overdressed," he said suggestively as he walked in. "As far as I'm concerned, you could have come to the door wearing a smile."

Would she have dared? Probably not, but a more sophisticated woman might have, and she didn't want him to know the thought hadn't even crossed her mind. "I didn't want to make everything too easy for you," she murmured.

Excitement gleamed in his eyes. "Challenges can be stimulating, too." Then he cupped her head in one hand and kissed her.

The magnitude of that kiss made her long to toss the roses to the floor and drag him off to the bedroom, but that wouldn't be cool. She was having a grown-up affair and she wanted to conduct herself as if she knew the routine.

Slowly he lifted his lips from hers. "Let's get rid of the roses and the champagne so our hands are free."

Then again, she might not have to worry about being a grown-up. How nice. "You brought champagne?"

"Yeah." He lifted the bottle. "For later."

"Are we celebrating something?"

"Absolutely." He glanced around. "Nice effect with the candles, by the way."

"Thank you." She wondered if he'd notice that she'd used masking tape to hold the candles inside little juice glasses. Now she had to figure out what to put the roses in. Her only vase was currently in use.

"I'll go find something for the roses," she said, planning to dream up a solution on her way into the kitchen.

"I'll come with you."

"That's okay. I'll be back before you know it." She really didn't want him to watch while she rummaged through her meager supply of kitchen stuff.

But he followed her, anyway. "I'm not letting you out of my sight, lady. I've been waiting all day to be with you, and I'm not wasting a single second. I can put the champagne in the refrigerator while you take care of the roses."

"Um, all right." So he'd watch her rummage. At least she'd be rummaging by candlelight. "So what are we celebrating?" she asked as they walked into the tiny space barely big enough for a sink and appliances. In her experience, champagne was saved for engagements, weddings and anniversaries.

"Another night of great sex."

Her heart leaped into her throat, but she tried to appear casual, tried to stop trembling with lust and anticipation. She turned to smile at him. "You're that sure it will be?"

"Would I bring champagne otherwise?" He pulled the bottle out of the bag.

"Oh, the pressure."

"I'm sure you can handle it." He waggled his eyebrows. "I'm sure you can handle everything very capably, as people kept saying this morning."

She rolled her eyes. "Now there was an embarrassing moment, my boss saying I had capable hands and you rushing to agree with him."

"He had no idea that I was talking about something besides your PR work."

"No, but *I* did. You wanted to get me flustered."

"Who, me?" He tried to look innocent and failed miserably.

"It's a good thing you're not coming in there anymore. Honestly, what were you thinking?"

"I can't think when you're around. That's the problem.

All the blood drains south and I turn into a randy teenager with only sex on the brain."

She couldn't help laughing. "You're crazy."

"About getting naked with you, yes, I am." He opened the refrigerator and laid the bottle on its side on the top shelf.

All this talk about sex wasn't helping her come up with a solution for the roses. She went through her cabinets, hoping a crystal vase would somehow materialize. All she found were water glasses. Even if she divided the roses and put them in the glasses, the glasses would tip over.

She had one thing that would hold them—her popcorn bowl—but they'd have to lie sideways in it. Finally, with a sigh of resignation, she pulled it from a bottom shelf. "Behold my flower vase."

He leaned against the counter and grinned at her. "Interesting. You must not be much of a pack rat. I'll bet you've had a gazillion flower deliveries in the past few years."

"Oh, not so much." She ran water in the popcorn bowl and unwrapped the roses.

"Are you telling me that guys have been that intimidated by your brains?"

Yes. But she didn't want to appear pathetically underdated. "It's possible I'm just choosy." She laid the roses in the bowl, resting the stems on the edge. Maybe she'd start a new flower-arranging trend with this look.

"You should be choosy." He closed the small distance between them and reached for her. "An incredible woman like you should have her pick."

She abandoned the roses to snuggle happily into his arms. With Sam, she felt like that kind of woman. This morning he'd begged her to let him see her again. A hundred times today she'd replayed that scene in the Coco's parking lot, impressed that she'd brought him to that state.

He pulled her in close, close enough to make his arousal obvious. "I don't mean to be pushy, but the flowers are in water and the champagne's in the fridge."

As her blood heated even more, she wound her arms around his neck. His implication that they should move on to other activities made her shiver with longing. "Would you like a tour of my apartment?"

"Yes."

"Then come with me." She slipped out of his arms and took his hand.

"Don't you think we should blow out the candles before we start the tour?"

"Oh." She glanced at the ten-inch tapers, which hadn't even burned down an inch yet.

"We'd better blow them out." Sam walked over to the counter and doused both flames. "And the ones in the living room, too." He turned to her. "I assume the tour of your apartment begins in your bedroom?"

She wanted him so much her mouth was watering. "Uh-huh."

"In that case, by the time we remembered the candles, we might have burned the house down."

SAM WAS DEVELOPING a fondness for Kasey's endearing lack of sophistication when it came to housewares. She had one cheap vase and no candleholders, judging from the juice-glass-and-masking-tape combo she'd used to support the candles. Even the swaybacked candles had seen better days. Yet he could see her clever mind at work in creating the holders, and she'd attempted to give her place atmosphere. He found that touching.

Obviously she didn't know that he'd built up such a case of lust for her that atmosphere was wasted on him. As far as he was concerned, they could be anywhere as long as there was a surface that would hold their weight. He ached for her, and nothing mattered except stripping off their clothes and getting horizontal. Actually, vertical would work, too.

In fact, this hallway she was leading him down would be fine, up against the wall or braced against a doorjamb or on the carpeted floor, for that matter. He was a desperate man with a rocket in his pocket. But maybe he needed to pull back and not appear so needy. He'd scared her off before. He didn't want to do that again.

She had the masking-tape-and-juice-glass candle arrangement going on in her bedroom, too. In the light from three flickering tapers he saw a double bed with the covers turned down. He liked imagining her in this room a little while ago, folding back the covers and thinking about what they'd do together on the bed.

A double meant less room to roll around, but it was cozier, in a way. He didn't mind a double bed. He wouldn't mind a sleeping bag thrown on the ground. Beside the bed were a lamp and nightstands of the same vintage as her living-room furniture.

He might ask her to turn the lamp on before the night was over. She was so beautiful, and he wanted another chance to enjoy the view. He wanted many chances. There were blinds over each of her windows, even in the living room and kitchen. Maybe he could talk her into drinking champagne naked.

"This is it." She led him into the room. "Nothing fancy."

"Are you kidding?" He nudged off his shoes as he edged her toward the soft expanse of her bed. "You make any bed fancy."

"I don't have a king-size mattress."

"The better to find you, my dear." He pulled her down to the bed and rolled on top of her. "See? Gotcha." Oh, man, this was heaven. With his package nestled between her thighs, he started working her out of her tank top.

"And I have neighbors on the other side of this wall."

"Have they ever complained?" He pushed her top up over the lacy cups of her bra. Yes, he wanted some of that.

"No."

He was so captivated by the way her breasts swelled beneath the white lace of her bra that her answer took a while to register. He looked into her eyes. "No? You've been that careful not to make noise?"

"I don't make noise."

"Oh, yes, you do. You may think you don't, but I've been there, and you definitely make noise. If you've had an orgasm in this bed, I venture to say the neighbors are aware of it."

She simply looked up at him and said nothing.

At last a possibility dawned on him. "No orgasms in this bed?"

Even in the dim light from the candles, her blush showed. "Not that kind."

"I'm not sure what you mean." Then he figured it out. "Oh. I guess when you make yourself come, you can control the noise level better."

"Uh-huh."

"You're blushing." He thought that was the cutest thing, a new-millennium woman who was a little bit embarrassed about the subject of masturbation.

"I can't help it. I've never talked about this subject with a guy."

"Good. I want you to talk about it with me." He was enormously pleased to discover something he could share with her that no other man had. "But first raise your arms so I can get rid of this tank top."

"We don't have to talk about it." She lifted her arms so he could pull the top over her head.

"But I would love to." He threw the piece of clothing on the floor and slid both hands under her back, groping for the fastening of her bra. That was another thing about her that intrigued him. Most women into seduction wore front-clasp bras, but Kasey hadn't picked up on that trick. He sort of liked that she hadn't.

"Why would you want to talk about it?"

"Because." He unhooked her bra and got that off. With a sigh of delight he gazed at her. His memory had served him well, but he'd forgotten the sweet little freckle right there, on the underside of her left breast. He leaned down to kiss it and she quivered.

So did he. Her skin was so soft. Although he intended to continue the promising discussion they'd recently left, first he needed to spend some time honoring her spectacular breasts. His penis throbbed, reminding him of what he ultimately had to have, but he thought he could hold off a little while longer. And her breasts invited him to play. He really hadn't had his fill the night before.

Propping himself on one arm, he caressed her, lifting and massaging her breasts while he listened to her breathing change. "When you masturbate, do you touch yourself here?" he asked.

"Um…"

"I'll bet you do." He stared into her eyes, which grew darker the longer he caressed her. But she still wore her blue contacts. Before the night was over, he'd coax her to take them out, so he could see the true color of her eyes. "Come on, 'fess up. You play with your breasts."

Her eyelashes fluttered. "Maybe."

"You do. I know it, because you like it when I touch you there."

"Uh…huh."

"But here's something you can't do for yourself." He cradled the weight of her breast in his hand and leaned down to feather a kiss over her nipple. The firm tip reminded him of a plump raspberry. He liked raspberries, but he'd take this treat over an entire bowlful. He drew her nipple in, then rolled it gently against the roof of his mouth and was rewarded with her soft moan.

Then he began to suck, loving the sensation, loving the taste of her and the flowery scent swirling around him. She moaned again and arched her hips. Much as he wanted to unzip both his pants and her shorts and take her right then, he had another agenda that would teach him more about Kasey. He wanted to know her better than anyone.

Releasing her breast with great reluctance, he rolled to his side. Now he had full access to her. He reached for the button on her shorts, unfastened it and pulled down the zipper. When he took them off, he deliberately left her panties in place.

"I have… I have condoms," she said in a husky voice.

"Me, too." He'd stashed several in his pocket, not willing to take a chance they'd be without. "You can never have too many."

Her answering laughter sounded breathless. "Guess not."

He slid his hand inside her panties. He had an idea, something that would excite him tremendously, but he didn't think she'd do it unless he left her panties on.

She was slick and hot, and his pulse hammered as he stroked downward, curving his middle finger so he could probe inside. "Is this how you do it?" He moved his finger slowly, knowing from the way her breath caught that she wasn't too far from a climax.

"I…sort of."

He pulled his hand back. "Show me."

She shook her head, but her eyes glowed with excitement.

"I want to see. Please."

"I…can't."

"Sure you can. Like this." He eased his hand under the waistband of her panties again and found her hot spot. "I would love to see how you make yourself come."

She groaned. "Please…just…"

"Do it for me." Once again he pulled his hand away.

"I want…"

"I know. You want to come. Make it happen. Show me."

She caught her lower lip between her teeth. Then she closed her eyes. Slowly, tentatively she slid her hand down over her stomach. After a slight hesitation, she worked her hand under the elastic band.

He would give anything to watch this when she was naked, but that might take some time and patience. He'd be grateful for this small concession, something she'd never done for another man. His heart pumped wildly as her hand, outlined by the smooth satin of her panties, began to move in a rhythmic way. With her other hand she stroked her breast and pinched her nipple.

Damn, he'd better be careful or he'd come right along with her.

Her lips parted and she gasped. Her movements grew quicker, and then she arched upward with a muted cry.

Sam watched through a haze of desire. He'd never wanted another woman this much, which told him Kasey could be the one he needed to share his life with. And she'd asked for a no-strings affair. Somehow, someday, he had to convince her otherwise.

CHAPTER TWELVE

BY THE TIME Kasey opened her eyes, she'd changed. The shy girl who'd been embarrassed to masturbate in front of a lover had left the building. In her place lay a sexual woman who enjoyed giving herself the extra thrill of having Sam watch. And now she was ready to make her own desires known.

Slowly she peeled off her panties. "Well? Did you like that?"

His voice rasped in the stillness. "Yes."

"Now it's my turn for a fantasy." She sat up. "I want you to lie on your back."

"Why—" He paused to clear his throat. "Why do you want me to do that?"

"I want to play. And all the interesting toys are in the front." Ideas came to her like lightning. She knew how she affected Sam. So she'd put him through his paces and revel in her power.

"All right." He kept his attention on her as he stretched out. "Clothes on or off?"

"I'll worry about that." She climbed off the bed. "I'll be right back."

"Where are you going?"

"You'll see." Discarding her first thought, which was to grab her bathrobe out of the closet, she walked down the hall and through the living room with nothing on. She'd never done that in her life. Tonight it felt perfect.

She went into the kitchen and flicked on a light. Once she'd opened the refrigerator, she snagged a can of whipped cream and padded back across the kitchen. To think that when she'd bought the whipped cream she'd intended to put it on the chocolate pie she'd brought home from the bakery. Wait a minute—the chocolate pie might come in handy, too.

Doing an about-face, she returned to the refrigerator and took out the pie. Sam might have a hammock in a private little patio, but she had whipped cream and a chocolate pie. The neighbors were liable to get an earful, but that couldn't be helped. That was apartment living for you. She turned out the kitchen light and headed back to the bedroom…and Sam.

On the way back down the hall, she called out to him, "Here I come."

His voice sounded a little bit strained. "How do you mean that, exactly?"

She laughed. "In the nonsexual sense, this time. This next episode will be about you, not me." She walked through the doorway and noticed from the jut of his fly that the flag was definitely up on his mailbox. "Just don't start without me, okay?"

His eyes widened. "Whipped cream?"

"Oh, yeah. And chocolate pie. I missed dessert tonight." She'd missed dinner, too, but who cared?

"Uh…I see."

"Maybe you're beginning to. First rule, I'm in charge." She sat beside him on the bed and put the whipped cream and pie on the nightstand.

"You walked naked through your apartment." With a smile, he reached out to cup her swaying breast.

She batted his hand away. "No touching me. I get to

touch you, now. And yes, I walked naked through my apartment. What of it?"

"I'll bet you've never done that before."

"Maybe not."

"How did it feel?"

"Good." She began unbuttoning his shirt. "Now hold still."

"I can't promise a thing."

"Then hold as still as you can." She tugged his shirt from the waistband of his slacks and spread it open. "There." He had such a great chest, lightly furred with dark hair and muscled enough to be manly without the overdeveloped physique of a professional bodybuilder. It was no wonder the women at Beckworth had spent most of the day watching him trim the mesquite tree.

Now she had the privilege of enjoying his body all by herself. Gretchen had tried to get her to spill the details of her relationship with Sam, but Kasey had claimed they were only friends. She'd told Gretchen that Sam was now a client and she shouldn't get involved with a client anyway. Gretchen had protested that this particular client would be worth breaking a few rules for.

Gazing down at Sam, Kasey had to agree with Gretchen. Smoothing her hands down his chest, she gazed into his eyes and watched them darken in reaction to her touch. Then she stroked his arms and lingered on his tattoo. "Why did you get this?" She traced the pattern lightly with one finger.

"In high school I had a reputation for being too nice."

"I can believe that." She brushed her palms over his nipples.

"I thought… I thought a big bad tattoo would help my rep."

She smiled. He was definitely getting more aroused with every caress. "And did it help your rep?"

"Oh, yeah. Instant tough guy."

"I'll bet." She leaned over him and nibbled on his lower lip. "By the way, I have neighbors, but don't worry about making noise."

"I can control it."

She trailed kisses along his jaw until her lips were right next to his ear. "We'll see." Then she gently nipped his earlobe. "We'll see about that, tough guy." Then she sat up and reached for the can of whipped cream.

SAM WAS FASCINATED by the transformation in Kasey. From the evidence, she'd passed some milestone by making herself come while he looked on. He'd meant to nudge her a little further down the road of sensuality. Apparently he'd launched her onto the superhighway of sexual adventure.

He wasn't complaining, but he would have to keep his wits about him if he intended to stay in the game. With her brains, she could outpace him in the innovation department in no time. And he was very much afraid that if she ever got bored, she'd be gone.

She wasn't bored yet, however, because she'd just discovered whipped cream. He gasped when she squirted a mound of the cold white stuff on his nipple. He hadn't thought that his nipples were overly sensitive, but when she started lapping at the whipped cream with her warm tongue, he changed his mind. She licked him clean before zapping the other side. Wild.

Incredible how her attention to that one little spot had him going. And he knew exactly what other target she had in mind for that squirt can. But he wasn't quite sure what she planned to do with the pie, or whether he'd survive it without coming in a very loud and spectacular fashion.

He knew that was her goal, to prove that she could make him lose all control and yell like a banshee. Because he wanted to continue to challenge her, he would fight like hell not to do what she expected. He sensed that the un-expected would keep her interested, and he very much wanted to keep her interested.

When she finished playing with his nipples, she took off his pants and briefs. He was supposed to lie there and let her undress him, and that was a whole new experience, too, because she wasn't very practiced at it. She fumbled around a lot and kept laughing and brushing her naked body against him. When she bumped his aching penis with her breast, he nearly erupted from that single contact.

"Are we having fun, yet?" she asked once she'd pulled off his slacks and briefs and dropped them on the floor. "How're you doing down here?" She wrapped her fingers around his shaft.

"Terrific." He clenched his jaw against the release that pounded at the gates of his self-control, begging him to surrender. He knew she'd pick up that whipped-cream can again, and he wondered how he'd make it through another tongue bath, especially if it involved that rebellious part of his anatomy she held in her hand.

But instead of the whipped cream, she picked up the pie. His brain stalled just thinking of the possibilities. Here he'd been hoping that before the night was over, she'd drink champagne naked. In the past half hour, she'd shot right past that mark and was on to more creative turn-ons.

"Do you like chocolate pie?" she asked.

"Sure."

"Me, too." She stuck two fingers into the center of the pie and lifted out a glob of chocolate filling.

He fully expected it to end up on some part of him, but instead she started licking it off her fingers.

"This is very good." She put both fingers in her mouth and sucked on them. Then she scooped up another glob and repeated the process.

He began to understand her devious plan. She was playing mind games with him, letting him watch her lick and suck her fingers while he imagined what she could do to his penis.

"Want some?" She extended her hand, a quivering bit of chocolate filling on her fingertips.

"Love some." He tried to pretend that he wasn't lying there completely erect and that she didn't have him right where she wanted him. He sucked the chocolate off her fingers and used his tongue to clean off every last morsel. Two could play at this game.

She definitely responded to the movement of his tongue. Her breathing quickened as she watched him slide it right between her fingers. "Want more?" she murmured.

"Sure." He met her gaze. There was plenty of filling in that pie. Enough for him to have a little fun, too. He took his time getting the chocolate off her fingers when she gave him a second helping. He sucked on her middle finger a little longer than was necessary, and noticed her shiver.

"Let's try something else," she said, and her voice trembled, revealing that she wasn't in complete control.

"Whatever you want."

"Let's see how this feels." And she smeared the filling over the tip of his penis.

He moaned. Couldn't help it. The cool, creamy texture against his hot, tight shaft drove him insane. He clutched the sheets beneath him, closing his hands into fists as his muscles bunched, wanting that climax more than life itself.

Then she began to lick.

He didn't last very long. "Kasey…" He writhed against the mattress. "Kasey, I'm… I can't stop…"

"Go ahead," she murmured, right before she slid her mouth down over him and sucked hard.

Oh, he made noise all right. All his macho pride went right out the window as he climaxed. He told the world about it, made sure everyone in the next county knew that he'd come. And when it was over, he lay panting, his eyes closed, his body drained of every last bit of energy.

He felt the moment when she released him, felt the silken slide of her body as she moved up the mattress.

Then she nuzzled his ear and nipped his earlobe again. "Gotcha," she whispered.

KASEY LAY DOWN next to Sam, put her hands behind her head and gazed at the dancing shadows created by the candle flame. So this was what sexual liberation was like. She'd always wondered if she had the necessary temperament to be a wild woman. Sam had helped her answer that question.

Even though they'd eventually have to part ways, she'd always be grateful to him. Maybe she'd needed someone older to guide her through this. A less experienced man might not have gently pushed her to explore her options.

What a good time she'd had with the whipped cream and the pie. The only unintended side effect was her own arousal. She wondered if Sam would drift off to sleep and leave her to deal with that on her own. If he did, then she would. He'd taught her to take what she wanted.

And she did ache for another climax. Being with Sam had cranked up her libido, and now one orgasm wasn't nearly enough. She glanced over at him and saw that his eyes were still closed. She'd worked him pretty hard the past two nights. He probably needed his rest.

Slowly she reached between her legs, where she was very hot and wet. Yes, she needed to come again, maybe even twice. She hadn't understood herself before, but the fact was, she was a highly sexed woman. And a highly sexed woman needed satisfaction.

"Can I help?"

With her hand still in position, she turned her head and found that he'd rolled to his side and was watching her. "That's up to you."

His chuckle was low and intimate. "What progress. You'd give me a repeat performance, wouldn't you?"

"Or I can let you sleep. Maybe you need to relax and take it easy."

His eyebrows lifted. "Oh? Are you questioning my stamina?"

"You seem kind of…wiped out."

"Well, I've recovered." He circled her wrist with his fingers and lifted her hand, guiding it to his mouth. "And hungry." He licked her damp fingers.

She quivered, remembering the scene in the hammock the night before. That might have been the true beginning of her transformation. No man had ever given her such unparalleled pleasure. Sam had elevated oral sex to an art form.

He nuzzled her palm. "Do you like chocolate pie with or without whipped cream?"

She gulped. "That depends."

"I'm not sure which I want, either." Releasing her hand, he shrugged out of his shirt. "Lift up."

"Why?" She thought she knew, and her blood ran hot.

"You had your turn. Now I want to play. Lift up."

When she raised her hips off the bed, he shoved his folded shirt underneath her. Then he reached for the pie and the can of whipped cream. "Choices, choices."

Her heart beat faster as he got up from the bed and walked around to the foot, surveying her the entire time.

Not long ago she would have felt vulnerable and exposed if a man had done that. Now she was proud of her body, proud of how completely she'd captured his attention.

At last he nodded. "I have a taste for both chocolate and whipped cream. I've found the perfect spot to enjoy it, and I want to be comfortable, so we need a small adjustment." After laying the pie and the can of whipped cream on the end of the bed, he leaned over it and grasped her thighs.

"Sam! What—" But she understood when he scooted her, shirt and all, closer to the end of the bed.

"Now hold still," he said, a smile in his voice as he repeated her instructions.

"Yeah, right." Her voice shook. "Like you stayed still while I did this." She lifted her head.

"Maybe you're stronger than I was." He sank to his knees at the foot of the bed.

"Maybe." She doubted it, especially considering what he had in store for her. She let her head fall back to the mattress.

"First, a little chocolate filling."

She thought she was prepared, but even so, she gasped as the cool substance settled over her hot vulva. The sensation was arousing in a way she never would have imagined. So this was what she'd let him in for a while ago.

And he wanted to return the favor. No, he wanted to up the ante. Whipped cream under pressure danced across her trigger point, making her moan with pleasure.

"Ah. I think we need more of that." He licked it away, which only drove her wilder. Then he hit her with another spurt, cleaned her off with his tongue and tried it again.

She began to tremble violently, closing in on her climax.

"Now for the chocolate," he murmured, and began lapping, finishing each stroke by paying special attention to the area he'd zapped with whipped cream.

She'd never felt anything like it. Almost without warning, an orgasm ripped through her, forcing cries of ecstasy from her throat. But he wasn't finished. He stroked on more chocolate and kept going. She was in for an incredible ride.

This time he had to hold her steady while he licked, because she thrashed around, driven out of her mind by his clever tongue and the powerful undulations that rolled through her again and again. One climax blended into another as she gasped and bucked in his arms.

When at last he eased her back to the mattress, she was sobbing with gratitude, totally wrung out with the force of her body's response. Her ears rang and every nerve quivered. She was his puppet, his slave. Had he asked her to run away with him, to give up everything to be with him and make love every waking moment, she would have done it.

Instead he crawled up beside her and gathered her quaking body close to his. Carefully he brushed her hair back from her ear and placed his lips there. "Gotcha," he whispered.

CHAPTER THIRTEEN

AFTER THE CHOCOLATE-PIE-AND-WHIPPED-CREAM incident, Sam had no problem persuading Kasey to walk naked into the kitchen with him so they could break out the champagne. "See, I told you we'd have something to celebrate," he said as he opened the refrigerator and pulled out the bottle. It wasn't Dom Pérignon, because he hadn't wanted to be too flashy, but it was a decent brand.

"You did tell me that." She set a couple of inexpensive wineglasses on the counter. "I guess you've figured out by now that I don't have a lot of the amenities."

He unscrewed the wire from the plastic cap on the champagne. "Lady, you have chocolate pie and a can of whipped cream. The amenities don't get any better than that."

"That was pure accident." Then she seemed to catch herself. "I mean, I knew they might come in handy, but I wasn't sure how you'd react if I suggested something that wild."

"Oh, come on." He laughed as he grabbed a kitchen towel and covered the top of the bottle so he could twist out the cork. "You don't have to pretend you were all prepared for something like that. I could tell that using the pie was a last-minute inspiration, just like my deal with the hammock was totally unplanned. I think it's great that you're spontaneous. So am I."

She paused, as if absorbing what he'd said. Then she

cleared her throat. "I'm not as sexually experienced as you are. I suppose you've figured that out, too."

"Well, that makes you just about perfect." He punctured that with the pop of the cork, then poured the champagne into the glasses she'd set on the counter, making sure he didn't spill. "Guys dream about finding a woman who isn't quite as experienced as they are but is ready to try anything."

"I can't be your dream girl."

That got his attention. He stopped pouring and looked at her.

"Well, I'm sorry, but I just can't." She looked like a stubborn little kid.

He sighed and put down the bottle. "Kasey, what's the deal here? This morning you were ready to ditch me because I came on too strong. Now I make an offhand remark about guys who dream about women like you, and you jump on me as if I've proposed."

She flushed and looked away. "I know you're not proposing, but it sounded sort of…definite, that's all."

"It wasn't definite, okay?" But he was sick of her acting like he had cooties. "The thing is, I can't help wondering what you find so objectionable about me that you have to keep reminding me I'm temporary entertainment. Is it my IQ? Is it that I'm not smart enough for you?"

"That's not fair."

Instantly he was sorry. She'd probably heard that a hundred times. "Yeah, you're right. I told you I thought it was fantastic that you're smart, and then I used it against you." He ran a hand through his hair. "But whenever you push me away, I can't help wondering why. I lost my temper. I apologize."

"Maybe I can explain." She took a deep breath. "Let's go in the living room and I'll light the candles."

"Yeah, let's do that." He hated that the mood was spoiled, but when she'd said, straight out, *I can't be your dream girl,* it had hit him where he lived. He thought she might be his dream girl, and he didn't like hearing her reject the idea so completely.

Moments later they were cuddling on her futon couch with the candles burning, and the mood had already improved. He couldn't stay mad at her for long. Besides, he liked snuggling with her.

He liked it too damn much, as a matter of fact. In a setting like this, he started thinking about how nice it would be to cuddle this way every night, and then go to bed and cuddle some more, and wake up next to each other. He could picture Kasey in that role. But she didn't want him to, for some reason.

She took an afghan that had been folded across the back of the futon and spread it over them to ward off the breeze from the air conditioner. Then she took a sip of her champagne. "It's good."

He touched his glass to hers. "So are you. Very good." He didn't make the toast he'd wanted to make, about many more nights like this. She might take it wrong.

"Sam, I haven't dated a lot, haven't had a bunch of lovers."

That made him very happy, but he tried to sound sympathetic. "Because of being so smart."

"That has a lot to do with it, yes. I, um, used to be sort of a nerd."

"Looking at you now, that's hard to believe."

"It's true. Last summer, my...a friend...helped me with a makeover. We did the hair, the clothes, the makeup—all of it."

He caught her chin in one hand. "So exactly what color are your eyes, really?"

"Gray. Totally uninteresting." Then she must have realized how that could sound to someone whose eyes were also gray. "Not that *your* eyes are boring. I like your eyes a lot. You have little flecks of gold in there, but mine are—"

"Would you take out your contacts so I can see for myself if they're totally uninteresting?" He had a hunch he'd like her better without the blue tint. The more she revealed the authentic Kasey Braddock, the more he liked what he saw. Her personality—part child, part woman—fascinated him.

"If I take out my contacts, I'll be blind as a bat."

"I'll bet you have glasses around here somewhere."

"Glasses!" She stared at him in horror. "As if I'd let you see me in glasses! Talk about blowing the entire image. I think not."

"Is that why you don't want me to get too close? You're hung up on creating an image? Because I don't care about that."

"Are you sure?" She skewered him over the rim of her glass. "Think about when we first met. Would you have been as excited about going out with me if I'd walked up to you wearing glasses, dressed in a shapeless denim jumper and with my hair in a braid?"

He wasn't sure he liked this discussion. "Maybe not," he finally admitted. "But—"

"See? That's my point."

"But that look is not you, not your personality. You wouldn't deliberately try to make yourself unattractive."

"Not deliberately, but that's exactly how I used to dress. Needless to say, I didn't have a lot of offers back then."

He studied her, trying to picture her the way she'd described. "I'll bet you looked better than that."

"I could show you pictures."

"Anybody can take a bad picture."

"Sam, face facts. If you'd met me a couple of years ago, you wouldn't have given me a second glance."

Unfortunately, she was probably right. He'd been attracted by her outward appearance, which made him just like all the other guys. He wasn't proud of that.

But he was nothing if not honest. "Okay, guilty as charged." he said. "I was hooked the minute I saw you get out of your little red convertible with SO REDY on the vanity plate."

"I'm not surprised...or even offended." She sipped her champagne. "I work in PR, remember? I understand the emotional impact of images. I just didn't have the nerve to apply the principles to myself until recently."

He could see where this was going. "So you want to catch up on all the fun you missed during your shapeless-denim-jumper phase?"

"Is that so wrong?" She held his gaze.

"No, of course not." But it shot the hell out of his dreams. "Now that you've explained the situation, I can't help wondering something. You don't have to answer, but I have a feeling this is important to the discussion. Since your makeover, how many guys have you, uh...been with?"

"You mean, how many have I had sex with?"

He sighed. "Yeah, that's what I mean. And I have no right to ask. That's a very personal—"

"One."

"Me?"

"You. I haven't been ready until now. I had to be mentally prepared to live up to my new image, prepared to take on hot guys instead of the nerds I was used to."

That was good news and bad news—he liked having the distinction of being the first hot guy, especially liked being labeled a hot guy. But she'd implied he would be the first of many. That was very bad news. Her casual-sex period could last for years. After all, his had.

"So that's why I said we were at different stages in our lives right now," she said. "Eventually I'll need to move on."

That thought depressed him, so he drank some more champagne.

"In the meantime, though…" She slipped her hand under the afghan and quickly put his penis on red alert.

"I see your point." He loved what she was doing under that afghan. "*Eventually* is a very vague word."

"But *orgasm* is not."

"Nope. Quite specific." And impending, too. He realized there was a problem with walking around naked. No pockets. Much as he hated to do it, he put a stop to her erotic stroking.

"Bring your champagne," he said, throwing back the afghan and standing. "We need to make an expedition back to where the wild condoms grow."

She laughed. "But I could just—"

"I know. You were about to accomplish exactly that." He grabbed the champagne bottle and motioned her to go ahead of him down the hall. "But I have a hankering to try this the old-fashioned way."

"No pies?" she said over her shoulder. "No whipped cream?"

"That's right." In the dim light of the hallway, he could just make out the inviting sway of her hips and the mouth-watering curve of her butt. He'd like to try doggie style some time, but right now, he had some bonding in mind. "And no contacts," he said as they stepped into the darkened bedroom.

"You're ridiculous." She set her glass on the nightstand. "Want me to light the candles?"

"I'd love you to turn on the lamp, instead."

She pushed the little switch and glanced at him. "Full light and no contacts. Are you trying to demystify me?"

I'm trying to learn who you are so I can somehow hang on to you. But of course he couldn't say that, so he gave her another reason that was almost as valid. "I'd like to watch your eyes when you come. I want to see what color they get for real."

She shook her head and smiled, as if unable to believe he could be so goofy. "Okay, if it means that much to you. But I won't be able to see you very well."

"Unless you put on your glasses."

"I draw the line at glasses. Be right back. These aren't disposable, so I have to take them out in the bathroom."

After she left, he took one more drink of his champagne before setting the bottle and his glass next to hers. He noticed how uncluttered the surfaces were in this room. She didn't have any framed family pictures sitting around. Most women he knew loved doing that. No doubt about it, Kasey was a puzzle, a puzzle he wanted to solve.

Stretching out on the bed, he was in a perfect position for her entrance. She walked in holding her hands out in front of her as if she couldn't see a thing.

Then she groped for the edge of the bed. "Where are you, Sam? I can't find you."

If he hadn't seen the corner of her mouth twitch, he would have believed her act. "I'm right here," he said, holding back a smile. "Keep looking."

"I see something...something *enormous.* There!" She grabbed his erect penis. "Got it!"

"Ah, yes, but do you recognize this large object you've found, my dear?"

"It does feel sort of familiar." She fumbled around some

more and cupped his balls in her other hand. "I think all this goes together."

"Good guess."

She fondled him some more, keeping her eyes unfocused. "This part feels like something I've touched before.... Sam, is that you?"

"Yeah, it's me, you faker." Laughing, he rolled her to her back. "And I love the color of your eyes."

"You're just saying that." But she was smiling, as if she liked hearing the compliment. "After all this hoopla, you wouldn't dare say anything different."

"Your eyes are the color of clouds before a rain."

"And dishwater before it drains."

He leaned down and kissed her. "Be quiet. We're going to have sex, now."

"I hope you can find the condoms, because I can't even see the box."

"Leave everything to me."

"All righty, then."

And she did leave everything to him. Maybe she sensed that he had a certain experience in mind, because he'd asked her to leave the light on and take her contacts out. Or maybe she felt sad because she couldn't give him any promises about their future.

She did give him all of herself, though, allowing him to kiss and caress every part of her, to map her body completely in the glow of the bedside lamp. And when he finally put on a condom and thrust deep inside her, she let him see the passion building in her eyes...her beautiful gray eyes.

He knew he was falling for her. No doubt she also realized what was happening to him. If only she'd let go of the agenda she was clinging to so desperately. Then she just might fall for him, too.

Sam stayed for breakfast, even though Kasey warned him she didn't know how to cook. He promised to take care of that situation. Then he set the alarm and roused her out of bed at an ungodly hour so they wouldn't have to rush.

While she showered, he borrowed a razor. He insisted he wouldn't kiss her until he'd shaved because he didn't want to give her whisker burn. Then he joined her in the shower, kissing her on the mouth and after that in places that quickly produced her first climax of the day. She returned the favor, and by the time they finally climbed out of the shower, she was very glad her utilities were included in her rent.

After they dressed, she watched in fascination as he poked through her refrigerator and located eggs and butter. He found a skillet she never used, took his time learning the idiosyncracies of her stove, and finally fried the eggs over easy, exactly the way she liked them. She made the coffee and managed to burn the toast.

Their division of chores felt dangerously domestic to her. The easy way they puttered around the kitchen together was a little unnerving, and she wondered if he'd comment on it. He didn't.

Sharing breakfast at her tiny table in a corner of her living room seemed way too cozy and comfortable, and she searched for a way to change the mood. She settled on discussing the project he'd hired her for. "You never did fill out that questionnaire I need for your PR campaign," she said.

"No. We got sidetracked." He winked at her and continued munching his toast. No guy had any business looking so appealing at seven-thirty in the morning.

"I could ask you the questions now." If she didn't focus on something else, she was liable to drag him back to the bedroom, and they'd both be late for work.

He took a swallow of coffee. "Shoot."

"What message are you conveying with your business currently?"

He looked blank. "Message? I'm not conveying any message."

"Yes, you are, whether you realize it or not." Right now he was conveying the message that he was available for some more mind-blowing sex.

"Then maybe you can tell me what the message is."

That you're hot. With great difficulty she refocused her thoughts and tried to picture the business card he'd given her yesterday. "What else is on your card besides the company name and your contact info?"

"Professional, courteous service."

"There's your message."

"And it's boring. It's not sexy enough."

Oh, but you make up for it. She wondered how many female customers he had. An ad featuring Sam without his shirt would triple his business in no time. But that wasn't the plan he had in mind.

"So that's what you want?" she said. "A sexy message?"

"Yeah." He gazed across the table at her. "That's why I came to you. You know that Springsteen tune 'Secret Garden'?"

"Uh-huh." It was one of her favorite songs in the whole world. She'd nearly worn out that part of the *Jerry Maguire* soundtrack.

"I want that kind of message to come across."

"The song's about sex."

"I know, and I want to help customers create a secret garden right in their own backyards, where they can…do whatever they want."

"Like have sex?"

He smiled at her. "If they want to."

"But of course you can't come right out and say that."

"No. It has to be implied, like in the Springsteen tune. But if you can think how to do it, I guarantee I'll get more business."

She sipped her coffee and turned the problem over in her mind. "How about using the implications of the Springsteen song? Your new slogan could be *Specializing in Secret Gardens*."

"You're a genius."

"Borderline."

He laughed. "That's close enough for my purposes. I love the slogan. I'm sure we can do lots of great things with it." He reached across the table and captured her hand. "Now let's talk about us, and my garden. I want you to come to my place again. We'll do it right this time, with a meal, candles, soft music and perhaps another visit to the garden."

Her body hummed in anticipation. "Last time wasn't too shabby."

"I can improve on it." He rubbed his thumb over the back of her hand. "Tonight?"

She should probably put him off. Three nights in a row was beginning to look like a serious commitment. Then she tried to imagine how she'd feel, staying home alone when she could be in his garden, in his arms, having multiple orgasms. "Okay," she said.

His eyes blazed with triumph. "Great. And now I'd better leave before I haul you back to bed." He squeezed her hand and released it before scooting his chair away from the table.

"What can I bring?" She stood and walked with him to the door.

"Yourself."

"No, seriously. I'm no cook, but I can pick up something at the deli."

He paused by the door. "There is one thing, but you might not want to get it."

"Sure I would. Bread? Wine? What?"

"Underwear from Slightly Scandalous."

CHAPTER FOURTEEN

KASEY DISCOVERED THAT strolling into Slightly Scandalous as a potential customer was very different from walking in as a PR professional looking for ways to upgrade the store's image. As a buyer, she looked at the displays in a whole new way. Her tummy jumped with nervousness as she tried to decide if she was woman enough to do this or if she was too chicken.

That emphasized exactly why the store needed an image change. If more women could shop for sexy undies with a degree of comfort, the business would survive, maybe even prosper. If too many women came here feeling as she did right now, sales would continue to slide downhill.

"Hi, Kasey!" Monique, a young salesgirl the owner had hired a month ago, smiled. From her pink-and-blond spiked hair to her multiple piercings, Monique fit the old Slightly Scandalous stereotype. She was nineteen, only a year younger than Kasey, but she made Kasey feel ancient.

"Hey, Monique." Kasey wondered if Monique would take kindly to a slight makeover herself, once the store changed its look. A California native, Monique was a free-thinker who didn't mind the risqué nature of the shop, but no doubt she wanted to keep her job and understood that business wasn't what it should be. She'd probably cooperate.

"I'll bet you're here to get some more ideas, huh?"

"Something like that," Kasey said. No changes had been

made to the displays or the merchandise pending Kasey's presentation of the proposed makeover. Therefore mannequins still wore peekaboo bras and thongs with no crotch. She wondered if that's what Sam envisioned on her tonight.

"I had an idea," Monique said.

"What's that?" Kasey had always thought Monique was creative, so she was more than willing to listen.

"Once the store has relocated with its new look, for some free publicity, you could do a fashion show for some of the businesswomen's clubs in town."

"With underwear?" Kasey wondered how that would go over at a downtown luncheon meeting.

"Sure. You could do it very tastefully, have the models wearing silk robes, and then they sort of flash the underwear. I mean, not like a flasher, but more sort of seductive. You know—sophisticatedly sexy."

Kasey laughed as she imagined how fun and flirty that could be, exactly the image she was trying to create for the store. "I get it. And I think it would work, too, presented like that. Thanks, Monique. If we do that, I'll make sure you get all the credit for the idea."

"Thanks." Monique flushed with pleasure. "And by the way, you'd make a great model."

Kasey gulped. "Oh, I don't think so."

"You would. You have the body for it. You might not want to, seeing as how you're with this big-deal PR company, but you'd be great. I've had some modeling classes. I could teach you how to walk."

"You could?" Kasey couldn't help thinking of a private runway in a secluded little garden with an audience of one. She wouldn't mind some tips on how to model whatever she bought today, *if* she worked up the nerve to buy it.

"I could definitely teach you. Whenever you want. Anyway, I've bothered you enough. You probably came here to prowl around and make notes, like you did last time. Don't let me stop you."

"Um, okay." If Monique hadn't made assumptions about Kasey's reason for being there this morning, she might have been able to confess the real reason. But now she felt obliged to look professional and busy. Taking her voice-activated recorder out of her briefcase, she started moving around the store.

"The leather thong and bra might be able to stay in the line," she murmured into the recorder. *"But the matching handcuffs need to be moved from the front of the store, perhaps to a special room in back. Ditto the riding crop."* She wondered if Sam was into any of that S and M stuff. She couldn't picture him taking it seriously, but as long as it was all in fun, then maybe…

Shaking herself out of an erotic daydream, she walked to another display. *"Silk teddies are one of the key items in a store of this kind, but the customer we're hoping to attract will not want her nipples to show, or her…other parts."*

Or would she? Maybe under certain circumstances she would. For example, if she were carrying on a high-energy affair with a sexy landscaper, she might want to flaunt her nipples. The more Kasey saw of this underwear with gaps in strategic places, the more she believed that was precisely what Sam hoped she'd bring to his private party tonight.

If she recommended eliminating all such items from the store, they might lose customers who wanted a special thrill connected to their purchase. *"Perhaps the answer is to make a private annex available to those who wish to shop for these items,"* she dictated into the recorder. *"Think video store, where the bulk of the offerings are for general consumption, and a special section in the back is dedicated to adult movies."*

No doubt about it, though, something had to be done about the store's curb appeal. She'd been there nearly thirty minutes and not a single customer had arrived. That might change anytime, though, and if she planned to buy anything, she'd better make her move. But what should she get?

Monique would be glad to advise her. Kasey walked over to the counter where the salesclerk was flipping through the pages of a magazine. Kasey cleared her throat. "Monique, I could use some help."

"Yeah?" Monique glanced up, her expression eager. "Great! I love coming up with ideas about how to promote stuff. I've been thinking I might like a career in PR. Maybe I'll take some classes."

"You'd be good at PR." They were back to business and Kasey almost lost her nerve. Monique was setting her up as a role model, so how could she ask for advice on crotchless panties? "I encourage you to give it a try."

"You know, I think I will. So what do you need help with?"

"Well, I... I, um, it's sort of a...a personal matter."

"Oh!"

"I need to buy some really sexy underwear." Kasey rushed on before she changed her mind. "And I want you to help me pick it out, and...and teach me the runway walk."

SAM DIDN'T HAVE TIME to make a meal for Kasey, so he picked up some Thai food on the way home. He'd decided to dismantle the hammock to make room for his latest purchase—a canvas gazebo with side panels that rolled down for privacy. He was struggling with the gazebo when Colin stuck his head over the alley gate.

"Hey, man!" Colin called. "I saw your truck out front but you didn't answer your doorbell, so I thought you might be out here in your favorite spot. What the hell is that, anyway?"

"It's supposed to be a gazebo, but right now it's a pile of canvas and metal pieces that won't cooperate." He abandoned the mess on his patio and walked over to unlock the gate. "So what's up?"

"Not your gazebo, apparently. Want some help?"

"Smart-ass. Sure."

"Then I'm your guy. I played at a gig where they had one of these contraptions." Colin fished a rubber band out of his pocket and put his long hair in a ponytail—his personal signal that he was getting down to work. "Got beer?"

"Yeah, but you'll have to drink it quick. I have a date."

"Cool. Is it that hot chick you brought to the Cactus Club?" Ignoring the directions sitting on the patio table, Colin started putting together braces.

"Aren't you going to take a passing glance at those directions?" Sam knew the answer, but he wanted to divert Colin away from the subject of Kasey. He'd promised her they'd keep their affair secret.

Fortunately Colin was easy to distract. That was one of his problems. The only thing he'd stayed with consistently was his music, and that was why Sam wanted to give him all the support he could.

Sure enough, Colin took the bait and gave Sam a withering glance. "Have you *ever* known me to use directions?"

"Nope. But there's always a first time."

"No, there isn't. Directions only confuse the issue."

"If you say so. I'll get the beer."

When he returned a few minutes later with a bottle of his brother's favorite imported brew, Colin had made good progress on the gazebo. The kid was so bright when he focused. Then something occurred to him. As a very bright person who seemed to have her act together, Kasey might be able to help guide him to stay focused. But Sam wasn't supposed to be fostering a relationship between Kasey and his brother.

"Pick up that side of the canvas top and we'll lift it over the frame," Colin said.

"How do you know that's it's facing right?"

"I channeled the gazebo maker over in China, dude."

Sam laughed, but sometimes he wondered if Colin was joking or not. The kid was amazing. Having Colin around had given him an appreciation for the workings of the right brain and had taught him to admire creative intelligence, not sneer at it.

Kasey might not find a lot of guys who could do that. He wondered how he could subtly point out to her that he, Sam Ashton, was the one for her. And he didn't feel like waiting around tapping his foot while she had sex with a bunch of other guys, either.

Before long the gazebo was finished and Colin claimed his beer. "You're not having one with me?"

"Nah."

"Gotta stay sharp for your gazebo-mate, huh?" Colin grinned at him. "Are you going to put the patio table in there? That would be classy."

"Uh, maybe." Sam wasn't keen on revealing his plans for the gazebo. They didn't involve putting the patio table in it. "When's the next gig for the Tin Tarantulas?"

Colin pointed the beer bottle at him. "Way to read my mind, bro! I swear you're getting better at ESP every day."

Not really. But he was getting better at changing the subject when he didn't want Colin to continue along a certain line of questioning. "So you have something coming up?"

"We do, and it's a big deal. We're booked into that new place, the Yucca Lounge."

Sam had heard of it, a trendy club in Scottsdale. "Isn't that a much bigger venue?"

"Most definitely. Which is why I need your help, man. I want you to call in all your favors for Saturday night, talk to anybody you know. We have to pack that place to the rafters, and I'm nervous. It's huge."

"You'll pull them in," Sam said. "There was standing room only at the Cactus Club."

"We're talkin' twice the number of seats. Please get the word out to everyone in your Rolodex, okay?"

"Okay." Sam nodded and tried to think of helping his brother instead of mourning the loss of a big chunk of his Saturday night. He and Kasey would have to meet afterward, because he couldn't take her, not if she really wanted to keep their affair quiet.

Colin still looked worried. "Like, can you put pressure on your guys at work?"

"Sure. I'll do that. I'll ask them to bring their friends. Don't worry. It'll be fine."

"I can't leave that to chance. This is the time to dredge up everybody you've ever known in Phoenix, man. Drag out your yearbook and start looking for dudes you knew in high school. Me, I can't do that because we moved and I've lost track of everybody."

"I'll find out who's still in town. I've been meaning to look in the phone book and find out if Jim Winston's still here. If he is, maybe he can help me round up some of the other guys."

"Thanks, bro." Colin clapped him on the back. "And bring your girlfriend, and all her friends, too."

"Uh, we'll see."

Colin peered at him. Then he waved his arm at the gazebo. "You just put up a frickin' gazebo for this chick, and you can't bring her on Saturday night?"

"It's complicated."

"Oh, I get it. It's the same chick from the other night, and she secretly hated our music."

"No, she loved your music. That's not the problem."

"Then it must be that she's hot for me and you don't want to take a chance that she'll jump ship."

Sam grinned. "You are such an egomaniac."

"It's true, huh?" Colin laughed. "Don't worry. I'll tell her you're a better deal. Chicks love the steady income."

"Gee, that makes me feel like such a man. I may not be much, but by God, I have a steady income. How sexy can you get?"

Colin finished his beer and handed the bottle to Sam. Then he glanced at the gazebo. "You tell me, bro." Chuckling, he headed for the back gate.

"Hey, thanks for the help."

"Any time. Just round up all the strays you can find for Saturday, okay?"

"Don't worry. I'll charter a bus if I have to."

"Sounds good." With a wave, Colin left.

AFTER BUYING THE UNDERWEAR and getting a quick runway lesson from Monique in the back room of the store, Kasey made one more stop at a dress boutique and found a wraparound silk dress. The ivory material slid over her skin like cool water and was held together by two small ties. Kasey practiced in the dressing room to make sure she could pull the ties apart in seconds.

The dress exactly matched the underwear she'd bought at Slightly Scandalous. She would have to drive very carefully over to Sam's house. If she got into an accident and was taken to the E.R. in this outfit, her mother would never forgive her.

She stowed her loot in the trunk of her Miata before returning to the office. Gretchen and the gang were already convinced she was keeping secrets about Sam. They didn't need to find a shopping bag from Slightly Scandalous to make them even more suspicious.

She spent the rest of the morning on the lingerie store's new image, and the afternoon dreaming up promo ideas for Ashton Landscaping. Sam's enthusiasm for her ideas felt good. Everything about Sam felt good. If she were looking for the perfect guy, Sam would be it.

But she was only twenty years old. She wasn't ready for the perfect guy. Life was so unfair. Now that she was ready to experience being a swinging single girl, she was supposed to find men who were fun, not perfect. She'd read the chick-lit books—nobody found Mr. Perfect right off the bat. Except her, apparently.

Maybe Sam wasn't as right for her as he seemed. She wasn't very experienced, so she might not recognize his imperfections. The fact that she considered him perfect should be a warning bell in itself. He was human—there had to be things wrong with him.

Maybe tonight she'd try to be more objective and figure out where Sam was lacking. It wouldn't be in the area of sex, so she could simply enjoy that part and look for flaws in other parts of his life. And she *would* enjoy the sex. She could hardly wait to show off her Bad Girl duds.

At last the day crawled to an end. She hurried home, showered and changed into her outfit. As she headed out the door, she picked up the folder containing her plans for his promo campaign. Because they'd agreed he wouldn't come into the office, she had to discuss business sometime during the night.

She was surprised at how natural that seemed, mixing their private and professional lives. Apparently he'd known what he was talking about when he'd insisted she could do his PR work even though they were having a hot and heavy affair.

The situation could change, though, if the affair ended before the promo campaign. They might not work together so easily if one of them decided to call off the fireworks. And someone would do that sooner or later.

But she refused to think about that now, while she was wearing underwear from Slightly Scandalous and contemplating Sam's reaction. She smiled as she turned into the driveway of Sam's cute little house. Tonight would be another outstanding night of sex. She should have brought champagne.

CHAPTER FIFTEEN

SAM BARELY MADE IT through all the preparations, but when the doorbell rang, he'd finished everything. Candles in glass containers ringed the patio and sat on the table, which was set for two. Exotic music drifted from his portable CD player.

He'd covered the floor of the gazebo with an egg-crate mattress topper plus quilts and pillows. Three sides were rolled down, but he'd left the fourth side up, so that Kasey could see what he had in mind for after dinner. He wanted to create some anticipation in her, too.

When he opened the door and saw her standing there in an ivory silk dress that looked like it would come off in no time, he wanted to forget about anticipation, forget about dinner completely, in fact. "Hi," he said. "I see you brought dessert."

"You think so?" She smiled and moved past him.

"Yeah, and it smells delicious." He loved dealing with a smart woman, someone who didn't have to ask what he meant by bringing dessert.

She turned and held out a folder. "I have more ideas for your promo plan, if you want to hear them."

"I do." He took the folder and put it on the coffee table. "Later. Much, much later." Then he slid his arm around her waist. Silk was so touchable, especially when it was wrapped around Kasey. "Right now, I want you to come with me. By the way, thanks for wearing your clear contacts tonight."

"Anything for you, Sam."

"Good to know." He wished he could take her statement literally, but he knew there were limits to what she'd do for him. Making a long-term commitment was out of the question, for example, at least for now. He had to stop thinking about that and focus on the present.

Fortunately, when he opened the kitchen door and guided her outside, her response to his efforts was exactly what he'd hoped. She laughed with delight.

"Like it?"

"I *love* it. Arabian Nights, here we come. But I forgot my seven veils."

"You won't need seven veils to get my attention." He leaned down and stole a quick kiss. One made him want more, but he forced himself to release her while they still had some control over themselves. "Have a seat at the table. I'll bring out the food."

"Can I do anything to help?"

He raked her silk dress with a glance. "If you follow me into the kitchen we'll end up having sex on the floor."

"Is that a bad thing?"

"Depends on how much you like cold lemongrass soup and spoiled chicken with peanut sauce."

Her eyes widened. "Wow. Sounds as if you went to a whole lot of trouble."

"No, the restaurant did."

She looked at him with affection in her gray eyes. "Even so, I'm impressed with all you've done, and I don't want to ruin your careful setup. I'll stay out here and let you serve the food."

"Okay. I'll be right back." He was dying to know what she was wearing under that dress and whether she'd accepted his challenge to pay a visit to Slightly Scandalous today. But anticipation would make the discovery that much sweeter. Even without audacious underwear she would be a joy to undress, as usual.

Moments later he returned carrying a tray loaded with the first course. But instead of walking straight over to the table, he paused to take in the scene. Kasey was facing away from him as she sat quietly, her attention on the candle flame in front of her. Her shining blond hair hung straight down, looking as silky and touchable as her dress. Although the dress was simply styled, the color reminded him of weddings, and he was hit with a longing that was as fierce as it was sudden.

In that moment he knew that everything he wanted was right here. If he could have Kasey, a couple of kids, a little house, a quiet garden and a decent job, he'd be a happy man. But if he told her that, she'd leave and never come back.

He cleared a lump from his throat. "Dinner is served," he said, and she turned to smile at him. Oh, yeah, she was everything he wanted and more. It might take a miracle for them to be together, but he wasn't giving up, not yet.

As they ate their spicy meal in the glow of candlelight, Kasey worked hard to come up with drawbacks to Sam Ashton. She wasn't having much luck. He was generous, sexy, hardworking and eager to please her.

Yes, he'd admitted that a woman's looks affected his judgment. So, that simply meant he wasn't any different from the majority of men on the planet. She thought it might be a function of the male mind-set, handed down from the caveman days.

Basically the only problem with Sam was his age. Even that was an asset right now, because his greater experience encouraged her to be sexually courageous. And he liked that she was smart. That was a refreshing change. She didn't have to hide her brains from Sam.

Oh, why did she have to meet Sam now? Why couldn't she have met him five years from now? But she knew the answer to that. Five years from now Sam would be married…to someone else. She hated that idea.

While they ate, Sam told her about Oregon, a place she'd never seen. He didn't suggest taking her there to see it, and she knew why. She'd made her rules very clear, and he was doing his best to abide by them.

Maybe he expected to change her mind about those rules with this elaborate effort tonight. If that was his intent, he was doing a damned good job. Sitting here drinking wine with Sam while music provided a sensuous background was the kind of romantic setting she'd often fantasized about. Maybe she'd be a fool to throw it all away so that she could have a series of unsatisfying sexual episodes.

She had to assume that sex with other guys would be unsatisfying. Sam had set the bar pretty damned high. After being with him, she couldn't imagine how any other man would measure up.

He set down his wineglass, stood and held out his hand. "Dance with me."

"Sure." And when she left the table and moved into his arms, the old cliché came true—they did seem to be two halves creating a whole. They moved together across the uneven flagstone as if the surface were glass.

He held her lightly, as if he didn't need to press her against his body to let her know how much he wanted her. The message was in his eyes and the tender way he circled her palm with his thumb. He seemed content to wait, knowing they'd soon be locked in passion, writhing sensuously on the quilts he'd laid down inside the gazebo.

He didn't speak, but his expression told her more than words what he was feeling. He wouldn't say it out loud, because she'd warned him not to tie her down. As they danced under the desert moon, she wondered what was so bad about being tied down to a guy as wonderful as Sam. She hadn't wanted to fall in love with him, but it was happening, anyway.

SAM COULD SEE the resistance melting in Kasey's eyes. Every second that passed, she was less afraid of her feelings, more willing to believe in her instincts. He allowed himself to hope, just a little.

Unimportant as it might seem to her, looking into her eyes while she wore clear contacts made a huge difference. He no longer had the impression she was putting up a barrier between them. She might be giving him a glimpse of the real Kasey, and that was very encouraging. When a woman did that, she was learning to trust.

Desire teased him, arousing him in lazy increments, becoming gradually more insistent. At last the slow dancing wasn't enough to satisfy the ache building inside him.

He tightened his grip on her waist. "I want you," he murmured. It was all he was allowed to say. It would have to do.

She ran her tongue over her lips. "I want you, too."

What he'd give for her to change the four-letter word in that sentence. But the night was young. His heart beat faster as he thought of what was ahead. "Then maybe it's time for the sheikh to take the maiden into his tent and ravish her."

"Or maybe it's time for the sheikh to wait in his tent and let the maiden come to him."

"Oh?" A shiver of excitement shot up his spine. "I thought you forgot your seven veils."

"There are other ways for a maiden to please her sheikh."

"And will I be pleased?" He had an idea that Slightly Scandalous had something to do with this. Hot damn.

"Yes, I believe you will be very pleased." She stepped out of his arms. "Go into the tent and wait for my entrance."

"An entrance, huh? This is sounding better and better." He walked over to the gazebo and took off his shoes before ducking under the canopy.

If she'd bought sexy underwear because he'd asked her to, that was an excellent sign. Then again, maybe he was still serving as her testing ground. That was such a depressing thought that he shoved it back into the pit where his other insecurities lived and slammed the lid shut.

He sat down on the cushy surface and glanced outside. She was gone. She hadn't been kidding about making an entrance. His pulse rate jumped several more beats per minute. He was probably supposed to play the bored potentate. He lounged back against a large floor pillow but kept his head propped on one hand so he didn't miss anything.

Then he saw her, poised about five yards away, her chin lifted, her feet bare. Her gaze locked with his as she started toward him, striding exactly as he'd seen fashion models walk. He wondered where she'd learned that. Then his brain went on overload as she slowly untied her dress.

Once the tie was free, the dress didn't fall open as he'd hoped. Apparently there was a second tie inside. Kasey paused and drew back the part of the dress that was loose, and he nearly swallowed his tongue. The ivory bra she wore was one of the cutout affairs. He caught a glimpse of one rosy nipple before she closed the lapel, holding it lightly against her body as she continued toward him.

Fascinated and incredibly aroused, he watched her slip

her hand under the shimmering silk to unfasten the second tie. Then she paused again and slowly drew aside the silk.

He forgot to breathe.

The view was more spectacular than he could have imagined in a hundred years of sexual daydreams. Her breasts thrust boldly through the openings in the ivory bra, but he'd been expecting that after the first teasing peek. He hadn't dared to expect the rest—a thong designed not to cover, but to set off and highlight that blond triangle where he would gladly lose himself for hours.

Then she drew her dress closed again, removing the visual treat she'd allowed him for a fleeting moment. He moaned in protest. She smiled and gave him another quick flash before pulling the silk back in place.

Then she turned and began walking away.

"No." His voice came out as an embarrassing croak.

She continued to walk, and he sat up, prepared to go after her. But before he got to his feet, he realized that she was letting the dress slide off her shoulders. He sank back to the quilt, his mouth going dry. The dress dangled from her arms, and in the flickering candlelight, he had an erection-producing view of her sleek backside as she moved steadily away from him. Nothing touched her there except the thin strap of the thong. He wanted to be that strap.

She stopped, tossed back her hair and glanced over her bare shoulder at him. He would take that image to his grave. As his heart threatened to jump clear out of his chest, she let the dress slip off completely, although she caught it before it hit the flagstone. She stayed that way, her back to him, for what seemed like an eternity.

Finally, with a flick of her wrist, she tossed the dress over her shoulder and turned to face him, giving him a full frontal view of that bodacious outfit. Like a jungle cat on the prowl, she sauntered boldly toward the gazebo. He wondered if he'd embarrass himself by having a climax before she arrived.

She walked straight into the tent and right over to where he sat. Standing with legs braced wide, she looked down at him. "Well, what do you think?"

He made some incoherent sound deep in his throat. Swallowing, he tried again. "Closer."

"Me?"

"You."

And when she complied, he cupped that delicious behind of hers and did what any man worth his salt would do when presented with crotchless underwear. He enjoyed his dessert.

From the way she moaned and clutched his head, she enjoyed serving it up for him nearly as much as he savored the fare. She began to shake, and he held her tighter, supporting her with both hands as she rushed toward her climax. How he managed to give her one without exploding himself was a true marvel.

Somehow he held off until her shudders eased, but she was still quaking in the aftermath when he urged her down to the quilt. In seconds he'd unzipped and grabbed a condom from the stash in a corner of the gazebo. He didn't take time to do more than open his fly and wrench down his briefs—the urgency was too great.

Then he was thrusting, stroking, pumping frantically, needing to bury himself deep while she still wore that crazy thong. A woman with no underwear was wild enough, but a woman with underwear built specifically for sex—that was the ultimate turn-on.

He felt her tighten and slowed a fraction to allow her to catch up. Braced on his outstretched arms, he blinked the sweat from his eyes so that he wouldn't miss the sight of her breasts, captured in satin yet brazenly exposed to her lover. He leaned down and tugged on her nipple with his teeth.

That must have put her over the edge, because with a gasping cry, she climaxed again. When her contractions began to roll over his hot penis, he thrust one last time and came in a delirious rush of pleasure. As his world spun out of control, he cried out in gratitude.

Long moments later, he'd recovered enough to shuck his clothes so he could cuddle with her skin-to-skin in a tangle of quilts. In that moment, he couldn't imagine how she'd think they would ever call it quits. With this performance it almost seemed as if she'd intended to make him her slave for life. If so, she'd succeeded beyond her wildest dreams.

KASEY FELT OUTRAGEOUSLY PROUD of herself. Talk about being a Bad Girl—she was a certified member of the club now. Poor Sam, he'd been a puppet on a string once she'd started untying her dress. She smoothed his hair as he lay beside her, his head pillowed on her breast.

The way he'd reacted had been adorable. But then, she'd known he would love whatever she tried to do. He was that kind of guy—appreciative. Fun to be with. *Easy to love.*

Oh, boy. There was the problem. Sam wasn't the sort to disappoint a girl, and he'd been doing a fantastic job of making her happy ever since they'd met. How was she supposed to keep from falling in love, when he insisted on being so terrific?

"You did it." His voice was rich with satisfaction. "You went there and bought this stuff. For me."

"Well, I got a little something out of the experience, myself."

"I hope so." He propped his head on his hand. "How does it feel, wearing something like this?"

"Kinky. It's not the most comfortable underwear I've ever owned, and I couldn't stand it for a whole day, but for a few hours, it sure encourages you to think about sex all the time."

"If I'd known you had this on, we wouldn't have made it through dinner." He stroked the exposed part of her breast. "In fact, I probably would have ripped the ties of that dress so I could get to what was underneath."

"I thought I might rip them, too, because I was shaking so much."

"You were? I couldn't tell. You looked like you had it all together."

She smiled. "That's what you were supposed to think. Anyway, on the off chance I'd rip the dress, I brought a change of clothes and left them in the car."

His expression brightened. "Does that mean you can leave for work from here in the morning?"

"No, not really." She noticed as the light left his eyes. He might not disappoint her, but she always seemed to be disappointing him. "I didn't bring makeup or my briefcase." She'd made that decision consciously, though. Coming prepared to spend the night and go directly to work from his place sent a certain message. Next he'd suggest she move a few things into his closet, and then—

"I didn't mean to push."

"I know."

"Forget I said that." He continued to toy with her breasts. Finally he leaned over and began running his tongue around her nipples.

Her worry about their situation eased with every swipe of his tongue. Sex didn't solve anything, but it pushed the problems away for a while. And she wanted him again. She couldn't believe how quickly her desire returned, even after she'd been so completely satisfied a moment ago.

"Keep that up and I'll forget my own name," she said.

His answering chuckle told her he was ready to change the subject back to sex, too. He raked her nipple with his teeth while he ran his hands over the bits of satin outlining her breasts. "I suppose you want to take this off, now."

"Not necessarily." Not while she was watching him caress her through the openings in the bra. It was quite a turn-on.

"How about this?" He ran his finger around the crotchless thong.

"Do you want me to leave it?"

"Uh-huh." He stroked his palm down over her damp curls and slid two fingers inside her slick heat. "It's like an open invitation. I'd never get tired of seeing you in this."

"Sure you would." Although when he rubbed his fingers back and forth, she wasn't sure of anything except that another orgasm was on the way.

"No. I wouldn't. And I do believe I'm going to accept that open invitation one more time."

"Good."

"Yes, it will be." He rolled away long enough to get another condom. Then he was back, moving between her legs, not so frantic as he had been earlier. And when he pushed deep, he held her gaze. "I'll only say this once, but I hope you'll think about it."

"Sam, I—"

"This sort of happiness doesn't come along every day." She swallowed. "I know. But—"

"Never mind, Kasey. Never mind anything. Just come for me."

And very quickly, she did. He kissed her while she climaxed, muting her cries of release so they wouldn't alarm his neighbors too much. Then he followed soon after, muffling his groans of completion against her shoulder.

And as they lay together, holding each other close, she knew he was right. Happiness was within her grasp. If she let it slip away, there was no guarantee she'd ever find it again.

CHAPTER SIXTEEN

SAM ACCEPTED THE idea that he had to be patient with Kasey. They spent the night making love, sleeping a little, discussing his promo campaign, finishing the last of the wine, eating ice cream he'd forgotten he had in the back of his freezer. With each passing hour, he believed he was making progress. She'd look at him for long moments at a time, and he could almost hear her thinking. That was good.

She was a smart woman, and smart women didn't make stupid mistakes—like giving up the best relationship they'd ever had. He certainly wouldn't make that mistake, but it wasn't all up to him. And he'd had more experience in this and knew how rare their interaction was.

Ever the optimist, he hoped she'd say something definitive before she left in the gray light of dawn. She'd changed into her spare outfit, shorts and a T-shirt, and she stood with him by the front door as they exchanged a few more sleepy kisses.

"You're sure you're okay to drive?" he asked.

"I'm fine to drive." She kissed him again. "We got some rest."

"Not much. But I'm not complaining." He couldn't worry about a little sleep when his whole future was on the line. "So what about tonight?"

"Let's see—it's Friday, right?"

He had to stop and figure it out. "Yes. Friday. Do you want to go somewhere? A movie?" If she said yes, then maybe she was giving up on the secrecy. He would be happy to give that up. They wouldn't flaunt their relationship around her office, but he didn't think anyone would have a problem with it, anyway.

She frowned as if turning the idea over in her head. "We could go away for the weekend," she said at last. "Not anywhere that costs a lot, but up in the mountains they have some—"

"I can't this weekend." And he sincerely regretted that. A whole weekend together might really change her mind about their relationship. But he'd promised Colin.

"Oh. Well, then—"

"Colin has another gig Saturday night. Do you want to go?"

He prayed she'd say yes, that she'd love to go. That would solve everything. They'd go hear the Tin Tarantulas and let everyone know they were together. But he didn't want to push the idea and risk scaring her away.

"Let me think about it," she said.

"Okay." He tried not to let his disappointment show.

He must have failed, because she slid her arms around his neck and stood on tiptoe to kiss him. "I'm confused right now, Sam," she murmured. "I thought I knew exactly how I wanted things to be, but now I'm not sure. I've been thinking about what you said. I really have."

"That's all I ask. Take your time."

"Let's go for a drive tonight, away from the city. We can sit and talk."

He wasn't above playing his trump card. He nuzzled her neck and cupped her breast. "And make out a little in the backseat of my car?"

She wiggled closer. "I could probably be persuaded."

"Then wear something that's easy to get off."

"Shall we say seven?"

He didn't want to wait that long. "Shall we say six-thirty?"

She laughed and kissed him full on the mouth. Then she released him. "Six. And this time I'll skip the underwear completely. How's that?"

"Lady, you don't even have to ask. Are you sure you have to leave right this minute?"

"Yes." She opened the door and blew him a kiss. "Six o'clock."

"I'll be there with condoms on."

She grinned at him. "Bye, Sam."

"Bye, Kasey." After the door closed, he stood there awhile and wished he didn't feel so damned unsure about where they were headed. He fought the urge to go after her and demand that she be completely honest about what she felt. Surely she'd have to admit that she was falling in love with him. She'd have to or risk lying. He'd seen love in her eyes thirty seconds ago.

Then he heard the sound of her little red convertible pulling out of his driveway. He'd lost the chance to force her to say something, and no doubt that was for the best. Thinking about her car brought up the memory of when he'd first seen her and noticed her vanity plate—SO REDY.

He'd thought it was a brazen invitation from a woman ready for adventure, sexual or otherwise. Now he realized it was a brave attempt to become something she'd never been. In some ways, like with the Slightly Scandalous underwear, she'd started living up to that plate. But in other ways, she was still afraid—afraid to trust herself to make the right decision.

After all, they'd only known each other a few days. He needed to cut her some slack, give her more time. Eventually, she'd come around to his way of thinking. He smiled.

Eventually. Such a vague word. *Orgasm.* Such a definite word. He'd concentrate on orgasms, and let *eventually* take care of itself.

BY ALL RIGHTS, Kasey knew she should be tired. Instead she was a mass of worries and wouldn't have been able to sleep even if she'd had the time. She loved Sam and wanted to be with him. She no longer cared about all the other guys she was supposed to get Bad Girl experience from.

And yet she was only twenty. How could she commit to Sam at such a young age? Her parents and Jim would probably hate the idea, although maybe not after they got to know Sam again. They'd liked him once upon a time, when he'd been Jim's buddy.

And that was the other thing—she was very afraid of how Sam would react if he found out how young she was. He'd fallen for a woman he thought was close to his age. Knowing the truth about her could change everything, but if she was seriously considering giving in to her emotions regarding Sam, then she'd have to tell him.

She needed advice, but she couldn't go to her friends in the office. Sam was a client, and the client issue was weird enough without bringing the whole office in on their love affair. Even more important, everyone in the office thought she was older, just as Sam did. They wouldn't understand the scope of the problem unless she revealed her age, which she wasn't about to do.

Only one person might be able to help, and Kasey hesitated to call her. Alicia and Jim had broken up several months ago, and Kasey had a bad feeling that she'd been part of the reason. Jim hadn't been happy with Kasey's makeover. A typical big brother, he was much more comfortable when she wore glasses and denim jumpers.

But after thinking about the problem for most of the

morning and getting very little done at work, Kasey decided to risk calling Alicia. She asked if Alicia would consider meeting her for lunch.

"I would love to do that!" Alicia said. "I've missed you!"

"This isn't about Jim," Kasey said quickly, afraid Alicia might misunderstand the call.

"That's okay. In fact, I was sad when we lost touch after Jim and I broke up. It doesn't seem fair that I should lose you as a friend, too."

"You're right. And the fact is, I desperately need some advice."

Alicia laughed. "According to Jim, I'm the worst person to give you advice."

"I don't see it that way. Can we meet at noon at the Coco's down the road from my office? That's about halfway between your work and mine."

"I'll be there."

"Great. See you then." Kasey hung up feeling much better. Alicia would help her figure this out.

As KASEY WALKED into the restaurant, she found Alicia at once. She'd cut her dark hair short, but otherwise she looked the way Kasey remembered her—tall and vivacious, with strong features and a ready smile. Kasey thought Jim had holes in his head for breaking up with her.

"You look fabulous," Alicia said when they'd settled into a booth. "Are the guys swarming around or what?"

"Well, one particular one is, but I haven't told him I'm only twenty."

"Ah. Afraid he'll freak?"

"Partly. Here's the weird part. I knew him twelve years ago, when he was in Jim's senior class."

Alicia's carefully made-up eyes widened. "And he

doesn't know that, either, I'll bet. Or remember you. And of course you have a different last name from Jim."

"Exactly. So I thought I'd just have some fun and then walk away. I had a crush on him twelve years ago, so it was—"

"Too tempting to resist."

"Right."

The waitress arrived and Alicia chose something quickly, as if not really interested in the food. Kasey picked the same menu item as Alicia to save time.

After the waitress left to fill their order, Alicia turned back to Kasey. "I completely understand why you'd go for him, even knowing the age difference."

Kasey sighed with relief. She'd made the right decision, calling Alicia. "The thing is, Sam's really a great guy. Everything between us is…wonderful. He's pushing for some kind of commitment, and to be honest, I'm falling for him, too. But I'm only twenty."

Alicia smiled. "You don't look it."

"Thanks to you, I don't. And Sam has no idea. I'm sure he thinks I'm at least twenty-five, maybe older. I told him that until recently I'd looked like such a nerd that I hadn't had many dates, and that now I want to find out what it's like to be single and attractive."

"I'll bet that went over like a lead balloon."

Kasey thought about Sam's struggle to understand her position. "He's trying to see it my way. But I'm not being fair to him. Plus, I'm beginning to wonder if I'd be stupid to break up with him so I could date a lot of other guys who wouldn't be nearly as great as Sam."

Alicia leaned forward. "Kasey, you have to tell him how old you are. Then see how he reacts. Right now he doesn't have enough information about you. He's falling for someone he doesn't really know."

What a depressing thought. But Kasey knew Alicia was right. The fantasy had been terrific, but she had to level with Sam and take a chance he'd dump her…or he wouldn't. "Let's say he doesn't run screaming into the night when he finds out I'm twenty and the kid sister of one of his high-school friends. Let's say he doesn't feel horribly betrayed because I misled him. Let's say he gets over both of those hurdles and still wants me. Am I crazy to consider tying myself down?"

Alicia studied her for several seconds. "Have you imagined your life without him?"

"Yes."

"And how does that seem to you?"

"Horrible. Sad. A complete waste."

"Then there's your answer, Kase. We don't always get to have things turn out the way we planned."

Kasey looked across the table at the woman she'd hoped would become her sister-in-law. "I know. It was mostly my fault that you broke up with Jim, wasn't it?"

"No, no, no." Alicia reached over, grabbed Kasey's hand and squeezed it. "Don't go on that guilt trip, Kase. If it hadn't been you, it would have been some other situation where I acted independently and disagreed with his take on things. But here's the punch line—I think he's having a change of heart."

"Jim?" Kasey sat up straighter. "When did this happen?"

"This morning. He called right after I talked to you. Talk about weird karma."

Kasey gasped. "You didn't tell him you were meeting me, did you? Because I don't want him asking questions until—"

"Sweetie, of course not. What's between you and me is private. But Jim asked if I'd go out with him Saturday night. It seems a friend of his called, and his little brother is playing in a band... Kasey, what on earth is wrong? You look positively green."

Her stomach pitched. This couldn't be happening. "Sam is the friend who called him. Sam's little brother has a band."

"Well, that *is* a coincidence. But it doesn't have to mean anything, does it? I mean, just because your Sam called Jim, that doesn't mean that they talked about you."

"Maybe not." Kasey tried to calm down, but she had a bad feeling about the whole thing. "It's just that Sam hasn't contacted Jim since he came back to town. If they talked on the phone this morning, Jim might have decided to fill Sam in on the family, tell him what everybody's up to."

"Or not."

"Or not. But I'd hate for Sam to find out who I am by accident from someone else. The truth is, I *did* mislead him, and I want to be the one who tells him so." They'd been dating only a few days, and she'd kidded herself that she had plenty of time to confess. She might already be too late.

"Of course you want to tell him yourself, and I'll bet you'll be able to tonight."

"I'll have to make it tonight. Jim will be seeing him tomorrow night."

"And will you be going to hear the band?"

Kasey looked across the table at Alicia. "I don't know yet. Listen, would you excuse me for a minute so I can make a quick call?"

"No problem. I'll check my messages, too." Alicia pulled out her cell phone.

Kasey did the same, located Sam's card and punched in his mobile number. When he didn't pick up, she left a message to have him call her. She needed to hear his voice before they met tonight. If he sounded completely normal, then he hadn't discussed her with Jim.

Sam didn't return the call during lunch. Kasey forced herself to concentrate on Alicia, who seemed thrilled that Jim was back in touch.

"He said he's had time to do a lot of thinking, and he was wrong to try and control me," Alicia said. "He's a good guy. He just had some growing up to do. Now maybe he's old enough for me." She laughed.

Kasey smiled, happy for Alicia even though worry about Sam was eating at her gut. Maybe age wasn't as important as she'd thought. Alicia and Jim were exactly the same numerical age but hadn't been the same mental age according to Alicia. Kasey had always been old for her years, so she and Sam might be exactly right. It felt that way.

Now if only he would call her.

BUT SAM DIDN'T CALL. Kasey tried every number she had for him, and he was always unavailable. The sick feeling in the pit of her stomach wouldn't go away. She told herself not to buy trouble, but by the time she drove home to get ready for their date, she was convinced that Sam knew the truth, and that was why he was avoiding her. Nobody liked finding out that a person they'd trusted had been deliberately hiding information about themselves, and hearing it from a third party was the worst way to get the news.

As she packed a small knapsack of munchies for the drive, she tried to think what she'd do if he failed to show up tonight. Finally she decided that if he hadn't arrived by six-thirty, she'd go to his house. If necessary, she'd scale the wall around his patio and wait for him there. He'd have to come home some time, and she'd make him listen. But maybe she wouldn't have to do any of that, because maybe

Sam would arrive as scheduled and then she'd have the whole evening to work up to her confession.

A good round of sex in the back seat of his car might make that confession easier. She'd had him wound around her little finger the night before when she'd flashed him with her crotchless panties. If she picked just the right moment to give him the news, he might be fine with it. She was probably stressing over nothing. He might even laugh and tell her she was silly to worry about such a small matter.

Nevertheless, she constantly checked through her living-room window to see if she spied his car pulling into the parking lot. When it did, at two minutes before six, she sighed in relief. Crawling over a patio wall seemed too much like stalking and it wasn't really her style.

Maybe Sam had been busy all day—simple as that. The important thing was that he'd shown up when they'd agreed upon. She'd done her part, wearing elastic-waist shorts, a T-shirt and no underwear whatsoever. If that wasn't co-operation, she didn't know what was.

When Sam rang the doorbell, her heart started pounding. Well, so she was a little bit nervous. Sometime before the night was out she had to tell him the very small details she'd left out. Surely they wouldn't matter too much, and he'd forgive her for the slight deception. She could explain it all in such a way that he'd understand perfectly. And then they'd have some more sex.

She opened the door with a smile. Her smile vanished the moment she saw his face.

"What in *hell* were you thinking?"

As she absorbed the fury in his eyes, she knew this was going to be bad. Very, very bad.

CHAPTER SEVENTEEN

SAM HELD TIGHT to his anger, ignoring a rush of sympathy for Kasey. She looked devastated, but he couldn't weaken toward her now. He walked into the room and slammed the door, for emphasis. She flinched. Too bad. She'd lied to him, and that hurt. A lot.

"Sam, I can explain. I—"

"I thought you had a little problem because you'd just gotten over a nerdy phase and wanted to spread your wings!" He glared at her. "I thought you might be younger than me, maybe by several years, but I never dreamed you were only *twenty*. You're just a baby!"

"I am not!" Her chin came up in defiance, but there were tears gathering in her eyes.

"Oh, yes, you are." He tried to block his awareness of the outfit she'd worn, an outfit he'd specified for back-seat sex. "I remember being twenty, and I didn't know shit from shinola back then." He turned away from her, unable to continue looking at the woman he still wanted and couldn't have. "Little Kasey Winston. And I sent you off to buy crotchless underwear."

"Don't call me that!"

He glanced back at her. "It's who you are, although I never would have recognized you. I guess I know where you got that little scar on your lip, don't I? Oh, and by the way, I didn't tell Jim anything about us. That's partly so he won't lecture you, but mostly so he won't beat the crap out of me."

"I wouldn't let him do that." Her voice shook. "Sam, you don't understand. Please let me explain."

"I probably do understand—at least some of it. Jim told me you charged right through school and had your Bachelor's by the time you were eighteen. He said you were trying to pass as someone older, especially at work, and I get that. But why in hell's name did you have to deceive me, of all people?" Damned if he didn't have a lump in his throat. He swallowed hard, trying to get rid of it.

She looked as if he'd propped her in front of a firing squad. She was obviously scared but determined to take what was coming to her. "You might as well know everything. All the women in the office watched you from the window. Then we drew straws to see who would ask you out. I got the long straw."

He'd thought he couldn't feel worse, but he'd been wrong. His throat hurt, and his voice rasped harshly. "You did it on a dare?"

"Sort of."

"Did you know it was me?"

"Yes."

"Oh, Kasey." He walked over and stared sightlessly out her living-room window. "So you knew all along that nothing could come of this, and yet you still…" He shook his head, unable to go on.

"I didn't…didn't mean for anyone to g-get hurt."

He didn't need to turn around to know she was crying. He felt like crying, too. "Well, I did get hurt. And at some point you had to know that was liable to happen. Damn it, Kasey, you as good as lied to me." He braced his hand against the wall and lowered his head, fighting for control. He wanted to go over there and comfort her, but he couldn't let himself do that. He hated hearing her cry. Worse yet, he still wanted her.

She choked back a sob. "You're right. I lied and I knew you could get hurt. There's really no excuse for that. I meant to end things that first night, but then I started to care for you, too. And I began to think that maybe it could work, after all. I was going to say that tonight, plus tell you how old I was."

"You thought maybe it could work?" He spun around, unable to believe she'd said such a thing. "I don't care how young you are, you should be old enough to know better than that. How could you think for one second I'd expect a twenty-year-old woman to give up all that precious time of exploring, finding herself—hell, *growing up?* Never in a million years would I ask that of you."

"But what if I don't want to—"

"You don't know what you want."

"Yes, I do!"

"Come on, Kasey. Two days ago you were saying you couldn't commit to me because you'd been a nerd and wanted to be a glam girl on the loose for a while."

She took a ragged breath. "So I've changed my mind."

"But there's one thing you can't change, and that's your age. If only you'd told me the truth that first night. If only you'd said *Sam, I'm twenty years old.* The commitment discussion would have been *over,* Kasey."

"And we…we would have been over, too."

"Yes, we damn sure would have. I'm way too attracted to you, and my days of casual sex are gone."

"Don't you see? So are mine! I love you, Sam!"

He winced. How he'd longed to hear her say that. And now she had. But he couldn't trust her to know her own mind. He sighed. "I know you think you do, but—"

"I do!" She hurled herself into his arms. "I didn't want

to love you, but I can't help it." Tears streamed from her eyes. "And I think I just lost one of my contacts and my nose is running and I need—"

"You need me out of your life." Gently he set her away from him. It was the toughest thing he'd ever done. "And you may not believe this, but I'm leaving because I happen to love you, too."

"Oh, spare me!" She swiped at her eyes. "Please don't tell me you're doing this for my own good!"

"Okay, I won't tell you that." He reached for the doorknob. "But it's the truth. Goodbye, Kasey." He went out the door and closed it behind him. As he walked away, he heard a thump, as if some object had hit the door. She'd thrown something. Well, after all, she was only twenty.

KASEY CRIED UNTIL her eyes hurt and her throat was raw. But gradually the tears dried up, and she was left lying on the carpet, staring at the door. She'd grabbed the closest thing to throw, which had turned out to be the little knapsack of goodies she'd packed for their drive out of town. Fortunately nothing in the canvas bag was breakable.

After getting to her hands and knees, she crawled to the bag, sat down and opened it. She'd put a package of Pepperidge Farm cookies in there, the kind with chocolate filling. She grabbed the package, broke the seal and took out a cookie. Cookies might make her think better, and she had some serious thinking to do.

According to all her test scores, she was nearly a genius. And if a woman who was nearly a genius, even if she happened to be only twenty years old, couldn't solve this problem and get Sam back, then what good were brains, anyway? So she would solve this problem, because she had to get Sam back. The minute he'd walked out the door, she'd finally known for certain that he was her forever-after man.

She also believed with all her heart that she was his forever-after woman. So by bringing them back together, she'd be doing both of them a tremendous favor. She smiled softly. Once she accomplished that she'd try not to remind him of it too often. Maybe just once a year, on their wedding anniversary. And they *would* have a wedding anniversary, because sometime in the next year they would have a wedding.

But first she had to convince Sam that he wanted to marry her. Actually, she wouldn't have to convince him of that part. He already loved her. He'd said so. And because he was thirty, he'd want marriage and kids and a life in that cute little house. She got all warm and fuzzy just thinking about it.

All she really needed to change was Sam's image of her, exactly the way she planned to change his company's image and the image for Slightly Scandalous. But she'd have to do it soon, and she'd have to make an indelible impression, one he wouldn't be able to get out of his mind, ever.

She'd recruit her buddies from work and Sam's brother, Colin. Although she'd met Colin only once, she'd felt an immediate intellectual kinship. She thought Colin would get a real kick out of helping her set a trap for his big brother. And tomorrow night would give her the perfect opportunity.

SAM AGREED TO go with Jim and Alicia to the Yucca Lounge, although he'd rather have had a root canal. Every time he looked at Jim, he thought of Kasey, and every time he watched Jim and Alicia getting friendly, he thought of

Kasey. On top of that, the whole time he listened to the Tin Tarantulas, he thought of Kasey.

Maybe it didn't matter who he was with or what he was doing. He was doomed to think of Kasey—Kasey on that first night in the hammock, Kasey pushing her sexual limits the second night in her apartment, Kasey prancing down an imaginary runway in crotchless panties, Kasey sobbing as he told her they were finished. He couldn't bring himself to picture Kasey moving on and feeling grateful to him that he'd had the good sense to break up with her. That image hurt too damned much.

One of these days he was bound to feel noble and virtuous for what he'd done. One of these days the pain had to improve—no one could continue to live for very long in this kind of agony. The worst of it was he couldn't tell anyone. The way he saw it, nobody else needed to hear about this, but that meant he couldn't vent, either.

Still, he had the definite feeling that Colin knew something was wrong. During the break between sets, he came to the table as usual and tried to act like his normal wisecracking self. But in unguarded moments he would look thoughtfully at Sam, and when Sam caught him at it, he'd turn away and make another joke. Maybe Kasey had gotten in touch with Colin, somehow. Maybe she was planning to show up here tonight.

The more Sam thought about it, the more likely it seemed that Colin was in on some scheme of Kasey's. Sam hadn't expected her to give up, although that's what she should do. If she thought Colin would put in a good word for her, she might have asked him to do that after the gig tonight. Well, Colin could talk until he was blue in the face. Sam was not about to ruin the future of the woman he loved, no matter how much the decision to let her go hurt.

After the band's final number, Sam braced himself, convinced that Colin would ambush him, somehow. Jim and Alicia were ready to leave, but Sam delayed them, just in case Colin had something to say. It wouldn't do any good, of course. But if the message had come from Kasey…aw, hell, who was he kidding? He wanted to believe that she'd talked to Colin. He wanted some evidence that she would try to get him back.

Nothing she could do would work, but still, if she tried, that would soothe his soul a little bit. He'd hold her off until she stopped trying and realized that they didn't belong together. In truth, they *might* have belonged together, if they'd met several years from now. Maybe he'd look her up after a long time had passed. God knows he wouldn't be with anyone. He couldn't imagine it, not after loving Kasey.

Colin didn't show. Sam finally excused himself from Jim and Alicia and went to find him. There was Colin, surrounded by his female groupies as usual. Sam waded into the middle of them and tapped his brother on the shoulder.

Colin glanced up. "Hey, bro! How come you're still around?"

"I wondered if you wanted to talk to me about anything."

"No, not really." But there was a gleam in his eyes. "Go on home, man. Guys your age need your rest."

Sam's heart leaped. Sure as the world, Colin had loaned Kasey his key to Sam's house, and she was waiting for him. He would bet money on it. "That's what you think," he said, just to test his theory. "Jim, Alicia and I are heading out for a late-night snack." They had no such plan, but he might smoke Colin out that way.

"Suit yourself, dude." Colin tried to look unconcerned.

Sam saw right through him, and excitement fizzed in his veins. Something was definitely going on, and he would find out what once he got home. "See you later," he said to Colin.

"Sure thing. And thanks for coming. The crowd was great."

"Yeah, it was." Sam was happy for his brother. The Yucca Lounge had been packed. But now he had to go home and tell Kasey he really didn't want to see her anymore. He shouldn't be looking forward to that, but the thought of talking to her one more time put a spring in his step as he returned to the table where Jim and Alicia waited.

"We're going out for coffee," Jim said. "Want to come along?"

"Thanks," Sam said, "but if you could drop me at home, I'm ready to turn in." He noticed they took the news with good cheer. No doubt they wanted to be alone, anyway.

When they pulled into his driveway, he looked for Kasey's little red convertible, but it wasn't there. The disappointment was so sharp he almost forgot to say all the usual polite things to Jim and Alicia. At the last minute he remembered to thank them and promised that they'd get together again soon.

Then he started up his walkway. He might actually have to sell the place. That would be stupid, because he hadn't lived in it long enough to build up much equity, but the house no longer interested him if he couldn't have Kasey. Coming home night after night, knowing she'd never be there again, would be pure torture.

After twisting the key in the lock, he opened the door. Monday he'd call a real-estate agent. Monday he'd...

He stood in the doorway, the key still dangling from his hand, while he stared at his living room. Vases and pots of flowers covered every surface. Roses, daisies, chrysanthemums, you name it. They sat on the coffee table, the end tables, even the floor. And sticking out of one bright vase of mixed blooms was a sign. He moved closer. *Let me color your world. Love, Kasey.*

"Kasey?" She must have used the time he was at the Yucca Lounge to set this up. He wasn't sure if she'd staged it and left, or if she was still here. But if she was here, she didn't answer.

Heart pounding, he walked through the living room, picking his way around the flowers. Then he smelled something cooking. Could she be in the kitchen? But she didn't cook. Following the delicious aroma of apple pie, he went through the dining room into the kitchen.

She wasn't there, but the counters were filled with pastries. The aroma he'd caught came from a chafing dish of warm apple cobbler. He leaned over a decorated sheet cake next to it. Was that a naked woman outlined in pink frosting? With little red nipples? It was. Next to it, lettered in red, was the message *Let me cook up some excitement. Love, Kasey.*

So she wasn't in the kitchen, either. He decided to check the bedroom, imagining her stretched out on his king-size mattress. Walking down the hall, he trembled, knowing he needed to be strong, and aware he was weakening fast. But she wasn't in the bedroom, either.

Instead, the bed was mounded with silk pillows. On his dresser and nightstands, dozens of votives in glass holders turned the room into a fairyland. Then he realized each pillow was stitched with a word, and taken together, they spelled out *I can set your nights on fire. Love, Kasey.*

He only had one obvious place left to look. Taking a deep breath, he walked back down the hall and through the kitchen. He opened the door, expecting to find candles there, too. But the area was dark and still. Sick with disappointment, he stepped onto the patio. He'd been so sure she'd be here, with some sort of grand finale.

Then he heard a click and Bruce Springsteen's "Secret Garden" drifted from somewhere nearby. Next the trees sparkled to life, the branches strung with hundreds of tiny white lights.

"Welcome home, Sam."

He spun around, and she emerged from the shadows wearing the skimpiest halter top and the tightest capri pants he'd ever seen.

He stared at her, at a loss for words.

But she seemed to know exactly what she wanted to say, as if she'd rehearsed it. "Sam, I can be everything you need—a partner, a playmate and a lover. You told me that this sort of happiness doesn't come along every day, and you're right. Are you willing to let me go and take a chance on losing what you've found?"

"But...you're so...young." She didn't seem young right now, though. She seemed exactly the right age for everything he had in mind.

She looked at him, her posture straight, her gaze steady. "I'm old enough to know that I've found the love of my life. Are you old enough to know that?"

He stepped closer, drawn to her by the certainty in her eyes. "I don't want you to regret loving me."

"Never in a million years."

With a groan of surrender, he gathered her into his arms. God, she felt so good. "I need you. I need you desperately."

She held him close and looked deep into his eyes. "We need each other, Sam. You know we're perfect together. We'd be fools to let anything tear us apart."

He trembled to think how close they'd come to having that happen, all because he'd allowed a numerical age to cloud what he knew about her in his heart. She was his equal in every way, more than his equal in some ways. "I was almost that dumb."

"That's why I had to save you…save us."

A smile of pure joy tugged at his mouth. "You did one helluva job, PR lady."

Her serious expression lifted and her eyes began to sparkle with professional pride. "You liked the way I displayed my message points?"

He tightened his hold on her. "I like the way you display all your points."

"You were one tough customer to deal with, but I have to say, this campaign kicked butt."

"I can't believe you did all this while I was at Colin's gig." And he wondered how easily this outfit of hers came off.

"I had help. I called in my buddies at the office. They gave me a ride here so you wouldn't see my car out front, and then they fetched, carried and decorated. They left about thirty minutes ago."

"So they know about us?" The happiness just kept coming.

"Yes, and it's only the beginning. I have Alicia working on Jim right now, and tomorrow we'll go over and see my parents. You'll need to get reacquainted, and we should take a trip to Oregon."

He started feeling giddy. "We should?"

"Of course. They should meet me before the wedding, don't you think?"

"You're going to marry me?" He forgot all about trying to get her clothes off as he contemplated this new miracle.

"What did you think that little speech of mine was all about?"

"Being perfect for each other. But I thought, since

you're so young, that you might want to—" He noticed she was glaring at him. "What?"

She blew out a breath. "First of all, if I never have to hear that phrase *you're so young* again, that would be just ducky. And my speech, you might recall, was about getting *married,* Sam. My message points were about getting married. This whole production is supposed to lead to the conclusion that we'll get married."

"Oh." Life was so good, he could hardly stand it.

"So are you going to propose to me, or not?"

He grinned and cupped her face in both hands. "Not while your face is all scrunched up like that. You might turn me down."

"I will not! I—"

He kissed her, and because she'd had her mouth open, he got immediate entrance, so he could use his tongue to best advantage. By the time he finished with her and lifted his head, her expression was exactly the way he wanted it, dazed and happy. "There," he said. "You hot woman, you. Will you marry me?"

She sighed and pulled his head back down. "Yes, yes, a thousand times yes. I love you so much, Sam."

"And I love you, Kasey," he whispered as his mouth grazed hers. Then he couldn't resist, because after all, she'd practically dared him. "Even if you are so young." Then he gasped as she grabbed his crotch.

"What did you say?" she murmured, laughter in her voice.

"That you're...old enough. Yeah, that's it. Old enough."

"And how about you? Are you old enough to know better?"

"Me, I'm old enough to know the best, and you're it."

"Good answer."

As her grip turned into a caress, he leaned down and

whispered a suggestion in her ear. Before long, they were in the bedroom tossing aside silk message pillows so they could set the night on fire exactly as she'd promised. Right before Sam thrust deep inside her, he remembered his words, the ones she'd tossed back at him. *This sort of happiness doesn't come along every day.*

He had a feeling that from now on, it just might.

* * * * *

SPECIAL EXCERPT FROM

 HARLEQUIN®

 *Blaze*®

New York Times bestselling author
Vicki Lewis Thompson is back with three new
sizzling titles from her bestselling miniseries
Sons of Chance.

Riding High

"Caution. Proceeding with it."

"You want to proceed?"

"I do." Her eyes darkened to midnight-blue and her gentle sigh was filled to the brim with surrender as her arms slid around his neck, depositing mud along the way.

As if he gave a damn. His body hummed with anticipation. "Me, too." Slowly he lowered his head and closed his eyes.

"Mistake, though."

He hovered near her mouth, hardly daring to breathe. Had she changed her mind at the last minute? "Why?"

"Tell you later." She brought his head down and made the connection.

And it was as electric as he'd imagined. His blood fizzed as it raced through his body and eventually settled in his groin. Her lips fit perfectly against his from the first moment of contact. It seemed his mouth had been created for kissing Lily, and vice versa.

He tried a different angle, just to test that theory. Still perfect, still high-voltage. Since they were standing in water, it was a wonder they didn't short out. He couldn't speak for her

HBEXP79803

Fires aren't all that's sizzling for this smoking-hot firefighter!

Firefighter Dylan Cross, aka Mr. June in the annual "hottie" calendar, is used to risking his life to save others. But he's not about to risk his heart—or his bachelorhood!—when it comes to sexy Cassie Price....

From the reader-favorite miniseries *Last Bachelor Standing*

The Final Score
by *Nancy Warren*

Available June 2014 wherever you buy Harlequin Blaze books.

Available now from the
Last Bachelor Standing miniseries by Nancy Warren

Game On
Breakaway

H HARLEQUIN®

Blaze®

Red-Hot Reads
www.Harlequin.com

HB79806

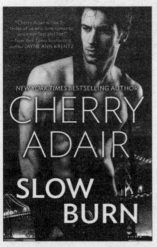